HEAVEN'S SMILE

Peter Ireland

Heaven's Smile

Copyright © 2016 Peter Ireland

All rights reserved. No part of this book may be used or reproduced without prior written consent.

The moral right of Peter Ireland as author of this work has been asserted by him in accordance with the Copyright, Designs and Patents Act of 1988.

This is a work of fiction. All names, characters, and events in this publication, other than those clearly in the public domain, are fictitious and any resemblance to real persons, living or dead, is purely coincidental.

First published in Great Britain in 2016 by

Libri Argoed

www.argoed.com

ISBN-10: 152342818X
ISBN-13: 978-1523428182

Nobody can doubt that this world will one day be the scene of dreadful struggles for existence on the part of mankind. In the end the instinct of self-preservation alone will triumph. Before its consuming fire this so-called humanitarianism, which connotes only a mixture of fatuous timidity and self-conceit, will melt away as under the March sunshine. Man has become great through perpetual struggle. In perpetual peace his greatness must decline.

The Great Leader

Pro Europa

Contents

ACT ONE: UTOPIA 1
    1.1 – Melting Pot 3
    1.2 – Machinations 26
    1.3 – Puppet Masters 40
    1.4 – Justice 50
    1.5 – Gods 90
    1.6 – Wormsign 111

ACT TWO: LEGIONES 123
    2.1 – Sverige 125
    2.2 – Blood Bound 166
    2.3 – Blueprint 187
    2.4 – Sentinel 196
    2.5 – The Turning of the Tide 209
    2.6 – Soviet City 212
    2.7 – End Game 228

ACT THREE: PHOENIX 245
    3.1 – Rebirth 247
    3.2 – Castel di Guido 256
    3.3 – Saturday 281
    3.4 – Dies Apollinis 322
    3.5 – Aryan Dawn 339

GLOSSARY: 345
Nomina Legionum: 359
Basic Legionary Organisation: 362
Intermediate Ranks: 363

ACT ONE:
UTOPIA

1.1 – Melting Pot

In the drizzle, the sharp, piercing November winds carry the *adhan* unsteadily on the gusting eddies of the North's chilly blasts. The minaret is clearly visible above the shop fronts in this once-prosperous part of town. The national chains had long gone, but a host of Pakistani, Arabic and African tenants had moved in, catering for their Pakistani, Arabic and African clientele – many of whom were now scurrying towards the mosque. White faces were rare in these parts: rare enough to excite more than one inquisitive glance, if not openly hostile stares from those earnest, bearded young men passing rapidly on their way to hear the imam's proclamations.

She moved purposely but gingerly, threading a path through the pavement crowds heading for the bus stop she hoped was at the far end of the High Street. In her early twenties, she had straight, black, shoulder-length hair and light-blue eyes set in a fresh, pale skin. She wore a padded Harrington donkey jacket whose collar had been turned up against the wind, along with a pair of pre-faded Levis and green DM boots. A rather expensive overnight bag was jammed tightly under her left arm.

She glanced furtively at the passing shop frontage in its myriad exotic manifestations, all the while trying to avoid direct eye contact as she pushed on through the bustling, alien streets of her hometown. Fully aware of her quixotic status, the question of native and alien struck her forcibly in this place, begging the question: who was who?

Her family had originally lived less than half a mile from the High Street, where she now found herself surrounded by alien bodies, in alien garb, speaking alien tongues in an alien setting. It was almost surreal: a caricature of all those government advertising campaigns singing the praises of multiculturalism – a sort of Faisalabad-on-Trent. She caught sight of a terracotta plaque above a shop front: 'A & J Sharpe, Drapers 1908' – below which, in harsh green neon lights, the shop's current status was proclaimed in golden Urdu script, complemented by the dulcet tones of Qari Saeed Chisthti Qawwal warbling through his rendition of *Gos-E-Aazam Zamane Ke,* emanating forcefully from the shop's innards. She hurried on through the *niqabs, burquas* and *pakuls,* punctuated by groups of conspicuous West Africans standing in shop doorways deep in conversation, the more important of whom wore the full *boubou,* others making do with the *dashiki.*

Her grandmother had told her stories about shopping trips to the High Street less than half a century earlier, before the family moved to the suburbs and their out-of-town shopping centres – Sharpe's? It rang a faint bell.

She squeezed past a group of four *hijab*-bedecked women moving slowly down the street, pushing buggies and lugging shopping. A crew of noisy Asian youths drew her attention to the opposite side of the road as they remonstrated with an unseen individual inside the doors of a large building with the descriptor 'Bangladeshi Cultural Centre' attached to the wall, side by side with the logo of the local council and its tired, hollow mantra, *'Working for communities'.*

She peered through the crowds for some sight of the fabled bus stop, but it was still too far away and there were far too many shoppers blocking her view.

At the next junction she was brought up short by a group of a dozen or so young men. All were bearded and wearing the traditional white garb of the Muslim under dark coats. The group's leaders were energetically engaged in exalting the shoppers through a handheld loudspeaker in a mixture of broken English, Urdu and Arabic. Above the speaker's head the now-familiar black

1.1 – MELTING POT

flag of Jihad flapped fiercely in the biting wind, with its Arabic proclamations etched in white flicking in and out of focus on the wintry gusts. One of the Jihadists, suddenly aware of an unfamiliar blur of white among the street's milling humanity, had automatically moved into her path. With a look that managed simultaneously to convey both contempt and lechery, he barked something into her face in Urdu. Hearing the raised voice, several other Jihadists turned towards her, their smug, chilling banter cutting through the hubbub of shoppers and background drone from the mosque. Despite her linguistic incomprehension, their body language spoke eloquently enough. She glanced rapidly around for a haven – but was met by a sea of Asian and African indifference, sprinkled with the odd glare of raw malevolence.

The straws came fast and furious ... the police? The idea was so ludicrous she almost burst out laughing, despite her churning stomach. A neutral shop, perhaps? Superman?

From the corner of her eye she noticed that a couple of the bearded Jihadists had detached themselves from the main body and were beginning to work their way behind her through the damp crowd. Every warning bell she possessed was jangling by now as wild panic began to well up inside her like a pregnant Vesuvius. Her eyes flicked frantically, scanning the alien townscape for an escape avenue.

The only truly neutral area was the road, where a steady flow of traffic moved slowly along the High Street. Her focused zeroed in on the limited number of vehicles visible from her hemmed-in position. The two Jihadist outriders had turned by now and were working their way back towards her; the jaws of the trap were closing fast. The bearded Jihadist who had originally blocked her path continued to berate her in an attempt to draw her attention from the outriders, all the while trying to grasp at her arms, which she batted away ever more frantically. She harboured no illusions as to her fate; despite the deafening silence of the politicians, the police, the courts, the national TV channels and newspapers – everybody knew the fate of European women who fell into Muslim hands.

Then, miraculously, like some unsuspecting archangel dumped unceremoniously into humanity's grubby little existence, a scruffy, battered, whitish van appeared among the busy traffic. It had ladders and various pieces of equipment strapped to its roof, while the words 'SPH Builders' were still legible on its dented flanks. Three White faces could be vaguely made out through the rain and wipers.

Her reaction was immediate. She swung around violently to her right, only to collide with yet another *burqua,* weighed down with shopping. A stream of expletives – some in English – broke from the masked face, while an overweight man in a *pakul* suddenly appeared at the *burqua's* side and began hitting out with a half-rolled umbrella. He carried no shopping. She took a blow to the side of her face, surprisingly painful, before reacting with a furious push at the *pakul,* who tripped over the *burqua* busily engaged in trying to save her spilled shopping from being trampled. The *pakul* fell back just as the first outrider stretched out to seize her; their comic collision buying a couple of vital seconds.

Heading pell-mell for the road, she burst between two indistinct figures huddled from the wind and rain in coats and billowing *shalwar kameez* and threw herself towards the railings that guarded the pavement from the traffic at the junction where the Jihadists were preaching. Powered by raw adrenaline, she vaulted the slippery railings.

The van had almost passed by now; she landed heavily straight into the path of an oncoming scooter, sending her expensive overnight bag sprawling across the greasy road. The Muslim youth riding the scooter slammed on the brakes and hit the railing, cursing the fleeing White woman – all in broken, heavily accented English. She turned towards the van, which was moving with the traffic. She dared not look behind, but knew instinctively that the Jihadists had also cleared the railings and were right behind her.

Running full pelt she launched herself at the van, grabbing wildly at the door handle which, to her horror, flew open under the weight of her body, swinging precariously outwards towards the pavement. As she hung in mid-air, her feet half-dragging on the tarmac the first Jihadist grabbed her, with a second joining his colleague almost immediately; she screamed and kicked out at the Muslims. The van stopped suddenly with a jerk; she fell, rolling to the ground, while the Jihadists crashed headlong into the open door. Out of the van spilled three White builders, the first of whom took one quick, confirmatory glance at the Jihadists before sliding open the van's side-door. Each of the three builders quickly grabbed whatever came to hand, before lining up along the van's side armed with assorted hammers, crowbars and a nail gun.

As she glanced up from the tarmac she got a first look at her unlikely saviours. The nearest to her was about average height, though solidly built, with light-brown hair and a strong jaw line. In his late twenties or early thirties, he wore a blue-chequered lumber jacket and brandished a well-worn, all-steel claw hammer in his right hand and a crowbar in his left. In the middle stood a taller man of just over six foot, in his mid-thirties. He had a square beard and black hair with the odd grey fleck; well-built, he grasped a long, heavy miner's crowbar in his right hand. Furthest away, wearing a brown construction jacket, was the third builder. Having curly flaxen hair and prominent chiselled features, he too was around average height though wirier than the other two and a little older, perhaps forty. He held a club hammer at the ready in his right hand and a large, orange nail gun in his left.

The Jihadists leapt to their feet, stung more by the indignity of having fallen down in front of infidels than the impact of running into the van's door. One of them shouted over to his comrades still preaching at the junction, while the second bent down to take hold of the girl. She kicked him away and scrambled to her feet.

'You all right, love?' came an English voice.

'Please, get me out of here,' she blurted.

A third Jihadist joined his colleagues; on the pavement a crowd of *pakuls* and *dashikis* was forming. The third Jihadist went to grab her arm, but the nearest builder, in the blue-chequered lumber jacket, pushed him away, brandishing his hammer; she retreated behind her saviours.

Angry, accusing voices broke out from the sodden pavement, mostly Urdu and bad English, though liberally sprinkled with Bengali, Arabic, Hausa and Pashto. The subtleties of Asian insults were lost on the bemused lads, but the message struck home with the first half-brick as it clattered against the van's side.

The Jihadists had by now been heavily reinforced; a crew of perhaps a dozen or more was forming into a half-circle confronting the three men. From behind the motionless van a chorus of blaring horns and angry motorists' curses merely heightened the tension emanating from the ugly mob assembling on the pavement behind the bearded Jihadists.

Her nearest saviour, nervously brandishing his claw hammer, eyed the rapidly swelling horde with trepidation: 'Steve, for fuck's sake let's get out of here before these bastards lynch us,' he pleaded in a low, urgent voice to the bearded builder. Steve glanced quickly behind him, then hissed to the girl through the side of his beard, 'Get in quick, through the side door … go!'

Needing no second invitation, she leapt into the van – a pigsty on wheels – landing heavily and painfully on a jumble of tools and equipment boxes. Immediately the side door was slammed home and the three men bundled into the van's front, accompanied by the baying of the mob watching their prey's attempted escape. As the van lurched forward a bright red fire extinguisher smashed through the nearside passenger window in a hail of broken glass, followed immediately by the frenzied face of a bearded Jihadist. A desperate struggle for the door ensued between the Jihadist, aided by unseen confederates outside the van, and the blue-chequered builder – one trying to force the door, the other to keep the jackals at bay. The flaxen-haired builder, sitting between Steve, who was driving the van, and the embattled lumber jacket defending the door, leant forward nonchalantly, seeking a better angle before bringing down his club hammer sharply on the crown of the intruding Jihadist, who tumbled away from the door grasping a cracked skull.

1.1 – MELTING POT

The sliding side-door was groaning under the weight of another unseen Jihadist swinging on its handle, trying to gain entry against the flailing efforts of the girl to keep it closed. The flaxen-haired builder now turned in his seat and took hold of a crowbar, which he proceeded to slam into the sliding door's floor track before hammering it tight against the doorframe. He looked down at the girl squirming painfully among the jumble of gear and grinned fiercely: 'Let's see the buggers get through that.'

She sat uncomfortably in the dark, listening to the cacophony of bangs and wallops as a deluge of missiles fell on the asthmatic van. Hands began violently tugging at the back door, causing the entire van to sway under the force of the attempted entry. With incredible violence a scaffold pole smashed through the windscreen, striking the flaxen builder and opening an ugly gash across his forehead. More Jihadists flung themselves at the van's doors and windows, all of which were met by hammer, fist or boot. Suddenly the back doors gave a screech and a chink of light flooded into the van's murky interior. She yelped involuntarily, but Steve's consolatory voice broke through her hysteria: 'Calm down, girl; it's padlocked with an Adus Security System – Christ, it cost more than the van. They'll have to rip the doors off their hinges if they want to get in through there.'

As the traffic speeded up the fury of the initial attack subsided. The bearded builder took the opportunity to introduce himself in snatched glances over his shoulder, 'I'm Steve, by the way; sorry for the mess in the van. What's your name, love?'

'Rachel.'

'Right, Rachel – would you mind taking a look at Alex here?' He nodded towards the flaxen-haired builder, who was holding his head, with blood oozing through his fingers and trickling down the side of his face.

Panicked by this unexpected request, she fumbled around for a response, 'But I haven't got anything, I'm no nurse – I lost my bag …' She suddenly remembered her expensive travelling bag. Oh no: it had all her overnight clothes, her handbag and purse, not to mention a brand-new mobile – shit!

'Just patch him up for now; we'll get him to a doctor as soon as we get out of this place.'

She couldn't really refuse. 'Have you got a first-aid kit or something?'

'I don't know – we used to have one.'

'It's under Rich's seat,' mumbled Alex distantly, from among the blood and pain. Rich immediately thrust his hand under his seat and began fishing among the jumble of empty disposable coffee cups and old newspapers before triumphantly pulling up a green plastic box with a familiar white cross emblazoned on the lid. Rich opened it; there was little to be seen, but Rachel found a piece of gauze and asked Alex to turn towards her – he was a mess.

'He'll need a hospital,' she said.

'There's an A&E not far away,' responded Steve. Rachel found a pack of tissues in the pocket of her Harrington and cleaned him up as best she could before placing the gauze over his wound.

'I've got no way of holding this gauze in place,' she complained. Without saying a word, Rich leaned over and began taping the gauze down with a roll of grey duct tape.

The van headed down to the far end of the High Street, but through the cracked wing mirrors Steve could make out a determined crew of Jihadists still pursuing along the edge of the traffic. Further back he noticed how the crowd had spilt right across the top of the High Street, blocking the traffic in both directions, with the black Jihadist banner fluttering triumphantly above the frenzied throng.

They had almost reached the T-junction that would allow the van to swing onto the main road for Lichfield. In front were two cars waiting for the lights to change. The lights, seemingly stuck on red, were making life very uncomfortable, each second dragging like an eternity. Steve and Rich glanced anxiously from the lights to the rapidly closing Jihadists running alongside the tail of traffic behind them – it would be a close call.

At last the amber winked, and Steve heaved the old girl into first, heading for the junction to turn right – but it was too late. Dark hands grabbed the inside of the smashed nearside window's doorframe while others, incredibly, came swarming around the van's far side attempting to enter, with the rain and wind, through the shattered windscreen. Yet others tried their strength once again at the back doors – all accompanied by demented cries of, 'Allah Akbar!'

Even as Steve pushed home the gear lever for second, the hands grasping the nearside doorframe were joined by a head and arm, which proceeded to resume the struggle for the door. However, it was the figure literally coming through the windscreen that caused the greatest concern. Having gained a handhold on the window frame he lunged at Steve with an evil-looking *janbiya* knife. Instinctively Steve turned his head at the last instant as the blade flashed by, ploughing into the remnants of the van's well-worn seat padding. Alex, nursing his bloodstained brow swaddled in duct tape, swung his club hammer at the figure, who parried the blow with his forearm then slashed out with the knife, opening a fresh wound along Alex's right cheek. The van, swerving uncontrollably, bounced off the nearest of the two cars at the traffic lights, narrowly missing a bus waiting to turn left into the gridlocked High Street. Steve had one hand on the steering wheel while the other wrestled with the Jihadist, who in turn was hanging onto his precarious perch on the van's bonnet with his left hand.

With a mighty heave the Jihadist swung around athletically, successfully hooking his right leg over the van's facia, then rolled himself half into the cabin, landing in Alex's lap. In an instant he'd slammed his right foot firmly against Rich's unsuspecting back then launched himself at Steve for a second time. The instant Steve sensed the flash of the blade he threw himself forward onto the steering wheel as the glinting steel flew narrowly above the nape of his neck, impacting heavily on the driver's side window, which miraculously remained intact.

The van, trailing an absurd gaggle of screaming Jihadists, staggered violently into the main Lichfield traffic. The windscreen Jihadist, ignoring the bloodied and groggy Alex, pulled himself up and, half-leaning against the steering wheel, snapped his left hand tight around Steve's throat, steadying his victim for the fatal knife thrust.

Through a haze of concussion and streaming blood, Alex's flaxen head bent down unsteadily to reach for the nail gun lying among the debris littering the van floor. He pulled the gun up and thrust it directly into the Jihadist's surprised face, discharging a nail at point-blank range. With an anguished howl the Jihadist disappeared out of the window, falling under the van, which shuddered as it bumped over the body. Steve slammed the gear stick into third and accelerated towards Lichfield. The Jihadist wrestling for the door, seeing the nail gun turn ominously towards him, leapt from the van, impacting heavily on the kerb where he slumped unconscious.

The van chugged away from the High Street, caught up in the main Lichfield traffic, its occupants stunned into silence. The enormity of the incident overwhelmed every other emotion. A low groan from Alex brought them back to reality.

'We need to get him to that A&E,' said Rich.

'Yeah, I know,' said Steve grimly. 'It's not far.'

They got more than a few quizzical looks as they pulled wheezing into the extensive hospital car park twenty minutes later. In an almost dream-like trance they fell out of the van and headed for A&E, with Alex half-carried between Steve and Rich. Looking back at the van, the reason for the quizzical glances became self-evident.

From where she stood Rachel could see that two of the van's three windows had been smashed – including the windscreen – and there were dents and scars from the stoning visible along the length of the van's body. There was a bright red slick running down the nearside door, and one of the ladders on the van's roof was protruding at a ludicrous angle. Part of the exhaust had come loose and was dragging on the road. The rear doors had been partially bent outwards at their tops – though as Steve had prophesied, the mighty Adus Security System had kept them firmly closed.

A sudden wave of guilt washed over her; she was responsible for all this. The van was probably their livelihood, and now it was wrecked. She turned towards Steve as he helped Alex towards the hospital doors. 'Look at your poor van,' she said, 'I'm so sorry ... I ...' – but before she could finish her sentence Rich cut in:

'Don't be silly, love; d'you think we'd leave one of our own to that scum? What do you take us for – coppers?'

Internally she recoiled – scum? Her conditioning was deep, and until now had carried her unquestioningly through all aspects of life to this present predicament. She had spent a lot of her free time at college campaigning with various green and anti-racist groups – as was the expectation of modern, progressive, middle-class students. Although she had no direct experience of living among Negroes or Muslims, she had attended a few anti-Nazi rallies with the college branch of the ARC – the Anti-Racist Coalition. Although hardly a front-line warrior herself, she had been attracted to the group largely owing to the fact that a certain Rhys Rogers was a leading member. Bearing a passing resemblance to Keanu Reeves, he spoke eloquently and passionately on the subject of racial equality, primarily during college parties. The combination of looks and ideology had proven very successful and as a result he had acquired a lively following among the ladies.

On one notable occasion, the group – all of whom were White – had travelled down to a squat in Brixton to experience the vibrancy of its majority Negro population. Rachel had gawked, spellbound, at the casual attitude to sex and violence displayed by the local population. However, what really took her breath away had been the sexually explicit dancing of the Black women. Wearing the skimpiest of clothing, they bent over with legs splayed wide, then thrust their gyrating booties hard into their partner's crotch and began grinding in rhythm to the music – little was left to the imagination. Secretly she had visions of performing the same ritual on Rhys herself.

The heady mix of casual sex, casual violence and the ever-present air of menace had proven intoxicating, especially as her visit to such a location was in direct violation of her parents' pleading before leaving for college. However, Brixton had provided more than an exciting ethnic experience; there had also been that dark business with Sam. Samantha Wheeler had travelled down with the rest in the ARC mini-bus and, like the other girls, had been exhilarated by the colourful locals – even experimenting in a little dancing herself. However, unlike the others, who after tasting an approximation of the forbidden fruit had retired to the comparative safety of the squat, she had stayed out with the locals. Sam had reappeared the following morning just in time to catch the mini-bus home, looking dishevelled and strangely reticent to recount her exploits – even though it was a good two-hour drive back to college. Up to that point Sam had been a regular and enthusiastic participant at ARC meetings, but she never came again. Indeed, following a short interlude she disappeared entirely from campus.

Rhys had organised the Brixton trip after attending one of the ARC's biannual meetings in London with officers of the Freedom Guild to discuss progress and campaign targets. The Guild helped lots of organisations like the ARC, co-ordinating activities and giving advice on matters such as how to handle the media or disrupting meetings of political opponents. More to the point, the Guild also distributed funds to 'worthy causes', like the ARC and, as Rhys discovered, the Guild's activities were not confined to Britain. The Freedom Guild operated throughout Europe – even in Russia. The source of the funds was not discussed, though five minutes' digging on the internet would reveal that a certain George Chanos was the ultimate figure behind the Guild, providing both its finance and its overall direction.

The visit to the Brixton squat had been offered to the ARC by a sister movement, the South London Campaign for Racial Equality. Rhys had taken up the SLCRE's thoughtful offer under prompting from Guild officers keen to see greater cooperation between the different groups they financed. None of these matters was discussed openly within the ARC, and most of the rank and file were either unaware or unheeding of the mechanisms behind the organisation. It certainly was not a topic that interested Rachel.

The ARC, true to its roots, being composed entirely of White, middle-class, well-educated, financially comfortable students, was very particular concerning the right look: urban grunge was *de rigueur*. Although to their parents they might appear to have been clothed entirely in items discarded from charity shops, such a philistine lack of understanding hid the well-crafted reality of their dress. This look was not only carefully cultivated, but surprisingly expensive, served by internet shops and certain outlets in the larger cities dedicated to self-proclaimed avant-garde fashion. Rachel's green DMs alone had cost enough to feed a family of four for a week.

The ARC – or Rhys to be specific – had been the primary reason why Rachel had been in the High Street at all. Rhys had a core group of female admirers who tended to swirl around him, one of whom was a certain Libby Mason. Libby, with her hourglass figure and striking strawberry-blonde hair, had made an impact on Rhys from the moment she first joined the group. Emanating from a solid middle-class family, she had been sucked into the heady world of the ARC by Rhys' film-star looks, in due course becoming one of his favoured few via the traditional female path.

Incongruously, both Rhys and Libby – and the rest of the harem, for that matter – were committed feminists.

Rachel's decision to make an attempt at joining the chosen few had come after a particularly fine performance by Rhys during a lively party in the digs of one of her fellow Sociology and Politics course members. That he had the makings of a successful politician was undoubted; he spouted all the expected platitudes with a heart-rending superficiality that had his largely female audience in raptures. They squatted around him engrossed, swigging heartily from their alcopops and puffing earnestly on the circulating spliffs.

That Rhys was merely the well-groomed public face of the ARC never crossed the minds of the ladies, whose thoughts tended to be elsewhere. Rhys was not one of those hard-core members, typically battle-clad in black with red bandanas, who waged constant guerrilla war against their nationalist foes. The spearhead of these New Right forces was formed by National Resistance, referred to as the Nixons by their enemies. The 'Nixons' label was an indirect reference to the town where National Resistance had first emerged as a fighting force – Billericay in Essex. 'Billericay Dickie' had been an old Ian Dury hit from way back. These new Billericay Dickies soon found themselves being compared to the disgraced former US president, 'Tricky Dickie' Nixon, by their Marxist adversaries. The former president, a man who'd been stitched up by the insidious Georgetown set and those inglorious hucksters Woodward and Bernstein, was by now primarily remembered as a crazed talking head in a popular cartoon show. The adoption of the label, 'Nixons' by the college-based ARC to describe their enemies was an attempt to portray them as deceitful liars – supposedly like the ex-president. That linkage may have failed, being far too obscure for the general public, but the tag stuck.

National Resistance, like similar groups across Europe, fought to defend the *patria* from the rampant Marxist social-engineering programmes promoted by the likes of the ARC and their establishment allies. The irony of the situation was lost on the bulk of the ARC's membership. They saw themselves as class and equality warriors: revolutionaries battling against a corrupt, racist society. None of them had any real contact with the working class, and their knowledge of the ethnic groups that comprised multiracial Britain was farcical in its superficiality and abject naivety. In truth, the ARC was only revolutionary in the strength of its adherence to mainstream politics dominated by Marxist ideology – a glaring truism which explained their parents' ease with the idea of their offspring cavorting in such company.

However, the ARC bubble was burst from time to time, and it was Rhys, with his slick words and political spin, who was obliged to explain away any nasty little hiccups. One such problem was the rapidly expanding militant Muslim groups, who more than once had turned on the ARC, their erstwhile allies, and beaten them – quite literally – in the streets. There was also the occasional member who wandered unchaperoned into dangerous areas of open knowledge – like the internet. Once beyond the tightly controlled universe of the MSM – Main-Stream Media – all sorts of horrors came crawling out of the woodwork, such as videos of the bloody butchery used in Muslim countries to enforce Sharia, or some of the colourful ethnic traditions practised by Black Africans, like FGM – female genital mutilation – or the quaint tribal custom of 'necklacing'. Rhys had much to explain away, but his silver tongue was invariably up to the job, whatever the task.

In reality, the ARC knew as well as National Resistance did the real raison d'être for the actions of the Jihadists. Islam simply did not recognise Western ideas of Left and Right; to them one was either a believer or a *kafir* – there was no middle ground. However, this inconvenient little truth was not to be relayed to the college faithful, who remained steadfast in their loyalty to the twin towers of multiculturalism and multiracialism.

Libby had decided to acquire a flat near the High Street because of the area's large Muslim population. Although dangerous, it gave Libby major street-cred within the ARC – something Rhys greatly appreciated, much to Libby's delight. This was how Rachel's request to stay the night at Libby's place first came about. Superficially it was to experience the glories of enrichment in a multicultural area; in reality it was to get a closer look at Rhys' current number-one concubine.

Libby was well aware that her visitor was a competitor rather than the friend she purported to be. Well, if Rachel wanted to play games so could Libby, who organised the whole event with military precision. She'd also planned a little sting in the tail as a going-away present for her inquisitive guest. Thus the visitor had arrived late at night in a car organised by Libby, when the area was quiet and the full impact of its Muslim character hidden. The following day, Libby had nonchalantly informed her guest that the bus stop was at the far end of the High Street – forgetting to mention that she herself had never used it. Over the short period Libby had been in the flat she had seen enough of multiculturalism to realise that all the dire warnings – spoken quietly and out of earshot of third parties – were fully justified. She always took a taxi, paid for by her parents, to and from the flat whenever venturing out. She never used local taxis – there were three such companies in the High Street – as the drivers were all Muslims. She called in taxis from Darnby, as that company and its drivers were all English. It was expensive of course but, as Libby reasoned, one cannot put too high a price on safety. In practice she spent as little time as possible in the flat and considered the whole area and its population ghastly.

Thus it was that in stepping out alone onto the pavement to head for the bus stop that fateful November day, clad in her expensive donkey jacket and carrying her up-market overnight bag, Rachel came face to face with the grim reality of multiculturalism for the first time in her life.

'Scum'? Even now, after coming within a whisker of experiencing the full warmth of Islam's appreciation of European womanhood, she still instinctively leapt to their defence. Scum? It jarred heavily on her indoctrinated nerves. She turned to Rich, 'I can't thank you enough for what you three did today – but I'm sure not all Muslims are as predatory as those fanatics who attacked us.'

Steve glanced at her, smiling, 'I'm sure you're right. They were just biding their time before coming to your aid – bless 'em.'

The other two grinned ironically as they pushed through the hospital door.

They told the hospital receptionist that Alex had had an accident on a building site, slipping off some scaffolding and hitting his head – which was partially true.

While killing time in the crowded waiting room, Steve and Rich took turns to go outside for a roll-up. Steve went first, as Rich was busy helping Alex. On Steve's return Rich got up and left for his much needed smoke. Steve turned to Rachel, and in a rather perplexed voice asked, 'What exactly happened to us today? As introductions go it takes some beating.'

1.1 – MELTING POT

Rachel scrambled for a response, 'It came out of nowhere. I'd been staying at a friend's nearby …'

'You've got friends in the town centre?'

'Yes, in the flat above the laundrette.'

'What kind of friends? There's nobody in the centre of town except Muslims: even the Blacks have been pushed out – unless they're Muslims, of course.'

'Oh, just a college friend.'

Steve's eyes narrowed. 'And she's a Muslim? I take it your friend's female?'

Taken aback by the tone of the question and its probing into her private life, she retorted hesitantly, 'Well yes; my friend's a girl, but she's not a Muslim – she's from Little Hurst,' Rachel had made it her business to learn a great deal about Miss Mason.

Incredulity filled Steve's face. 'She's from Little Hurst and she lives in the town centre?'

'Yes, it's just a flat for college – why, what's up with that?'

'There's something wrong here,' he said in a low voice. 'Muslims don't tolerate *kafirs* – or didn't you notice?'

'You're being too black and white – excuse the pun; as I said in the car park, not all Muslims are the same, and my friend does live in the town centre. You can't condemn all Muslims for the actions of a minority.' The vacuous words poured out of her on autopilot, but even as the hackneyed soundbites tumbled from her lips she felt their impotence keenly.

'I don't care; I stand by what I said. I'm not spouting some slogan here, I've seen plenty of trouble from Muslims; I've got mates up in Bradford and Dewsbury.'

Bradford and Dewsbury: the names leapt accusingly at Rachel. In both locales the Muslims were by now in the majority. Following a host of accusations of grooming young White girls by Pakistani men – none of which had been taken further by the local police – a more general campaign to form homogeneous Muslim communities had been taking place. Using a number of different tactics – some semi-official with local government connivance, others organised ad hoc by local mosques – a de facto ethnic cleansing of the English from both areas had taken place. Neither campaign had been reported in the news – standard procedure by now – but a mountain of video footage, blogs and eyewitness accounts had appeared on the internet. Bradford and Dewsbury now sat among a growing list of European cities slipping from indigenous control – Malmö, Marseilles, Rotterdam, Roubaix, etc. – where any remaining native Europeans who'd not either fled or been expelled, clung on in embattled enclaves.

The internet had long been a thorn in the side of progressive forces like the ARC, and every mainstream political party in Europe for that matter, with its open forum for all sorts of independent ideas. Its unregulated output allowed nutters of every persuasion the freedom to expound the most outrageous views without first having obtained the permission of responsible authorities to do so. Who did these people think they were, expressing their own opinions?

Rachel held decidedly mixed views concerning the internet. It was great for the important stuff, like talking to friends on Facebook and Twitter, or illegally downloading music and films. She hadn't paid much attention to the medium's other uses other than research for the odd piece of college work – though she was aware that pornography and gambling constituted two of the internet's greatest contributions to Western civilisation.

Disappointingly, she found the ARC's official website both hectoring and boring in the extreme and, even worse, it inexplicably contained no pictures of Rhys. However, she had also become acutely aware of a large body of 'fascist' websites, often named and verbally attacked during ARC meetings. These insidious sites had slowly begun to eat away at her careful conditioning through directly questioning everything she held sacred. Although fascists like the Nixons were a constant danger, against whom members of ARC had to be vigilant, the membership were reliably informed that they were only few in number, composed mainly of uneducated working-class White thugs who were little better than knuckle-dragging Neanderthals.

Yet confusingly, on closer inspection virtually all the revisionist and nationalist sites she visited contained probing essays, obviously written by educated Europeans, attacking the religion of multiculturalism with facts: powerful, all-pervasive facts that appeared to undermine the whole project. She dismissed the whole thing of course, but in the back of her mind little voices were beginning to utter heresy, and late at night she would often find herself staring at some dangerous website, reading an even more dangerous blog before snapping out of her trance and returning to YouTube for something a little less taxing. Stung by the impudence of these Nazis, she had dug a little deeper and discovered the scale of these dangerous websites; there were thousands of them. Even worse, having researched their stats she was forced to confront the enormity of the beast as highlighted in the astronomical number of hits they were receiving. She was dumbfounded.

As Rich returned from his cigarette, Steve announced, 'Rich, Rachel says that she's got friends living in the town centre.'

'What? How on earth …? No, that's impossible; what friends? Where do they live?'

'Above the laundrette, in a flat.'

'The laundrette? What's it called?'

Steve turned to Rachel.

'I think it's called Wishy-Washy,' she ventured.

'That sounds familiar.'

'You know the laundrette?' Steve could hardly believe his ears.

'Not personally, but I've heard of it. Alex mentioned it the other day.'

'In what context?'

'I can't remember exactly: something to do with Darnby.' Turning to Rachel he confided, 'That's where Alex lives.'

Alex sat silently, wrapped up in his own world of pain, with blood oozing through the duct tape and running down his front.

There was a pause in the conversation while two worried parents brought in a wailing boy holding a bloody leg. There was a rush of activity as nurses suddenly appeared and the boy was whisked away for treatment.

Steve turned to Rachel. 'There's no need for you to wait; we'll look after Alex. Shouldn't you phone somebody to come and get you?'

'No, I couldn't; you've done so much.'

'You've been through a lot; head home with our blessings before it gets dark. In any case, the police will be here sooner or later.'

The police? It had never occurred to her.

'But we're innocent; they … that particular gang of extremists, attacked us; we were just defending ourselves,' Rachel's words, though accurate, were nevertheless more a plea to her own scruples.

Steve cut in: 'Yes, but that was a pretty wild attack and people have been hurt – including Alex. There's also the matter of religion … there'll be a hell of a stink tomorrow; the press and police will be swarming all over the place. It's getting late, but I think you'd better report the incident either tonight, or early tomorrow at the latest.'

1.1 – MELTING POT

A million and one scenarios suddenly exploded in Rachel's mind. The police were the enforcers of her rapidly dissolving faith in multiculturalism and had a fearsome reputation for action against anybody they considered a blasphemer. As somebody who had spent much of her time in the ARC demanding ever more stringent action by the police in defence of the cult of multiculturalism, she was suddenly very aware of the public condemnation that fell on heretics, prior to them receiving their just deserts in state-run kangaroo courts. She had visions of herself on the front page of the *Guardian* – the ultimate disgrace; indeed, as she contemplated such a predicament a disturbing image started to form before her mind's eye. The lens focused on something close, too close to see clearly: then slowly the vision began to zoom out. The indistinct shape hardened into a copy of the *Guardian*, held in a finely manicured hand, while a female voice giggled somewhere in the background. The camera moved out a little further and slowly all became clear: there they were – Libby with her *Guardian* and Rhys, coiled around each other, naked on a splendid four-poster bed.

Bitch! Her mind zeroed in on Libby's radiant face resting contentedly on Rhys' muscular shoulder. She wore a broad grin, with her bright scarlet lips, slightly parted, 1940s' fashion. Her sparkling eyes were hungrily contemplating a photo blazoned across the paper's front page, above which the headline screamed, 'Evil Racist Apprehended'. Rachel's focus dropped from Libby's gleeful visage to the paper's front page. She froze, her eyes struggling to take in the sight that confronted them. There she stood, in a grainy black-and-white photo, her left hand defiantly planted on her hip, dressed in a black latex cat suit, wearing a Nazi armband and with a malicious leer on her face. Her right hand held a smoking nail gun, which inexplicably was coloured orange.

It was all simply too awful; what would her friends say? Her parents? Rhys? It was all the fault of that slut Libby; she'd planned this all along … Rachel's mind raced wildly, conspiring revenge after revenge, each more grisly than the last.

'Yeah, we're just goin' to take Alex back to his place – once he's patched up – then get some nosh; I'm starving. It's work again in the morning, depending upon the police,' added Rich.

Rachel mumbled her thanks; deep in thought she shuffled over to the public phones by the hospital reception to phone Daddy. Half an hour later a silver BMW saloon whooshed into the car park and in an instant Rachel was gone.

Another forty-five minutes later, despite the blood running freely down his face, turning the front of his once-brown jacket a dark claret, Alex was finally led off to get stitched.

It was dark when the three of them emerged from the hospital. They made their way over to the battered van in an ocean of parked vehicles. Alex's head had been heavily bandaged – it had already been agreed that he would not be in work tomorrow. They wrapped up as warmly as possible before setting out; the lack of a windscreen meant it would be a decidedly chilly trip home.

The journey would take around 40 minutes. They huddled against the icy wind, marvelling at the number of police cars and vans roaring up and down the Lichfield road, lights flashing and sirens blaring, before turning off for Darnby. It never occurred to any of them that the sodium lighting on this section of the road gave the van a distinctly yellow hue. Steve tried the radio, despite the howling noise from the wind. He wound up the dial in time to catch the end of *Wonderwall* before the local nine o'clock news came on:

'Police are still seeking witnesses after a serious incident in Bransborough town centre this afternoon. Following an initial stand-off between two groups of men, subsequent clashes saw a vehicle trying to leave the crime scene, which resulted in the death of one man and serious injury to another. Investigations are ongoing, with a news conference scheduled for 10 o'clock tomorrow morning by Mr Asif Azim, Chief Constable of Mercia. The police wish to question three men described as Caucasian in appearance, last seen in a white van travelling towards Lichfield on the A765.'

There was then a brief recording of comments made by David Greenberg, the local Socialist MP. 'This appears to have been yet another racist attack leading to the tragic death of one of my constituents. I urge the Chief Constable, Mr Azim, to leave no stone unturned in finding these men and bringing matters to a speedy and judicial conclusion.'

Other news saw Sally Kelly, the local singer from the hit television talent programme *Star Struck Britain,* arrested for being drunk and disorderly outside the Horse and Hounds public house in Broadway, Worcestershire …'

Steve turned off the radio. Dead?

1.2 – Machinations

Steve and Rich did not reach the building site the following morning until eleven, having spent almost three hours getting the van's windscreen replaced. Steve had phoned Geoff, the foreman, to explain the situation claiming that 'kids' had smashed the glass as a prank. The pair had been on site less than an hour when Geoff approached them.

'Hey boys,' he beckoned.

'I'm sorry we were late, Geoff, but as I explained on the phone: bloody kids …' Steve began – but Geoff cut him off,

'It's nothing to do with that.' Geoff paused, looking from Steve to Rich then back again. 'There's a couple of plods down by the main gate asking after you two.'

Steve glanced over towards the gate and saw around half a dozen uniforms loitering by the site office.

'Do I need to know something?' asked Geoff, doubt written all over his craggy face.

'No, it's fine, Geoff, thanks. We've been expecting them.'

The pair walked together down towards the gate, where a plain-clothes officer stepped from among the uniforms holding up his warrant card.

'Stephen Phillip Hall, Richard Jonathan Norman Cunliffe?' They nodded. 'I'm arresting you on suspicion of murder; you do not have to say anything, but it may harm your defence if you do not mention when questioned something which you later rely on in court. Anything you do say may be given in evidence.'

As he spoke, the uniforms closed in and handcuffed the pair before leading them off to a waiting van.

Neither of them had the slightest idea of what awaited them, but the scale of the beast's maw became apparent as the van approached Bransborough police station.

It was apocalyptic.

Vast hordes of baying Muslims, liberally sprinkled with ARC activists, filled the pavement directly in front of the police station. Protruding from the mob was a forest of placards and flags ranging from the standard, professionally produced ARC anti-racist polemic to home-made homilies charmingly proclaiming death to the infidel and Sharia for Britain – all knocked up in a local mosque. Among the large number of flags fluttering in the cold wind were the obligatory Palestinian examples, along with those of Pakistan, Bangladesh, Afghanistan and Iraq – to name but the most numerous – with assorted black Jihadist banners thrown in for luck. Around the frothing horde jostled an almost equally large scrum of photographers, TV cameramen and reporters, the entire mass kept in uneasy order by a thin line of police in full riot gear.

Steve and Rich could not see the horde from inside the van, but when the vehicle came into view they certainly heard the explosion of noise as the mob began ululating wildly; it was primeval. The van driver was heading for the side entrance of the spectacularly ugly 1960s police station, where prisoners were usually dropped off. The station's main entrance sat underneath a square prefab concrete office block, supported on the street front by spindly white concrete legs. Steps led up to the front door, while to the side was a long wheelchair ramp.

The most militant and noisy section of the mob was concentrated at the foot of these steps, with a further larger body across the street filling the car park opposite the police station. With the van's approach those in the car park broke ranks and surged across the road to join their compatriots at the foot of the steps, choking the entire thoroughfare and bringing all traffic to a halt – including the police van.

The mob now turned its fury on the stationary van in a virtual rerun of the original incident. The police driver was helpless; boxed in fore and aft, he desperately radioed the regional controller in Stafford for help from Bransborough Police Station, which was literally 200 metres from where he was sitting. The mob hit the van in a wave, surging around the vehicle trying to rip open the doors, while others rocked the van violently from side to side in an attempt to tip it on its side.

While the storm raged outside, something far more introspective and spiritual was occurring inside the van, for one man at least.

Builders are not famed for their religiosity, yet the need for a higher purpose touches all eventually – or at least that was Steve's belief. He had been raised an Anglican, in theory, though to the best of his knowledge he had only ever entered a church once, and that was for the wedding of his sister Liz. It had been a fabulous day and he'd enjoyed it immensely, but there was precious little religion involved.

He probably would have spent the rest of his life as a disinterested agnostic – like almost everybody else – if he had not met Elaine. He'd had numerous girlfriends over the years, but nothing ever jelled, and once he turned thirty he began to wonder whether he'd ever find a suitable partner. Although his academic record looked poor – a handful of mediocre GCSEs – this doleful scholastic picture did little justice to his real abilities. The school he'd gone to had been a fairly tough place, with plenty of tension between the various races – Asians, Blacks and Whites; lessons had been the least of his problems, and received the least of his attention as a consequence. In truth Steve was basically a pretty bright individual, often finishing crosswords during the morning tea break, and these were not the moronic red-top variety, but full broadsheet versions. He read continually – at home, never in front of his mates – and spent most nights surfing the internet, keeping abreast of the crumbling economic situation. Like everybody else, he had scant faith in the MSM, taking little notice of the thinly disguised propaganda pumped out on the main TV channels.

He'd finally given internet dating a try, and after a few duds had met Elaine Clark. From the very beginning he realised that he'd found somebody special in Elaine, prompting the question: could this be it? Could she be the one, after all these years?

Elaine had been equally smitten with the catch she had unexpectedly landed, quickly grasping there was more to Steve than the bluff builder; here was a man capable of taking the journey with her – for Elaine had begun to explore alternative religious routes, down old Pagan paths.

Elaine first broached the delicate business of religion in bed – *post coitum* – a time when a lady is at her strongest in propositioning her man. Steve at first expressed incredulity and disbelief, all tempered by the delicacy of the situation. However, it actually turned out to be a fairly simple task to hook him, since once the seed had been planted he set off under his own steam to learn as much as possible about Paganism. As he soon discovered, there was far more to it than he had realised.

In practice they ended up taking a far bigger journey than either could have imagined. Elaine had initially been infatuated with Wicca and the nature-based belief systems connected with such totems as the Green Man and the White Witch. However, Steve found himself drawn to the Old Gods, and the moves afoot in various corners of Europe to reignite the ancient traditions and resume the journey interrupted by the Christian hiatus. For the first time in his life he came across mention of the *Liber Iuliani* – the Book of Julian - that was being hailed as a new beginning for Paganism in Europe. At first Steve had no idea what the *Liber Iuliani* was, but after reading some Pagan blogs and asking around in Pagan chat rooms he came across various inaccurate references to it as some sort of Pagan Bible, based on suggestions made by the Roman emperor Julian the Philosopher back in the fourth century.

Julian had delineated the philosophy pertinent to Pagan teachings: Stoicism, Neo-Platonism, Pythagoreanism, etc., which a group of Pagan academics had begun collating, along with the iconic Pagan poetry of Homer, Hesiod and Virgil. The volume would also include such works as Sallustius' *On the Gods and the Universe* and Julian's own *Against the Galilaeans* – both of which Steve had searched out and read online, as had Elaine.

Intoxicated by the world opening before his eyes, Steve found himself hooked, and his infectious enthusiasm soon sucked in Elaine as well. Although the proposed creation of the *Liber Iuliani* would furnish Paganism with an unsurpassed body of philosophic teachings, the old myths remained central to interpreting the nature of the Gods. More importantly, the myths spoke to the reality of the Gods, something normally referred to as 'faith', while philosophy was its intellectualisation. Steve took his cue from English and Germanic Paganism and began reading the *Prose Edda*, while seeking out local Pagan groups.

Elaine had once asked Steve why, if he found a religious itch developing, he hadn't got the Anglicans to scratch it for him. Since he had never considered the question before Elaine broached the subject, he couldn't answer – indeed, he asked himself why he was turning to the Old Gods: what was wrong with Christianity? By then, having read Julian's attack, he was fully aware of the core weaknesses of Christianity from a Pagan point of view, but that didn't of itself answer the question. There was something else eating away at any loyalty he might have felt towards the itinerant, charismatic, Galilean rabbi – but he couldn't name it or explain it.

1.2 – MACHINATIONS

These things were very much private affairs, something restricted to himself, Elaine and their new circle of friends; they most certainly were not for discussion on building sites. However, as the van wound its way towards the police station and the howls of the mob broke out, Steve's mind returned to the words of Sallustius he'd scribbled on the back of a pack of Rizla papers:

'It is impious to suppose the Divine is affected for good or ill by human things. The Gods are always good and always do good, never harm, being always in the same state and true to themselves. The truth simply is that when we are good, we are joined to the Gods by our likeness to them; when we are bad, we are separated from them by our unlikeness.'

Steve glanced over towards Rich, who, wide-eyed, was desperately listening to the assault on the van. Steve's mind went back to the words of Sallustius, and a wave of calm enveloped him.

The van jerked suddenly to one side.

'Are you religious?' Steve's voice, calm in the eye of the maelstrom, was directed at the clearly distraught Rich, as the van bucked frenetically to and fro.

'What? Are you friggin' mad?'

'Come on, Rich: are you religious?' Steve was as calm as a summer picnic on a lazy August afternoon. Rich just stared at him in bewilderment. The van squirmed again, violently, almost going over.

'I don't go to church or anything, but I know the Gods are real enough.' Steve was talking more to himself than to his friend, who was struggling to control his racing passions. The pair of them suddenly found themselves thrown forcibly against the van's side – which miraculously still refused to topple.

'When your gran died last year,' Steve continued, as if nothing had happened, 'did you go to the funeral service? Yes, you did. Why? Did she care? Did she know? Would she have noticed if you hadn't bothered? Did you feel her presence? Was she there? Come on, Rich, tell me: what do you believe?'

Drowned by the screams of the mob and sounds of the attack on the van, the two prisoners had not heard the sharp blast of the whistle that signalled the charge of every police officer in Bransborough nick against the mob. Other vans were already racing to the scene, full of extra police from every station in the county, but they would not arrive in time to save the prisoners, as Bransborough's commander well knew. Although heavily outnumbered the impact of the police, backed up with a mixture of baton, CS gas, tasers and mustard spray, cleared the immediate area long enough to drag out the two bedraggled inmates and bundle them back towards the station as quickly as possible. The decision had already been taken to seal off the road in front of the station at both ends to protect the building from direct assault.

The whole event was filmed, photographed and recorded by every TV station and paper in the land; it was glorious stuff – charging riot police battling wild Jihadists and Marxist ARC 'revolutionaries'.

It took another six hours of running battles and heavy reinforcements – initially from across the county, but soon expanding to involve men from neighbouring counties – before order was finally re-established. But for London's political elite it was already far too late; Bransborough had become a public-relations disaster.

The following morning, every TV channel in the country had reporters on site, standing by the now formidable concrete barricades sealing off both ends of the road on which the police station was situated. The barricades were heavily manned with equally heavily armed riot police, sporting every piece of kit allowed under the law. The streets around the police station showed the signs of battle: discarded placards and flags, vast amounts of rubble and glass that had been hurled at the police, along with scores upon scores of empty CS gas canisters and discharged rubber bullets. About twenty cars had been torched during the night, some of which had been pushed into police lines ablaze in the hope that the fuel tanks might explode. All this had been caught on camera, but would never be screened by the MSM. Interestingly, the police's own camera crews had also recorded these events, but their video would join the rest locked away from public scrutiny. Unfortunately for these bastions of the public interest, local National Resistance members had also captured these incidents on their mobile phones and proceeded to post revealing clips on the internet.

All the hospitals within a thirty-mile radius overflowed with the wounded, but nobody had been killed – much to the MSM's disappointment.

Although both Muslim and Marxist continued to maintain a vigil against the 'racist killers', they had been pushed back so far by police cordons that they'd became largely irrelevant. Mercia Police maintained a very high presence on the streets, determined there would be no further disturbances. Some in London actually suggested moving the defendants to more secure premises in the capital, but the chief constable politely, yet firmly, rejected the suggestion.

Rich and Steve were informed by their court-appointed brief that both Alex and Rachel had been brought to the station earlier that morning. What they didn't know was that Basil Kynaston, Rachel's father, had already instructed the family solicitors, Jarrett and Taylor, to appoint a private brief to arrange bail for his daughter.

Events started to move fast. At 3:00 pm they were informed that the injured Jihadist had gone into a coma. They commenced on a round of official police interviews, in which each gave his version of events. Crucially, the CCTV cameras on Bransborough High Street had been switched off after complaints to the chief constable from the Central Mosque that the police were unjustly spying on innocent worshippers. Nobody mentioned that unfortunate incident two years earlier, when a member of Bransborough Central Mosque, along with three other Jihadists, had been shot dead by German police in Cologne, while trying to place explosives on a commuter train.

Since there was no video of the incident the police had to rely heavily on the extensive interviews of those present that day. However, things did not go smoothly. Progress was painfully slow owing to the number of witnesses unable to speak or understand English, with most requiring an interpreter. Soon there were interpreters transcribing evidence in seven languages. Initially, the stories coming back varied extremely, with some more or less agreeing with that given by the builders and Rachel. Others, however, spoke of a White girl sexually provoking a group of Muslim men with her obscene dress and lewd suggestions. When the men tried to move her on before her profanities were heard by their good Muslim womenfolk and innocent children, three heavily armed Nixon thugs turned up to defend her. Although the brave and pious Muslim men did their best to rid their God-fearing community of these *kafirs* by driving out the devils, they were met with utterly disproportionate violence. Unarmed Muslims had been attacked with heavy hammers, crowbars and a nail gun.

After the local imam had spoken at Friday prayers, this second version of events became universal among the local Muslim population.

This was the version that seeped back to the press, and was soon being broadcast verbatim as if true. David Greenberg was not long in jumping on the bandwagon, demanding protection for Muslim communities throughout the county. He also reiterated a call made earlier at the Socialist Party's annual conference that the state ban the Nixons as a threat to social cohesion and racial harmony.

Greenberg's words were widely reported in the press and TV, having been cleverly crafted to dovetail seamlessly with the prevailing political orthodoxy, as disseminated by the press and TV.

Chief Constable Azim was sympathetic to both of Greenberg's suggestions, not so much for their practicability – which was zero, as he well knew – but for their political kudos. However, the investigation was actually in chief detective Andy Wallace's care, and he was far from convinced by the mounting pile of identical affidavits claiming Rachel was some sort of wanton harlot, and the three builders were all members of the Nixons.

There were other sources of evidence beginning to emerge, primarily from drivers and passengers in passing cars and buses. Their snippets of testimony, and video clips caught on mobile phones, had one thing in common: they virtually all agreed with the version given by the builders. Wallace already knew in his heart that the builders were innocent, and had merely defended a girl in distress. Under ordinary conditions this would have been a fairly open-and-shut case, and legally it still was – but the politics were something else. Politics and politicians were not interested in the truth; they were interested only in power and its maintenance. Huge forces were clamouring for a sacrificial offering to sate the gods of anti-racism, and these three builders and their female charge had been lined up for the gig. Politics demanded one thing, the facts another. Wallace could feel the heat rising with every publicity-seeking exhibition of bleeding-heart politics reported in the MSM.

That afternoon Zakia Gandapur, Azim's secretary, phoned; Wallace was to report to HQ for a full briefing at 10:30 the following morning.

Wallace duly arrived at the County Constabulary's HQ for his interview, full of foreboding. He was acutely aware of the mounting pressure from the press and TV channels that something must be done to avert further outbreaks of racial violence; heads would have to roll. He steeled himself and entered Azim's outer office, where Miss Gandapur was expecting him.

'Ah, Mr Wallace, the Chief Constable will be available shortly – can I get you a tea or coffee?'

Wallace found a seat in the corner and sat down. Five minutes later Azim's door opened, and a familiar-looking documentary maker emerged with a film crew in tow. The minor TV celebrity and Azim shook hands like old buddies, while Miss Gandapur held the outer door open for the crew to shift their gear. After an extended period of laboured bonhomie, stylised backslapping and insincere mutual appreciation, the fantasy world of the mediasphere exited the building. For the first time Azim, somewhat bemused, noticed his fellow policeman sitting in the corner of the outer office. Had he forgotten?

'Ah, Andy, there you are.'

'Chief Constable.'

'Please come in; we have much to discuss.'

'Sir.'

They entered the inner sanctum. Azim loitered by the door long enough to order Miss Gandapur to rustle up a couple of coffees, 'Something decent, not that instant muck.'

They sat down either side of an impressive mahogany desk with a splendid panoramic view out of the window; Azim made himself comfortable, then began his questioning.

'Good morning Andy – sorry for the slight delay with the film crew. You know how it is: everything stands still to catch the deadline. Anyway, back to the here and now. As I'm sure you're aware, there's a great deal of interest in the Bransborough case, necessitating that I be kept up to speed on developments. I'm sorry for having to call you over like this when you're so busy, but I have an appointment tomorrow with the minister in London; he wants a full report on our progress and some idea of our chances of securing a conviction.'

'A conviction, sir?'

'Yes – for the murder of Mr Abdullah Qazi, and the serious injuries to Mr Yunus Jilani and Mr Umar Arain, plus common assault on Messrs Khan, Chodary, Hussaini and Siddiqui.'

'Sir, our evidence for such a prosecution is weak – in my opinion very weak.'

'Weak? I've seen with my own eyes piles of affidavits stating unequivocally that these three builders attacked and injured the gentlemen I've just named.'

'Yes sir, that's correct. However, I must point out that almost all this testimony is suspect. It's all identical, word for word in many cases. It is no secret that the imam of the Central Mosque ordered the local Muslim population to report as they did; indeed, sir, we have obtained recordings of his Friday sermon when he instructed his followers to toe the Brotherhood's line. As you know, sir, the Islamic Brotherhood has consistently claimed that Miss Rachel Kynaston acted in a lewd and suggestive fashion, and that Hall, Cunliffe and Fuller are all members of National Resistance.'

'You mean the Nixons?'

'Yes, sir.'

'I see. Is the imam's sermon admissible?'

'No sir; we obtained it through unofficial channels.'

'Then there's no problem.'

'With every respect, sir, a good barrister would tear our case to pieces.'

'I suspect the minister will be the judge of that.'

'There is also corroborative evidence to support the case of the defendants from drivers and passengers in vehicles travelling along the High Street at the time. There's even some crude video footage taken on mobile phones, which again is supportive of the defendants' claims. Sir, with the greatest respect, there is no case in law.'

'Was not Mr Qazi shot at close range with a nail gun, and subsequently died under the wheels of the defendants' van?'

'Yes, sir.'

'Was that same nail gun pointed at Mr Jilami, causing him to crash to the road at high speed? He's now in a coma, I understand.'

'Yes, sir.'

'Did not …' Azim reached for the file to check he had the correct name, '… Mr Fuller strike Mr Arain on the head with a club hammer, causing him grievous bodily harm?'

'Yes, sir.'

'Wasn't Fuller the same man who used the nail gun on Mr Qazi?'

'Yes, sir.'

'I see. And were not the other gentlemen I mentioned earlier, hospitalised with various injuries due to the actions of the defendants?'

'Yes, sir, but in every case – including Fuller's – the defendants were acting in self-defence. To be frank, sir, we have a far stronger case against the purported Muslim victims than the defendants in question.'

'Come, Andy, let's not be silly – prosecution indeed! Just remember who had the weapons, and who were unarmed.'

'Sir, can I remind you that Fuller sustained a nasty injury to his forehead from a scaffold pole smashed into the van's windscreen? He was also slashed across the face with a knife by Mr Qazi.'

'Are there any witnesses to the throwing of the scaffold pole?'

'All the defendants, sir.'

'I meant independent witnesses.'

'No, sir.'

1.2 – MACHINATIONS

'Has this knife Mr Qazi was supposed to have used been found?'

'No, sir.'

Wallace knew that Azim understood the situation perfectly. The defendants were innocent, as Azim well knew. But this was no longer a police case or even a legal case; it had become a case of political chicanery. It would end in tears, thought Wallace; the case was so weak, and he was well aware that Rachel Kynaston came from a well-heeled family. They would make sure there was a sharp barrister on their bench. The prosecution would be torn to shreds.

1.3 – Puppet Masters

Just before 1:00 pm, Danny Morgenthau arrived at Hershel Blumenfeld's plush eatery in the West End to be shown through to the private dining suite. Ten minutes later, Ben Kaplan arrived, and he too was escorted to the secluded room where Morgenthau was waiting.

After exchanging small talk and catching up on mutual friends, they ordered lunch and a bottle of fine wine. Both enjoyed those little extras that habitual wealth could provide, which included gourmand dining in convivial surroundings such as these – along with the impeccable service provided by the restaurant's most experienced staff.

Danny, as one of the senior partners in Morgenthau-Yellen Associates – Europe's largest media conglomerate – was taking the opportunity afforded by this little tête-à-tête to discuss a couple of issues with an old and influential friend.

Ben Kaplan was deputy chairman of Global Social Strategies, a London-based think tank with close connections to both the main British political parties. Founded fifteen years earlier by George Chanos and David Molodovsky, GSS had become a major player behind the scenes in shaping Britain's public policy strategy. Such heady success did not come cheaply, but as most Westminster insiders were aware, the pockets of Chanos, a merchant banker, and Molodovsky, a hedge-fund manager, were deep; indeed, both were multi-millionaires. Despite the unquestioned wealth of these gentlemen, shrewd observers suspected that even greater powers lurked in the background.

None of this was considered suitable for public consumption, which explained why GSS's activities were hardly ever reported in the press, nor featured in any current-affairs programmes. Occasionally, some nosy-parker who'd spent too much time digging around on the web would get the opportunity to lob an awkward question in the direction of the controlling interests. However, over the years the machinery had been well honed, and by now very little managed to ruffle its feathers. Faceless, shadow-dwelling executives made sure that a stock response was always to hand for every situation.

The vice-president for public relations at Morgenthau-Yellen Associates, Bill Sonnenfeldt, had recently been obliged to make one such statement in response to a tenacious young reporter's continued interruptions of his prepared statement on corporate responsibility. The young man had been energetically querying a series of unsubstantiated reports claiming that the Education Minister had been visited by a string of call girls during the recent European Education Summit in Barcelona. Yet the media had inexplicably remained silent – what was going on? It was time for Bill to earn his generous pay. When one is in bed with the political establishment, uninvited curiosity can be a very dangerous pastime. The trick for Bill was to extricate oneself while maintaining the myth of media neutrality.

Bill was an old hand at these shenanigans. He turned patiently towards the earnest young man and, as if talking to a wayward child, explained that responsible news outlets – like those controlled by Morgenthau-Yellen Associates – did not report potentially slanderous rumours arising from unaccountable sources. With virtually every other reporter present working for concerns controlled by Morgenthau-Yellen Associates, the message reached its intended target audience.

As it turned out, the 'slanderous rumours' of the Education Minister's misdeeds were subsequently confirmed in spectacular fashion. A graphic video of the Minister performing with one of his lady friends in a Barcelona hotel room surfaced on the internet. The establishment didn't blink. Having been aware of the truth of the accusations from the beginning, a corporate response had long since been prepared – just in case.

Within the month the idealistic young reporter's position unexpectedly became surplus to requirements. After unsuccessfully seeking a new position with every paper in the land, he finally concluded that his reporter days were over. He eventually found employment driving a delivery van for one of the national supermarket chains.

Of course, this refusal to deal with rumours 'arising from unaccountable sources' did not apply when the target of speculation was somebody opposed to Morgenthau-Yellen Associates' corporate policy position. Although all Associate news outlets actively promoted homosexuality, multiracialism and feminism, as specified in their 'One World' corporate policy document, the infamous case of Roger Fraser had seen all this moral posturing unceremoniously flushed down the toilet. Fraser, a leading member of the Rolling Dice Club – the intellectual arm of National Resistance – had been accused by an ex-Club member of being a closet homosexual, and of having relations with a Black Nigerian man.

Fraser was a fierce critic of the contemporary fetish for beatifying sodomites, while his opposition to immigration and the whole concept of multiculturalism was well documented; therefore the claim that he was a homosexual, and with a Black man to boot, was just too good to be true. The informer claimed he had solid proof, which consisted of an indistinct, low-quality video of a Negro and a White man apparently engaging in lewd acts under a poorly lit canal-side bridge. The corporate powers-that-be decided that was enough, and right across the board, on every medium available, the news was proclaimed that the 'arch-Nazi' Fraser was nothing but a 'homo' who enjoyed a bit of Black male booty when he wasn't calling for them to be deported – the irony was so sweet it almost hurt.

Fraser made it to the front pages of most papers and for two days even managed to be the leading television news item. However, within seven days Fraser's lawyer had slammed injunctions on half a dozen papers and four TV channels with cast-iron proof of the false nature of the accusations. It emerged that the accuser, Jason Snow, had been expelled from the Rolling Dice Club for having a Negress girlfriend, and Roger Fraser had been foremost in calling for his expulsion.

Snow, stung by the public exposure of his penchant for illicit brown sugar, had concocted the whole story, obtaining the dodgy homosexual DVD from a German website of dubious reputation.

The news of Fraser's innocence did not make the front page. If reported at all, it was safely tucked away deep in the paper's innards – though eventually Fraser's lawyer succeeded in forcing the papers to publish an apology. All too late, of course; as the old adage goes, 'mud sticks' – which had been the intention from the beginning.

GSS had been chief consultants to Morgenthau-Yellen Associates when drawing up their flagship 'One World' policy document, and had used many of the same ideas when approaching members of the government. It was amazing how well a proposed policy change was received when the selfsame idea was being openly lauded in the press and on television.

Whatever the ultimate source of GSS' finances, the organisation would never have enjoyed so much success without access to substantial funds. The greasing of wheels was a seriously expensive business, and the greater the wheel, the greater was the amount of grease required.

GSS had originally found a foothold in government after the then British Foreign Secretary, Harvey Barrett – Eton and Magdalen College, Cambridge – was referred to them by Eliot Ledeen, an influential member of the Washington Foundation for Overseas Policy. The Foundation had already established a firm foothold in the corridors of US foreign-policy decision making via the large number of US members of Congress who supported its mission. The Washington Foundation tended to concentrate on foreign policy, but other kindred bodies, like the Institute for National Regeneration and the David Levy Yulee Center, spread their influence into most areas of domestic social policy.

The Washington Foundation for Overseas Policy had an extensive list of associate members, consisting of pressure groups, non-governmental bodies, various media companies and sympathetic corporate concerns. All these bodies received regular briefings from the Foundation, and more generally subscribed to the policy positions laid out by the group.

Coincidentally, although over 90 per cent of Morgenthau-Yellen Associates' business was conducted in Europe, it did own two regional papers in the US, both of which happened to be corporate members of the Washington Foundation.

So it was that GSS began briefing the British Government on foreign affairs, though unlike the Washington Foundation it was prepared to expand into other fields under its own banner. Thus it came about that the influence exercised by GSS grew to include huge swathes of government activity, though social, financial and business policies received most attention.

This expansion had occurred irrespective of the colour of the government. Indeed GSS, along with several fellow travellers of a similar ilk and background, had managed to bring its influence to bear on every facet of British public life in one way or another.

Ben wiped his mouth with his napkin, having enjoyed an excellent *Sambocade*. It was time to broach a tiresome irritant.

'Danny, we've been getting some unfortunate resistance to our expanded population programme; the recent news from Bransborough hasn't helped much. However, as I see things we are faced with a situation that might prove beneficial, if handled deftly. David's already set the scene locally; we just need to support him as best we can. What do we know about the situation, and how can we move the agenda forward in a positive direction? I don't need to remind you that handled badly it might fuel a backlash – something we'd prefer to avoid if possible.'

'Yes, we gave David a fair bit of coverage with his 'Nixons' accusations – always a good tactic, as it forces the native xenophobic elements to justify themselves, which is psychologically a virtual impossibility. This is all standard practice, though that Asian policeman, er …'

'Azim.'

'Yes, Azim … well, without openly pointing the finger at anybody he seemed to imply that David's claims were true, thus throwing further doubt – albeit indirectly – on the testimony of the builders and that silly girl. If we can manage to discredit them in the eyes of the general public – especially their own people – the fewer problems we'll face in moving forward with the expanded population programme. I can assure you, Ben, we at Morgenthau-Yellen Associates are as heavily committed to the programme as you are.'

'What do we know about the principal actors in our little drama?'

'Rachel Kynaston, the girl at the centre of the incident, is daughter to Basil Kynaston, owner of the Countryside Living chain, selling rural-style clothes and accessories – they have around 25 branches, if I remember correctly. It's more Sloane Ranger than Farmer Giles, if you ask me, and the prices certainly tend towards the Range Rover and grouse-shooting end of the market. Having said that, the company's fairly successful and Kynaston's not short of a bob or two.'

'Tell me more about this Basil Kynaston.'

'He's quite a character; rumour has it that he half-fancies becoming a Tory MP – he's big among the county set. He has an impressive pile out in Warwickshire, where he likes to entertain, plus the usual London flat, Cotswold cottage and beachside villa on the Côte d'Azur.'

'How serious is he about becoming an MP?'

'From what I understand he's quite keen; it's definitely common knowledge among local party bigwigs. I'd say he has a better than average chance of becoming an official candidate by the next General Election.'

'Which means it's important for him to remain in Central Office's good books.'

'Yes.'

'I'll have to have a word with Rupert.'

'Rupert Hayes-Smyth, party co-ordinator?'

'It so happens that Rupert's coming down to Longlea Manor next weekend, with a couple of other dignitaries from the Conservative Party. It'll be an excellent opportunity to discuss a few topics, and perhaps solve the odd problem – it should be interesting. Is there anybody else we need to be aware of?'

'The main investigating officer is called Wallace. He's no more than lukewarm in his support for prosecuting the three builders, as he claims there's no real evidence.'

'Is he right?'

'Yes, but that's a mere technicality – there's still a case and an argument to publicise.'

'Is there anything that can be done about Wallace?'

'We've got to tread carefully with the police, but if some pressure can be applied via the Crown Prosecution Service and perhaps the chief constable, we might get a more committed response. We've been digging around in his background; as you can imagine there's not much to report – after all, he is a policeman – however, there is a story of him puffing on a joint when he was in college at some student party.'

'How often did he indulge, and how far back are we going?'

'Only the once, and fourteen years ago.'

'I take it this is merely a backup; you're not going to publish it, are you?'

'No, it's far too incendiary at present, but if things start going badly for us it becomes an option. We'll continue to give this Azim plenty of coverage; he seems to know the script, and is making all the right noises. There'll be a number of pieces, both in print and on television over the coming weeks, highlighting the problems immigrant communities are facing from Nazi thugs – like the Nixons.'

'That sounds excellent; good work, Danny. Though I've heard unofficially that you have something special in the pipeline.'

Danny laughed, 'You're well informed as usual. Yes, we've almost finished a documentary on the financial hardships faced by the widow and family of Abdullah Qazi, the man murdered by Fuller, and another piece on Yunus Jilami, who's currently in a coma. We've already had lots of interest shown in the programmes and I think it's safe to say they'll receive a wide airing, both here and abroad.'

'Well, I have some good news too. GSS has a number of senior contacts within the judiciary and at the Home Office who are open to the policy directions we're all working so hard to see implemented. I'm fairly sure I can guarantee that Mr Wallace will soon be left in no doubt as to what is expected of him – d'you know, I'm beginning to get a distinctly positive feeling about this Bransborough business?'

Danny smiled.

'Right, Danny, I've literally got to fly; I have a meeting with the chairman of the EU's foreign-affairs committee tomorrow in Strasbourg. It looks like the criticism on the West Bank issues can be contained. Incidentally, thanks for your support, especially that piece in *Analyst* magazine; it was inspirational – who wrote it?'

'Nathan Cohen – he's coming along nicely; we use him a lot for important syndicate pieces, like the widows-and-orphans-of-Palestinian-terrorism article you're talking about. He has a knack with words and his photographer, Sam Klein, is brilliant at catching emotion in people's faces.'

'Well, it certainly did the trick this time.'

'Our pleasure. Incidentally I'll need to see you again soon concerning some hiccups we're experiencing in Hungary. We've been expanding rapidly in Eastern Europe, but recently our attempts to acquire two Hungarian newspaper titles and a commercial radio station were blocked – I tell you, Ben, there are distinct nationalist undertones at work there. The objections listed by the Hungarian authorities are all contrary to EU regulations; we're a London-based outfit with offices in all the major European commercial centres, a fact which gives us every right to operate in Hungary, or anywhere else within the EU for that matter. This needs addressing; it's impeding our whole strategy for expanding coverage across the Continent.'

'That's a disturbing development,' admitted Ben, 'I'll get the office to work on it right away – we have excellent contacts in Brussels. I'll also have our Eastern Europe field officer take a closer look at what's going on in Hungary.'

'Thanks, that would be greatly appreciated; hopefully this problem can be solved swiftly and we can all get back on track, spreading the programme from Cork to Krakow.'

'Right; before I go we were talking about pleasure, were we not? I believe it's my turn to buy lunch next; how about getting out of town for a change? Do you fancy a table at the Riverside Inn? I've heard good things about it.'

'So have I – that sounds great. Get your secretary to email the details to Janet as usual – I don't know where I'd be without her. Next Tuesday, around 1:30?'

'It's a date. Oh, I nearly forgot: Robin Donnelly, the shadow spokesman on home affairs, will be joining us, I thought it might be a good opportunity to meet and greet, as they say.'

Danny chuckled at the thought, 'Yes, invite Donnelly; after listening to his "British jobs for British workers" tirade in Blackpool he's obviously in need of a little tutoring. Let the process begin over a bottle of decent wine, though I suspect the oaf couldn't tell the difference between a claret and a can of Vimto.'

1.4 – Justice

The date was eventually set for the case, which would be held at Bransborough Crown Court before Justice Alan Hoffman. The prosecution was in the hands of Joshinder Chaggar, an upcoming star in the Crown Prosecution Service. Alex was charged with murder, attempted murder and GBH; his solicitor had approached Elliot Callaghan to represent him, while Steve and Rich, both charged with manslaughter, were represented by local Darnby barrister Aaron Walters.

Rachel faced charges of causing an affray, and behaviour likely to incite racial or religious hatred. She was represented by the very expensive Jonathan Eisenhower, senior partner in the swanky London chambers of Williamson, Koch and Eisenhower.

In the weeks running up to the case the media had cranked up the heat, in effect demonising the three, albeit indirectly. The press printed a host of damning articles concerning the rise of fascist groups in Britain. The far more powerful medium of video did its bit too, with a series of hard-hitting documentaries highlighting the uneducated, animalistic virulence of the working-class White thugs who comprised the bulk of these extremist parties. The case for firmer government action was incontestable. All the MSM channels ran programmes in support of further immigration, lauding the valuable contribution these hard-working citizens made to the UK's economy.

1.4 – JUSTICE

The elephant in the room remained firmly off limits: namely, why were nationalist groups springing up like mushrooms all over Europe? And why were they garnering so much support in the face of an unrelenting avalanche of negative publicity from the MSM? Something was out of synchronisation, and logic suggested it wasn't the public.

The *pièce de résistance* in this process was the main state-financed station's deeply moving portrait of the families of Abdullah Qazi and Yunus Jilami, showing the hardships they endured following the loss of their menfolk. During the programme both families openly blamed the White, infidel builders for the murder of Qazi and injury to Jilami. They also expressed grave doubts that there would be a fair trial, owing to the institutional racism that everyone knew was endemic in Britain's police and judicial system.

None of the women in either family could speak English, requiring that their surprisingly erudite and technically accomplished complaints be translated via subtitles. In contrast, all the men could get by in English, though the standard was universally poor, requiring frequent recourse to the film crew's interpreter. Although the youngest children in both families constituted the third generation living in Britain, none had English as a first language, even after going through the state education system.

England was, and remained, an alien country to all of them.

The fateful day finally arrived. The prosecution would concentrate on two areas, namely, Rachel's appearance on the High Street, and the physical clash with the racist builders. The list of witnesses to Rachel's allegedly inflammatory behaviour was very long; however, pride of place went to the four hospitalised men – Rahat Khan, Surabhi Chodary, Muhammad Hussaini and Fouad Siddiqui. All these gentlemen, plus another eight witnesses from among the passing shoppers, were available to give what was essentially the same story. Rahat Khan, a leading community leader, was first into the witness box; his testimony would set the tone for the remainder of the prosecution.

Joshinder Chaggar began by asking Khan to describe the behaviour of Rachel Kynaston that day, and explain why it caused such consternation. He coughed, cleared his throat and began to recite what was self-evidently a well-choreographed account. He painted a colourful picture of an arrogant White woman, pushing her way impatiently through local shoppers going about their lawful business in the howling wind and driving rain. As she crossed the street that led to the Central Mosque, she bumped into a group of male worshippers – including Khan – on their way to the mosque. It was then that the full enormity of the situation struck home. Khan was stupefied by the sight that met his eyes. This haughty White female stood before them displaying utter contempt for their traditions and religious beliefs. She had come among devout Muslims with her face painted like a harlot, and worse still, her blouse shamelessly open, revealing a full bosom. Khan struggled to find words to describe the enormity of the insult to the community; this was nothing less than a display of raw wantonness. Westerners might accept these shameless displays on their streets, but no community of loyal, God-fearing British Muslims could tolerate such moral depravity.

When the men tried to reason with this Jezebel, they were subjected to a tirade of verbal abuse, followed by a number of explicit sexual invitations. Enough was enough; she was asked to leave the community with a suitable escort that was quickly thrown together to ensure her compliance.

Khan half-turned towards the jury – a third of whom were Muslim – to make his appeal. 'Why do righteous British Muslim communities have to suffer from the decadence and obsession with sex that consumes these people? Do not honest British Muslims have the right to defend themselves and Allah's revealed path to salvation from these godless sinners? Where's the local council, where's the government – where's our protection?'

Chaggar then turned to the builders. Khan described how the girl tried to run away from her escort, when a van suddenly pulled over and three White men jumped out. Totally unprovoked, they reached into their van and pulled out an assortment of heavy weapons – hammers, crowbars and a nail gun. The

1.4 – JUSTICE

Muslims were stunned; what had they done to merit this display of raw aggression? The three men proceeded to threaten local Muslims with extreme violence. No explanation, or cause for their actions, was offered by the builders.

The girl, seeing that the her Muslim escort had retreated to face this new threat, ran back to greet the armed thugs, and whispered something into the ear of the leader – the description of whom left no doubt in the minds of those in court that he was referring to Steve.

The three men then happily allowed this strumpet to climb into their van; only one sort of woman climbs unaccompanied into the back of a vehicle with three strange men.

Khan then described how one of the builders – 'the yellow-haired one' – had first assaulted a good, peaceful Muslim with a hammer before jumping into the van with the other White men; Khan claimed the injured man was Umar Arain. The family and friends of Umar Arain had then tried to prevent the van from leaving the crime scene before the police could arrive. Khan agreed that the builders' vehicle had sustained damage during this failed attempt, but insisted that the fault for any material or physical damage lay squarely with the thugs; all the Muslims present assumed these creatures were Nixons. They'd had dealings with Nixons before, attacking the Central Mosque with paint and leaving hurtful stickers and posters on buildings and lamp-posts in the vicinity.

Khan finished this first day of evidence with a long description of the efforts by local Muslims to detain the van and its criminal occupants. He described how some men had tried to wedge a scaffold pole in the van's front wheels to jam the steering mechanism. Unfortunately, the pole worked itself free and flew up, smashing the van's windscreen. Other men had tried to physically stop the White thugs from driving away, but as they pulled open the doors of the van to remonstrate with the builders they were met with heavy weapons, sustaining injuries that required hospital treatment – including his own.

Most had given up chasing the van by the time it reached the lights at the bottom of the High Street, but a few of the bravest and most devout in their love of Allah had continued. They were met, however, with the utmost violence. The holy martyr, Abdullah Qazi, was brutally slain with a nail gun by 'that yellow-haired devil'. Another brave Muslim, Yunus Jilami, having been hurled unceremoniously from the vehicle, was left comatose after smashing heavily onto a kerbstone.

The press and TV had a field day. Khan's evidence was treated as if it were the revealed truth of the Prophet himself, while the three builders were universally condemned as fascist goons. Rachel was all but called a whore; certainly that was the underlying implication. Being old hands at the game, nothing was said or printed that would hold in a court of law, but the message to the public was clear enough.

The following day, Eisenhower cross-examined Khan. Pressed to explain who exactly were these men who had 'escorted' Miss Kynaston from the High Street, Khan admitted there had been six men assigned to the task. He went on to praise the men's steadfastness in carrying out such an onerous task under trying conditions. Asked how Rachel reacted to being led away by this posse of men, he said she'd accepted the situation passively.

'Why, then, was her overnight bag found on the far side of the road by the police?' enquired Eisenhower.

'She'd tried to run away from her escort – into the main road – but lost her footing and lost her bag,' he explained.

'But you've just claimed she left the High Street willingly; now you're saying she tried to run away – why?'

Khan said he didn't know, but admitted that some White women feared Muslim men. When questioned why, he responded, 'We're painted by your racist media as monsters, killing people with suicide bombs and molesting young White girls. But it's all lies, meant to discredit us Muslims and the

1.4 – JUSTICE

word of Allah. The problem doesn't lie with the Muslim community, but with sick, godless Westerners – like this girl – sunk in moral depravity, continually striving to blacken that which is holy and righteous.'

Aaron Walters stepped in to continue the questioning. Did Mr Khan have any explanation as to why the builders decided to stop their van? Furthermore, were there any examples of the builders offering violence to the local Muslims prior to the attempts to detain the van?

Once again Khan was forced to admit he had no idea as to why the builders had decided to stop. The suggestion by Walters that perhaps it was in response to the way Rachel's 'escort' were treating her, was dismissed out of hand. These were devout Muslims; they neither offered violence without provocation, nor had any interest in corrupt Western females.

Finally Callaghan took up the baton. Before addressing Khan directly, he listed the injuries sustained by Alex Fuller: forehead opened by scaffold pole, requiring eight stitches, right cheek opened by knife thrust from Mr Qazi, requiring a further five stitches. Alex Fuller, the so-called 'mad dog' according to some of the less scrupulous tabloids, had sustained 13 stitches worth of damage – why? Was Mr Khan really trying to claim that Mr Fuller would risk sustaining this level of damage just in order to pick a pointless fight? Or was it pointless? What was really going on with Mr Khan's 'escort' of six heavies? Did the builders see something Mr Khan is forgetting to mention? And what right did Mr Khan and his strong-arm men have to escort anybody from the public highway – wasn't that the responsibility of the police? Indeed, were not these six 'escorts' merely kidnappers in turbans, illegally forcing a citizen off the street through sheer physical force?

Khan said he was no expert in the law of *kafirs*; as far as he, and all good Muslims were concerned, there was but one law: Sharia – the law of God.

One by one, Surabhi Chodary, Muhammad Hussaini and Fouad Siddiqui came forward to give what was little more than a rewording of Khan's original testimony.

A number of doctors were then called to describe the injuries sustained by the hospitalised Muslims. The autopsy on Abdullah Qazi confirmed he died from a nail entering the brain via his right eye-socket. However, the pathologist was unable to say whether or not he was dead when the van ran over his body; Qazi was pronounced dead on arrival at North Mercia A&E.

The prosecution finished its case with the detective in charge of the case, Andy Wallace, taking the stand. He described the sharply varying stories being touted by the builders and the Muslims, and while there was no denying the death and serious injuries sustained by a number of the Muslims – and Alex Fuller, for that matter – there were other sources of evidence to consider. Although the CCTV system in the High Street had been deactivated in response to requests from Muslim community leaders, some of those passing the incident in their cars took pictures and film clips on their mobile phones. Having admitted there was no clip showing the key moments of the incident, the clips that did exist tended to chime closely with the account given by the builders.

The prosecution wound up, but already it was apparent that things were not going well. Unless something extraordinary happened to the defence case, Chaggar feared the worst.

While the builders were kept in custody, Rachel's lesser charge, in conjunction with influential family connections, allowed her to be released on bail. Every evening after the day's events came to an end she jumped into her Mini Cooper and drove down to Warwickshire to stay with her parents. At the end of the third day she was surprised to discover a strange man ensconced in the study, discussing 'important matters' with her father, while her barrister, Jonathan Eisenhower, kicked his heels in the Blue Reception Room.

Eisenhower's acceptance of this case had surprised many from outside his chambers who knew him well. As a rule he rarely travelled outside London and normally would never touch a dangerous political case like this – lucrative commercial disputes were more his line.

Six weeks earlier it had been decided that Louis Fortas, one of Ben Kaplan's senior executives, would visit the chambers of Williamson, Koch and Eisenhower once it became clear that Mercia Police and the Crown Prosecution Service were ready to start proceedings. GSS's own in-house legal department had already gone over the case themselves, concluding it couldn't be won.

GSS and the 'One World' ideology needed the prosecution to succeed – or at least not to explode in their faces. A damaging public airing of yet another example of Muslim violence against a White woman would only fan the simmering anti-Islamic sentiments held by the beleaguered White population. The 'One World' project was key not only to GSS's long-term development, but the maintenance of the entire, carefully crafted NWO paradigm. The selling of this paradigm to Western populations constituted the most breathtaking example of naked audacity since the French Revolution. It was the acceptance, through media manipulation, of the NWO's global vision that allowed the functioning of the vast social-engineering programme that was busily dismembering every White society on the planet. Ever since the 1930s, when the current version of this long-standing insanity was conceived on the banks of the Main, the project's academic midwives had known that the biggest threat to their success stemmed from White European identity. Aryans were the only force the scheme's authors considered strong enough, both intellectually and morally, to challenge their goals – they, therefore, became the number one priority for disposal. The sooner White populations could be reduced to irrelevance, the sooner the chosen ones who controlled the NWO's programmes could fulfil their calling.

The project's extremely well-financed tentacles spread far and wide, into every crevice where power or ability might lurk. Unsuspecting dupes, usually very intelligent and well-educated individuals but whose greed and egos were easily manipulated, found themselves recruited unwittingly to the cause in considerable numbers. Jonathan Eisenhower was a case in point.

Eisenhower's career path had been one long sequence of success stories; indeed, success had become so ubiquitous that Eisenhower had almost reached the point of self-delusion where he thought this progress reflected his genius. In truth he was a very good lawyer: but nobody's *that* good. Occasionally he had become vaguely aware of indeterminate manipulation by some shadowy body or other; at other times he merely sensed something out of sight.

He cast his mind back to the starting point of his extraordinary journey. On completing his final law examinations he had been approached by an executive planning agency called the Juniper Foundation, offering what they described as a 'bespoke career path for senior executives'. The deal was very favourable to Eisenhower, who once on board the programme found doors opening and new opportunities springing up at an impressive rate. Within five years he'd become a full partner in one of London's most prestigious practices, his name adorning the practice's brass nameplate and corporate stationery. Membership of a particularly influential Freemasonry lodge had fallen into his lap, followed by rapid promotion, considerably expanding his network of influential contacts.

Although superficially Jonathan Eisenhower revelled in his incredible good fortune, he was no fool. In his heart he knew his success was all part of a bigger game, and that he was merely a piece on somebody else's chessboard. Often, while being driven to his Central London office in the morning, he'd find himself reading with mounting empathy the endless stories of poor, young, working-class White girls being groomed for sex by predatory Muslim gangs.

Louis Fortas was known to Eisenhower as a senior figure in the Juniper Foundation. If Eisenhower was aware of the existence of GSS at all, it was merely as some faceless consultancy with an obscure relationship with various government departments mentioned occasionally in the broadsheets. Legally, the Juniper Foundation was a wholly owned subsidiary of Vienna Trust of London, an international investment bank – which incidentally was itself wholly owned by various holding companies belonging to the controlling directors of GSS.

1.4 – JUSTICE

When Fortas' secretary booked the fateful appointment six weeks earlier, Eisenhower had realised immediately that something important was afoot. He had never met Fortas face to face, but was fully aware that he was a powerful operator, a fact that only stoked his curiosity further.

The meeting was held mid-morning. Fortas arrived on time and was led through to Eisenhower's private suite in the partnership building. After a perfunctory shaking of hands the pair settled down on a couple of modern comfy chairs, with a silver-and-onyx coffee table between them on which was a pot of steaming coffee along with two Wedgwood china cups. There followed a general chat on Eisenhower's current position and plans for the future – a subject on which Fortas appeared to know almost as much as Eisenhower himself – before broaching more pressing concerns. Here it comes, thought Eisenhower, who'd had the uncomfortable feeling of being stalked since the meeting first began.

Fortas drew himself up formally, his voice assuming an authoritarian crispness as he came to the crux of his visit: the Foundation felt it was an appropriate time for Eisenhower to repay some of the considerable investment that had been made in furthering his career – which brought them neatly to the Kynaston case.

Eisenhower was aware of the case; it had been in all the papers, along with numerous documentaries highlighting the background racial and religious issues involved – but what had this to do with him?

Fortas, judging the moment ripe, took a quick sip of his coffee, then broke the news. 'The Foundation has come to the conclusion – for corporate policy reasons – that you could make a significant contribution to this case. Although at this juncture we're not in a position to discuss wider issues, the Foundation, with its working partners, is keen to prevent the British Muslim community from being tarred by yet another unfortunate incident of an interracial character. In furtherance of this goal, it has been suggested, indeed recommended, that you be appointed defence counsel for Rachel Kynaston.

In anticipation of your consent, contact with the Kynaston family solicitors – Jarrett & Taylor – has already been made on your behalf; the various technical and financial arrangements have been agreed upon with the Foundation. All that's required now is for you to meet the team and get up to speed.' He pulled a business card for Jarrett & Taylor from his jacket pocket. 'Here's the solicitors' card; I believe a Mr John Glaspole is dealing with the arrangements.'

Eisenhower was thunderstruck. What about his current workload and commitments? He felt angry and used, but Fortas hadn't finished, 'While you were in Taunton last week at that country house you frequent, a meeting was held with the other senior partners of the practice; I do hope you don't mind. I explained to them the importance of such a high-profile case and the potential prestige that could accrue to the partnership with you playing such a key role in proceedings.

'I also took the opportunity to go over the practice's plans for the new branch in Chester, a very interesting development in which the Foundation would be more than happy to invest – as I indicated.

'They seemed very happy with your appointment, and quickly agreed to reassign any outstanding cases to other members of the chambers. I can assure you, Jonathan, this case will be of benefit to you in every way conceivable – including financially.'

Internally Jonathan Eisenhower was furious; he was no odd-job boy to be ordered here and there at the whim of others – but then he realised that was exactly what he was. The Foundation had prepared the way thoroughly, his partners in the chambers fully supported the appointment, and once the news hit the evening's papers he had been inundated with congratulatory messages and calls. He was trapped like a fly in a web. Facing the inevitable, he at last bit the bullet, picked up the phone and rang John Glaspole, who'd been expecting his call.

That had been then; now, with the third day of the case having just finished, things were not going well for the prosecution – as Eisenhower well knew. He had been troubled with Fortas's arrangements from the beginning. During that initial meeting it had become clear to Eisenhower that Fortas's main concern was for the Muslim version of reality to triumph; therefore, logically, that meant discrediting the defence case. At the time he had not questioned the inconsistency of his appointment, owing to his anger at being railroaded into the case. However, the chickens were coming home to roost and Jonathan was at a loss as to the ultimate intensions of Fortas and the Foundation. If anything, his cross-examination had been instrumental in undermining Khan's testimony, and that of the other Muslim manikins, upon which the prosecution had relied so heavily.

Therefore it came as something of a cautious relief when, at the end of the third day, he received a phone call from Fortas's secretary to say he'd like to see Eisenhower that evening at Basil Kynaston's place in Warwickshire.

By the time Eisenhower arrived Fortas had already been in the house for some hours, locked in deep discussion with Basil Kynaston. Eisenhower faced the indignity of having to wait until Fortas was ready to see him. Basil eventually emerged from his bargaining and signalled Eisenhower to enter; he noted how even here Fortas had taken control, commandeering Basil's study for his own use. On entering, Eisenhower was met by a very traditional scene of oak panelling and bookshelves filled with leather-bound display editions of the classics. Fortas was sitting by an open fire in a leather chair; he gesticulated for Eisenhower to sit opposite.

They reviewed the case and once again Eisenhower was impressed at the depth of Fortas's knowledge. In reality, of course, the Foundation kept a young intern in the public gallery who sent detailed daily reports to Fortas.

Eisenhower's mystification as to how he, as a defence counsel, could help the prosecution was now to be revealed. For Fortas the task was simply to skin the cat: he was unconcerned as to the procedure. To him the result was everything – regardless of cost. To that end Eisenhower was now introduced to a whole raft of issues and considerations whose implications were potentially devastating in unscrupulous hands.

Fortas revealed Basil Kynaston's craving for a safe Tory seat and need to gain planning permission for a proposed new store in York. Fortas assured Eisenhower that, conditional on a suitable outcome in Bransborough, Basil Kynaston would be confirmed as Tory candidate for the safe rural seat of Upper Tame, while the planning permission for York had already been agreed in principle. As soon as Fortas's office had phoned the chief planning officer and chair of the planning committee to finalise certain financial arrangements, planning permission would become automatic. Eisenhower was left in no doubt that Fortas meant every word and could deliver on both counts.

However, this entire scenario hinged on one key ingredient: Rachel Kynaston's testimony. It would need to be doctored to achieve the desired result.

Then there was the issue of Rachel herself.

She had been expelled from the ARC, accused of being a confederate of known racists. She had also been suspended from her Sociology and Politics course – the college hierarchy being ultra-sensitive to any accusations of breaking PC taboos. Her social life was dead, as were her prospects for the future, with her having been cast as some sort of closet 'fascist' – the pariah of the West's utopian dystopia.

Fortas could get Rachel back into the ARC and onto her course – though he conceded that of themselves these inducements would not suffice. However, he was in a position to organise a number of highly supportive articles to be published in the press emphasising Rachel's commitment to multiculturalism and her horror at being associated with the actions of known racists. She was to distance herself as far as possible from the three builders; this was important,

1.4 – JUSTICE

since the media would fall upon them like feeding piranhas once the court had issued the correct judgment – with the help of Rachel's revised testimony.

Eisenhower was charged with delivering Rachel's testimony. She would have to repudiate the builders' story and do all in her power to support the version of events being peddled by the Muslims. A Muslim victory would secure for Rachel the promised path out of this nightmare, with redemption via the media, and deliver to her father a safe Tory seat and a shiny new store in York. In essence it was a straight quid pro quo.

Eisenhower was unsure; he knew that Rachel was furious at the Muslim claim that she was some sort of brazen hussy. He also suspected, quite rightly, that she'd come to loathe Islamic society and its denizens. He knew, too, that she felt a deep sense of gratitude towards the builders for their bravery and honour. However, the astute Louis Fortas was not paid a hefty six-digit salary for nothing. He gently reminded Jonathan Eisenhower that his penthouse overlooking the Thames at Battersea was currently held on a business account registered to Finances de Genève of Switzerland – one of the financial-services arms of Vienna Trust. It would be a pity, would it not, were the company to find the flat surplus to requirements? – though Louis assured Jonathan he would be given plenty of notice to quit if this unfortunate situation were to arise.

The flat had come to Eisenhower originally as part of the partnership settlement at a peppercorn rent. The thought of losing it caused him to blanch; an acquaintance of his who worked at the higher end of the London property market had confided to him that it was worth at least four million.

Fortas got up to leave, but before summoning his driver – who was in the Kynastons' kitchen having a tea – he had a final message to deliver.

'Hopefully we understand each other. I fully grasp the difficulty of your position, but those of us who command large remunerations also carry large burdens, and this is yours. I wish you luck in your endeavours; the Foundation will be looking on with the keenest interest.'

As if by magic, the driver appeared at the study door as Fortas exited. The pair crossed the classically tiled reception area, where Fortas bid a perfunctory goodbye to Basil Kynaston, then hurried across the gravel drive to Fortas's parked Bentley. He glanced at his driver as they crossed the gravel. 'Any messages, Johnson?'

'Mr Kaplan would like you to phone as soon as you get back to the office.'

Fortas nodded, more to himself than Johnson. He looked at his watch; it was 10:30 – they wouldn't be back at the office until after midnight. As it turned out, the call wasn't made until nearly 1:00, but Kaplan needed to know the state of play. Fortas duly reported that the die had been cast, just as had been planned over six weeks earlier; it was down to Eisenhower now to deliver the poisoned chalice. Kaplan mused to himself how much he enjoyed these little tableaux: the flush of betrayal, followed by the explosion of rage thirsting for revenge – all so barbarous. These were the futile reactions of cavemen, not the subtle efficiency of a Machiavelli. Kaplan was a great admirer of the brilliant Italian, even if he had been a *goy*.

There were times when Eisenhower questioned everything – the wealth, the prestige, the brass plates, the ludicrously extravagant Thames-side penthouse, his speed-of-light Mercedes AMG, the plush executive boxes at Ascot and Stamford Bridge – all of it. As he sat at the heavy oak table in the corner of Kynaston's study opposite Rachel, he felt these doubts gnawing at him. The weight of his task was slowly crushing what little humanity he still possessed – is this it? Is life just a collection of toys and a childish peacocking of wealth? According to the slime oozing from every television and newspaper in the land, he was living the dream; every advertised must-have was his, therefore he was happy – right?

He looked up into Rachel's tortured face. He felt anything but happy.

Tears ran down her cheeks from red-raw eyes, her trembling lips almost as bloodless as her pallor. Next to Eisenhower, among the burnished wood and leather hides, sat Basil; the pair of them had been hard at work trying to persuade Rachel of the advantages in 'modifying' her testimony. This distasteful exercise in mental torture had been going on for the best part of two hours. Eisenhower felt exhausted, not merely physically, but spiritually. At times he drifted off, fleeing mentally from such dirty work.

Basil's insincere pleading droned on, as it had for the last twenty minutes, Eisenhower's mind slipped into the Mercedes parked outside and his Thames-side penthouse; that would be a relief after this. He imagined himself cruising through London's streets in his over-engineered flying machine – what function does a 200 mph car serve in central London? – before parking in his underground compound, electronically sealed and guarded by a private security company. His mind turned to the enigma of his penthouse. He had no partner, though he'd had plenty of one-night stands and casual flings, but nothing that could be called a relationship. Not even a goldfish shared the cavernous splendour of the penthouse with him – in truth, it carried as much human warmth as an undertaker's waiting room. And yet its obscene opulence still seduced him – it consumed him, despite his better judgement. It was his opium.

Basil was still arguing his case. 'Look at the advantages you'll acquire – you'll be back in college, the newspapers will have rehabilitated you and we can even get you back into the ARC, if that's what you really want.'

Rachel had been listening to this for a long time by now. Eisenhower had confirmed all the details, making it clear that the powers pulling the strings could deliver on every promise and more if need be. The goodies promised to Basil hadn't originally been part of the discussion, but in a fit of rage with his stubborn daughter earlier in the meetings, he'd thoughtlessly bewailed the loss the 'family' would suffer because of her refusal to play the game – namely his proposed safe seat and new store for the comfortable burghers of York. Needless to say, this revelation did nothing to help persuade his recalcitrant offspring of the merits of their proposed little stitch-up.

Everybody involved in the plan was fully aware of the illegality of their actions: in theory Eisenhower could be charged with perverting the course of justice, professional misconduct and a dozen other misdemeanours. He could theoretically go to prison, be kicked out of his profession and lose everything – but as he'd learnt over the years, if you control the media you control the game. Such abstract nonsense as justice, the rule of law, democratic accountability and the rest of the liberal claptrap was putty in the hands of a good TV producer or sharp leader writer. Eisenhower knew how impotent these institutions really were; the Foundation and its myriad tentacles were the real power – they were the ones who could unleash a public maelstrom at will, via their control of the organs of mass media. He'd witnessed the beast in action on numerous occasions against individuals claiming the right to free speech, who'd been publically crucified by the press and TV for expressing an opinion contrary to PC theology and the Marxist dogma of the 'One World' project. The legality of expressing such thoughts might exist in theory, but a legal right to express an opinion didn't guarantee you could exercise that right; a straight fight between the judiciary and the media had but one winner. Eisenhower had seen the law changed twice over the past four years to fall further in line with corporate social policy.

No, the danger of prosecution and charges of misconduct were not a concern for Eisenhower – but life was.

Rachel's knowledge of the English working class, other than the laughable stereotypes found in the media, was on a par with her knowledge of Negro culture – if that wasn't an oxymoron. When the incident in Bransborough had brought her face to face with real, native Englishmen it had been a startling discovery to experience unquestioning loyalty, and a genuine sense of honour. These were not the usual characteristics found in the social circles her father typically frequented, where duplicity and the stab in the back were almost an occupational hazard.

True, she'd also been taken aback by their fierce sense of racial identity, and realisation that they certainly did not consider the various non-European populations to be part of the fabric of British society. Before the incident Rachel would have found such attitudes repugnant, having been brought up in an atmosphere of multicultural and multiracial political correctness – always praising the alien, always criticising the native; it had become second nature. But the fly in the ointment was the fact that for all her lauding of the other, she had no experience of these peoples and mixed exclusively in a wealthy, White environment of yuppie conformity to a doctrine drawn up by non-Europeans specifically for the purpose of destroying Europeans. Yet the conditioning had been so thorough that anyone pointing out the obvious was immediately attacked for breaking the social rules specified by the diktat of PC conformity.

Bransborough had changed all that for Rachel, both in her feelings towards her own people – the working class in particular – and towards the much lauded Muslim community. Now her father and her lawyer were doing everything in their power to persuade her to betray three men whom she admired beyond words. She felt physically sick.

Eisenhower leaned back in his chair as a lapse in the pleading ushered in a welcome wave of silence. He found looking at Rachel difficult, as the pain on her wracked face was beginning to turn his stomach; he needed closure. Rachel was obviously feeling the pressure – her physical condition showed that clearly, but she was not cracking; something stronger would be required.

It was getting very late, Eisenhower called a break while everybody got a drink and took the opportunity to answer the call of nature. Hanging around in the tiled reception area outside the study sipping coffee, Eisenhower started questioning Basil about those closest to Rachel – hardly Basil's strong point. He managed to call to mind the names of a couple of friends Rachel had brought to the house, even the odd boyfriend – but none of it sounded particularly promising. They finished their coffee and began drifting back towards the study when absent-mindedly Basil said, 'Of course, the one person who's always been very close to Rachel is her mother, Connie.'

Gotcha.

'Really, Basil? Tell me more.'

Eisenhower brought the session to a close with no agreement having been made. He bid farewell to Basil, then got into his Mercedes – but instead of driving off he pulled out his mobile phone to call Louis Fortas.

The following day's legal proceedings were dominated by technical accounts of the van and the damage it sustained. The defence, led largely by Callaghan, argued that the damage had demonstrably been inflicted during the incident and seemed far in excess of what might have been expected from the version of events expounded by Khan and the other Muslims.

Eisenhower played little part in proceedings; instead he had a junior member of the practice's staff on standby, awaiting a crucial message from Fortas's office. During the afternoon session – discussing how the rear doors of the van had been bent outwards – the junior intern slipped Eisenhower a message saying the 'package' would be delivered to Kynaston's place later that day by registered courier.

That evening Eisenhower was back at the table in Basil Kynaston's study, giving Rachel another mental battering. Basil was away on business, leaving Eisenhower with a free hand, but as he suspected all this pressure merely hardened Rachel's resolve to remain loyal to her saviours. Okay, so be it, thought Eisenhower; it was time to play his ace.

'Have you ever considered the repercussions for your family if your current status as some sort of Nixon sympathiser remains? Even if the defence is successful, and you and the builders are acquitted, the mud of fascism will stick. I've got to tell you, Rachel, the powers that be who control much of this country's media would not let it rest; as you well know from your ARC days, they hunt down and expose "racists" for public pillorying.

'There'll be no let-up; they'll dig about in your personal life and attack anybody close to you. You've been offered an escape route; the newspaper articles reaffirming your commitment to multiculturalism and multiracialism would reinstate you into politically correct society, free from persecution by the media.'

Rachel considered for a while then answered, 'I understand what's being offered, but those men stood by me when I needed help, I will not abandon them now when they need me.'

'But Rachel, it's not you we're talking about – it's your family.' As he spoke he opened the package the courier had delivered earlier and pulled out a piece of paper, which he slowly pushed across the table. She sensed its danger even before she picked it up.

It was a mock-up of the front page of the *National Courier*. The headline shouted, 'GUILTY'; underneath were five photographs – on one side police mugshots of the three builders plus Rachel, on the other a picture of Connie Kynaston standing by the front gates of their Warwickshire home. Below her mother's photo the caption read: *Constance Kynaston, mother of Rachel Kynaston, suspected Nixon sympathiser and confederate of Cunliffe, Hall and Fuller, convicted racist murderers of Abdullah Qazi, photographed yesterday outside her Warwickshire mansion.*

Rachel's fierce glare shot across the table and bored, laser-like, into Eisenhower; he could feel the raw hate and pent-up fury directed towards him. Struggling to control her voice, she hissed, 'But we might be found innocent.'

Eisenhower smiled coldly. 'What does that have to do with anything? Just rearrange the caption. It's the mud that counts, not the truth. But why am I bothering to tell an old hand like you all this? As an ARC activist you've done plenty of these character-assassination jobs in cahoots with the press.'

'It wasn't me; it was Rhys – he dealt with the press.'

'And you and your other ARC comrades attacked this Rhys, I take it, for spreading his lies and falsehoods?'

She went quiet, her lowered eyes hovering over the picture of her mother; in a voice hardly above a whisper she half-pleaded, 'Why are you involving my mother? She's got no part in all this. What's wrong with you people – aren't you human?'

'With the greatest respect, Rachel, I seem to remember the case of a certain Roger Fraser – member of the Rolling Dice Club, as I recall – who was accused of being a closet homosexual, which, incidentally, is not a crime. Of course, as a member of the Rolling Dice Club he was considered fair game, and the media went after him irrespective of the fact that all the accusations had been shown to be false. Did not the ARC have something to say concerning Mr Fraser?'

'Yes.'

'Which was?'

'Those who preach hate and intolerance do not have the right to anonymity.'

'Wasn't that your Rhys again?'

She nodded.

'And what happened next to Mr Fraser?'

'The press picketed the school of his eldest son.'

'Who was forced to move school, was he not?'

'Yes.'

'And what did the noble ARC have to say about that?'

'There's no hiding place or quarter for the enemies of humanity and their fellow travellers.'

'I take it that "fellow travellers" includes the immediate family? It certainly seemed to be the case with Mr Fraser's poor son.'

Rachel didn't respond; she just stared at the table top, awaiting the inevitable *coup de grâce*.

Eisenhower smiled to himself, 'There, Rachel: you seem to have answered your own question – shall we get back to your mother?'

Unable to control herself any longer, she erupted in rage. Slamming both hands down hard on the table she screamed, 'You will not persecute my mother! Is that clear?'

'Then you will have to change your testimony.'

'I can't.'

'It's one or the other, Rachel – your call: the builders or your mother?'

She suddenly leapt to her feet and ran for the toilet, both hands clamped tight over her heaving mouth. But the decision had been made; the front-page mock-up had broken the logjam. That night Eisenhower and Fortas had a long chat on the phone; the powers that be were very pleased with Jonathan's efforts. Things were looking up.

As the case entered its second week, all the builders were called in turn. Their testimony was uniform in describing the Muslims chasing Rachel and their efforts to protect her from the excited mob. Many of the incidents they described were caught, or partially caught, on mobile phones; their version of reality appeared to be gaining credence.

On the Wednesday of week two it was Rachel's turn to take the stand.

Eisenhower had a tricky problem: to defend Rachel from the charge of inciting racial or religious hatred through her actions, while confirming most of the Muslim testimony concerning the builders. These three men had been earmarked for sacrifice, and it was Rachel's job to cast these good men into the maw of the horned beast.

She made her way slowly, and rather unsteadily, towards the witness box. The media, having been pre-warned by the Foundation, were present in large numbers, heightening the sense of expectation in court. After swearing on the Bible she took her place. The three builders watched intently; Steve was the first to notice Rachel's state. She was drawn and haggard, with beads of sweat already forming on her brow; her voice, hardly above a whisper, was slow, low and reticent, causing the judge to ask her to speak up on several occasions.

Eisenhower asked her to give an account of her journey to the bus stop that fateful winter day.

'I was heading out of the flat above the laundrette for the bus stop at the far end of the High Street. I've not been into Bransborough for years, since I was a little girl – it's changed a bit since then. It was busy; I had to almost push my way through at times and I suppose it could have looked rather cocky, but everyone else was doing the same thing – it was the only way to make progress.

'I eventually bumped into a group of men on their way to the mosque – I presumed that's where they were going, as the call from the minaret was clearly audible and there were similar groups heading in the same direction. They looked at me strangely; that was when I noticed that the top of my coat was open. It seemed a bit inappropriate, so I buttoned up the top two buttons in response to their obvious unease with my dress.'

In the accused dock the three builders listened with mounting unease – what was this fairy story she was spinning? Rich, his head held low by his knees, whispered through the side of his mouth to Steve, 'It was bloody wet and freezing; when I saw her she had that dark coat of hers buttoned tightly – no way would she have gone out in that wind with the thing open.'

Steve glanced back at Rich; he was beginning to smell a rat.

Rachel paused for a second. 'Could you speak up a little? You're very faint,' interjected Judge Hoffman. Rachel smiled wanly and nodded.

'The whole situation was getting very confused; the worshippers were disturbed by my presence and I wanted to leave the area anyway, so a few of them showed me the way towards the bus stop.'

Alex spun his head around in disbelief and mounting fury. He was about to blurt something out when Steve, sensing his anger, took a firm grip of his arm and whispered, 'Calm down, mate; there's something odd going on here – let's just see where this yarn leads.' Alex temporarily relaxed.

'As we moved along the High Street a white van pulled up, and three builders jumped out – some fracas began between them and a group of Muslims. Soon the men with me ran back to join the commotion – things were getting very heated. I ran back to see what was going on, and slipped; I lost my overnight bag, which slid across the road. The three builders were armed with hammers and things; harsh words were being exchanged with the local worshippers. The situation was getting very heated, and I felt I needed to get out of there as quickly as possible, so I thought if I could get the builders to give me a lift it would serve my purpose and hopefully defuse the tension.

'I asked one of the men for a lift and he agreed; all the time words were being thrown back and forth between the two groups, hammers were being waved about, then missiles thrown at the van by some of the Muslims. I saw one man lying on the road with his head bleeding.

'I jumped in the van and as it pulled away, one of the builders shouted at the Muslims, who shouted back. This exchange sparked a fight with some of the worshippers trying to grab the builder inside the van. All sorts of things were being thrown, windows were broken and the van sustained damage to its doors – one of the builders was injured when the front windscreen was smashed.

'This continued all along the High Street with both sides abusing each other. I thought by the time we'd reached the far end things would have subsided, but they didn't. The Muslim worshippers were still incensed by the words being bandied about by the builders. They tried remonstrating with the builders, but that merely led to another attempt to force the van door. Eventually some Muslims forced a partial entry into the van, but were met by hammers and a nail gun.

'I saw Mr Fuller discharge the gun at Mr Qazi, who fell off the van's bonnet under the wheels – it was horrible. I believe Mr Jilami fell away from the van when he was threatened with the nail gun.'

Rich and Alex stared blankly at Rachel, utterly dumbfounded by what they'd just heard; Steve, however, had seen the light. 'She's been nobbled,' he stated quietly, shocked by the implications. 'The bastards have stitched her up somehow; I'd put me mortgage on it.'

Rachel was having major problems keeping everything together. Her quaking knees were on the point of giving way, while beads of sweat speckled her sickly pallor. She stood unnaturally rigid, facing forward in an iron grip of terror. She didn't dare look at her co-defendants; she was acutely aware that were she to set eyes on their accusing faces she'd literally crumple, wracked by shame, self-disgust and an overwhelming feeling of worthlessness.

Chaggar was amazed and exhilarated by the unexpected turn of events. When first appointed to prosecute the case a senior member of the Crown Prosecution Service had assured her matters were in hand, and that she could look forward to a famous victory. She'd dismissed the words as mere bravado; apparently she was mistaken.

It was now Chaggar's turn to question the defendant. 'Tell me, Miss Kynaston, have you any knowledge as to why the builders suddenly decided to stop in the High Street and begin berating the local Muslim community? In your original testimony you claimed that you ran to the builders fearing some danger from local Muslims. This does not appear to be your recollection now; would you like to clarify the situation?'

'Of course: there seems to have been a misunderstanding. I didn't approach the builders initially. As to why they decided to stop, and what they were arguing about with the Muslims, I have no idea. But certainly, by the time I ran up to them, heated words were being exchanged on both sides – it was getting pretty nasty.'

'Did you hear the builders using racist, or Islamophobic language?'

'I can't recall what exactly was being said, though from the reaction of the Muslims I'd say it was pretty strong.'

'The three builders claimed they were attacked for no obvious reason other than trying to save you from an alleged assault by local Muslim worshippers. Are you suggesting another reason for the obvious violence seen that day?'

At this Rachel's head fell forward and her shoulders sagged. Judge Hoffman interjected, 'Miss Kynaston?'

She pulled herself together. 'Yes, it was as I've just mentioned; the two groups had been arguing and it seems things escalated out of control.'

'Was violence or the threat of violence offered to you by members of the Muslim community at any time that day?'

'Not directly, though I was in the van when it was under attack.'

'Without the threat of violence to yourself, the claim of the builders that they were acting in your defence seems to be false – wouldn't you agree, Miss Kynaston?'

Walters immediately stood up, 'Objection M'lud: the prosecution is asking the witness to speculate on my client's motivation.'

Hoffman smiled; he knew the seed of doubt had already been planted. 'Objection sustained.'

Walters, still in shock from Rachel's volte-face, tried to mount a counterattack. 'Miss Kynaston, you've just given us an extraordinary account of events in Bransborough High Street. The most startling facet of this new account lies in the fact that it bears no relationship whatsoever to the statement you gave the police at the time of the incident. Would you like to explain to the jury how this substantial difference came about?'

Rachel had been expecting this question; Eisenhower had told her it would come and had prepared accordingly. 'The builders had been extremely kind in helping me escape a dangerous situation. I felt obligated to them, and so gave a statement in support of their claims; in reality, as I've explained, I didn't see or hear much of what actually occurred.'

Elliot Callaghan got to his feet, glancing askance at Judge Hoffman, whose duty it was to maintain court procedure. 'You do realise, Miss Kynaston, that telling lies under oath is a criminal offence, and that you could be facing a charge of perjury were it discovered you had purposely given false evidence?'

Rachel groaned inwardly; would this nightmare ever end? 'Yes, Mr Callaghan, I am aware that perjury is a criminal offence. I stand by my testimony.'

The following day both the press and TV news bulletins had a first run at a feeding frenzy – the full-blown version would have to wait until after the expected guilty verdict was delivered. The mud was piled high on the three builders, but as Eisenhower had promised, Rachel's name no longer figured among those for public pillorying. Now she was the 'brave witness', telling of her ordeal, caught in the middle of an ugly racist incident on Bransborough High Street.

On arriving home after her hellish day, Rachel headed for the back parlour where her mother could normally be found. She burst through the door to find her mother watching the early-evening news, which was dominated by Rachel's extraordinary testimony – a testimony that her mother knew to be at odds with that heard from her daughter on the night of the incident.

1.4 – JUSTICE

Connie Kynaston looked up, startled by her daughter's sudden entry, only to be shocked even more deeply by the sight of Rachel's drained and wracked face. Mothers sense the pain of their offspring; Connie knew instinctively that her daughter was in trouble and that something, somewhere, had gone horribly wrong.

Rachel collapsed on the couch sobbing, burying her head into her mother's bosom. The two sat like this in silence for a good ten minutes as the news droned on. Connie's mind turned over recent events for a clue. Her husband had been acting oddly, and there had been those surprisingly frequent visits of Eisenhower – how did that man get appointed as Rachel's barrister anyway? The family had always used Dennis Formby; not only was Dennis a QC, but he was also an old family friend. And now Rachel sat sobbing on the couch. What in heaven's name was going on?

Then there was that shifty character who'd turned up and virtually commandeered the whole house. She forgot his name, but with her daughter's tears forming a damp patch on her dress she knew instinctively that his presence spelt trouble.

After a while Rachel lifted her head. 'Do you want to talk?' asked her mother.

'Not yet.'

'Okay, but when you're ready – any time, day or night – just call.' Connie kissed her daughter tenderly on the forehead. 'Julie phoned earlier; she's invited you round tonight, if you fancy getting away from all this – or will it be too much? If you can't face her tonight I'll phone your excuses. Everybody understands you're under a lot of strain.'

'No, it's fine – a glass or two of plonk with Julie is exactly what I need right now.'

'Well, if you're going to drink I'll phone Marshall's for a taxi – and don't stay out too late.'

Julie was an old friend from way back, all the way to primary school in fact. She came from a solid, middle-class family, mother a teacher and dad something decent in the council. They'd always been close, discussing each other's hopes and fears. Rachel had come to depend upon Julie's sound judgement - her rock in a landscape of shifting sands. Whatever hare-brained idea Rachel picked up from the trendy gadflies that tended to flit around wherever they smelt money, Julie put her right in blunt language of few syllables. Most of Rachel's biggest regrets stemmed from having ignored advice given by Julie; God's teeth, she needed a dose of common sense now.

Julie's parents lived in a detached house on a pleasant, leafy avenue in one of the town's more attractive suburbs – all prim and proper, with well-presented houses set in well-manicured gardens. A little pride in one's surroundings speaks volumes about those who live there. Rachel's mind drifted momentarily back to the third-world squalor of Brixton, and scruffy hovels off the High Street in Bransborough. She remembered when she was small being taken to one of the houses off Bransborough High Street, where an ancient aunt of her mother's used to live. The house was terraced and only had two bedrooms, but it was spick and span, with a tiny, well-cared-for garden at the back. How things had changed, mused Rachel; but of course it wasn't the things that had changed – it was the people.

The two girls went up to Julie's spacious bedroom, where they flopped on the bed. Julie had a bottle of white waiting on the dressing table, and some chick-flick, if Rach fancied it; she didn't. Instead, she wanted a glass or two and a heart-to-heart with her oldest and closest friend.

They started with the latest news regarding Tom, Julie's long-time boyfriend. It was all getting rather serious; at present Tom still had two more years in Newcastle Uni, where he was taking a BSc in Earth Sciences, while Julie had one more year in Bristol Uni before hopefully taking up an internship with one of the big pharmaceutical companies. But what really interested Rachel was the personal stuff. What about her and Tom: was there an engagement in the offing? A marriage, perhaps?

'Wow, we're getting a bit ahead of ourselves, aren't we?' giggled Julie. 'We're off to Greece for a couple of weeks in August – rather hot for Tom's taste, but I love the sun. I'll be finishing Uni next summer; let's see how the land lies then.'

As Rachel glanced at the numerous photos of Julie and Tom on the dresser she felt a tinge of self-pity; how she'd adore getting away to Greece for a couple of weeks with a lover. She finished her glass and poured herself another large one.

'I was in court again today, giving evidence.'

'Yeah, I know; it was on the news, and in the evening papers.'

'What do you think?'

'Of what?'

'Of what I said.'

'I know it wasn't the truth. You told me the truth the same night it happened – remember?'

'Yes. So what do you think now?'

Julie looked at her oldest friend coldly, 'I don't know, Rach. Where did all those fairy stories come from? I remember you in tears, telling me you were terrified that those Muslims were going to rape you. I remember you literally thanking God – right here in this bedroom – for those builders, who saved your skin. I was convinced you were going to phone the Pope and have them made into saints.

'So Rachel – what's happened? What's all this bull about you not knowing why they stopped the van? I have no idea what's going on, but I'm beginning to think I don't understand you any more. Where's the old Rachel gone? She might have been a bit scatty, but at least you knew where you stood with her, and you could talk openly to her. Can I talk openly to you? Or will you start twisting things, as you've done with this fairy story of yours?'

Rachel was horrified, 'No, no, please, Julie; you don't understand – it wasn't me saying all those things. It was them – they forced me.'

'It came out of your mouth.'

Rachel was staring wide-eyed at her friend; she'd come for succour, but even here her perfidious actions were having their consequences.

Julie pressed on with her questioning. 'And who's "they"? What do you mean, "forced you" – how did they manage that? Surely your dad could have sorted things out; he's got plenty of money and plenty of clout.'

Rachel started crying. 'Dad was one of them.'

Julie stood stunned. 'Your dad?'

'Yes. They promised he could become a Tory MP, and he'd get planning permission for his new store up in York.'

In a rather more conciliatory voice Julie probed a little deeper. 'You said "they" – who else was involved?'

'Eisenhower, my barrister – and some other man; I never really met him properly, but Mum saw him briefly. They concocted the story about Bransborough and twisted my arm to repeat it in court.'

'What does that mean, "twisted your arm"?'

'Eisenhower said if I didn't do as they wanted, the press and TV reporters would come after us. It happens – I've seen it when I was in the ARC.'

'I told you to stay away from those creeps; I did warn you.'

'Yeah, and you were right, as usual.'

'You said he threatened "us" – who's "us"?'

'The family; that's what I was trying to explain to you. Eisenhower had a mock-up of the front page of the *National Courier,* with a photo of Mum and the builders and me on it – the headline read, "Guilty" and under Mum's picture it said something like, *Connie Kynaston, mother of suspected Nixon Rachel Kynaston and friend of the murderers Cunliffe, Hall and Fuller, photographed in her garden today.*'

'Oh my God; that's terrible – how dare the bastard! What did your mum say?'

'I haven't told her. I can't say to her that Dad was part of all this just so he could get his lousy seat and planning permission. Oh Julie, what should I do? I feel terrible; I've betrayed those men who did so much for me, and for what? To keep the press off my family, and a couple of bribes for Dad.'

'Rach, I know it's hard with your dad and everything, but your mum's the most sensible, feet-on-the-ground person I know. She won't turn on you; she'll be calm and collected – she always is. Some of my other friends sometimes ask me about you, you know, with your dad being rich and all that. They think I'm jealous of your money.'

Rachel laughed. 'They don't know you as well as I do, then – money!'

'But I am jealous.'

'You are?' Rachel was aghast.

'Yes, but not of your money: your mum – she's absolutely fantastic. You can confide in her, and she's so warm and approachable; but more than that, she's a priceless fountain of common sense. I'm not saying I'd swop my mum for her – all mums are unique - but she's your real wealth, Rach, not your dad's millions. Tell her everything; you'll see, she'll know what to do.'

As Marshall's taxi took her home Rachel pondered first Julie's words, then those of her mother earlier – day or night, she'd said. She looked at the clock on the taxi dashboard; it was 1:30 in the morning.

She'd had the best part of a bottle of Riesling, without which she'd never have had the courage to slip into her patents' bedroom to gently shake her mother awake. Connie opened her eyes sleepily and focused uncertainly on her daughter's face. 'What is it?' she rasped. Rachel just beckoned her to the door. Connie sighed and swung out of bed. Basil momentarily muttered something; Connie just rolled him back onto his side and whispered quietly, 'It's just Rachel; go back to sleep.' The pair stepped out onto the landing.

'What's up darling?'

'You said "day or night", didn't you?'

'I did.' The sleep was clearing fast now. 'Come, let's go down to the back parlour – I'll make a cuppa and you can tell me what's going on.'

So they sat through the wee hours as Rachel told her mother of the promises made to her and her father, of the threats to the family and the photograph of Connie herself on the front page of the *National Courier*. It took almost two hours to go through the whole story and the inevitable questions – not merely of Eisenhower's conspiracy, but to clarify and confirm the real story of the builders to the best of Rachel's recollection. By the end Connie had all she needed.

She stood up and took Rachel into her arms, giving her a kiss on the cheek. 'Try and grab a couple of hours' sleep. Tomorrow's going to be unpleasant; the air will need to be cleared and you're going to face the consequences of having lied in court. Don't fret, darling; we've both learnt something far more important than the court and your dad's money – family, friends, love and honour. Those are the true virtues, and tomorrow we as a family are going to declare our loyalty to them.'

1.4 – JUSTICE

With the aid of the white wine still in her veins Rachel managed to snatch a few hours' sleep, despite any lingering worries she might have felt concerning her mother's words.

When Basil rose at 6:30 he found his wife already up, dressed and busy. He reminded her he'd be late that evening, as he had an afternoon appointment with the architects for the new store in York.

'I've cancelled it.'

Basil stared at his wife in disbelief. 'You've cancelled my appointment? Why?'

'Not only have I cancelled your appointment: I phoned your secretary as well, rather early I'm afraid - please give her my apologies when you see her next. You're not expected in today – family business.'

Basil's hackles were up now, 'Family business? What bloody family business?'

'Your daughter's sanity and the future of our marriage.'

'What are you talking about, woman? Our marriage?' Basil was in utter confusion; then suddenly a bolt of clarity struck him. He vaguely recalled Rachel waking Connie in the middle of the night. So that's it: the cat was out of the bag.

'Basil Kynaston, if you think for one second that I will remain your wife while you put your own daughter – *our* daughter – through a living hell for your damned store and a bloody seat in Parliament, then I'm afraid I've got bad news for you. I'll miss this place, but I can move back to Tyrone Grange if need be. In any case, my sister's been badgering me for years to take an extended stay at her villa in Cyprus. It's beginning to sound more appealing by the day.'

'Look, Connie – I admit what you say is true; the seat and the store were offered, and for Rachel they were going to get her reinstated into college, and newspaper articles would be published saying she wasn't really with those builders. The deal was good – considering.'

'The deal was not "good"; those builders saved our daughter and we've repaid them with treachery and lies. What sort of people are we, Basil? Is this your idea of decent behaviour? Well, it's nothing of the sort; it's appalling – the worst kind of lily-livered, money-grubbing deceitfulness imaginable.'

There was a slight pause as Connie collected her thoughts, 'What was that you just said – "considering"? Considering what?'

'Considering who was behind it. You think it was all that Eisenhower's doing, don't you?'

'Wasn't it?'

'Do you think Eisenhower has the power to order articles in the press, or programmes to be made on television? Do you think he can rustle up safe Tory seats at the drop of a hat, or twist planning committees around his little finger? These are the actions of far bigger fish than Mr Eisenhower. Our visitor – Mr Fortas – do you recall the gentleman?'

'I recall him taking over the study.'

'Now there's a pretty big fish. He gets things done, however impossible they may seem – though I suspect there are even bigger fish in the mix somewhere.'

'I don't care how big the fish are: you and this Fortas character are not going to destroy our daughter or, frankly, betray those men who acted in her defence. If I may remind you, they were the only ones to lift a finger – she's our flesh and blood, Basil!'

Her husband found a chair and sat down. Connie brought him a mug of tea and a piece of toast and marmalade. Basil could be something of an enigma to those on the outside. Some took the affable front as a sign of befuddled amateurism, a man who had fallen into wealth, but in reality was no businessman – more a country gent. Basil rather liked the front and played up to it constantly. However, in truth, when his father passed on the family business, Countryside Living only had two stores, whereas it now had twenty-five. There was far more to Basil Kynaston than the outward passive appearance would indicate; he was a predator, and a successful one at that.

As he ate, he thought deeply about the predicament in which the family found itself. He understood better than his wife, or his daughter, how dangerous were people like Fortas, and those for whom he worked. Basil had spent enough time rubbing shoulders with powerful movers and shakers to know there was real power behind the throne of state, and that the seats occupied by the country's democratic representatives were merely window-dressing – albeit prestigious window-dressing.

Basil finished his toast. 'Well, Connie: where do you suggest we begin?'

'I'm not happy with that Eisenhower fellow – never was. I want him gone. Would it be possible to get hold of Dennis Formby at such a late stage in the game?'

'Perhaps.'

'I know it'll mean serious trouble for her, but Rachel must retract those lies she spouted yesterday – if only for her sanity. Did you see the state of her, Basil? I warn you, she'll have a breakdown if things continue as they are.'

'If we're going to pull up the drawbridge, I'd better get cracking.'

'Meaning?'

'The men who make kings can break kings; I can't be left exposed with an interest in a Tory seat or planning for a new store in the offing. All these things can be turned against me. I'll resign from the party and revoke the planning application. I'll have to find alternative paths for expanding the business.

'I'll also need to get over to Dennis' place, so, darling, could I ask you to contact John Glaspole over at Jarrett & Taylor, and inform him that Mr Eisenhower's services will no longer be required? You can tell him that a new appointment will be made by the end of the day. He'll probably warn you about all sorts of financial penalty clauses I signed as part of the original deal, but there's nothing that can be done about that now – just get rid of him.'

'My pleasure, Basil; I suspect Rachel will be mighty relieved to see the back of him. Shall I warn your office that the proposed York branch is being shelved?'

'Yes, good idea – phone through and get hold of Jim Hunter in the back office. Tell him we're going forward with his original West Country Plan and that York's dead for now. He'll understand.'

By now Basil's mind was in overdrive; he'd accepted his wife's plea to place matters in their proper perspective – family first. He got on the phone to Dennis to confirm he was home before driving over. He arrived just after breakfast. They had an interesting meeting; at first Dennis was less than keen after having been passed over for Eisenhower. However, after Basil had told him the full story – which interestingly, didn't entirely surprise Dennis – his old friend and eminent QC agreed to pick up the pieces.

In the meantime, he'd also arranged lunch at the Wellington Arms with Lord Priestholm – or Johnny, as Basil liked to call him. Johnny was chairman of the local Conservative Party Association; Basil would be handing in his notice over an excellent plate of Dover sole. It was a pity; he got on well with Johnny, and had hoped for great things from his parliamentary career – but as he now realised, without his family it would all be so much hollow junketing.

The change of barrister and rearranging of some of the testimony was enough for Judge Hoffman to order a twenty-four hour adjournment, which Formby would need to prepare his client. Rachel was to return to the stand.

That evening, just before she went to bed, there was a gentle knock on Rachel's bedroom door.

'Come in … oh, Daddy it's you. What's up?'

Basil came into the bedroom holding an old, black book, and sat down on the edge of the bed next to his daughter.

'I need to speak to you, Rachel, to apologise for my despicable actions over the last few days, I can't tell you how disgusted I feel with myself. I'm so sorry, darling.'

'It's done, Daddy; let it go.'

'I just got so caught up in the business and my career; sometimes you lose sight of the big things in life when you're running around, chasing your own tail. Your mother sorted out all that nonsense, you know, I don't know what I'd do without her.'

'I'm sorry you've lost your chance to be an MP, and the new store in York.'

'You've got nothing to be sorry about, darling; my stupidity and greed aren't your fault. It might not be much, but were you to accept this gift' – he handed over the old book to his daughter – 'it would make me feel a little better.'

Rachel stared inquisitively at the old book. Across the battered cover was written 'The Holy Bible', the gold leaf having all but worn away.

'What's this, Dad? I know it's a Bible – and an old one at that – but why have you given it to me?'

'Kin.'

'Kin?'

'Perhaps this is my fault as well. Has nobody ever explained to you that us Kynastons originally came from the Welsh Marches?'

'Really?'

'Our branch came from Bishop's Castle, in Shropshire. This Bible belonged to your great-great-grandmother; I'm not entirely sure, but I think she was the last of us Kynastons to live in Bishop's Castle.'

Rachel opened up the ancient book and flicked through some pages, glancing at its archaic English and difficult typeface.

'The best bit is just inside the cover: look here.' Basil flicked the Bible to the second page, where a family tree was laid out, with an 'Emily Parry' having married a 'John Kynaston' as the last entry, near the bottom of the page.

'That's her, Emily Parry – Parry was her maiden name; she was your great-great-grandmother.'

'And I'm related to all these people on this page? They go back to the eighteenth century!'

'Yes, they're all your kith and kin.'

'So what are we doing in Warwickshire?'

'My grandfather, Frank, who was Emily's second son, first moved here to work in engineering – but he eventually drifted into retailing in Birmingham. We've been here ever since.'

Rachel gazed in amazement at the list of her forebears going back over 250 years. This was her family: the history of her blood.

'I hope you like it, darling; it's been in the family a very long time and in recognition of your mother's wise words – "family comes first" – I've decided it's time to hand on this family heirloom to the finest daughter any father could wish for.'

Rachel was close to tears by now; she threw her arms around Basil's neck and kissed him on the cheek, 'Thank you, Daddy. It's the most wonderful gift I've ever had – I'll guard it with my life, I promise!'

Basil chuckled again. What's life, he mused, without family?

Eisenhower had phoned Fortas as soon a he'd been informed of his dismissal as brief for Rachel Kynaston. Fortas in turn phoned GSS' legal department, who immediately dispatched one of their in-house lawyers to keep an eye on developments – a necessary precaution, though neither Fortas nor Kaplan were overly concerned. Rachel Kynaston may well retract her earlier testimony, which Eisenhower's sacking strongly implied, but her new testimony would be worthless – who'd believe the word of such a witness? Even if the builders were ultimately found innocent, it could be sold to the public as a mistrial – all caused by Miss Kynaston's revolving-door attitude towards swearing oaths and giving evidence. Better still, she might go to jail for perjury. The builders would remain guilty in the eyes of the media, and therefore, by default, in the eyes of the public too. The aim of the whole exercise had been to avoid a charge of molesting a White woman from being levelled against Muslim society. Whatever happened now in Bransborough Crown Court, they had won. The long-standing claim made by the press and TV channels, that Muslims posed no threat to Western society, had been vindicated. Thus there would be no need for any moratorium or tightening of regulations on further immigration – as had been threatened at one stage. The expanded population programme was free to roll on unscathed.

Mission accomplished.

1.5 - Gods

As Steve sat in his cell in Bransborough, contemplating the fickleness of fate, he felt very much at peace with himself and the world. Rich and Alex thought he'd gone barking, but he'd discovered the key to scratching his spiritual itch. His mind travelled back to the previous summer – before the nightmare of Bransborough.

He and Elaine had been on a spiritual journey; they had joined an Ásatrú group, thinking to explore Germanic Paganism. For a while they had fun, caught up in the rush of new ideas and strange customs. They attended the odd *blót* making offerings to the Gods under the guidance of a Pagan priest, who led the group. However, after a while things began to go flat, rituals felt forced and the Gods were keeping their distance; there was something wrong – something missing.

During one such *blót* Elaine remarked on her lack of spiritual engagement to one of the other girls who, having listened carefully, mentioned a member who had left six months earlier for the same reason. The word was that he'd gone to seek a Pagan shaman, who apparently lived up in Yorkshire near a hamlet called Skyreholme. The shaman went by the title Fell Follower, but his real name was Phillip Stavert. Perhaps he could help.

Elaine was intrigued, as was Steve after hearing the story. They both felt they'd lost their way and were in concert in believing it was time to seek a more substantive path to the Gods. They resolved to find this shaman.

Their first task was to contact Fell Follower – or plain Phillip Stavert. However, this proved far from simple. There were no listings for him in any of the various phone directories; neither did his name appear on the internet search engines. Nobody in their Pagan group knew how to contact him – indeed, only two had ever heard of him.

Eventually, hours of patience paid dividends. Late one night, deep in conversation with another Pagan in a chatroom called The Wyrd Way, Elaine found someone who knew Fell Follower and how he could be contacted.

According to the contact, a note to 'Phillip Stavert' was to be sent care of the Craven Arms, in Appletreewick, Yorkshire. Elaine was warned that Fell Follower would consult the runes before deciding whether or not to meet her. Should the runes fall favourably under the influence of Freya, Fell Follower's chief guide, a note would be sent back with an invitation for an exploratory meeting.

Much time was spent in wording their request – producing a rather long explanatory affair – which was duly dispatched to Appletreewick. The weeks slipped by, and Elaine and Steve had all but given up on receiving a reply, concluding that Freya had rejected their plea.

But a month after sending their initial letter, a handwritten envelope dropped through the letterbox with an invitation to meet Fell Follower over the first weekend of the following month. A pent-up surge of enthusiasm passed through the pair of them, a fact reflected in the heavy circling, in red ink, of the much anticipated weekend on the kitchen calendar in their semi-detached home. Steve got onto the internet and booked a double room for Friday and Saturday nights at the New Inn, Appletreewick.

As the old sayings tell us, waiting time is hard time; the days dragged slowly, inching their way, snail-like, towards the audience with the Yorkshire shaman. However, at long last the appointed morning dawned.

The drive to Yorkshire was long and tiring after a day's work, but just before ten in the evening they entered Appletreewick and found the New Inn.

They'd wisely eaten en route, having stopped for a perfunctory bite at a motorway stop north of Manchester. They unloaded the car, then settled down in the bar; Elaine ordering half a cider and Steve a pint of the local brew. The lady of the establishment, Janet, was serving behind the bar. As she pulled Steve's pint she handed over an envelope bearing their names in a distinctive hand they'd seen before. It was a note from Fell Follower.

They were invited to meet him outside Parcevall Hall Gardens at 10:00 the following morning. Unsure of the geography, Steve checked with Janet, who informed them the Gardens were about 15–20 minutes' walk up the road in Middle Skyreholme. If they went by car they could get there in 5 minutes.

Steve decided to quiz a little deeper. 'Do you know a Phillip Stavert?'

'Phil? Yes, I've known him for years – he teaches folklore and stuff. He has people calling fairly regularly; quite a few of them stay here. You'll be seeing him tomorrow, I expect. He's a nice chap, always very polite and very knowledgeable about lore, nature and history.'

Steve and Elaine thanked Janet, then moved from the bar to sit in the corner for a private chat.

'It's quite exciting, isn't it?'

Steve looked longingly at Elaine and blessed the day the Fates had brought such a special woman into his life. 'Yeah: I feel like we're really only just starting our journey, and all that other stuff we got up to was merely a preamble.'

Elaine, aware of Steve's gaze, took a sip from her cider. 'It's a bit cloak-and-dagger, don't you think?'

Steve felt immensely content with his lot, seeking the Gods in this wonderful corner of England with the woman he loved – does it get any better? 'Perhaps, though everyone in the village seems to know him; it's not exactly James

Bond. Have you noticed how all these shaman characters – like Fell Follower – live out in the wildest places? It's almost as if they need to feel nature at her most raw and tangible to connect with the Gods.'

Elaine, like Steve, had great expectations of the weekend. 'I can't wait to see what happens; I feel like a little girl again on Christmas Eve, trying to guess what presents Santa will bring.'

Steve grinned, then finished his pint, tired after the long drive from the Midlands. As he got up to return his empty glass to the bar he gave Elaine a kiss on the cheek. 'And what presents will Santa be bringing me tonight?'

'You cheeky bugger!' laughed Elaine, getting up to follow him. Steve placed his and Elaine's empty glasses on the bar and turned for the door. Elaine took his arm and led him towards the stairs for the bedrooms. 'Let's see what we can find in that sack – but only for good little boys.'

'I'll do my best,' promised Steve, still grinning.

The following morning, after a hearty breakfast, they plumped for the walk – it was a beautiful day and they both fancied a blast of fresh country air and a chance to savour the striking scenery. After marching up to Middle Skyreholme, they forked left and headed for the Gardens. Nearby, a rather unprepossesing character in a faded blue shirt and brown cotton trousers stood in the shade of a tree, watching their progress.

'That'll be him,' said Elaine intuitively. The man looked to be in his mid-thirties, perhaps a year or two older than Steve. He had short, dark hair with a hint of grey starting to colour his temples. He had tanned skin, showing the effect of long hours spent in the elements, as his shamanic name indicated, and a short goatee beard and trimmed moustache. The most striking feature of the face that turned inquisitively towards Elaine was the calm intelligence of the hazel eyes; here was a man who radiated wisdom, a man comfortable in his own skin, content with life and the path he'd chosen to walk.

He stepped from the shade and offered his hand to Steve, being the closer, then Elaine.

'Welcome to Skyreholme. I'm Fell Follower, though plain Phil's fine if you prefer. Fancy a cup of something? There's a tea room here we can have a pot and discuss your requirements of me and your hopes for the weekend.' An easy smile broke across Fell Follower's countenance that both Steve and Elaine instinctively reciprocated.

Having settled down with some tea, it was time for a general chat as they got to know each other better.

'Why do you think I can help you? You said in your letter that the group you're with isn't working for you – what's the problem and what ultimately are you searching for?'

Elaine spoke first, 'Personally, I've yet to feel the Gods; I've done all that's been asked of me, but nothing seems to have any effect. Is it all just interpretation? I thought being touched by a God would be something electric, something life-changing. Steve and I have done a few ceremonies and made offerings to the Gods during *blóts* – we've done around a dozen or so – but it all feels a bit superficial, a bit pointless. Where have we gone wrong?'

Fell Follower turned to Steve. 'And you? What's your take on all this?'

'I agree with Elaine; whatever's supposed to happen, once you embrace Paganism, hasn't had any impact on me. It's strange; I sort of know there's more out there, that there's some sort of presence, but I can't reach it; it's like a shadow in the fog – as you stretch out towards it everything just dissolves. As Elaine said, I was expecting to have my life changed by accepting Paganism, but it's all been rather disappointing. I'm willing, keen even, to make the effort and do what it takes, but we need guidance; the people who run our current group simply aren't cutting it. I suspect they're either charlatans or are fooling themselves as to their real knowledge of the Gods.'

1.5 - GODS

Once they'd finished Steve paid the bill, then Fell Follower led the pair out of the building and down towards Skyreholme Beck, which climbed into the hills behind Parcevall Hall. They followed the beck's course to an impressive ravine called Troller's Ghyll. They walked beside the beck, passing grazing sheep and green trees, going deeper into the gulley, until they reached a point where the impressive rock features came into full view. The ravine went deeper, but Fell Follower decided to stop. He glanced about; Troller's Ghyll was a popular site for ramblers and he wanted to make sure nobody would disturb them. Once he was happy they were alone, he stretched out his hand and, with a sweep of his arm encompassing everything in sight, said, 'What do you see?'

He turned to Steve, who replied, 'Rocks, a few sheep, couple of trees – grass?'

Then Elaine: 'The same as Steve, though there's the beautiful sky as well, of course. Look at those birds up there.'

Fell Follower looked askance at them both. 'Surely, however poor he may be as a leader and guide, your priest has managed to instruct you concerning the Being of things?'

Both Steve and Elaine gave non-committal nods, indicating they'd come across the idea, though their reluctance to volunteer further information suggested strongly to Fell Follower that their understanding of the concept was limited in the extreme.

He sat down on a large boulder and pulled from his back pocket a battered black book. He opened it almost on the first page. Then, when he was happy that Steve and Elaine were listening, he began to read:

'Then God said, "Let us make man in our image, in our likeness, and let them rule over the fish of the sea and the birds of the air, over the livestock, over all the earth, and over all the creatures that move along the ground."

'Have you heard those lines before?'

They both nodded.

'And what, as good Pagans, do you make of those lines?'

Steve was cagey and didn't respond, but Elaine had a few things to say, 'As Pagans we don't believe in the one God, and the way the Bible describes how Man is to rule over the Earth is not sustainable. Look what's happened with overfishing and the number of species going extinct.'

Fell Follower sat still for a while, listening to these ramblings before finally raising his hand in exasperation. 'Enough.'

'Steve, Elaine: you've not grasped first principles. You still carry around the mythology and mental baggage of those who wrote the Bible. This sort of arrogance might work for Semitic desert dwellers, but for us Indo-Europeans – or Aryans, if you prefer – this is not, and never has been, our way. To those who wrote the Bible, the Earth is as I've just read from Genesis – a storehouse to be plundered and exploited. To such a mindset the Earth of itself has no merit or essence; it is merely a gift of Yahweh's to be disposed of as we mighty humans think fit.

'However, this heedless, piratical attitude towards the Earth and Nature is not shared by us Pagans. A well-respected modern Pagan summed up our attitude succinctly in the immortal phrase, "There is nothing dead in Nature" – meaning we are surrounded by a living mosaic of fellow Beings. We are not the only ones with a Being; Nature has almost limitless variations – each one, in its own way and for its own purpose, as perfect and well-formed as we are.

'To progress, you'll have to first remove the blinkers: stop looking at animals as walking microwave meals, or mountain sides as unfinished ballast for the local bypass. Look at them afresh, as entities in their own right, as Beings with their own essence, created – like us – by the eternal force of Nature.

'Both of you expressed a wish to know the Gods. Before we start, I must warn you: there is only so much that can be achieved, for the Gods are beings beyond human understanding. They are unchanging, unbegotten, eternal, incorporeal, and exist beyond the confines of time and space. As the makers, they preceded the made; they, the eternal Gods, created Nature. As I've already mentioned, Nature itself has an essence – an essence to which we need to attune ourselves, for it is our living environment, and gives us a window into the desires of the Gods, who so closely identify with their creations.

'If it helps, you can view Nature as our given habitat; we live in Nature as fish live in water. In the unnatural world, the man-made world, we can't live; we're out of our element – we're fish out of water. The best we can manage in an urban world is to exist. Unfortunately, vast swathes of our people today are obliged to "exist" rather than live, which explains the almost universal malaise one finds throughout the lands of our people.

'As I've already mentioned, the Gods are eternal, therefore they're always with us; they never left – and they never will. However, if we are to receive them we need to ready ourselves. The first step in this process is to open ourselves to the Being of Nature – in all her varieties. Once we begin to sense these Beings, in whatever form they touch us, a path to the Gods begins to open within us. The Gods, as creators, are far mightier than Nature, but they manifest themselves through Nature and the forces of Nature. You may walk in the deep forest, visit the hidden riverside pools, climb the lonely mountain tops and drink mead offerings to the Gods until you collapse drunk – but unless you're capable of opening yourself to the Being of Nature, to the fact that every part of Nature has a Being, an essence, you will never create the internal space to experience the Gods. They cannot enter that which is closed behind the unnatural dogma of Genesis, be it in its original religious guise or its myriad secular scientific offspring.'

Steve, slightly taken aback, looked agog at Fell Follower. 'You seem to be half-suggesting that Pagans are a species of New Age Traveller – you know, getting back to Nature, living in tents and worshipping Mother Earth and all that. Are we basically just Odin-worshipping hippies?'

Fell Follower chuckled softly, 'Not quite. I'm not saying we shouldn't use Nature – of course we must, otherwise our civilisation would collapse and we'd cease to exist. Pagans have always used Nature; the Greeks and Romans were Pagans, and look what they built. However, there's a world of difference between using the fruits of Nature for our immediate needs, and the raw exploitation seen today in an age dominated by unrestrained greed and rampant corruption. A good Pagan takes what he or she needs, and tries not to squander the gifts the Gods offer us.'

Elaine now interjected: 'You speak about the Being of the different parts of Nature; does everything have a Being? And are they all connected and of equal weight and power?'

'Good question, Elaine. Firstly, let's contemplate the Being of different parts of Nature. The simple answer to your question is "yes" – all of Nature's works have a Being, an essence. They are also connected, since Nature is all-encompassing and creates an entirety. Our world is an entirety, a work of Nature in which all the parts work in accordance with their own Being. However, these Beings reflect the essence of the part of Nature that gave rise to them – figuratively speaking. They are not, and can never be, the same, nor equal. Take us humans: we are not as strong as bulls, or as fast as greyhounds; we can neither match the salmon in water nor dream of matching the hawk in flight. The Being of salmon, greyhounds and bulls must be different from ours, reflecting the difference in their essence. The bull is strong, the greyhound fast; but our gifts from the Gods lie elsewhere. We have an intellect the like of which no animal can match. Animals too, sense the Gods; watch them closely the next time you walk in Nature. However, they can never communicate with the Gods as we can; that is our great gift, if we can but open ourselves to the majesty of that which is all around us.

'However, I don't want you to get the idea that the Gods are merely the spirits of Nature, a sort of personalisation of natural phenomena. They are, in fact, the complete opposite. Nature is a reflection of the divine power that brought it into existence, and when we attune ourselves to the essence of Nature we're attuning ourselves to the Gods who created it.

1.5 - GODS

'In attuning ourselves to the essence of Nature we open ourselves to the Gods, whose work Nature is. Once you begin the process of opening yourself, you'll become ever more aware of the Gods; they lurk in their works. Remember, the Gods do not seek us; we seek them. This is not just me spouting these ideas; Pagans have always been aware of the relationship between Nature and its creators. Steve, I believe you're familiar with the work of Sallustius?'

Steve nodded.

Fell Follower pulled a sheet from the Bible he still held. 'Well, this is what Sallustius wrote about Nature:

"To say that these objects are sacred to the Gods, like various herbs and stones and animals, is possible to sensible men, but to say that they are gods is the notion of madmen."

'I'm not asking you to worship the spirits of Nature: I'm asking you to open yourself to their essence in order to connect with that which some refer to as the Greater Spirits. Once you feel yourself opening to Nature, the receiving of the Gods takes a giant step forward.'

The sound of voices alerted him to the approach of a group of ramblers heading for Troller's Ghyll. Fell Follower got up and began making his way back towards Parcevall Hall, which they passed following the beck, before re-emerging in Middle Skyreholme. Turning left they entered High Skyreholme, where after passing the first set of buildings they turned into a field entrance, then followed a dry-stone wall down towards Bland's Beck. 'You should try this in the winter mud,' bemoaned Fell Follower. They then trekked upstream along Bland's Beck until, having passed the last farm in High Skyreholme, they crossed over on a rickety bridge. Finally they cut through a copse to a farm building surrounded by a small compound. The utilitarian building looked like a cattle shed from the outside – which it had once been – though inside it had been modified enough to constitute reasonable, if basic, accommodation.

'I get it at a cheap rate from the farmer,' explained Fell Follower. 'I do odd jobs for him and help out at lambing. It's a great location, and allows me to get up onto Simon's Seat – the big hill that dominates this whole side of the valley.'

Elaine scanned Fell Follower's scant possessions. 'You've got no television!' - an observation that won a little chortle. 'No, afraid not; I need all my time to study and prepare spiritually for my other tasks – though I've got a radio.'

Elaine cast an eagle eye over a large bookcase standing against the far wall, flanked by a couple of interesting tapestries, behind which was bare stone. She knew enough to recognise Odin on one of the tapestries, while the other portrayed a female deity, who Elaine assumed was Freya.

'What other tasks?'

'Ah, you mean the burden of knowledge. You see Elaine, whatever our title – teacher, elder, shaman, guide – we shoulder a common duty to pass on our knowledge. The greatest failure would be for the knowledge we carry to die with us. You and Steve would not be my only students; there are others whom I see at various times, all at different stages of development. Some, like you, are on the first rung; others are more advanced, while the best are almost ready to accept their own students.'

Steve and Elaine sat down on a couple of rustic chairs by the sparse kitchen table as Fell Follower brewed some tea on a simple gas stove. While he pottered around, Steve and Elaine spoke softly to each other. They concurred that this was indeed the real deal; they were in no doubt that this man could lead them to the Gods. However, they also suspected it would be no easy journey; the spartan surroundings spoke of devotion and single-minded determination.

Fell Follower placed three steaming mugs of tea on the table and joined his guests. As they drank he began to outline the road ahead. It would entail much studying; ignorance was a major stumbling block for so many 'weekend

Pagans'. He told them that Judeo-Christian dogma had penetrated so deeply into the European psyche that without a thorough grounding in the basics of Paganism, most who wished to walk with the Gods became entrapped in their Christian cultural backgrounds. Without breaking free of this baggage a way could never be opened for these people to receive the Gods.

Fell Follower had already decided he would accept Steve and Elaine, though for now he'd keep the news to himself. He'd also decided that their first steps should be directed towards reading the runes; he would insist they make their own – he'd not tolerate a set of commercially produced rune stones bought anonymously online from some 'Pagan Shop' in America.

It was nearly lunchtime and Fell Follower asked if they wished to return to the New Inn or Parcevall Hall for something to eat – or, conversely, remain in the lodge with him. He didn't have much: bread, cheese, butter, half a cured sausage, a few tomatoes and a cucumber plus a pot of local chutney. They could have some bread and honey for afters – plus more tea, of course. It was a long way back across the fields, so they decided to share Fell Follower's modest fare. They continued to talk throughout lunch, clearing up questions of terminology and the exact meanings of words. He told them that Ásatrú was for those who followed the Æsir, Odinism for those who followed the Alfather. He considered his teachings to be Theodish, or Spiritual Nordic Paganism – where all the Gods were recognised and honoured.

He clarified another important issue of semantics: namely, in his opinion Paganism was not a religion; as far as he was concerned 'religions' were dogmas of the monotheists. He referred to Theodish as a spiritual belief. Paganism had no holy books, no 'Word of God' with which to beat and persecute others. Steve asked about where the *Edda* fitted into his teachings. He confirmed they were valuable accounts that had to be read. However, he also warned that by the time the *Edda* was written down, Christianity had already taken control in Iceland. The *Edda,* had to be treated with a degree of circumspection; it almost certainly did not tell the whole story of Norse Paganism, having been compiled under the nose of Catholic clerics.

However, he also admitted that not everybody shared his views concerning the nature of Germanic Paganism; some, in particular the various Ásatrú groups, considered it a religion.

After lunch they returned to Troller's Ghyll. The place was alive with ramblers and casual visitors from Parcevall Hall Gardens. Fell Follower said he wished to speak with each alone for an hour or so. While he did this, the other partner could explore Troller's Ghyll, find a quiet spot, sit down and relax. Once comfortable they should allow themselves to drift mentally, remaining open to whatever feelings they encountered. Nothing major would happen – there were far too many people around to allow anything of significance to occur – but it would be a good exercise in attuning oneself to the Being of Nature's various manifestations.

He questioned each in turn about how much they knew of their ancestors and their family history. Elaine knew a few facts about her great-grandparents, Steve only his grandparents. Both were told that those who follow Theodish teachings, besides believing in the Gods, also revere the folk – their folk. How could they take their place among the folk if they knew so little about themselves and their lineage?

He gave an example. He was not a Sioux: he could not just turn up in Dakota and claim a place in their spiritual traditions – his place wasn't among the Sioux and never would be. Steve and Elaine were English; this fact not only defined their folk, but it defined their Gods too. Folk, land and Gods went hand in hand; the Gods they sought were English Gods – albeit from a general Germanic pantheon. It was in recognition of their own identity as members of the folk that they needed to know the depth of their roots; once again, knowledge was key. He instructed both to start seriously working on their family trees.

It had been a long day, but they all thought it had been very productive. Fell Follower sent them back to the New Inn for their evening meal, while he returned to his lodge. He asked to see them again at ten thirty the following morning.

1.5 - GODS

The food was good; Steve and Elaine felt tired after such an intense day, yet buoyed by the prospect of finally encountering the Gods. One of the local girls serving table came over to collect their plates and with a smile said, 'I hope you enjoyed the meal, Mr and Mrs Hall – would you like some dessert? Here's the menu; I can recommend today's special, raspberry cobbler.'

The girl handed out the dessert menus, collected the dirty plates and returned to the kitchen; Elaine, in a daze, watched her disappear through the double-hinged kitchen doors – 'Mrs Hall'. Steve caught her wistful look and knew immediately what it meant, and how the girl had come to assume they were man and wife; after all, the place had been booked for two in his name.

'Would you like me to have a word?' he asked sheepishly.

Elaine looked him straight in the eyes. 'Why? I have no issue with anything she's said or done. Leave the poor girl in peace and order your cheesecake.'

Steve felt the unvoiced implication acutely; he knew the future beckoned, but for now he contented himself with a lame, 'How do you know what I want?'

She leant forward with feline grace, the unconditional love she felt filling her countenance as she placed her hands gently over his. 'Because, darling, you always order cheesecake – hadn't you noticed?'

That night a very content 'Mrs Hall' followed Steve upstairs to their room.

The following morning Steve and Elaine trekked once again over the fields to the lodge, just in time to catch a brief glimpse of Fell Follower at the edge of the copse holding aloft a rune cup making an offering – not dissimilar to the artificial affairs they had witnessed in the *blót*. Feeling acutely like interlopers straying unwittingly into an intensely private affair, they hurried along into the building, leaving the shaman to finish his devotions.

Fell Follower wasn't long in coming after them; he quickly returned the rune cup, and bottle of mead, into a corner cabinet, while making a cursory apology for being tardy. He then sat down by the table, having already decided to broach some further basic tenets of Pagan spiritual belief with his new pupils.

'Once you're received a God, or Gods, it will change your life. This relationship between you and the Gods is a strictly personal affair – it's for nobody else. As you know, Freya chose me – why? I have no idea – but she's always close to me, and she's the one who responds whenever I seek advice. Those people, in your Pagan group, trying to commune publicly with the Gods, are simply wasting their time; such things can't be done publicly - it's a nonsense. You must follow your own path, irrespective of others. The Gods will always guide you as to what's required.'

'Does that mean,' interjected Steve, 'that joint worship can never happen for Pagans?'

'A couple of things, Steve. First, I'm not too happy with the word "worship". Personally, I honour the Gods, I make offerings to the Gods, but I don't worship them. Now, once again this is a personal matter – perhaps even a Theodish matter, since we lay such emphasis on the spiritual dimension. I'm fully aware that Ásatrú groups do worship the Gods; ultimately it's down to the individual to find his or her path to communing with the Gods.

'To me, "worship" is a submissive act carried out within a religion. And what exactly is a religion? If I remember correctly, the Oxford English Dictionary defines a religion as *a system of faith and worship*. To me the key word here is "system" – religion is organised and systemised. These are the characteristics of the large Semitic sects that have dominated our spiritual landscape since the fall of the Roman Empire. As hopefully you've realised by now, Paganism is not systemised: not just Germanic Paganism, but none of the other schools of European Paganism either – Celtic, Slavonic, Baltic, et cetera. If you want to lie prostrate in supplication before some potentate, you'd best rejoin the Christians, or one of the other Semitic, monotheistic religious cults.

'Your bigger question, regarding communal activities, is very interesting, especially at a time when Paganism is growing. Certainly for celebratory purposes Pagans should come together – weddings, funerals, naming ceremonies for babies, honouring the ancestors on Forefathers' Eve, coming-of-age ceremonies, et cetera. Also at the eight points of the calendar, to celebrate the turning of the sun's cycle. These are all joint activities, concentrating on a single issue that I would consider legitimate causes for Pagans to celebrate as a group. As long as it doesn't impinge on the individual's relationship with the Gods, it is a valid, and I would say a constructive, activity. I was actually in a Yuletide celebration two years ago; it was pretty good – big turn-out and very spectacular, with everybody holding a flaming torch. They had also adapted some of the Wassailing songs for Pagan use. This all worked reasonably well because they concentrated on the turning of the sun's wheel – namely, having reached the deep point of winter. I must admit it felt good to be among a community of fellow Pagans.'

The rest of the morning was spent giving advice on creating a set of runes. Fell Follower noted the permitted materials for constructing runes: bloodstone, antler horn, bone, or wood from a fruit-bearing tree. He mentioned the best sources of information on how to read the runes, and how the runes were to be kept safe. He emphasised to both that they were to read the necessary books and make their own runes. He would only see them again once this task had been completed.

Steve and Elaine were scheduled to leave at around 3:00; it was a fair step back to the Midlands. However, Fell Follower had one last thing he wished to show them. They were going for a short walk further up the valley; he'd made some cheese-and-chutney sandwiches and had a flask of tea with some spare cups, which he threw into a rucksack and led off.

'Where are we going?' asked Elaine.

'Up near Stump Cross Caverns – you'll see.'

They got up onto the higher ground with the ubiquitous dry-stone walls running off in every direction. Fell Follower's path, however, never faltered. He soon found what he was seeking – ancient stones. Some were lying on the ground, isolated; others embedded within dry-stone walls. He pointed out each in turn, one huge rock after another, every one of which carried strange markings – some with discernible patterns, others with man-made indentations in the stone. Steve stared down in awe. 'How old are these?'

'Hard to say; they're all prehistoric.'

'Are they religious?'

'I suspect that's exactly what they are – indeed, I'd go beyond that: I'd say they represent our prehistoric forefathers' attempts to honour the same Gods I've been talking to you about all weekend. Oh, they'd have had different names, and no doubt they held different visions of the Gods from us – but in essence it was the same process, responding to the majesty of the immortal, unchanging Gods, omnipotent creators of Nature in all her myriad manifestations.'

Fell Follower stood back for a second and scanned the staggering beauty of the wild country about them, 'Look at it: Nature in all her glory. It's literally awe-inspiring, is it not? Yet if this grandeur leaves you humbled – as it should – how is one to react to that far greater eternal entity that forged all this?'

Elaine touched one of the indentations. 'Do you think these were once used for magic?'

'I hope not. There are Wicca groups around today claiming to practise magic, but thankfully most of them are nothing more than an opportunity for a bunch of women to go running around the woods naked. I've got nothing against that; if they're happy, I'm happy – no problem. However, magic is real – it's also suprahuman. Magic is literally a force beyond the ability of humans to wield. Those misguided fools who try are playing with forces far in excess of their capacity to control. Don't touch magic, or get close to it –

it's a force of the Gods, not men. Magic is very, very dangerous, and unfortunately those who decide to play with fire will get burnt.'

As they made their way back to Skyreholme Elaine posed one further question. 'When I told my sister I was a Pagan, she just dismissed the whole thing out of hand. I remember quite clearly her saying it was all mumbo-jumbo, invented by a load of bored men with nothing better to do with their time. I've heard similar things from Christian friends. What do you say?'

Fell Follower bent his head back to catch the sun's warmth and smiled.

'Have you tried it?'

'Tried what?'

'Making up a god.'

'No.'

'But if our forefathers could – according to your friends – why shouldn't you have a go? Look there, at that buzzard over by Simon's Seat. Let's make up a god of buzzards, or birds if you prefer – have you got a name for our new god?'

'Um … Windborn.'

Fell Follower stifled a laugh. 'Right, now all you've got to do is persuade everybody that "Windborn" is a god worthy of their devotion and respect.'

'Nobody would listen to me and my god – they'd laugh me out of court without a second thought.'

'And yet your friends hold that's exactly what happened. Were our forefathers idiots? Has there been some sudden leap in human IQs since ancient times? Did the Greeks and Romans build those staggering temples of marble to fictitious gods? Have you ever been to Athens?'

'No.'

'Go. Get up onto the Parthenon – I jest not: it is utterly breathtaking. The Parthenon is the temple of the Goddess Athena; are your friends telling me that this masterpiece of European architecture and culture was built on the whim of Stavros down the market, who decided to invent a goddess called Athena to protect the city? Not only am I to believe that Stavros made up this goddess, but he persuaded the people of Athens to swallow his fairy story – the Athenians, of all people! We're being asked to accept that men like Pericles, Plato, Socrates and Herodotus – despite being among the greatest minds in all European history – were so gullible that they happily coughed up a fortune to build this stupendous temple in honour of a fake goddess. Does any of this sound remotely realistic to you?'

'No.'

'Your question actually touches on a very important point. The Gods were not "invented" by anybody; they were, and always have been, here with us. The relationship between the Gods and the different peoples who honour them through making offerings is as unique as is the relationship between the individual and the Gods. This explains why the various peoples of Europe have their own pantheons; it is their unique response to the divine – thus we have various schools of Paganism across Europe: Germanic, Celtic, Roman, Greek, Slavonic, Baltic and so forth.

'Some call us Neo-pagans, as if we are reinventing something. We are accused of being little more than a religious re-enactment society. I reject all that. We are not reinventing anything; we are merely resuming our relationship with the Gods. It may not be done exactly as it once was, but that's not important. What is important is our relationship with the Gods. Do Methodists and Presbyterians have to mimic Catholics in order to be considered Christians?

'I am not a Neo-pagan. I am a Pagan, as were my forebears; we traverse the same spiritual ground for the same spiritual reasons. In order to be a Pagan I don't have to make offerings to Freya in exactly the same way as was done a thousand years ago – any more than the minister down in Skipton Methodist Church needs to hold mass, or listen to confession, to be considered a true Christian.'

At the turn for his lodge, Fell Follower bade farewell to Steve and Elaine, charging them to contact him again once they'd studied their rune-lore and made their own set of runes. He would also want to know how their family histories were progressing.

Thus began the real journey to the Gods, in the secure hands of Fell Follower. Over the next six months Steve and Elaine travelled to Yorkshire five more times, every visit opening more doors, and exploring deeper into the essence of Paganism.

Three months into his tutoring Steve was working on a new roof for a renovated pub on the outskirts of Clifton Campville. It was a hot day and he was alone on the roof, fashioning a new set of joists. Lunchtime wasn't far off. The sun had been beating down relentlessly all morning, turning everything white. Steve glanced at his watch; it had just passed one o'clock. He slumped down by a pile of timber to eat his sandwiches, though the sun was so bright he had to squint to see the catch on his butty-box.

He'd just finished eating and was considering pulling out his thermos for a cup of tea. Everything was quiet, birds chirped vaguely in the background and a welcome breeze wafted lazily across the sun-bathed roof. Steve was very much at ease; he slowly extended his left hand to reach for the thermos when he became acutely aware that he was not alone. The hairs on the back of his neck stood up and every nerve of his being began tingling: time froze as the birds fell silent. He turned his head, very slowly, to his left, with the blazing sun filling his entire world – yet behind the sun's shimmering whiteness he sensed a greater light, a greater entity of terrible potency. Without moving, the Eternal entered him, filling his being, engulfing him in its fathomless majesty.

An overpowering sense of love washed over him as the words of Sallustius drifted across the front of his mind: *The Gods are always good and always do good, never harm.*

He sat there for what seemed like hours, just drinking in the essence of the Being filling him. Everything else around him had faded into greyness – even the sun. Eventually, the hoot of a passing train somewhere far in the distance broke the spell. With an inane grin on his face he staggered unsteadily to his feet, and absent-mindedly tried to resume work: but everything had now changed – everything.

The next day he donned the Mjölnir that Elaine had bought for him on his last birthday, and which he had been keeping in his bedroom drawer. At last he felt ready to wear it.

1.6 – Wormsign

Rich was in the bar of the Saddler's Arms; it was early afternoon and already he'd had three pints of Old Bob. A couple of men were sitting at a table by the window, talking quietly while taking an occasional sip of their beer. If Rich had been paying a bit more attention, he might have noticed that they were keeping an eye on him.

One of the two got up and walked over towards the bar against which Rich was leaning, lost in a wave of self-pity mixed with a large dose of anger, 'Mr Cunliffe?'

'Yeah, it's me: Mr Richard Cunliffe – *the* Mr Cunliffe of Bransborough fame.' The words tumbled out in a heavy, world-weary sigh.

As somebody who had become famous, or infamous, depending upon your politics, for crossing the system's PC race fetish, he had experienced two schools of response. The first, from those who'd had enough of multiculturalism – which was the vast bulk of the indigenous population – tended to consider him with guarded sympathy. Conversely the second, comprising members of the establishment intelligentsia and the ethnically controlled media, were far more circumspect and usually openly hostile. By now Rich had picked up the term 'merdia' for media; it always made him chuckle. Of course, the first time he heard it he'd failed to comprehend the joke, until somebody with a little French explained.

He turned his head towards the questioner. Facing Rich was a man with dark hair, around six feet tall, of average build and with brown eyes. He looked intelligent – perhaps he was a member of the merdia. 'And what can I do for you?'

'Mr Cunliffe …'

'It's Rich.'

'Rich: my colleague and I have been hoping to have a word with you regarding your recent unfortunate experiences with the establishment. My name is Nick Poulton.'

'How many times do I need to repeat myself? I'm not interested in giving interviews and I don't want your poxy money; just get out of my life and leave me alone – sod off!'

'We're not reporters.'

Rich looked at the man again, slightly confused – who was he? What did he want? Nick checked over his shoulder with his colleague, who nodded. He turned back to Rich.

'We're from a small group who try to help individuals in your position. You may think your experiences in dealing with the legally enforced diktat of multiculturalism and the predatory state machinery are unique. Unfortunately, they're not. We have associates right across Europe, and I can assure you this is not merely our little domestic problem here in Britain; it's occurring everywhere, from Portugal to Austria.'

'Is it? I've never see any reports on the telly, or in the papers.'

Nick smiled. 'Yes, I know – and for one very good reason.'

Rich paused; there was obviously something going on here he didn't understand. A local walked through and caught Rich's eye. 'Scott.'

'Rich.'

Rich watched Scott go through to the bar next door, then turned slowly back to Nick. 'So what is it you want from me?'

'At this time, nothing. Indeed, we would like to offer you something.'

'What?'

'Knowledge'

'Knowledge?'

'We need people to understand what's going on, and for that to happen we need ambassadors – people who can communicate at different levels to different groups of people. You've been through an unpleasant experience, but you've also witnessed at close quarters the problems which are destroying this nation – and all Europe, for that matter.'

'You want me to be a spokesman? Who are you, bloody Nixons? Don't you think I've got enough problems without running around with a bunch of head-bangers scrapping with Pakis and Commie wankers?'

Completely unruffled, and in a gentle tone, Nick continued, 'No, we're not connected with National Resistance, nor would we advise you to get involved in any form of direct action – as you've quite rightly said, you don't need any more trouble or attention from the authorities.'

Nick paused for a second before continuing: 'Though I would point out that if members of National Resistance had not videoed the incendiary attacks on the police outside Bransborough police station, and posted them online for all the world to see, there would have been nothing to counteract the anti-White media campaign and the whitewashing of the Jihadists and Marxist ARC. It had a huge impact on the public's perception of events, and was largely responsible for the widespread refusal to accept the obviously engineered evidence against yourself, Mr Hall, Mr Fuller and Miss Kynaston.'

'Yeah, that's true.'

'You do realise, do you, that despite being acquitted by the court, the establishment and its organs of propaganda will never give you up? They have decided you are guilty, and will hound you for ever. The establishment will do whatever is required, even changing centuries-old legal precedents to entrap you – and they can wait as long as it takes. As I said, you're not unique and you're not the first; neither will you be the last.'

Rich already had an inkling of this from the tone in which the acquittal had been reported, and the coverage given to those calling it a miscarriage and demanding a retrial – Mr Greenberg, MP, being particularly prominent in that respect.

'So what are you, some sort of political party? We've seen them all before: National Front, BNP the EDL – they've all been and gone. They always seem to fall apart after a while.'

'Again, there's an explanation for that, and no, we represent no party. You see, Rich, forming parties and campaigning within the current structure is pointless. The parties and organisations you mentioned have all tried and failed. How can you operate through a system dominated by a media that is openly hostile and largely controlled by our enemies? The general public sense the gravity of the situation, but are continually reassured that all is well by the politicians, the papers, the television – by everyone. It's all a pack of lies, of course, but Joe Public is ignorant of the facts and, let's be honest, although many of the answers are out there on the internet, you need to be determined, astute and reasonably well educated to access the material.

'Our way is different. We say if the people can't, or won't, access the truth, we will bring the truth to them. We are, if you like, the sowers of seeds that, with care and hard work, will blossom into a new dawn – a golden dawn.'

'Okay: so how do I fit into all this? It's Nick, isn't it?'

'Yeah. Our first task is to explain to you how the world operates and what's happening here in Britain – and most importantly why it's happening. I'll start us off, but my colleague here, Jon Carroll, will also contribute. You won't remember everything we tell you – indeed you'll forget the vast bulk of the detail – but I hope an overall picture will form and begin to stick. Don't worry about any of this; if after this meeting you wish to continue you'll be seeing a lot of us, and other colleagues, who will help you grasp the bigger picture.'

By now Rich was intrigued and ready to hear more.

'It's a nice day, so let's go out to the beer garden; there's a bench down by the back wall where we'll be able to talk in private.'

The three of them wound their way out through the back door to the garden, found the bench and sat down. Certain questions had bothered Rich ever since the trial; he decided to pitch a couple of these concerns to his guests.

'There's one thing that's been bugging me through all this. We were obviously innocent from the beginning, yet the papers and especially the telly have consistently painted us as villains, although they never crossed the line of openly accusing us.'

'Yeah, it's good, isn't it? Effective, does its job well,' retorted Nick.

'What do you mean "good"? What the hell are you talking about?'

'Rich, open your eyes. What do you think television is? And the papers? Surely after all you've been through you don't still think they're some sort of mythical fount of truth and unbiased reporting? They're propaganda machines, controlled and owned by the enemy. When during the Second World War some German pilot shot down fifty British planes, did the old BBC report "Excellent German ace scores again"? Factually that would have been accurate; such a pilot would have been an ace, and from a neutral perspective deserving of praise. But the BBC was no more a neutral source of information during the Second World War than it is now. To its masters you are the enemy; you are, and always will be, the German pilot.'

'But I'm no enemy of this country.'

'No, you're not.'

'Then why are they attacking me?'

'I think, Rich, if you stop for a second, you've just answered your own question.'

'I have?'

'If you are not the enemy of the nation…..'

'Oh … no, that can't be right; they *are* the country.'

'Who are?'

'Those who run the BBC and the other stations – and the papers and all.'

'Are they? Tell me, Rich: who runs the BBC, who owns the TV channels and the papers?'

'I don't know, I just assumed …'

'Don't. You'll be wrong 99 per cent of the time. It's a vast subject, Rich, but we need to start somewhere – so let's begin with one very important part of the jigsaw. It's not the entire story, but constitutes one of the main driving forces behind the project. We can look at other parts of the hydra's head next time – perhaps the industrial–military complex, or the nasty story behind GM crops. Today I'd like to revisit a very old problem, which has been causing trouble for us and our people for as long as anyone can remember. Jon?'

For the first time Nick's partner spoke. He was obviously well educated and had been waiting to intervene ever since Nick suggested coming out to the beer garden.

'There are powerful influences in the world, which control basic institutions that impact on the entire global system – and in particular our part of the globe: the White, European part.'

Rich's eyebrows twitched. 'White European? Can you say that? I thought the anti-racists had banned people using language like that.'

'Have they banned Blacks calling themselves Black? Do not Muslims run their own Muslim organisations? So what's wrong with the word "White"?'

'Well, that's different …' Doubts crowded in on Rich's befuddled mind.

'No, it's not. Stop repeating the propaganda you've been fed on TV or in the papers. Every time you hear some zombie mouthpiece, or robotic representative of the media, use the cover term "anti-racist" - counter attack. Use mantras like, "Anti-racist is a code word for anti-White," or, "Diversity equals White genocide." They'll call you a racist, but just answer, "In your opinion I'm a racist because I'm White," then continue your point, or better still, start talking about the alien invasion of Europe or North America – White lands – and ask why it isn't occurring anywhere else in the world. Always throw it back in their faces; never let them set the tone or agenda.'

Rich took another swig from his pint; he'd heard a great deal already but his interest had been whetted. These men were showing a path through the maze of disinformation – a way to grasp the nature of the unseen enemy he'd always felt lurked just out of sight, hiding menacingly in the shadows.

'Our enemy is very powerful and well dug in at the summit of Western society. As I said a minute ago, there are certain groups who have invested heavily over a very long time in the great project – the New World Order.'

Rich glanced at Jon with disbelief in his eyes.

'Yes, I know – it's all conspiracy nonsense, even though both the Bush presidents, Obama, Clinton and prime ministers Brown and Blair have all spoken of it openly, and videos of their pronouncements are there for all to see on the internet. Yet it's all imaginary. Even Wikipedia says so ..,' – Jon's voice dropped as he leant forward towards Rich, smiling to make his point completely clear – '... therefore you know it's true. You have also learnt another important lesson about organisations like Wikipedia. In this war, Rich, nobody is neutral.

'One of the major backers of the NWO is a group – a tribe – whose aristocratic banker families control 99 per cent of the entire global central banking system. The same group owns every major film studio in Hollywood, as well as the vast bulk of the West's publishing houses and papers. The social-engineering think-tank of this group, originally based in Germany but now mostly active in America, has fomented every element of the social revolution that has ripped the guts out of Western civilisation over the past 70 years. They have been the starting point of every assault, from gay rights to feminism. Their offensives have struck at every bastion of civilised life, attacking our very existence as social beings. They've sought to dismantle the family, alienate kin, belittle faith – well, Christianity to be specific – and have promoted the liquidation of every White nation on the planet through mass third-world immigration. Every one of these cancers originated from within this group. I take my hat off to them: although they are the enemy in every sense imaginable, and I hate them utterly, I also admire their skill in manipulating target societies and the success they've had in destroying them – including Britain. We must learn from them, Rich; as with all weapons, they're capable of cutting in both directions.

'It's the same with the current financial crisis – are you aware of the scale of Western debt? You realise that it can never be paid back, don't you? It's simply too vast.'

'So what will happen?'

'There'll be a huge crash; the entire global financial structure will implode – the dollar, the yen, the euro and all the other currencies will go to hell, and us with them.'

'I don't understand; why do these people want to see the collapse of our economies? Surely it'll hurt them as much as us?'

'Keep your eye on the ball, Rich. What's the end goal of the NWO? It's not rocket science; it's right there in front of your eyes – it's exactly what it says on the box: New World Order. And what does this crew of megalomaniacs need to accomplish the project? What did they do on their dry run in Europe?'

'Dry run in Europe?'

'What do you think the EU is?'

'I thought it was about trade and …'

'How quaint. The EU is an NWO construct from stem to stern. And it was in the EU that they made their biggest step forward to date: they introduced a single currency for an entire continent – the euro. Money is power. Their next trick is to introduce what will be in effect a single global currency; it already exists in an embryonic state. It's called SDR and is issued by the International Monetary Fund, another central plank of the NWO project. But that's merely a starting point; they're not there quite yet.'

'You've lost me.'

'What I'm trying to explain is that a global financial collapse is not a bad thing if your goal is to introduce a new global currency to replace all those "failed" national currencies. The fact that the entire process was engineered is obviously not openly advertised, even if true.

'You see, Rich, the pot at the end of the rainbow for these guys is unbelievable. Their companies and corporations will dominate the entire planet – that's the whole point of globalisation. Who needs factories in Britain, or France, or anywhere in the West when we can get the goods made more cheaply in China or Bangladesh? If they control the issue of money, they will in effect have the whole population of the planet working for them to earn their new currency. They are the ultimate human vampires. I tell you, Rich, either we destroy them, or they will consume us utterly.

'Rich, we want you to help us. You'll be speaking to small groups, no more than a dozen, and usually more like five or six. There's no need for you to teach them anything, or explain developments; we, or our colleagues, will do that. But you're a real person who they've seen on TV. All you need to do is tell your story, what happened to you and how the system reacted.

'We'll organise your speaking schedule, perhaps once a week or even less. We'll transport you, and if need be arrange any stopovers – but obviously only if you're happy to take on these responsibilities. Does this sound like something that might interest you? You'll need further background information, the sort of stuff we've been discussing today, but that's relatively easy for us to arrange once you've agreed to take part.'

'Who are you working for again?'

Nick cut in here. 'We didn't say, Rich, but we're part of the Nova Europa movement. We operate in most countries in Europe. We're anti-globalist and anti-centralist. We're nationalist and believe in the existence of nations and national groups. Let's not beat around the bush here; we're White Europeans seeking a future for White Europeans in our own homelands – in Europe. There's probably a war coming, Rich, and we need to prepare our people – who include you, hopefully.'

Nick held out his hand. 'Are you in?'

Rich took first his hand, then Jon's, and shook on the deal. Yes, he'd be happy to tell of his experiences at the hands of Islam and what passed for justice in pluralist, multicultural Britain.

Thus began Rich's education and contribution to the resistance.

ACT TWO:
LEGIONES

2.1 – Sverige

The ten tired *legionarii* milled about at the back of the vast concrete agricultural warehouse, looking for a place to flop down. It had been a hard tab up to this desolate site, which would be their jumping-off point for the assault on the main agro-industrial complex five klicks to the east – a grim, soulless expanse of concrete that the men had dubbed 'Soviet City'. There was still an hour and a half of daylight left; but the word was they wouldn't be moving out until dawn.

All the men were members of the 7th *Decuria* under the command of *Decanus* Vasily Nikonov.

The legionary structure that emerged in Europe in response to the Eurabian War was based on the *legio* – legion – with a nominal strength of 5,000 men; each *legio* was subdivided into ten cohorts of 500, which in turn were divided into five *centuriae* – hundreds. Each *centuria* was further divided into ten *decuriae*, each of ten men. Vasily Nikonov's unit was officially the 7th *Decuria* of the 3rd *Centuria* of the 6th *Cohors* (cohort) of *Legio XXV Gediminas,* or 7, 3, 6 – XXV in shorthand.

Three legions, *Legio XXV Gediminas, Legio IX Scipio* and *Legio XXII Zrinski* had originally been assembled to form the *Exercitus Thracius* (ExThrac), which was currently engaged in trying to take the Thracian industrial city of Zorolus. This key city, located halfway between the Greek border and the *legiones'* ultimate goal of Constantinople, was rapidly becoming a serious bottleneck. The main Turkish force opposing ExThrac had dug in among the smouldering ruins of Zorolus, under the command of Hakan Yilmaz, who held aspirations of replicating the Communist Red Army's vaunted victory at Stalingrad. Were Yilmaz's dreams to come true, *Imperator* Aeschiliman – commander of ExThrac – would be honour-bound to stand his ground, come what may; a test so infamously failed by Paulus.

Beyond Zorolus' immediate urban environs, secondary rural locales – like Soviet City – acted as concentration points for hostile Muslim auxiliaries, such as Albanian irregulars and various Jihadist groups. These forces specialised in hit-and-run operations, in particular attacking supply convoys and landing sites used by legionary aircraft. As a result of these activities Soviet City had become a throbbing thorn in the southern flank of ExThrac – a thorn that *Impertator* Aeschiliman wanted extracting.

Soviet City's Jihadists were a mixed bag. At the beginning of the Eurabian War, when Europe's Muslim population had first exploded out of their ghettos and sprawling estates, it seemed as if the whole continent would fall to the New Euro-Caliphate. Europe's pathetic democratic leadership simply crumbled, paralysed like rabbits in a car's headlights, while their fantasy of a liberal Utopia died in a long-prophesied tsunami of racial violence. Under conditions of life or death, Mother Nature always reasserts her sway; indeed, there's no other possible response, bar suicide. Europe's native Aryan population found themselves forcibly reintroduced to reality at the eleventh hour, the vast majority opting for the warm bosom of nationalism and identity. For the first time since 2698 AUC Europeans found themselves fighting their own cause again; the relief had been palpable.

That all happened back in 2782 AUC. In the five years since the outbreak of war the *legiones* had reasserted European authority over the continent. The forces of Islam, along with hordes of heavily armed, but comically disorganised, African militias, had been either exterminated or driven out. It had been a bloody business: survival of the fittest always is, but now this last corner of Europe, Thrace, was being liberated. The Jihadists who infested Soviet City were a mixture of Eurabian veterans – hardened, proficient warriors who'd seen it all – and fresh, keen idealists shipped in from North Africa and the Middle East. Many of these religiously charged newcomers were seeking martyrdom, a wish with which the *legionarii* were more than happy to comply.

The task of cleaning out Soviet City had been given to *Legio XXV Gediminas*. The legion's command structure then passed the buck down internally to 6th *Cohors,* who in turn delegated the job to 3rd *Centuria,* under the command of *Centurio* Henk de Witt – whose assault was scheduled to begin in ten and a half hours.

De Witt had given each of his ten *decuriae* an assembly point, dotted among the dozen or so warehouses which formed a western outlier to the main Soviet City complex. On paper De Witt had 100 men, but after subtracting the wounded, the sick and other extraneous absences, 3rd *Centuria* was left with 86 active combatants – although of course, he also had elements of 1st *Centuria* at his disposal. The first *centuria* of every *cohors* was a support unit, in this case supplying 3rd *Centuria* with eight medics, two Wiesel III mortar carriers firing heavy 120 mm rounds, two BPM armoured carriers armed with Kord 12.7 mm heavy machine guns, a couple of lorries with extra ammo, a field ambulance and twenty sappers. The sappers would be particularly useful, as the individual *decuriae* intended blasting through the concrete warehouse walls as they advanced through Soviet City's maze of buildings, rather than taking the direct frontal route. This course of action had been largely dictated by intelligence reports indicating that the Jihadists were aware of 3rd *Centuria's* deployment and had prepared accordingly.

De Witt had set up his HQ in a derelict gatehouse, a stone's throw from two warehouses each of which housed a *decuria.* All units were securely in place and had reported in to De Witt's command centre; so far, so good. He ordered his second in command, *Optio* Luka Popovic*,* to physically check each *decuria* to make sure there were no problems of which he was unaware.

As Popovic exited the gatehouse De Witt activated the hologram on the COMS band wrapped around his right ear, to check with Henri Beaupré, *Tribunus* of 6ᵗʰ *Cohors,* that the promised support units were in place. Both men spoke in the language used throughout the *legiones,* namely standard military Latin, or VVM (*Verba Vulgata Militaria).* Beaupré confirmed that a Mil *Pilum* attack helicopter, armed with air-to-surface missiles and heavy machine guns, plus a Kamov Mi-97 general-purpose helicopter for evac purposes, were on standby. For the assault on Soviet City he had also managed to acquire the promise of a powerful Sukhoi Su-39X ground-attack aircraft from the legionary air arm, together with a battery of six Caesar 155 mm mobile howitzers from the legion's central artillery pool. De Witt thanked the *tribunus* warmly for his diligent work, in particular the extra support units. Once finished with Beaupré he contacted all his *decani* – including Nikonov – to finalise plans and to pass on the good news regarding the beefed-up support for tomorrow's operation.

The boys of 7ᵗʰ *Decuria* tried their best to earwig as Nikonov spoke to De Witt on the COMS system in his helmet, and although nobody succeeded, everything pointed to the expected dawn kick-off. There was little they could do for now other than check their kit, knock up some chow from their portable rations and then find a decent place to bed down – though the concrete floor looked anything but inviting.

Vasily Nikonov was a solidly built citizen, with deep-blue eyes and black hair. A Russian, he hailed from Pskov, not far from the Estonian border, though St Petersburg was his preferred destination for more serious partying and long weekends. Many of the men wore personal T-shirts under their armour; in Vasily's case it was a striped, light-blue Telnyashka of the elite Russian VDV paratroopers. He was a tough man who took his duties seriously. He was also ambitious and looking for promotion to *optio* rank before long.

Having wandered halfway down the warehouse while talking to De Witt, Vasily turned about and returned to the unit. With all eyes on him he smiled, then said, 'We move out at 06:00. Vargas, Batista – you're on first watch.

Scope out the surrounding area and find a suitable observation post; radio in when you're established. Black and Klukowski will relieve you at 22:30 – Nyberg and Stoger, you're on at 01:30.

'Dioletis, you're to patrol the warehouse perimeter until Vargas and Batista are relieved, Bellini will take over while Black and Klukowski are on watch, then Eberhardt will have the warehouse until Nyberg and Stoger are finished. I'll give the final rotas at 04:00 to those concerned. Any questions?'

Nobody said a word, then without further ado the two Spaniards, Alvero Vargas and Carlos Batista, got up and slipped out of the warehouse's side entrance to begin sweeping the surrounding area. Simultaneously Theo Dioletis shouldered his GA-6 and began checking the warehouse perimeter and patrolling its cavernous interior. All the men were old hands; they knew as well as Vasily what was required.

Over in one of the huge storage bays lining one side of the warehouse, Axel Nyberg and Rudi Stoger were busy brewing up tea and heating some rations. Vasily had paired them for the third watch, starting at 01:30.

Axel was a typical blond, blue-eyed Swede who'd recently turned 29. A large man standing at six-foot two and sporting a campaign beard that would have to be removed once back in barracks, he had a slightly serious countenance – though a mischievous smile lurked boisterously behind the external façade. He had a taste for heavy metal and often wore a tasteful Motörhead T-shirt under his armour. His partner, Rudi Stoger, was an Austrian of average height at around five-foot eleven, of medium build with finely chiselled features. Although Rudi was three years younger than Axel he had actually seen more action than his Swedish colleague, having experienced the fierce fighting in Upper Austria, the Tyrol and southern Bavaria.

Rudi's great-grandfather, Wolfgang Stoger, had won the Iron Cross first class during the Second European Civil War, while defending Vienna from the Red Army. Tens of thousands of civilians had managed to flee due to the bravery of men like Wolfgang, before the full horror of the Soviet Hellstorm descended on the stricken city. In memory of his great-grandfather's actions Rudi proudly wore a 4th SS Panzergrenadier *Der Führer* T-shirt under his armour. Wolfgang Stoger subsequently perished of starvation and disease, one of an estimated 1.7 million German POWs to die in America's genocidal Rhine Meadows internment camps.

Axel and Rudi had been more or less permanently paired since the beginning of the Thracian Campaign, swopping stories and histories even before ExThrac had taken Adrianople. As Axel watched the vacuum-packed spaghetti bolognese boil on the portable stove his mind drifted back to the previous winter, the first time they'd been paired. The pairing, new at the time, had come about after 7th *Decuria* had lost their long-time *decanus,* Niilo Kettunen, in a tragic military air crash. The new *decanus,* Vasily Nikonov, had decided to reorganise the *decuria*, which signalled the beginning of Axel and Rudi's partnership.

They had been sent to an old cabin high on the remnants of the Rhodope range overlooking the Evros valley; it was late December and had been raining off and on all day. Their breath steamed in the chilly air: it looked, and felt, like snow – not perhaps the best weather to be holed up in what was basically a dilapidated shed. Soufli wasn't far off, its roofs visible to the north. They weren't expecting any trouble; the two armies below them, eyeing each other across the Evros – the joint legionary and Greek forces on this side, the Turks opposite – had been static for the previous six weeks. How much longer the phoney war would continue was anybody's guess, but for now all was quiet.

They had taken it in turns to watch over their allotted section of the valley, though the whole exercise soon deteriorated into a long and very tedious chore. *Legio XXV Gediminas* had been one of three legions sent by the *Curia* in Bonn to bolster the Greek army: the same *legiones* that would soon be formed into ExThrac. It was no secret that the *Curia* had decided to free all Thrace from the Turks, and further legions were expected soon. None of this surprised anybody; Turkey had used the outbreak of the Eurabian War to cynically strengthen her military ties with Albania and Bosnia, prompting speculation of a second coming of the Ottoman Empire – which everyone assumed was Ankara's ultimate goal.

However, for Axel and Rudi the here and now took priority. They would probably be stuck in their miserable shack for two to three days, before being relieved and returning to the legionary base outside Komotini. The chances of anything happening to alleviate the drudgery were virtually nil, especially if the threatened snow finally arrived. Komotini itself had once contained a sizable Muslim presence, prior to the war, but by now they had all fled over the Evros back into Turkish-controlled territory.

The pair of them were *evocati*, or senior *legionarii*, sporting a single *gladius* motif on their arms, neither having sought promotion to *decanus*. That HQ considered their surveillance a decidedly low-risk affair was confirmed by their equipment, for neither was wearing *arma proeliaria*, just ordinary fatigues, with extra thermal underwear and heavy jackets stuffed into their bulging backpacks. Nor did they carry the standard legionary weapon – the GA-6; its impressive firepower was considered a bit much for sitting in a derelict cabin. In its stead they had been issued with the lighter Flobert 9 mm submachine gun. However, they were both wearing *gladii*, treating their iconic charges as badges of identity and status as *legionarii*. These modern carbon-steel blades were almost always worn under every condition short of full battlefield combat, when they became discretionary – though most still liked the option of the *gladius* for close encounters. *Gladii* were neither toys nor pieces of useless decoration; the men were trained in their use and were all aware that a carbon-steel blade thrust through a torso was every bit as deadly as a bullet from a GA-6.

All *legionarii* received a *gladius* on the completion of basic training. However, both Axel and Rudi kept two *gladii*, having adopted the practice used by most of the older hands of buying a second *gladius* to be kept pristine for ceremonial use. Those who stuck to the standard issue soon found that day-to-day use – especially under combat conditions – and the requirements of ceremony did not mix. Trying to get a battle-scarred *gladius* up to a standard that would pass a *centurio*'s inspection was no mean feat.

As is the way of men having been newly paired, they commenced with a spot of shadow boxing, exchanging banalities and dry military procedures, before turning to more personal matters as each tried to weigh up the other.

It was 13:00 on a grey, overcast day; both had eaten and Rudi was on duty scanning the Turkish side of the valley for any sign of activity – all in vain, of course. Axel was lounging on some timber, his back propped against the lower, stone-built part of the cabin, giving his *gladius* a wipe over. After one more scan of the Turkish positions, Rudi turned to his companion and popped the inevitable question: 'So what got you into the legion?'

Axel knew it was coming, but even so it was a lot to dredge up. He glanced over his shoulder, through the gap in the cabin wall where Rudi was scanning the valley, but there was little to see except the odd trail of smoke from the forward Turkish bunkers.

His eye caught a drone flitting tentatively above the two armies. Drones had not evolved into the decisive weaponry once envisioned and here in Thrace one could see why. Both sides had good anti-helicopter and anti-drone equipment that took a heavy toll of the expensive toys. The Legions were equipped with the excellent Swiss-built Bollingen & Sartori *Federschwert* system, while the Turks used the ubiquitous VAC – Vannevar Aerospace Corp – *Potomac* system.

While Axel contemplated the drone a short, low growl barked out across the valley, followed by a plume of smoke from the hapless drone as it plummeted to earth. Axel turned slowly back to Rudi and said, 'You've heard it a thousand times before, or some version of it. They're all the same.'

'Yes, but I've not heard *your* version – and anyway, they're not all the same; each has his own personal nightmare.' Sharp words indeed, thought the big Swede. What's his story, I wonder?

2.1 – SVERIGE

He had no stomach for reopening old wounds, yet these were the reasons why he was sitting in a damp, cold cabin on a Thracian hillside staring at Turkish troops. In any case, protocol obliged him to open up to his partner; after all, as he had just admitted, it was a common enough tale, told in a thousand variations right across Europe.

'The legions came later; much happened in Sweden before that.'

'Okay, I'm listening: so tell me about Sweden.'

So be it, thought Axel. He took a deep breath. 'Well, it all started back in Malmö.' In his imagination a picture began to form of the fateful events that would stay with him for the rest of his life. 'I'd had my eye on this girl down in the university – Elsa Mattiasson; she was a curvy lady with auburn hair, and a flatmate of Ebba, my best friend Viktor's girlfriend. They were on the same course studying languages – French, I think.'

There was a short pause as Axel gathered his thoughts. 'I'd known Viktor for years; we met as kids playing junior ice hockey in Malmö. We had fun, but knew we would never make it professionally; most of the kids dreamed of playing for the Redhawks – as we did – but it was only ever a dream.

'Eventually, Viktor went to the local college in Malmö to do a degree in Information Systems; networking was his area of interest. That's where he met Ebba, and she of course was a flatmate – or corridor mate to be more accurate – of Elsa.'

'And what were you doing while your friends were in university?'

'I was working in a furniture shop – giant shed, really – on the outskirts of town. I'd hoped to persuade my bosses to pay for me to do a degree, and if that hadn't worked I'd probably have joined Viktor and the rest at my own expense the following September.'

'Meaning your parents' expense.'

'Well, I'm sure they would have contributed,' grinned Axel. 'Anyway, one weekend there was this party down in Rönnen, where the college had some residential blocks. Officially I came as a friend of Viktor and Ebba, though both knew I fancied Elsa; I just thought it was an opportunity not to be missed. In any case, I'm pretty sure Ebba had already hinted to Elsa of my interest – you know, to check out her reaction. The fact that the invitation still stood was a good omen, in my opinion.'

'So you'd met before?'

'Yeah, we'd seen each other up in town when Ebba and Viktor were having a coffee, or even occasionally in the evening – though students tended to find the centre of town a bit expensive. Having said all that, we'd never actually been introduced nor had a proper conversation.

'The party was being held in the winter, with weather like this' – he motioned towards the gap in the wall facing the sodden Evros valley – 'but windier and if anything even wetter than the Rhodopes in December.

'Well, I rolled up, joined in the merriment and started to chat with Viktor; then after a while Ebba sort of nonchalantly sauntered over with Elsa in tow. She introduced me properly, as one of her and Viktor's friends. We made a big show of the introduction, and started to chat. It was all very pleasant and restrained – everybody was still relatively sober. Our little exchange didn't last long, as one of the students powered up the room's speakers from his tablet and soon the tunes were blasting out; then one of Elsa's friends called her away for something trivial and that was the end of round one.'

'What's she like, this Elsa of yours?'

'She's quite tall, with rosy cheeks, auburn hair as I said, and blue eyes.'

'And curvy?'

'With curves and bumps in all the right places.'

Rudi smiled. 'Okay, carry on.'

'Well, I sort of floated around, drinking lots and trying hard to "bump into" Elsa again, as innocuously as my inebriated state would allow. I hadn't been particularly successful, but at last I got a dance with her. We were all in the communal kitchen, as it was the only place big enough to even try dancing. God, I was drunk by then!'

'What were you drinking?'

'Trying to be big and trendy, I was giving this bottle of *Jägermeister* a real hammering, but unfortunately it was hammering back even harder.'

'Thus is the nature of alcohol,' voiced Rudi philosophically.

'What I hadn't realised at the time was that Elsa was pretty hammered herself. I successfully navigated the dance, but the *Jägermeister* was gaining the upper hand, and after another unsteady attempt at dancing I had to vacate the kitchen and head for the block door. Some of the other students were outside huddling from the wind and rain in the entrance, smoking and swigging various beverages; I just stumbled straight past them towards some trees about a hundred metres away and threw up all over the place – I felt like shit. There was no way I could go back to the party – God, I felt embarrassed and my legs were turning to jelly, like my guts. Booze is weird stuff; although my higher brain functions were in the process of closing down, there were still enough grey cells working to decide it was time to head home – and to do so without any conscious input from me.'

'So you left the girl? After all your hard work and scheming?'

'Believe me, if I could have stayed, I would have, but I was utterly wrecked and knew it. I had no choice. My flat at the time was in the Norra Sofielund district, which meant walking along the Nobelvägen. It was late and dark, and frankly I have no recollection of the journey or getting home. It was all done on auto-pilot.' The tone of Axel's voice changed, taking on a harder edge.

'You need to understand, Rudi, that the Muslims were well established in the east of the city, in the Rosengard district – but their presence had fanned out way beyond there, into neighbouring districts like Hermodsdal, Nydala and over towards Mollevangstorget market. In the evening you would find gangs of them up in town causing trouble around Gagatan and Torggatan, even in the Kungsparken. You know the police were afraid of them? They refused to enter Rosengard unless in large numbers. The fire brigade were another lot that refused to enter Rosengard without a police escort; it was surreal, and of course the spineless politicians did nothing.

'The Muslims had a terrible and terrifying reputation locally; the rape statistics for the city were a national disgrace – not that the papers or television ever mentioned such things.'

'Sounds familiar.'

'I awoke the following morning to this colossal noise; it was Viktor beating frantically at the door. I was lying on top of the bed, fully clothed; the front of my shirt was a mess and my hair was caked in spew. I stank. I heard, or perhaps I should say felt, this massive banging – at first I assumed it was the *Jägermeister*. It took a while before it sunk through my thick head that the pounding was coming from the door and not inside my skull. I shouted, "Sod off," but that only made the pounding and hollering worse. I tried to move, but every time I lifted my head from the pillow a wave of vertigo swept over me, causing my guts to heave in unison. But the banging continued, along with Viktor's persistent voice. I forced myself off the bed only to collapse on the floor; Viktor was screaming, "Axel, Axel, open the damned door!"

'Well, I finally dragged myself along the carpet, stretched up and released the latch. The door swung inwards violently under Viktor's weight and slammed into my alcohol-sodden corpse – not that I felt a thing. I remember afterwards Viktor saying I looked terrible, with a grey pallor and a sheen of sweat over my face and body as the booze seeped slowly out of my pores.

'Even in my state I could tell from Viktor's face and frantic banging that there was something wrong. "What's up, what's happened?" I rasped. He just looked at me, prostrate on the floor; then suddenly disappeared into the kitchen before reappearing with a tumbler of water.

'"Drink!" he commanded. He made me drink three of them before I fled to the toilet, where my body started expelling the previous night's intake from every orifice I have. I half fell into the bath afterwards, and did what I could to clean myself up with a rubber showerhead attached to the taps.

'Viktor helped me out and I managed to dress in some clothes that didn't honk of puke. He finally got me sitting back on the edge of the bed; I was sweating even worse by now, and felt cold. I dragged a blanket over my shoulders, but my guts had calmed down: the worst had passed.'

Axel's voice began trailing off, his words coming ever fainter as that terrible morning re-emerged in his mind's eye. He continued barely above a whisper.

'Viktor looked serious and started talking slowly, in a low voice, the emotion of the things he'd been holding back etched in his face. He leant forward slightly and spoke directly at me, retaining eye contact throughout.'

Subliminally the scene started to reform in Axel's mind; it was almost like watching a film, only from his perspective. All was crystal clear. He saw Viktor peering directly at him … 'Last night, Axel, when you left the party, Elsa went to look for you.'

'I'm sorry I left, Viktor, but really, I was wrecked; and – what … Elsa? What d'you mean, she came looking for me?'

'She came down to the front of the block and asked the boys in the entrance if they'd seen you; they told her you'd thrown up then headed for the Nobelvägen. She already knew you lived in Norra Sofielund – Ebba had told her.'

Axel shot bolt upright, his eyes wide open. 'No, she mustn't – it's not bloody safe …'

'She was drunk, Axel - perhaps not quite as far gone as you, but she'd put away more than her fair share.'

Through the alcohol and complaining bodily functions, Axel felt a premonition of disaster looming ominously. 'Viktor, what's happened? Where's Elsa?'

'She's in hospital, Axel. The police found her this morning on some waste ground, down by the tracks in Lönngarden.'

The universe condensed into that one point of devastating information, leaving Axel hanging powerless, gripped by the horror of the images his mind conjured up, his brain overwhelmed by their enormity and chilling implications. His senses couldn't hold the mounting emotions indefinitely; sitting rigid, frozen in indecision, his body reacted through pumping adrenaline into his alcohol-filled veins; then suddenly, spluttering in a mixture of self-anger and remorse, the dam broke.

'Whaa …? What happened? What do you mean, "found" – is she dead?'

Viktor looked into Axel's pleading, bloodshot eyes. 'No, but she's in a bad way, Axel.' There was a pause as Viktor steeled himself. 'She's been gang-raped and beaten badly – broken arm, couple of ribs, both eyes closed, nose bust …'

A vast howl wailed out from Axel's throat, filling the flat, before subsiding into stunned silence.

The vision faded; he was back again in a damp shed on the slopes of the Rhodopes, overlooking the Evros. Rudi was staring at him with almost as much concern as Viktor had on that terrible morning.

'You okay?'

'Yeah. Sorry – I was lost in my thoughts for a moment. She'd gone looking for me on the Nobelvägen, you see. That's no place for any White person on a dark winter's night, let alone a single White female. They came out in the evening, you see, like vampires – cruising the streets looking for easy meat; and that night they found what they were looking for.'

'The Muslims got her?'

Axel nodded. 'She had been found early that morning by some man walking his dog.'

Then after a slight pause, in a dark, granite-hard voice he added, 'You have no conception of how much I hate them.'

'Use it wisely, friend.'

'At every opportunity.'

'Good. So let's make a finish; complete the tale. Did they get them, the Muslims?'

'Oh, the police knew who'd done it almost immediately, but proving it was another matter.'

'Was there any public reaction? And what about Elsa's family and friends? What did they do?'

'The public in Sweden had been heavily indoctrinated regarding multiculturalism – but you already know this. The media were very wary about reporting crime involving Muslims, whose identity and names were never given. Everybody understood the code, of course; no name or details immediately meant Muslim. As was typical at that time the authorities tried to brush everything under the carpet: business as usual, with as little fuss or publicity as possible.

'We went down to the hospital, me, Viktor and Ebba, plus a couple of others from the university. We spoke to her – she was a mess, Rudi, all bandages, plaster and tubes, and she seemed both embarrassed and crushed by events. Eventually we boys left, leaving the girls to talk amongst themselves. Do you know what Ebba told me afterwards?'

'Go on.'

'That Elsa blamed herself. She should never have gone running off like that: it was silly and dangerous, asking for trouble; she blamed herself! So now if a Swedish girl walks down a street in a Swedish city after dark, she's asking to be raped; this was the sick mentality of Swedish society. The Muslims could do no wrong, however evil – and we natives could do no right.

'Elsa's parents arrived from Uppsala; they stayed a couple of nights in a local hotel, then collected her once she'd been discharged. She didn't return to college.'

'Have you seen her since?'

'No – well not to talk to properly, though I caught sight of her at the trial.

'Eventually two were convicted of rape and assault, though there were actually four of them – as I said, the police knew everything from the beginning, but couldn't get charges to stick on the two that walked. Up until that night I too had been a good little Swede, swallowing all that crap about multicultural enrichment and the joys of living in a multiracial society, and that only Nazis and ignorant thugs ever objected to our colonisation by third-world dregs. Even now I can't believe how stupid and naïve we were – accepting those endless lies, in direct contradiction to what was happening before our very eyes.

'Opposition to the state's viewpoint was very difficult in the Scandinavian countries; it was a sort of soft dictatorship. You were free to do as you pleased, until you expressed the wrong opinion – then God help you. If the general financial collapse hadn't occurred I would probably have joined the opposition Sweden Democrats, or even something a little stronger, and would've ended up losing my job and being put on some secret state blacklist.'

Rudi glanced over. 'All this sounds very familiar: the same lies, the same cover-up. And the joke is they went about bragging about their precious democracy and how wonderful it was. Apparently, it wasn't the fact that we, the people, were getting shafted by corrupt, lying shysters that was important, so much as the pretty words they used to justify their sick deeds. The national details may have been different, but the treachery was the same everywhere. Sorry, you've not finished, have you?'

'No: far from it. The real trouble hadn't even begun; Elsa had merely been a small-time personal disaster, but things were soon to get really bad.'

'But it's the small-time personal disasters that count, is it not?'

'That's what fuels me – but as I said, the bigger picture was only just forming. About six weeks after the end of the trial, the Global Meltdown occurred. In Sweden we had the krona, and initially it was assumed that having an independent currency would save us from the economic fallout caused by the crash of the euro – and it did, for about two weeks. Of course our third-world "guests" had been kept all this time by the generosity of the state, and the docility of the Swedish taxpayer. Now, rather inconveniently for them, the state was in the process of collapsing, along with the free ride for our "guests"; they were not amused. As soon as the Muslims realised there was no longer any police or, more importantly, state welfare funding, they went on the rampage, looting and stealing. Almost immediately there were clashes with Swedish youths, and soon both sides were reaching for weapons.

'That was a dark period. Both groups were still living in close proximity to each other; the fighting and killing became very personal. Any Swedes living in predominantly Muslim areas either fled or were killed; it was like existing in a nightmare, with the smallest task became a major issue. Need to go to the local shop to buy bread? Is the shop still there? Does it have bread? Will the shop accept kronor? And how do I get to the shop? You'd need to know the racial geography of the area to the inch to even attempt such a journey.

'A friend of my brother Anders ignored that last point; he heard there were some shops with basic supplies willing to sell to Swedes – brave people, obviously heavily armed. Anders' friend thought there would be a rush for the goods and so took a shortcut between two blocks of flats, coming out by the side of some council tennis courts – bad move. The area had been mixed, but even this early on most Swedes had left. I don't know the whole story, but it appears that as he came out by the courts he was faced with half a dozen Muslim youths; he turned to flee back down the alley, only to find three others had magically materialised behind him. They all had knives, and one a meat cleaver, Woolwich style. They took photos of his head atop one of the corner supports of the tennis courts and posted them on the internet. He was one of the first in Malmö.

'It was mayhem in those early days – so many different people trying to do different things at the same time. Some of the police tried to continue as if they were still a force. They found the going easier in Swedish districts, and for a while even tried to arrest those of us who protected our homes and family with weaponry. They couldn't police the Muslim areas before the Global Meltdown, and afterwards they didn't even try. Any policeman caught by the Muslims was normally executed.

'Lots of the trendy, liberal middle classes called for calm and when the fighting started, automatically blamed their own people – old habits die hard. Of course the Muslims just laughed up their sleeves, and took from these idiots whatever they could – their cars, their plasma screens, their daughters – you name it, they took it. Once there was nothing left to steal, they simply killed them. Thus died the utopian dream of the Swedish liberal elite, dashed to pieces on the rocks of racial reality.

'The churches were exactly the same. They came out declaring brotherly love and distributing free food – while it lasted. Not a bad idea in theory, but as usual they hadn't the discipline, or focus, to care for their own flock – which of itself was more than they could manage. No, it was the same old universalist twaddle, as if they were the holders of divine truth and the judges of the world's morals; their conceit was bottomless. It was all so predictable; they went out of their way to send vans of food into the Muslim districts, but few ever re-emerged. Most of us Swedes just got ever more angry with them and their naivety in the face of such contempt and violence. They ran around preaching tolerance and cajoling food from us gullible Swedes, playing on our conscience with pictures of starving Muslim children – none of which was taken in Europe. But we were in serious trouble ourselves, and could ill afford misplaced generosity. The churches handed the bulk of the contributions to the immigrants, who then set about raping our women, burning our city and killing anybody without the weaponry to defend themselves.

'Most people think the turning point occurred when Sjostrand was hacked to pieces in front of his altar by a bunch of drunken Somalis; the whole incident was medieval in its barbarity.'

'Sjostrand?'

'He was head of the Church of Sweden in Malmö – they killed him in St Petri's cathedral.'

'So that was the turning point in Sweden?'

'Well, yes and no.'

'What does that mean?'

'Well, perhaps for the general public Sjostrand was a major turning point, but for us doing the fighting it was something else entirely. This is going to sound crazy, but I witnessed these events with my own eyes – it's all true. One day this wild figure, with long, matted blond hair and a huge bush of a beard, turned up out of nowhere. He must have been around 50 or so, a big, powerful man carrying this long ash staff covered in Norse runes. He had hypnotic deep-grey eyes and runic tattoos covering his arms. He was a man impossible to ignore, emanating an almost supernatural presence. An absolute Viking to his fingertips, and definitely not a man you'd mess with.

'He said his name was Kråka.

'He started berating us fighters for being a bunch of girls and poofs; he told us we'd spent too long under the blight of false gods, worshipping money and our dicks. He had come in the name of Odin and Thor, as a true servant of the Old Gods, and commanded us, to our faces, to stand as men like our proud forebears, to fight for the folk and win back our fatherland. Burning with raw passion, he demanded that we annihilate the aliens completely, to the last man – no prisoners; it was to be them or us. He wasn't joking either; he meant every word of it.

'There was one incident in particular which left us all absolutely thunderstruck; it also sealed our allegiance. It happened around a month after he first appeared; he'd called a meeting. There must have been a couple of hundred of us, all sorts really, mostly civilians but with a fair sprinkling of ex-police and soldiers; they stood out as they tended to wear their old uniforms. None of this mattered to Kråka; he didn't speak to policemen or bakers or electricians – all he cared about was Sweden. He spoke to Swedes and expected all, as men of Sweden, to respond as one. Utterly black-and-white: you either stood 100 per cent with Kråka, or you got out; there was no middle ground. We were sitting on what had been the playing field of a local secondary school; there was a natural bank at one end of the field, which allowed the men to see Kråka as he spoke. It was a reasonable day, a few clouds but sunny and quite warm. As Kråka began speaking I noticed the wind pick up, moving his long hair about his face and beard; his eyes, as always, were unblinking and set on the horizon.

'There's a tipping point in the affairs of men, Rudi, and Kråka was about to cross ours. We'd all been brought up on a diet of bubble-headed American sitcoms and self-gratification. Nobody had ever seriously put to us anything of value; I don't mean the false value of money, but real value – the sort of stuff that inspires men to stand their ground even when they know it means certain death. To the bubble-headed generation such things were either laughably naïve, or the actions of nutters – meaning Muslims. It was never taken seriously, and therefore could never motivate anybody. Kråka, by the strength of his presence, broke all that. He not only preached uncompromising loyalty and sacrifice for folk and fatherland, he demanded it. Early on a couple of mouthy, know-all teenagers challenged him; why should they die for somebody else's mother-in-law? I knew immediately that these two idiots had stepped into oblivion; Kråka was not a character anybody sane would cross.

'"So you are not prepared to fight for the folk? You're telling me these men here are not your kindred?" he growled, pointing to the rest of us.

'"What folk? Get real, old man; we're all just people."

'"We're all just people, are we? And you're not part of the folk? Neither are you kindred? In which case, you're not of this blood or of this soil – are you?"

'"That's right."

'"Then what are you doing here, cockroaches? These men are of the folk, who fight for the folk: you are merely people. This is not a problem for us; gentlemen – your 'people' await." Kråka then pointed towards Malmö and its Muslims. "Go and join them!"

'"No way, man: we're not going there."

'"By Odin's beard, nor are you staying here to defile our work. We require warriors, good Swedish stock who fight for hearth and kin, not worthless parasites – in the name of the Alfather, be gone!"

'The two of them looked to the rest of us for support, but nobody said a word. The Muslims already knew the truth of Kråka's words; they fought for their

Ummah, and most certainly did not treat everybody as mere "people" – as we well knew to our cost. The pair of them were thrown out, but at least they had the common sense to head away from the city.

'The thing with the bubble-heads – and I openly admit I was one – is that the only defence they have for their world of consumption and individualism is ridicule and disbelief. Once ridicule fails, and belief is established, the bubble-head balloon explodes into a shower of superficial emptiness. Kråka filled that vacuum with uncompromising faith.

'Back on the sports field, the weather started deteriorating as the fire in Kråka's preaching grew. It was electric, driving deep into our souls, appealing directly to heart and lineage; he had that rare ability, which few possess, of seemingly addressing everyone individually at the same time. I've never seen anything like it. The only thing I can compare it to is one of the Great Leader's speeches in the previous age.

'So there we were, sitting on this bank, the atmosphere bristling with anticipation – even the weather seemed to obey Kråka's command. As he approached the climax of his speech, clouds started racing wildly across the heavens and thunderheads suddenly filled the sky – it was nothing short of supernatural. Completely spellbound, we turned in unison to face the mounting storm, and Kråka instinctively threw wide his arms and bellowed, "Honour the Gods of our people with your blood and sword, and the Gods will honour your sacrifice with victory for the folk," and as his injunction pierced the wind a lightning bolt split the heavens, followed by a clap of thunder so loud it made our ears ring – it was that close we could feel the static crackling in the air. Kråka stood motionless, silhouetted by the flash from the lightning, and at that moment we knew he was everything he claimed to be; he was truly Thor's chosen servant, sent in answer to our cries for salvation. The Old Gods had at last stirred from their long sleep. Despite centuries of betrayal to an alien god, they'd come to retrieve their lost folk; you could feel the ages roll back to a time when our forefathers honoured our rightful native Gods.

'We were stunned. The whole incident was messianic; the hair on the back of my neck was standing on end. It put a healthy fear of the Gods into most of the younger lads, while it seared a deep respect for the Old Gods and my Swedish identity into me. After that, there was no further talk of holding "discussions" or coming to terms with the invaders; we were Kråka's, body and soul, and within a couple of days I noticed that most of the men were wearing the Mjölnir.

'This was long before any widespread Pagan revival had started; nobody had heard of the *Liber Iuliani* – in fact I don't think it even existed at that time. In any case, Kråka wasn't about to start quoting Socrates or Cicero at us; he most certainly didn't represent the philosophic side of Paganism. He was raw, native faith.

'I remember on another occasion, in a first-aid station, one of the attendants – a Christian – was tending a Muslim. Kråka marched over to the duty doctor to demand what was going on. The doctor said all were treated there according to the Hippocratic oath. Kråka was furious. "Is this how you betray the fatherland and our precious folk, by giving succour to those who would butcher us? Those who would gladly wash in the blood of our fallen warriors and feast on the flesh of our women?" The doctor, somewhat taken aback by the verbal assault, nodded in confirmation. Kråka turned to face him and with a shuddering crack of his rune staff knocked the doctor senseless to the floor.

'Once we were organised and had fully adopted the attitudes and beliefs Kråka had taught us, he vanished. However, stories soon started filtering through from Göteborg, Uppsala, Vasteras, Norrköping, Stockholm – everywhere. It was Kråka, and he was Lord of the Storm Crows, as he was now universally known to the fighting men of Sweden; he'd become a living legend and we'd become his Storm Crows.

'So as you can see, for us Kråka was the real turning point. We didn't have the weapons yet to dislodge the Jihadists, but through Kråka the Old Gods had shown us the spiritual path forward. We were ready.

'Malmö was the first Swedish city to fall to the Muslims, though the violence soon reached epic proportions in other cities, like Stockholm and Göteborg. We Swedes now found ourselves in the same boat as everybody else in Europe. We too had become accustomed to being protected by police and army – the warm embrace of the nanny state from cradle to the grave. But once nanny ceased functioning, we were as helpless as new-born babes. Kråka had said the same thing, only in blunter terms – and he was right. Our third-world guests simply reverted to practices they used back in the old country – you've seen the clips from Malmö? Dragging those poor girls by their hair out of the flats over in Södervärn, then … you know, and afterwards butchering them like cattle. It was horrific.'

Rudi had seen the video, as had virtually everybody else in Europe, and all had come to the same conclusion regarding Muslims. Axel picked up his story again.

'As I said, in the beginning there were riots night after night, with buildings set alight across the city. As things escalated, the Muslims slowly gained the upper hand, driving the remainder of the native Swedes from the city. Some areas hung on grimly, surrounded by hostiles and battling every night to maintain their position, but it was hopeless; eventually we decided to abandon the city and pull back. It was during the nightly rioting and arson attacks that we lost Viktor.'

Another pause. Axel adjusted his sitting position before continuing his narrative,

'I'm not sure of the details, but he was found among the dead in Rönnen – after the Muslims had burnt down the residential blocks. Thankfully Ebba had already gone, at Viktor's insistence. He forced her to leave as soon as the first serious fighting started; she went home in tears to her parents' place outside Tollarp. I had the grim task of breaking the news to her: not an experience I'd care to repeat.'

Once again his mind travelled back to those dark days. He'd managed to get a lift in a car of one of the men in the association – all the men in Axel's unit knew of his friendship with Viktor, and the reason for his journey. They drove out of the city past Lund, heading towards Hörby. The roads were very quiet; there was little petrol or diesel available and most people tried to avoid the cities. Axel had only been able to arrange the trip after talking to the association commander, who gave him a ration ticket to draw fuel from the association's central store just outside the city.

The area around Tollarp is pretty – perhaps not stunning enough to feature on adverts, but a green and deeply Swedish place. Forested, with buildings set back amongst the woods, the town was typically small-town Sweden, with its neat estates and small business parks. Ebba lived outside town, a mile or two to the north.

After passing through the town and out into the countryside, along Träne Byaväg, the car eventually turned left at the junction with Uddarpsvägen – Ebba's house was on the left, set back in the forest just before the lake. The road was narrow, and on its right were open fields, but to the left it was all dense forest – Kråka country, thought Axel.

The house suddenly came into view among the trees on their left; there was no drive – just a piece of grassland in front of the house, which otherwise had forest on three sides. Axel stared spellbound at the house – by Odin, look at it! He slowly slumped forward in his seat, quietly suppressing his emotions. Jan, his driver, looked at him in surprise. 'Are you okay?'

Axel didn't answer. Quite simply, the beauty of the rustic house had struck him a hammer blow: how could it be so perfect? It was almost as if Kråka himself had planted it there among the trees as a sign – 'This is Sweden.' It was, in every respect, quintessentially Swedish. To Axel at that instant it represented everything lost, the essence of Swedishness and Swedish identity, all wrapped up in that simple, rural and deeply beautiful house. His mind flitted back to Malmö, and the hellhole estates and rampaging mobs of murderous, alien youths. At every turn, at every opening of his eyes, he saw the truth of Kråka's words – and now he had to enter that house, and tell sweet Ebba that her lover, and his best friend, had been slaughtered. Jan persisted, asking again, 'Are you all right?' He swung the car onto the grass in front of the house and parked up.

Axel smiled at him stoically, then pushed open the door of the battered Golf to get out. 'Are you coming?'

'To tell your college friend her boyfriend's been butchered? I think not – thank you, but no thanks. I'll stick to the driving.'

'As you please.'

'Good luck.'

'Thanks.'

He knocked on the door, which after a wait that seemed like an eternity, but in reality was but a few minutes, was opened by a smiling, neat, middle-aged lady. 'Hello – can I help you?'

'Hello: I'm sorry to bother you. I'm a friend of Ebba's from Malmö. I've travelled down because I need to speak to her; it's rather important, I'm afraid.'

'I see. Well, come through to the sitting room. Ebba's been out and is just having a shower; she'll be down in a minute. Can I give her your name?'

'Of course. I'm Axel – Axel Nyberg.'

'Would you like a coffee, Axel? What of your friend in the car – is he coming in?'

'No, thank you, and my friend is fine in the car for now; the business I need to see Ebba about is very sensitive. Are you Ebba's mother?'

'Yes, I'm Mrs Söderström.'

'I'm afraid what I have to tell Ebba will cause her considerable upset. Will she be long?'

'Perhaps I can help?'

'I'm sorry, Mrs Söderström, but it's private, for Ebba's ears.'

Mrs Söderström looked at Axel full of foreboding. She invited him to sit, then hurriedly disappeared out of the door, her footsteps clearly audible on the stairs. In the corner of the room a television was on with the volume turned down, but the voices could still be discerned. Two suited men were discussing the background to the Global Meltdown that had sparked the long-expected war now raging throughout Europe. The start of the fighting had also marked the end of the old political classes' control of the media. This programme was being broadcast by the new SPG – Swedish Provisional Government – and came as a refreshing blast of reality after the stifling political correctness of the old, corrupt establishment. The older of the two speakers was obviously on the offensive; Axel listened with one ear, though nothing actually penetrated his conscious mind, which was filled with Ebba and the terrible task confronting him:

'Oh come on, let's be realistic; the whole situation had been brewing for decades and was inevitable under an international central banking system built around issuing debt. Although the dangers inherent in such an irresponsible practice had been expounded upon by many great men – look at Ezra Pound – the scale of the profit flowing into commercial and central banks overrode all such concerns. After all, for the bankers it was literally a case of creating your own money out of thin air, which you then lent to governments at interest – the über-scam of all scams. Frankly the ethnic bankster clans that ran the whole thing deserve nothing but our deepest contempt.'

He heard muffled voices from upstairs, and the sound of doors banging and people moving about.

'And thus the spiral of debt grew ever greater and deeper – it was insanity …'

Suddenly he heard another exchange of voices; then his heart stopped. Two pairs of feet were coming down the stairs. He glanced up to the ceiling, closed his eyes briefly and offered a short, silent prayer to Vör for guidance – as Kråka had shown them. He glanced around the room for a suitable place, deciding on the mantelpiece. Time was very short; he'd found a two-kronor piece in his pocket, which he deliberately placed carefully on the mantelpiece with the merest of nods to signify the deed, then sat down.

'Of course the whole concept of using money – a means of exchanging goods and services – as a commodity was not merely flawed, but positively evil, as indeed is state usury. Under healthy regimes money is a service which allows economies to function correctly, the presumption being that a government operates for the benefit of the nation – an archaic and naïve idea by the time of the Meltdown, I acknowledge.'

The door opened. Ebba's eyes drilled into Axel; there was only one reason why he would have travelled all this way in the middle of a war. She didn't speak at first, but walked over to the couch opposite Axel and sat down. Her mother followed, and sat down beside her daughter, the two holding hands and looking at Axel. Ebba spoke first: 'It's nice to see you again, Axel; mother tells me you have some news for me.' There was a slight pause before she continued in a trembling voice. 'Come now, Axel, we're ready; what have you to say?' The defiance of her brave words was betrayed by her fingers, white from her mother's iron grip – not that either seemed to have noticed.

'Hello, Ebba; I'll try to be brief.' He pulled himself together and took a deep breath. He'd already decided there was no point dancing around the point; he would lay out the truth immediately. 'Two days ago the association made a sweep of the northern part of the city, reaching as far as Mollevangstorget; in the process we passed through Rönnen.'

He paused again and looked at Ebba; she knew it was coming – he could see the storm mounting in her eyes. The mother knew as well, her head slightly bowed, awaiting the blow.

'Rönnen had been destroyed, burnt to the ground. In and around the shell of the buildings were numerous bodies. Those in the building we couldn't do much with; there was no way to identify the charred remains – but those in the grounds we collected: around 37 in total. We identified those we could. Viktor was among the dead.'

Ebba's head fell forward, her face buried in her hands as her body heaved silently, while her mother did what little she could to console her daughter. Axel was at a total loss. Was he to stay or leave, speak or remain silent? The conversation on the television had moved on to China's role in the crisis; this time it was the younger man speaking. Axel tried to concentrate on the speaker in an effort to bring his own raging emotions under control; he felt as if he were in a straightjacket, confined both physically and socially by the pathos and agony of the situation.

'The ensuing economic troubles brought stress to the entire global economy, impacting particularly heavily on China and causing huge economic and political troubles. The fact that the government was Communist played no part in the grave crisis that faced the country, despite the attacks from the corrupt West, whose economies were in an equally poor condition. Although the Chinese government was warned by its own financial experts that the dollar would collapse if a major call was made on the mountain of dollar bonds held by China, the politicians had little choice. The country was unravelling at a frightening pace, with serious riots in Shanghai, armed nationalist uprisings in Tibet and Xinjiang, and a growing autonomous movement developing in the south fuelled by the economic crisis.'

Axel felt an acute sense of embarrassment, but as he absent-mindedly watched the two suits discussing the scale of the disaster emanating from the NWO's machinations, he suddenly realised that the embarrassment was all his. Ebba and her mother were only vaguely aware that he was still there. He decided to wait for an opportune moment before making any move.

'So it was that China announced that it intended making a partial draw on its dollar bonds. In practice no further step was needed: the news of itself proved enough to send the dollar into freefall. The economic fallout was global, with the euro being the first major casualty. The American economy collapsed, and it was only the US Government's limpet-like adhesion to the petro-dollar agreement with OPEC that bought the country a few extra months in which politicians and bankers scrambled around searching for a way to patch up their sinking Titanic.*'*

The suits droned on, but nothing had changed opposite him; Ebba was still locked in her own private nightmare. Axel felt perhaps it was time to go, but had no idea how to extricate himself from the situation. Then he remembered what was in his pocket. He leaned back slightly and started fishing around in his jacket.

'It came as little surprise, therefore, that the USA jumped at the chance to sell billions of dollars' worth of military hardware to Saudi Arabia – once the Saudis had signed an undertaking not to re-export the weapons to any third party without US agreement.'

He found it, and gently removed the item from his pocket. Now he was in a position to bring events to a close, and perhaps leave as unobtrusively as possible. He glanced over at Ebba and her mother, deep in their own world of hurt. He took a deep breath. 'Ebba.' She looked up, her flushed face sporting two pain-filled reddened eyes and a streaming nose. 'I have something for you.'

At this her mother also looked up, her face ashen, and in its own way as distressed as her daughter's.

'It's unusual to find items after they've … anyway, we found this on Viktor's body.' He handed Ebba a black plastic watch, which probably explained why it was still on the body. She recognised it immediately and took it with shaking fingers from Axel's hand.

'Within 24 hours of the first planeload of hardware landing at the Prince Sultan

Air Base in Al Kharj the weapons had been redirected onto SAF – Saudi Air Force – cargo planes to be dropped by parachute just outside Marseille.'

Ebba managed an ironic smile from the debris of her life and love. 'I bought it for him last year after he kept complaining he didn't have a watch. I got it in the market; it was just a cheap thing.' She held the watch almost in awe; this insignificant piece of plastic represented an ocean of memories and dashed hopes.

'I'm so sorry, Ebba. It sounds so pathetically inadequate, but there's nothing else I can offer but my sympathy.'

'I know. He was your friend as well; we've all been hurt.'

Mrs Söderström got up and left the room; soon she could be heard busying herself in the kitchen, boiling a kettle. Neither of them spoke.

'The Saudis claimed there was no re-export since nobody had bought the weapons; technically they still belonged to Saudi Arabia. The Saudis were merely lending the weapons temporarily to their allies – their allies being the myriad Islamic Republics springing up all over Europe, and all immediately recognised by the Saudis and the rest of the Arab League. In order to camouflage their de facto re-exporting of American arms, the Saudi Army started sending small groups of men to the new Islamic Republics. Officially all the Saudi weapons, now in the hands of the Eurab Jihadists, were under the control of Saudi military advisers. It was total fiction, but served as a short-term fig leaf.'

Mrs Söderström re-emerged with coffee which, unasked for, she placed in the hands of all, keeping a mechanical smile on her face throughout. The initial storm had passed, though looking at Ebba, Axel was in little doubt that there were more to come. Mrs Söderström's chores would certainly extend beyond the coffee.

'The Arab League and the rest of the non-Arabic Muslim world then went to work on condemning the newly emerging nationalist governments across Europe as

fascist regimes bent on destroying the legitimate aspirations of Europe's Muslim population. Their main platform was the rump UN, still sitting in New York, shorn of all its European members.'

Axel took a quick sip of the hot coffee then said, 'Thank you very much, Mrs Söderström, but I must be returning to Malmö with Jan. It's a very dangerous place once the sun goes down.'

Axel glanced at the television for the last time; the programme appeared to be coming to an end.

'The Americans knew what the Saudis intended doing with the hardware from the start. The talk of creating Eurabia had been floating around the Arab world since at least the days of Gaddafi. The Israelis were up in arms, not so much concerning Europe's plight as at the perceived danger of arming the Saudis so heavily. Their complaints, channelled via the well-worn and powerful connections long used by Israel in dealing with the US, led to America offering the Israelis an equally impressive array of arms as a sop to the Saudi purchases.'

Ebba sat subdued, oblivious to the world, having retreated into her inner vortex. Her mother delicately got up from her side, took Axel's coffee mug from him and placed it on a small table at the side of the couch. 'Come, Axel – can I call you Axel? Let's walk to the car. Ebba's quiet now; we'll give her a bit of space.'

'Certainly, Mrs Söderström.'

'Call me Catrina. Tell me, Axel – how's it going in Malmö?'

'Well, Catrina, they have the city, but we have the countryside and outer suburbs. I think we can win …'

During the lull in Axel's narrative, Rudi gave the valley below another scan. Nothing had changed; he watched a delivery van implausibly drive along the deserted road, following the course of the river on the Greek side – how odd.

2.1 – SVERIGE

Surely some Turk would take a pot shot at it? The van eventually disappeared from view, heading north – nobody, neither Greek nor Turk, having taken the slightest interest in its progress. He looked towards Axel, who was deep in thought, totally unaware he'd stopped speaking or that Rudi was staring at him. Rudi reached out and gently touched his arm. Axel started as if from a deep sleep, his eyes rapidly flicking from side to side as he reoriented himself.

'Sorry, Rudi; I was miles away.'

'Yeah, I could see. Are you ready to continue?'

'Continue?'

'Sweden?'

'Yes, of course: sorry. Where were we?'

'You were telling how society fell apart following the Global Meltdown – as it did everywhere else, incidentally.'

'Yeah, well in Sweden the police force disintegrated, most of them joining the rapidly forming defence associations. We held most of the suburbs, and all the countryside, of course – but the city was lost. At first the fighting was barbaric: kitchen knives, hammers and shotguns, with the odd hunting rifle. But soon the first army deserters began arriving, along with ex-policemen, and they brought real weapons.

'The Muslims tried to expand their area of control out into the suburbs, producing some heavy fighting. They also tried to link with their Danish allies over the Öresund Bridge – but the Danes had no intention of allowing Malmö's plague to spread into Copenhagen. They had enough on their plate already. What a wake-up call that was; it knocked us for six.'

'What did?'

'The Öresund Bridge – longest in Europe – the Danes blew it up to stop the Muslims from crossing over. I'll never forget it; symbolically it was a huge wake-up call for us. Now, at last, we understood there would be no help from anywhere; the entire continent was fighting for survival, and if Sweden was to emerge again we would need to start fighting – or convert to Islam. I presume something similar happened in Austria?'

'Same story, different details – though of course help did come.'

'Yes, but at the time we didn't know that, and would never have looked in that direction – though by today it's obvious. We were so heavily indoctrinated by the globalist vision of a utopian future we couldn't see the wood for the trees, despite the fact that their poisonous vision was materialising right before our eyes, slaughtering our kinsmen and declaring loyalty to alien deities and alien cultures. We were brainwashed to a degree that beggars belief. How could a people be so stupid? We swallowed their blatant lies and fell for their underhand tricks.' Bitter rage was hovering just behind these words; Axel paused again to rein in his racing emotions.

'How many friends and family have I buried, or seen murdered, because of this utopian brainwashing and elite treachery? And of course, the all-encompassing role of our Levantine friends in this horror story.'

Axel paused again as he brought his thoughts into some sort of order. 'Anyway, we tried retaking the city after a month or so. We'd been beefed up with more police and soldiers, and that's when we got our first inkling of the scale of the problem. No more kitchen knives and shotguns – they now faced us with machine guns, artillery and even tanks. We had to flee for our lives; luckily the police and soldiers did enough to slow up the Eurab counterattack, otherwise we'd all have been slaughtered.

'Generally the whole situation was getting very grim: food was scarce, power and water were intermittent, and people were dying – not just in the fighting, but through crime and neglect. The elderly and little ones had it worst. Hundreds of thousands were sleeping in village and school halls – or rough – living off handouts that were rapidly drying up. The areas controlled by the Eurabs were systematically cleared of Swedes – or any Europeans, for that matter – who were shot on sight.'

Rudi took another quick scan of the valley; then asked, 'I've heard a couple of stories about what happened in Sweden; wasn't there some general who turned himself over to the Eurabs? Or is that just a myth?'

'Ah, you're talking about Eckdahl.'

'What was his story, then?'

'Eckdahl was typical of Sweden before the Meltdown. We were modern, sophisticated globalists; we didn't need defence forces as we were part of the global community, as could be seen in any major Swedish city – not that the talking heads who spouted this hogwash lived anywhere remotely close to their beloved enrichers.

'We lived under the most incredible system of control. We had the most rigorously enforced anti-discrimination laws imaginable – all in the name of free speech. Of course, if your free speech infringed upon the state's defence of any of more than two hundred named protected groups under Swedish Law, you would be prosecuted, and even sent to prison. But that wasn't the end of the matter: you could also be sent to a retraining centre to have your incorrect opinions corrected – just like the old USSR. Ah, democracy – wasn't it grand? The best government money could buy.'

'And Eckdahl?'

'Well, as you can imagine, any government that lived in this fantasy world could not grasp the necessity for armed forces – nasty dangerous things, with all that testosterone and boy-scout mentality.

'The Swedish army had been cut continually over the preceding decades; by the time Eckdahl was appointment it stood at the grand total of 17,000 men. 17,000! Do you know how big Sweden is?'

Rudi did not answer.

'Not only were our forces verging on the non-existent, they were also gelded with the most extensive and complex rules for engagement under the sun. In complete contrast, the Swedish police were by then the most heavily armed in Europe – and needed to be.

'General Eckdahl was appointed chief of staff to our toy-town army more for his progressive political views than any perceived military ability. He was the one who pushed for racial quotas on recruitment into the services, women in the front line, mixed barracks, lax uniform regulations – a "modern" outlook for the new globalist age of eternal peace. And where was this Disneyland world of peace? It seems that all the wars that had been filling our television screens and newspapers for decades didn't exist for Eckdahl. As far as he and his political masters were concerned, they weren't real wars – merely "local disturbances"; though I'm not sure the dead would have agreed.' Axel was talking more to himself than Rudi by now, carried away on another wave of disgust towards the old elite.

'When the Meltdown came, Sweden managed to stay afloat for a couple of weeks on the krona, but even then things in the cities were beginning to disintegrate – riots, fighting, looting.

'It was a surreal time, watching the elites on television trying to explain away the end of the universe as if it were all a hiccup, and that normal service would be resumed shortly. No film of the troubles was shown on television; there was barely a mention in the papers – even as central Malmö burned to the ground! But it was too late for them. The internet was full of videos and reports of the fighting, nobody paid any attention to the official channels – we all knew the real story.

'In rural areas defence associations soon formed to counter Eurab scouting parties leaving the cities to look for food, raiding farms and shops in Swedish-controlled areas. Even as the ship went down the politicians were decrying the associations as being reactionary, fascist and un-Swedish. They were even repeating their pleas for racial harmony minutes before boarding their jets for the USA – well, Marie Lundberg did.'

'Marie Lundberg?'

'Our beloved Minister of Education. She had proposed the creation of mother-tongue schools for our "guests" – of course, her own kids went to a private school: no rubbing shoulders with Somalis and Moroccans for them.'

'Yet more *déjà vu*,' voiced the bemused Rudi.

'By then Eckdahl was panicking, as both the police and army were starting to break up. But worse than that were the rumours – all true – that most of the men were openly sympathetic towards the associations.'

Axel turned to Rudi to emphasise his next point, 'You've got to bear in mind what was occurring at the time. The Saudi-purchased gear was pouring into the Eurabian forces right across Europe. Rotterdam had just fallen; we'd all watched the footage on the web in disbelief. The Dutch were well organised, certainly better than us; they'd formed their Dutch Defence Force from volunteers and police and army remnants like us, but already they had brigades and a formal hierarchy in place – but it wasn't enough. In Rotterdam they came face to face with real military power. The Eurabs had M5-106 Obama main battle tanks, and a vast array of heavy gear landed by the Saudis. Watching it on line we thought Armageddon had arrived.'

'Yeah, I remember watching the same stuff myself, holed up in Vienna. All those disturbing videos of them clearing the city of its Dutch population, and decapitating people on the streets. And the rank callousness of the Eurabs in filming and posting such scenes.'

'It's done for a purpose.'

'Yeah, I know, but all it does is make me even more determined to destroy them. So what happened with your Eckdahl?'

'In southern Sweden the Eurabs had gained control of both Malmö and Göteborg, though things weren't easy for them as most of the territory between the cities was held by us. We'd turned off their water, electricity and gas – what there was of it. They used to send heavily armoured convoys between the two cities, Göteborg having been proclaimed provisional capital of the new Islamic Republic of Sweden.

'All Eckdahl cared about was keeping his politically correct credentials nice and clean, and in order to achieve that he needed the army to comply. Some – the senior officers mostly – had largely kept aloof from the mayhem, though that was more a case of confusion than anything deeper. Incredible as it may seem, most of the senior officers still believed that order would be re-established – despite the fact that the police had all but ceased to exist. They imagined that the correct, enlightened political programme actively pursued by Sweden's political elite prior to the troubles would resume its course – a staggeringly naïve standpoint even for them.

'General Eckdahl's world finally collapsed when he was informed that the two largest military bases in Sweden had joined the newly established Swedish Provisional Government (SPG) – whose programme was based on the re-establishment of a Swedish Sweden and rejection of all multicultural and globalist policies. The rank and file of the army had been growing ever more restless with the inactivity of their senior officers. Time was running out; indeed, large numbers of soldiers had already deserted, most of whom had joined the associations, particularly after the SPG programme was announced. It came as little surprise that it was a group of middle-ranking officers who finally led the bulk of what remained of Sweden's army into the SPG's camp.

'Eckdahl, beside himself with rage, contacted the media and, in an interview shown on all Swedish TV channels, stated that Sweden was a modern, progressive country, not some medieval ethnic enclave for troglodytes. The peoples against whom the SPG was illegally plotting were good Swedish citizens, every bit the equal of those fascists in the associations and SPG – he failed to mention that they were also armed, murderous Jihadists – and to prove his point, he was going to Göteborg to discuss peace terms with the head of the Islamic Government in Sweden.

'Eckdahl was caught on camera entering Muslim Göteborg on a bright, clear morning in a Swedish Army Hummer HX by a local film crew, who wisely refused to enter the city themselves. He was not seen again for ten days. No news emerged from Göteborg, even though there was a torrent of Islamic rhetoric pouring out of the Eurabian-controlled radio and TV studios in southern Sweden. The general had vanished.

'On the tenth day, a scouting party of SPG rangers – all ex-army special forces – broke through the eastern perimeter of the Eurabian lines. It was only a probing action, but it actually managed to penetrate the whole way to Göteborg City Hall – the famous Stock Exchange – before having to pull back. But that was long enough. On the balcony above the main entrance was a row of poles, each topped with a severed *kafir* head – amongst which was that of General Eckdahl. Photos of the good General's head appeared within hours on the internet, and adorned the front pages of those papers and magazines still functioning the following day. There were other pictures, too, such as Gustav Adolf's statue lying at the base of its plinth, having been hauled down with a chain attached to a refuse lorry – and of course there was the obligatory black banner of jihad fluttering defiantly over the Stock Exchange.'

'So that's the story of the famous Swedish general; frankly he got his just deserts in my opinion – but still no legions?'

'No, the meeting in Bonn hadn't taken place yet, though I think the Declaration of Rouen had been drafted – not that we knew of its existence at the time.'

'I take it the SPG picked up the pieces and started the counteroffensive?'

'Well, sort of, though it wasn't quite as simple as that. Democracy had failed, hijacked by elites and plutocrats; our new government was basically an ex-general – ironic really, considering what I've just told you about Eckdahl –

who ruled with an advisory council. But this general was no Eckdahl. Thord Nordenskiöld was an unapologetic nationalist, who held the welfare of his country and its people to be the government's highest calling. True, he could be a little stuffy at times, but he was no globalist; he was one of us – a Swede to the very marrow in his bones.

'The SPG brought order to those areas they controlled. This was a more traditional form of justice to that followed under the globalist elites, but at least people knew where they stood and how they would be treated. For all its punitive teeth it was actually very popular, far more so than the previous regime. Now all were held to account for their actions; those found looting were shot, and murderers – if found guilty – were hanged. The government issued a new krona to jump-start the economy. However, as in Rotterdam, we were facing the fearsome firepower of the Eurabs. They were getting helicopters, jet fighters, drones, everything – though they struggled to find anybody capable of operating the equipment or controlling the drones. Did you see the clip of that Eurab F-22 Raptor trying to take off from Amsterdam?'

'Certainly did; it's a classic. The fool hadn't a clue what he was doing, though he managed a very impressive corkscrew before ploughing into the ground. That was also a pretty spectacular fireball he created.'

'Yeah, the 'Dutch Shish Kebab' the boys called him. Well, it was much the same in Sweden; they couldn't use half the equipment they were given because they simply didn't have anybody capable of operating it – thank the Gods. But eventually it was our friends from the East who pulled our fat from the fire.'

'Yeah, it was the same story in Austria. God bless Mother Russia, I say.'

'Amen to that.'

'And the legions?'

2.1 – SVERIGE

'Well, the news came through on the internet of the formation of the legions to help counteract the Jihadists moving men around over borders. It was an incredible step, really exciting, which fired up a lot of us who wanted to finish the job and clear all of Europe. At about the same time I got a first look at the Declaration of Rouen on the web – it was dynamite. At last, a declaration for the future of European man; I was totally sold. As you know, the legions started opening recruiting offices in the working capitals of the European countries. In our case, although Stockholm never fell entirely under Muslim control – unlike Malmö and Göteborg – the SPG decided to operate from Jönköping for the first eleven months of its existence, and that's where I joined up. They flew me down to Bonn about a week afterwards. And you?'

'Much the same, though there was more than one office in Austria, I joined in Gleisdorf, not far from Graz.'

2.2 – Blood Bound

The sun had gone down, as had the temperature. Axel and Rudi sat in their concrete bay, eating spaghetti bolognese from steaming mess tins. Light was a problem; the men needed to see what they were doing without alerting any Jihadist patrols probing towards Zorolus. All the men had pulled back into the numerous bays in the warehouse, as it shielded them to a degree; even so all were acutely aware of the light given off by their stoves. For further light the men utilised their combat head-torches. Anybody who showed too much light got a swift rebuke from Vasily.

Rudi excused himself, and slipped out of the warehouse side door for a call of nature. When he returned Axel asked him if he'd seen or heard anything.

'No – it's pitch black out there and quiet as the grave.'

'You didn't bump into Alvero or Carlos, then?'

'No, in any case I probably wouldn't have got any sense out of them; they always speak Spanish when they're together.'

Axel chuckled.

The pair of them got as comfy and warm as possible before trying to snatch a couple of hours' sleep before their watch. However, despite the fatigue and need for sleep, Rudi's throwaway comment regarding Alvero and Carlos' use of Spanish had started the cogs spinning in his head.

All *legionarii* were given a full account of the formation of the *Curia* and the adoption of Latin as the working language of the *legiones* in their basic training. However, in truth much of this dry background history fell on deaf ears, or was quickly forgotten as more practical and exciting topics arose – like the fitting and care of their *arma proeliaria* or maintenance and firing of the legionary standard weapon, the GA-6.

Intellectually, Rudi was a cut above the average grunt and had been fascinated by the adoption of Latin, ever since those perfunctory lectures during initial training. However, the best and fullest account he'd ever heard had come from a totally different direction. As he tried to ignore the bone-chilling cold seeping through from the warehouse's concrete floor, his mind wandered back to a surprise evening encounter in Rome, 18 months earlier.

He had entered a bar on the Via del Monte della Farina, to meet some old comrades serving in *Legio XII Palaiologos*. After a couple of beers their conversation began to drift towards various sexual and drinking exploits – all standard fare – and some small talk about the war in general. By now the bar was thick with alcohol-charged Latin, when a suited man entered. He was middle-aged, tall with greying hair, but held himself erect and was in obvious good physical condition, with a certain air of assuredness about him. A few of the men glanced up before continuing with the banter and incessant leg-pulling. They weren't aware at the time, but the gentleman in question was American.

An American? The position of Americans in Europe had become strained since the start of the Eurabian War. Officially the USA had remained neutral – a strange position to adopt in the opinion of most Europeans, considering America had been allied to virtually all of them since the end of the Second European Civil War.

Once fighting began the USA refused to sell any further weapons or spare parts to Europe, even though European armouries were full of American equipment. Washington claimed that since the Muslims, along with the West Africans and other groups involved in the fighting, were all European citizens, equal in every respect to the native populations under international law, these disturbances were strictly speaking an internal affair. In other words, America judged them to be civil wars. Since civil wars did not pose an exterior threat, as specified by NATO, the State Department decided that the US had no mandate to intervene with arms sales.

It was in response to this position that, on being formed, the legions made several key long-term strategic decisions. Regarding arms, the legions announced that they would only buy weapons designed and manufactured in Europe, from bodies managed and controlled by European interests, be they commercial or state-run.

It was also decided to withdraw from all international bodies that harboured universalist aspirations – in particular the UN. The fledgling Pan-European Conference (P-EC) – which later became the *Curia* – had already decided to accept as its guiding ideology the tenets expounded in the Declaration of Rouen. In following these tenets the P-EC stated, logically, that it was self-defeating to fight for the survival of a national group, only to subsume ultimate authority over that group to an internationalist body. Such bodies, by definition being internationalist, could never hold the interests of any individual national group as their highest priority. Since under the Declaration of Rouen the first and primary duty of a national government was the well-being of the nation to which it was responsible, it became constitutionally impossible for such a government to belong to any international body that claimed some form of authority over it. The nebulous term 'nation' was clarified by the Declaration of Rouen, which defined it as the combination of a genetically unique group of self-recognising people inhabiting a historically designated territory. The Declaration also stated that the nation was the core identitarian entity of all European Aryans, and should be recognised as such, by creating self-governing political institutions – regardless of size or historical precedents.

Rudi, returning from the gents, headed towards the bar for another bottle of *Peroni*. The middle-aged gentleman in the suit was sitting on a bar stool close to where Rudi ordered his beer. As the bartender went to fetch a bottle from the cold cabinet the suited man turned to Rudi and, in good, though clearly accented Latin, said, 'I see you boys are having a good time. I don't blame you; all soldiers need a little R&R if they're to operate to the best of their abilities.'

'I couldn't agree more. That's an interesting accent you've got there – where are you from?'

'Mississippi.'

'An American?'

'Personally, I consider myself a citizen of Dixie. It's the Yankees and their New York handlers who are responsible for this mess, not us.'

Rudi smiled and took his beer from the bartender. 'Still fighting the Civil War? Isn't it a bit late in the day for that?'

'Just because we lost don't mean we were wrong and they were right. This current war in Europe is in its own way just another spin-off from the Yankee victory.'

'Really?'

'Let me tell you a little-known fact concerning the Civil War.'

'I'm listening.'

'The Confederate Army was 91 per cent native-born White American; the Union Army 45 per cent. Tell me, son – who really won the Civil War? It sure as hell wasn't the Nativist Americans, north or south. You see, the roots of this evil go way back.'

'Are you seriously trying to suggest that there's some sort of connection between the Muslim butchery in Rotterdam and Grant's defeat of Lee – what was it, 150, 160 years ago?'

'Nearer 170. However, the point remains that the good people of Rotterdam were slaughtered because their existence as an indigenous population on their own historic territory – just like us Southerners in Dixie – stood in the way of the great blending, which as I've just illustrated, was already under way during the Civil War. If you take the bigger picture, you'll see there's no fundamental difference between the fate of Dixie and that intended for Europe prior to the current Eurabian War.'

'Mass immigration and multiculturalism, you mean?'

'Yeah, call it what you like: it's the destruction of identity, aimed eventually at creating a homogeneous mass of rootless, rudderless consumers of pleasure through a programme of universal miscegenation and mongrelisation – all driven by governmental and corporatist interests. It's a perfect recipe for the globalist aspirations of our dear friends in New York. Believe me, whatever's good for those bloodsuckers is very, very bad for the rest of us.'

'But we're fighting Muslims and Blacks; what's that got to do with your Yankees?'

'The Muslims were merely convenient material for dumping into Europe; of themselves they're irrelevant. They're easily manipulated – look at the way the Neo-Cons tore through them in all those endless engineered conflicts in the Middle East. The whole laughable game was an open exhibition of Islam's impotence in the field of geopolitics. Did they even realise they were being led by the nose? And why were those wars fought at all?'

'To save people suffering under tyrannical governments?'

The suited man almost fell off his stool laughing. 'Really? That's a good one. You've just described half the governments in Africa, but I don't seem to recall any calls to intervene there. I wonder why?'

'I don't know,' answered Rudi honestly.

'It's not really that difficult soldier. What makes the world go round?'

'Money?'

'I was thinking more of a certain black, sticky substance; let me enlighten you. In reality the Yankees have been technically bankrupt for decades – since at least the days of the Vietnam War. So what was to be done? A certain Henry Kissinger came up with the brilliant scam of the petrodollar. The US guaranteed the security of the OPEC countries who in exchange agreed to sell their oil exclusively in US dollars. In consequence of this agreement all the world's successful industrial countries, like Japan, Germany and later China, were obliged to acquire dollars in order to buy oil.

'Because in effect the whole world needed dollars – for what country can survive without oil? - the currency's value was maintained irrespective of the vast debts America incurred. The New York and London-based bankster clans ran riot. A more dangerous financial state of affairs would be hard to imagine. These parasites could print gazillions in *fiat* money, whose worth would be underwritten by the world's oil stock.

'Now, what would be the consequences if an OPEC country disregarded the agreement, and tried to sell oil via some other currency? For America and its ethnic banker masters it would spell disaster. Any such move would have to be nipped in the bud immediately, irrespective of the consequences. Which leads us to Iraq and Libya. What was Saddam Hussein planning to do?'

'I don't know.'

'Sell oil for euros. And what was Colonel Gaddafi going to do?'

'I don't know.'

'Sell oil for his new, gold-based African dinar – both these gentlemen seem to have come to a sticky end after making their decisions; pure coincidence I'm sure.

'Iran was next on the list; they'd also started selling oil for gold – but there was a problem with Iran. Unlike Iraq and Libya, Iran had powerful friends in China and Russia. Engineering some spurious war with hired mercenaries and forged evidence was not going to work this time. So our Neo-Con friends decided to set an example. Who was Iran's closest ally? Syria, and suddenly, *voilà*, there was another war. Aren't these coincidences amazing? The only group in the Arab world that showed any understanding of the real situation was Hezbollah.

'Now I admit Muslims can be dangerous, but dangerous like wild animals – like a lion. A lion's potentially very dangerous, yet once you master the appropriate techniques, and use due caution, you can get it to do almost anything – jump through hoops, balance balls on its nose – you name it.

'However, like all dangerous animals they must be kept securely under lock and key; can't have lions running loose around the place. The Global Meltdown threw open the cage doors, and our lions went on the rampage – would have done a lot of damage too, if the Russians hadn't intervened.'

Suddenly through the door came an attractive, slim, middle-aged lady dressed in a rather smart deep-blue dress. She quickly glanced around the bar, raising an eyebrow at the legionaries, before heading straight for Rudi. Who on earth was she? Walking rapidly with a confident and rather alluring swagger she approached Rudi, who felt something approximating panic begin to well up inside him – but she kept coming, smiling broadly, her pale-blue eyes sparkling in the bar's lights.

Ever closer she came. Rudi was on the verge of saying something he'd probably regret, when from behind him he heard in a foreign language – English? – 'Hello, Belle darling; see you've found the place alright.' He turned his head just in time to see the man rise from his bar stool and embrace the woman, who kissed him warmly on the cheek.

'I thought you said it would be quiet here tonight,' she continued in the same language, eyeing the crew of *legionarii* critically.

'It normally is mid-week, honey, but it appears some of the boys are getting in a little R&R earlier than usual.' Rudi was pretty sure the language was English, or some dialect of English.

Suddenly switching into heavily accented Latin, which was not quite fluent, she continued, 'And who's your handsome friend?' – turning to Rudi with a broad smile and extending a gloved hand.

'I'm Rudi, Rudi Stoger – nice to meet you,' he replied, taking her hand and making a slight bow. 'May I enquire as to your name?'

'Well, I'm Maybellene, of course – Mrs Foreman.'

Rudi looked blank. Maybellene turned to her husband in mock anger, 'Vernon, haven't you introduced yourself to this gentleman yet? You haven't, have you?'

Vernon smiled.

'Rudi, please forgive my husband; he tends to get carried away with his thoughts, forgetting the courtesies of civilised life, like introducing himself. Allow me – Vernon Foreman, this is Rudi …'

'Stoger.'

'Yes, Stoger: I was just about to say that.'

Still smiling broadly, Vernon held out his hand to Rudi and the two shook. Vernon offered his stool to his wife, who responded with a plastic smile. 'Please, Vernon, we're not teenagers – really; let's take a table over by the far window. It's a bit too noisy here. Will you join us, Rudi?'

As she moved towards the empty table she addressed her husband, again in

English, as he got up to follow. 'Thanks, honey; I'll have a glass of *Falanghina*.'

Vernon turned to Rudi. 'Would you like a drink?'

'No thanks, I've just bought this,' he said holding up his *Peroni*.

Vernon turned back to the bartender as he finished the drink in his hand. 'Another Jack Daniel's and a glass of *Falanghina*, please.'

Rudi obediently tailed Maybellene over to the table and sat down on her left, leaving the chair opposite free for Vernon. 'Your husband tells me you're from the South.'

'You'd better believe it, honey, I'm a Louisiana girl myself, and Vernon's originally from Georgia – we're both true Southerners. My granddaddy's great-granddaddy fought under Bragg, you know, at Murfreesboro and Chickamauga – where some Yankee laid him in his grave. However, it remains a point of honour within the family that the Confederacy won every battle in which we Hallenders fought. That was my maiden name, you know.'

'Congratulations; that's some family history you have there.'

'I realise this don't mean much to you over here in Europe, but back home in Dixie we wear our identity with pride – well, some of us do.'

Vernon came back with his wife's wine. 'Belle, I was talking with Rudi here about the situation with the Russians just before you came.'

'Honey, I've heard it all before – all those seminars and conferences you drag me to; but if you want to continue don't let me stop you. I have some catching up of my own to do. But remember, you've only got around 45 minutes: our table at *La Tartaruga Cantina* is booked for eight.'

Maybellene leaned back and crossed her legs; then, after making herself comfortable, took a sip of her *Falanghina*. Satisfied with the wine, she proceeded to pull a rather smart mobile phone from her blue leather Gianni Chiarini handbag and started to read through her text messages, replying to those deemed worthy.

Vernon turned to Rudi and picked up where they'd left off.

'Talking of the Russians, I can assure you, Rudi, that any country that spent 250 years under the Mongol yoke needed no introduction to the perils of Islam. They'd watched the rise and rise of Eurabia with growing alarm. What sort of future faced Russia, if the rest of Europe was absorbed into some greater Eurabian caliphate?

'Of course, the alien population inflows which created Eurabia were just another element in the NWO project, like globalisation and the formation of supranational bodies like the EU and NAFTA. However, it was the megalomania of another branch of the project – the central bankers – that caused the Meltdown. However, all these various elements have one thing in common: they're all engineered constructs incapable of independent existence outside the institutional machinery of government – and war destroyed that machinery.

'Which brings us to the here and now, and this Eurabian War – since what happens next is crucial. There are two paths open to us, and when I say "us", I mean all White European peoples. One path, in my opinion, leads to hell; the other to salvation – but I reiterate, these are merely my own subjective views.

'If Europe wins the war and re-establishes herself and her identity as a collection of unique Aryan peoples living on their own historically recognised territory – as laid out in the Declaration of Rouen – then the path to salvation opens up, for such a road is natural.

'There's a scientific term for these feelings of belonging to a specific group and holding altruistic impulses towards fellow members. It's called GST – Genetic Similarity Theory, which at its most basic level says people naturally prefer to be with others like themselves.

'It's natural for groups to want to live, procreate and interact among their fellow group members; mankind has a strong natural inclination towards creating homogeneous societies. It's no coincidence that all the leading examples of successful societies are homogeneous ones – diversity breeds conflict, and always has done.

'Once one grasps the reality of GST, the perversity of multiculturalism and multiracialism becomes self-evident. They are, quite simply, wholly unnatural. They are, in fact, weaponised ideologies fashioned by their originators to degrade Aryan society. Their mission was to create a model of society – or lack of society – conducive to the operation of the NWO project. With society effectively liquidised into a shapeless goo there would be no nasty little problems such as national preferences, or governments adopting policies that might hinder the formation of a global market fit for global exploitation. Always bear in mind the wisdom of our forefathers - *cui bono?*

'On the other hand, if Europe loses, or fails to carry through the required national rebuilding programmes based on the Declaration of Rouen, the old NWO forces will re-emerge, for they still exist. Wherever you find great power and wealth enveloped in a web of secrecy, you'll find the NWO – for that is the natural habitat of the ethnic group that controls the project. They will claim that the failure of the first attempt at utopia was due to a lack of rigour. The great goal of a harmonised humanity fit for exploitation by a globalised economic elite simply wasn't carried through to completion. I guarantee they will try again if given the opportunity.

'You've got to remember that American culture and influence had dominated Europe since the end of the Second European Civil War; but all that changed with the outbreak of the Eurabian War. Suddenly, a golden opportunity arose for Russia to re-enter European life – something that had failed to occur even following the fall of Communism. I know many in the West had contended that the Russians were not true Europeans, but semi-Turkified outsiders, following the dream of the Steppes – that is, endless expansion. The joke in all this was that the peddlers of these jibes, mostly the likes of Britain and France, were old global powers themselves. A distinct case of the pot calling the kettle black.

'In truth, once Communism fell, Russia remained far truer to the European tradition of independence and maintenance of the nation than the grovelling servitude of Western Europe, snared within the EU, little better than lackeys of the NWO and its destructive globalist project.

'Russia retained the concept of an independent *imperium*, something she once shared with the rest of Europe. Under American cultural occupation Europe had diminished into nothing more than a Yankified pastiche of herself – as had always been the plan. Don't believe me? Get yourself some education, soldier; have a read of Elliott Roosevelt's book. He was Franklin D. Roosevelt's son, you know.'

'I don't doubt it.'

Maybellene, without looking up from her texting, interjected, 'He may be dry enough to spin cotton, but Vernon knows his facts; I'd listen good if I were you, hun.'

'I intend to, Maybellene.'

Maybellene looked up and smiled at Rudi. 'Don't let me interrupt. Vernon, time's moving on.'

'Thank you, Belle, but I think we have a few minutes yet.'

Rudi continued. 'Getting back to the Russians – tell me, Vernon, am I right in thinking the Germans were the first to seek their help?'

'That's correct. There were already quite strong links between Germany and certain members of the Russian leadership. At the time, the National People's Government of Germany was locked in a war of incredible barbarity with its

Turkish colonists – though the situation generally was very complex. Not only were there Turkish and Arab groups running around, but also a strong Marxist group who looked to the social disintegration as a means of furthering their own agenda. In the larger cities, like Berlin and Hamburg, there were Muslims fighting Nationalists fighting Marxists, with other free-ranging factions – like the West Africans and Somalis – making a bad situation even worse.

'Following a tentative approach by a small German delegation, Russia decided to make formal contact, expressing sympathy and support for the NPG's aims. The two sides held initial discussions in Schwerin before a second round of talks was held in Kaliningrad. The final agreement of friendship and co-operation was signed in the NPG's provisional capital at Lübeck. Two weeks later, the first shipment of Russian weapons landed in Rostock. Significantly, the eastern half of Germany had fared much better than the west in defending its territory from the Turkish onslaught – though Berlin had fallen.

'From that point onwards, Russia played a key role in the liberation of Europe, supplying weapons and advice – even sending units of specialist troops to help where and when requested. Although many remained cautious of Russian aspirations, her underlying wish to see Europe remain a cultural and economic entity was never in doubt. In contrast, the aspirations of the Yankee elite had always been towards the liquidation of cultural and social markers in the name of universality and globalisation – the essence of the NWO project.

'The Russians had decided that they needed Europe to survive, not as an outpost of globalist American policy, or an Islamic offshoot of Saudi money, but as a European entity, inhabited by Europeans espousing ideas and concepts drawn from European culture. Without Russian help many European countries would have fallen, or at the very least suffered catastrophic damage from Eurabian forces.

'Europe woke up to the fact that although relations with an entity as powerful as Russia were never going to be easy, at least it was a European beast.

America's leadership had moved very far indeed from its European cultural roots, as the plight of her shrinking Nativist White population, holed up in their Mid-Western and North-Western strongholds, clearly showed.'

Vernon paused for a second to take a sip of his Jack Daniel's.

'That last part, incidentally, concerns my people. We are in a hole every bit as deep as that you faced before the war, and just like you, if salvation doesn't come soon, we'll succumb to the ocean of Latinos and Blacks devouring our beautiful country and my sweet, beloved Dixie. We've arrived at an historical turning point; it's make-or-break time for the White man in America.'

One of Rudi's friends from *Legio XII Palaiologos* came over to their table to see what was going on. Looking rather sheepish, he politely asked, 'Rudi, everything okay? Your friends were wondering what had become of you.'

Maybellene turned a beaming face to the youthful newcomer. 'Sugar bun, don't stand on ceremony; take a seat here next to me. What's your name, honey pie?'

Looking very uncomfortable and self-conscious, the young *legionarius* gingerly squeezed himself between Rudi and the bubbling Maybellene. 'My name's Martin Verbeck, ma'am; I just came over to check up on Rudi here.'

'Ma'am! I ain't Maw Bundrum yet – call me Maybellene, pumpkin. Oh, I think you'll find that Rudi is doing just dandy, fine as a frog hair split four ways – ain't I right, honey?'

'That's right, Maybellene. Martin, let me introduce you to Vernon Foreman, Maybellene's husband.'

The pair shook hands.

Rudi continued, 'Vernon's been discussing the situation here in Europe and some of the problems our fellow Aryans are facing over in America.'

'Are you some sort of expert, then?' asked Martin indelicately.

'He most certainly is,' responded Maybellene.

'My wife's very generous, though I do have some knowledge in these matters. As I was explaining to your friend Rudi here, I'm from the South; not all of us in Dixie have been over-enamoured by the antics of the Yankees up in Washington and our friends in New York. I work for a Southern organisation championing the interests of the South. We Southerners are not like the Northern Yankees; we have a different heritage and different cultural values. We also suffer, much as you do in Europe, from Yankee hubris and cultural arrogance. They think everyone south of the Mason–Dixon Line is a country hick chewing tobacco, sleeping with his first cousin and going to weekly meetings of the Klan.'

'I mean really, boys – have you seen Vernon's first cousin? And white so shows the stains, don't you think?' offered Maybellene provocatively, with a sly grin.

Rudi, chortling, turned back to Vernon and asked, 'So what's your role in this organisation?'

'I'm their European agent; I keep them informed of developments here, from the Russian intervention to the formation of the legions and the views of the *Curia* towards events as they evolve. We have a lot riding on this war; your defeat would condemn us to defeat as well – the globalist steamroller would crush us all.'

Martin piped up again, 'What's the name of this organisation of yours?'

'The Cemetery Ridge Foundation.'

'Never heard of it – Rudi?'

'Nope.'

'Allow me to enlighten y'all concerning matters Southern,' interjected Maybellene, searching for the organisation's website on her phone.

Vernon smiled and took another sip of his whiskey.

'Here we are,' announced Maybellene, handing her phone over to a worried-looking Martin. 'Don't fret, sugar: it's in Latin as well as English.' Martin glanced down at the screen and started reading the entry.

"The Cemetery Ridge Foundation is an organisation promoting the cultural and historical identity of the Southern states of America, usually referred to as Dixie. The organisation has been outspoken in its condemnation of Federal bodies that ignore the unique heritage of the South. In more recent times the Foundation has publicly attacked US foreign policy towards Europe. It also has a controversial record of championing White Nativist causes, in particular the plight of poor Whites."

'Is that where the foundation is located, Cemetery Ridge?' asked Rudi.

Vernon smiled wryly. 'My friend, it's obvious they don't teach American history over here in Europe. No, we're not based at Cemetery Ridge – Cemetery Ridge is at Gettysburg. I'm sure you're heard of Gettysburg?'

'I've found him!' It was Martin again, getting rather excited as he clutched Maybellene's phone.

'You've found him?' asked a bemused Rudi.

'Yeah, look: there's a list of the Foundation's officers here. "European Secretary: Vernon Foreman"; there's a photo as well.'

'You doubted me?' enquired Vernon.

'Forgive Martin: he gets a bit carried away at times. He's probably had a beer or two too many.' Martin ignored the slight.

Rudi picked up the thread of his previous questioning. 'But wasn't Gettysburg a defeat? Why name your organisation after a defeat?'

'True, Lee's army finally broke on Cemetery Ridge; it's really a case of "lest we forget". You asked earlier, am I still fighting the Civil War? Of course I am, and so is every Southerner worth his salt. Defeat doesn't remove the feeling or desire for your own country. I've stood many a time on Cemetery Ridge, looking down to where Pickett's brave boys gave their lives for their country – for my country. I can tell you, Rudi, it's reduced me to tears on more than one occasion. If ever you get over to America, give Gettysburg a visit. Ignore all the Yankee propaganda and get yourself up onto Cemetery Ridge – if you go in late fall, or the winter, you'll probably have most of the place to yourself. You can almost feel their presence when the sun's low and the cold wind whips through the naked trees. You see, Rudi, their ghosts are not at rest; they twist and turn, writhing in the chains that shackle Dixie to this day. I swear to God they call out to those with ears to listen, or perhaps I should say "accuse" – and I hear them: "Were our lives of such little consequence? We fell, we sacrificed our all for Dixie; what have you done?" No, Rudi, this Southerner at least has no intension of turning his back on Cemetery Ridge, or the plight of his people.

'The Greeks still celebrate Thermopylae – it was a defeat, but told you everything you needed to know about Greece's indomitable spirit. Yes, we lost, but as the old saying goes, the South will rise again – especially if I and The Cemetery Ridge Foundation have anything to do with it.'

'You tell 'em, honey. We ain't Yankees and never will be. Vernon's folks fought under Jackson and Lee in Virginia, like mine did under Bragg. When a nation lays down the lives of her sons and husbands, as Dixie did, it don't forget just because some damned Yankee politician up in Washington says so.'

'Thank you, Belle.' Vernon reached into his breast pocket and pulled out a couple of cards. 'Here, take one.'

The card merely confirmed everything they had learnt, though the Foundation's logo was quite striking in two-tone blue with the silhouette of a ridge under an elongated and flattened Confederate battle flag. The ridge and the bars of the stylised flag stood out from the lighter background. The Foundation's geographical location appeared to be Corinth, Mississippi. Rather ironic thought Rudi: over by the other window, where the boys from *Legio XII Palaiologos* were drinking and joking, was a man from the original Corinth. Small world.

Martin hadn't finished yet. 'I'm sorry to bother you again, Vernon, but as you're something of an expert I just need you to confirm something for me. We were originally formed to move around Europe quicker than the local forces, weren't we? How exactly did that come about?'

'No problem, Martin. Yes, the legions were formed for a very specific reason. Initially, after receiving Russian aid, each country tended to fight its own patch. Although an understandable reaction, this left individual national forces vulnerable to Jihadist concentrations, which were shuttled from one hotspot to the next, irrespective of national borders. The Europeans realised that they too needed a mobile military body. Thus was born the Pan-European Confederation or P-EC – forerunner of the *Curia*. In its inaugural meeting, held at Bonn, it was decided to create a pan-European military force to counter the mobile Jihadist Eurabian columns; their answer was to form the legions. *Legio I* came into existence with 100 men from twelve countries about five weeks later. They, being the first, were given the singular honour of being named after the Grand Old Man himself – *Augustus*.

'As the total strength of a legion had been set at 5,000, you can see how modest this initial effort was – a single *centuria*.

'The choice of language of operation was to prove inspirational, giving Europe a unique linguistic mode of cooperation without showing preference to any pre-existing national body. It's the language, gentlemen, we're speaking now, and is used throughout the entire *Copiae Legionariae Europaeae* – as you're well aware.

'Incidentally, the adjective *Europaeae* is inclusive. Although Russia decided to remain outside the political structure, nobody wished to suggest that Russia wasn't part of Europe – especially as she had just saved the continent. In practice Russians have always played a major role in the evolution of the *legiones,* with large numbers serving loyally, many having reached senior positions.

'The whole topic of Latin has long interested me. Do you know, we Southerners had quite a reputation at one time as Latinists? I wrote a detailed paper for the Foundation on the adoption of Latin by the legions – it's an amazing tale. Have we time, Belle?'

'If you're quick, honey.'

'You see, initially Bonn witnessed a whole series of ferocious arguments over which language the legions ought to use – it had already been decided that sending military units into battle using more than one language was suicidal and militarily unsustainable. The fact that the Bonn Conference itself had to rely on a small army of translators to accommodate the various national groups merely underlined the problem any multi-national force would face. That the force would have to operate through the medium of a single language was, therefore, an undisputed fact – but which language?

'On the first day, in particular, there were verbal dog-fights with English, German, French and Russian all being touted as an answer to the conundrum – with the Italians, Spaniards and Poles making it pretty clear that they would never accept any agreement which ignored their languages. It was stalemate. When somebody first raised Latin as an option most of the representatives subjected the idea to open ridicule – even if it would have solved the linguistic impasse. The torrid experience most had of school Latin made such a proposal frankly incomprehensible.

'Reports of the proceedings appeared both on the P-EC's official website, and in various unofficial blogs and tweets. Therefore the news that the idea of using Latin had been floated, only to be rejected, was known almost immediately. A group of enlightened Latin pedagogues decided to respond. The question they had to answer, and answer urgently, was: could Latin really shoulder such a burden? Were the stinging comments made at the Conference justified? The group consisted of a Dane, two Italians, a Czech and a German. They knew each other well, having circulated in the same academic institutions for most of their professional careers. An email was sent out by Ejnar Roby, the famous Danish Latinist – who incidentally, gentlemen, I had the honour of interviewing in Paris last year – inviting the other four to an online video conference that evening at 18:00 CET. After a short discussion all five agreed to meet the following morning in Bonn, Ejnar having provisionally booked rooms in the Hotel Rheinland. Travelling through Europe at night during a time of general social disintegration was challenging, to say the least, requiring the skirting of larger cities to avoid the worst of the fighting – though even this did not guarantee one's safety. Other more mundane problems, such as obtaining fuel, also loomed large. Improvisation was the order of the day, but one way or another all made it to the relative haven of Bonn by 11:00 the following morning.

'They had to act fast before the Bonn Congress came to a final decision. A plan was hurriedly concocted which proposed to base their new legionary Latin on late Vulgar Latin, and to use a combination of the Hebrew Ulpan methodology and the more direct method used by the French Foreign Legion to introduce the French language to its new military speakers. Using personal contacts, the group managed to schedule a presentation to the Congress for the following day when they could make their historic pitch for the use of Latin. The Congress was still deadlocked over the issue of language, and having thrown out Latin earlier seemed to have run out of alternatives – yet the pressure for a pan-European force was actually increasing as the fighting intensified. Owing more to the impasse than any faith in the assembled Latin professors, it had been decided to allow the ancient tongue a second crack of the whip.

'The next day the main assault was headed by Professor Lucca Mari, a native of Naples – incidentally, another gentleman I've had the pleasure of meeting.

A nicer man you could not find anywhere, and as keen a Latinist as exists in Europe. He proved a lively and persuasive speaker, making a number of significant points in support of Latin. The others followed suit, and by the end they'd collectively said enough to suggest that such a project might work. Some of the Congress representatives began to revise their former doubts. Lucca Mari got to his feet for a second time to pose a key question for the Congress. Standing confidently and speaking Italian in a powerful, clear voice he asked the assembly bluntly: if the state of Israel could resurrect a working version of Hebrew, why did they consider it impossible for Europe to do the same with Latin – a language, incidentally, which had a far stronger record as a general mode of communication than Hebrew ever did?

'After an hour or so of further discussions, a clear majority of the members agreed that if it could be made to work, Latin would solve the language problem. The Latin Group was given six months to produce results – a very tight schedule. Many delegates wondered whether Europe *had* six months; the fate of Rotterdam still reverberated among the delegates, reminding everybody of the need to act.'

Maybellene stood up. 'Okay, honey, that's it. If we don't leave now we'll be late for our booking, and I'm ready to eat.' She turned to face the two *legionarii*. 'Remember Vernon's words, boys: it ain't just Europe you're fighting for, but Dixie and all the lands of us White folks. Remember those brave Greeks at Thermopylae, and my papa's great-great-granddaddy laying down his life at Chickamauga. I ask just one thing of you – bring us victory!' She leaned over each in turn and kissed them on the cheek; Vernon followed, shaking hands with both of them for a second time. The pair gathered their belongings.

'You ready, Belle?' asked Vernon in English; she nodded and they headed for the bar door, waved a final farewell and disappeared into the Roman evening. Martin and Rudi rejoined the boys of *Legio XII Palaiologos,* their heads spinning from the encounter.

2.3 – Blueprint

Vasily Nikonov was leaning against the wall in one of the warehouse's numerous bays, putting together the final watch rotas before the *decuria* moved out at 06:00; the temperature had fallen quite sharply by now, even for a hardy Russian. Vasily had only been back in the *decuria* for a week since spending three days at the legionary education centre at Nevers, in France. His trip to France had been prompted by the requirements of seeking *optio* rank, one of which was a reasonable grasp of the tenets laid out in the Declaration of Rouen.

To reacquaint him with the finer points of the declaration, *Tribunus* Chris Jones – *Legio XXV's* education and training officer – had decided to pack off the aspiring *optio* to Nevers, where he'd shadow a new intake while receiving a number of individual tutorials from the centre's staff.

So it was that Vasily found himself sitting in the back of the main auditorium at Nevers, with six other candidates seeking *optio* rank, as *Legatus* Marcel Dubois stepped out to address a group of new recruits. Today's topic would be an introduction to the core tenets of the Declaration of Rouen. In front of him were 300 men of *Legio XLII Silva*.

After a cursory glance at the assembled *legionarii*, Dubois began: 'The principles on which the Legions function, via the *Curia*, are laid out in the Declaration of Rouen, a copy of which can be found in the back of your introduction booklet. I don't intend reading through it section by section; you're free to do so in your own time, but I shall be summarising some of the key points in today's introductory talk.

'Europe is our homeland, and when I say "our" I mean specifically White European Caucasians – sometimes referred to as Aryans. Africans have Africa, Asians have Asia – well, gentlemen, Europe is our native soil. In the past, as you're all aware, evil and corrupt elements within our own peoples, in alliance with another ethnic group, have connived and plotted, not only to deliver what was not theirs into the hands of aliens, but to replace us as the inhabitants of this continent.

'The Declaration of Rouen states unequivocally that Europe is European, under all circumstances – now and forever. No politician, no king or queen, no company nor corporation, no religion, no state bureaucracy, no *anything* overrides this principle. Any individual or authority that tries to offer up our indigenous territories to the alien – for whatever reason – can, and will, be declared *contra patriam*. Such an attempt will be deemed an act of cultural, racial and social genocide. Those accused will be obliged to appear before the standing Nürnberg II Commission, which as you know was originally constituted to try the old democratic political and corporate classes responsible for causing the Eurabian War. We've all seen the videos – those one-time self-important politicians and arrogant EU mandarins, trying to excuse their actions by throwing the blame on each other. It's pitiful stuff; they can't even lie convincingly. Most of them are now rotting away in the *Curia's* penitentiary in The Hague.

'Again, as you're aware, the Declaration of Rouen actually echoes the old UN Conventions. Now I know that by today no European country is a member of the rump UN, but I think it important for you to realise that even under the old NWO regimes, these democratic politicians were knowingly breaking the then international laws.'

The *legatus* then opened a small book he had been holding.

'Let me read to you a piece from the old UN Convention on the Prevention and Punishment of the Crime of Genocide, dated 9th December, 1948. Article 1 confirms that genocide can be committed, quote:

… in times of peace or war.

'Then in Article 2, genocide is defined as:

… acts committed with intent to destroy, in whole or in part, a national, ethical, racial or religious group.

'Article 2 goes on to give five categories of such acts, labelled A to E, the third of which, labelled C, says:

… deliberately inflicting on the group conditions of life calculated to bring about its physical destruction in whole or in part.

'Article 4 states that anybody responsible for any of the acts listed in Article 2 will be held accountable, including:

… constitutionally responsible rulers, public officials or private individuals.

'Incidentally, it was decided to prosecute the old democratic pluralist political elite under the rules of the UN Convention – even though by then Europe had abandoned the UN for the Declaration of Rouen, and strictly speaking these internationalist agreements no longer had any authority in Europe. To circumvent this problem the UN Convention was reinstated by a vote of the *Curia* for the duration of these specific cases. It was fitting, don't you think, that the political oligarchs who came to power under the corrupt democratic system and betrayed their own people, becoming immensely rich and powerful in the process, were finally brought to justice under the rules of one of their own utopian, globalist institutions? Should any of them ever be released – an unlikely event, I admit – any native European would be free to accuse them anew under the Declaration of Rouen and have them brought before the Nürnberg Commission a second time.'

Marcel finished off his introduction, then handed over to an experienced *centurio* for more practical instructions concerning the cleaning of weapons and the correct procedure for maintaining a suit of *arma proeliaria.*

Vasily and the other six trainee *optiones* filed out of the auditorium, leaving the *legionarii* of *Legio XLII Silva* to enjoy the *centurio's* presentation. Vasily headed over towards the officers' lounge, where he was supposed to meet Marcel Dubois for a tutorial; however, he was met instead by *Tribunus* László Csikos, organiser of the centre's training programmes. Rather diffidently, he explained:

'I'm sorry, *Decanus* Nikonov, but *Legatus* Dubois has had to cancel your tutorial owing to the arrival of an official from Bonn to discuss a couple of matters concerning *Curia* policy. The *Legatus* has rescheduled your meeting for 08:30 tomorrow morning. I presume that will not be a problem?'

Vasily had no choice but to agree.

Largely invisible to Vasily and the other *legionarii* was the academic work conducted in the background by the centre's staff. They were a collection of specialists whose services were constantly being sought as policy advisers by Bonn. In Marcel's case his particular speciality was the interpretation and operation of the principles laid out in the Declaration of Rouen. Since both the *Curia* and the entire *Copiae Legionariae Europaeae* functioned according to the Declaration, it was important to have a working interpretation of its meaning – and any resultant consequences.

Marcel Dubois was recognised by most as being a leading figure in the Declaration's interpretation, and had had numerous articles on the subject published in *Aquila Aureua* – the in-house magazine of the legions. Today an old sparring partner, James Wilson, a senior official in the *Curia,* had come down from Bonn to speak with him. As old acquaintances they operated on first name terms – James and Marcel. It was always the same topic, of course: the interpretation and implementation of the Declaration. Marcel already had an inkling of what was afoot; it concerned language and identity within European states – a delicate matter in some places. James arrived and the pair of them enjoyed a coffee and biscuit in the officers' mess, catching up on chitchat before Marcel suggested they remove to his private office for the business end of the meeting.

'Marcel, I appreciate that the Declaration states that the nation, not the state, is the core unit within Europe, but in several cases – France, Spain and Britain, to name but the most obvious examples – there has been in effect, a long-standing multinational state. Are you suggesting this situation is no longer tenable under the Declaration? Should the likes of Catalonia, Scotland and Brittany no longer be considered parts of their respective larger states?'

Marcel was aware that many of the Declaration's tenets were ruffling long-established feathers, a growing concern which was being directed ever more forcefully towards James' office in the *Curia*. That's why James was here: to chew over the challenging implications of the Declaration with one of Europe's leading interpreters of the visionary document.

'That would be my reading of the text: Europe is a collection of sovereign nations. The requirements of the nation – that unique group of people – override all other considerations, be they political or commercial. Neither is the suppression of one European nation by another acceptable. Typically, within multinational states the political and bureaucratic requirements of the state's largest national group override all other considerations. You mentioned Catalonia and Brittany; okay, let's take Brittany as an example.

'You might argue that business in Brittany is run in French, or even English if we're discussing international companies. You might argue that if Brittany remains within the French state, any attempt to use the Breton language would cause bureaucratic problems. You might even argue that the majority of the population would prefer to be French rather than Breton. The Declaration would counter by saying that the nation's interests come first. The word "interests" means far more than mere financial considerations; it encompasses a wide range of factors that impact on the social health of the nation as a living, organic construct. If, for example, commercial interests refuse to use Breton in Brittany, demanding to use French or English, the tenets of the Declaration would dictate that they find other locations to operate and the Breton government develop domestic enterprises as a matter of priority – which, incidentally, is one of the proper duties of a national government laid down in the Declaration. If the French state has a problem with the Breton language, Brittany should run her own affairs independently of France. Incidentally, any bureaucrat openly advocating the suppression of Breton to the benefit of French, from his office in Paris, would be sailing very close to the wind in regard to the Declaration; he might well be asked to explain to Nürnberg what exactly were his intentions regarding the Breton nation. Remember, such a man operating directly or indirectly to subdue a national group, is actually engaging in an act of genocide – the destruction of a people. That is undoubtedly the position the Declaration would support, and I suspect Nürnberg would as well.

'If the majority want to be French, rather than Breton, I would reply that the Breton nation obviously does not reside in such people. As long as a viable population of Bretons exists, the nation resides in them, and their requirements become pre-eminent.'

'They – the majority – would argue that's not democratic,' countered James.

'That's a dirty word, James; let's not have the stain of democratic greed and corruption touch the workings of the Declaration. It's an empty argument anyway; the larger will always override the lesser. If we were still under the iron boot of the oligarchs and their democratic dictatorship, where all were equal, we would have by now hundreds of millions of equal citizens with us from every corner of the globe. Would it not then be democratic for a Muslim majority in Paris, or a Muslim majority in London, to declare Sharia law? After all, they would be the democratic majority, would they not?

'And if you think about it logically, it can't be any other way. Were you to say a simple majority should decide policy, does that mean if I imported 100 million Chinese into France I could democratically call on the French state to adopt Chinese as the official language? That's globalist talk – the cancerous falsehood that we're all one. This mythology was created as a weapon by our enemies to use against us. The Declaration is built on the bedrock of identity – Brittany is Breton as France is French. The importation of Chinese is an act of genocide, as indeed is the importation of an overwhelming number of French into Brittany.

'You see, James, if it was corrupt and evil for the democratic charlatans to attempt to destroy the nations of Europe through massive third-world immigration, why is it any less a crime for a French bureaucrat to plan the gradual erosion of the Breton nation for the benefit of a French bureaucracy? In both cases Brittany ceases to exist, either under a tsunami of third-world immigrants or through linguistic and cultural colonisation by France.

'Neither do crude commercial arguments cut any ice with the Declaration. The Declaration would never succumb to any argument suggesting that the pursuit of profit by a private commercial concern overrides the right to existence of the Breton nation. Under the old NWO governments, commercial concerns were absolute masters – entire states went to extraordinary lengths to placate the desire for profit among an economic elite. This situation begged the question: who was serving whom? One obvious result of this unholy alliance between business, politicians and state bureaucracies was that nobody was looking after the interests of the citizens who theoretically elected these governments.

'As you know, the pooling of sovereignty is also not allowed under the Declaration; that's why no European nation today is a member of the UN, or any other inclusive international body. We may meet in the *Curia*, but only independent nations are allowed to sit – if you subscribe to pooled anything you'd be asked to leave; what do they call it up in Bonn?'

'"Big boys only".'

'That's it. But the Declaration also states that every European nation has the right to a seat on the *Curia*, which implies that every European nation has the right to sovereignty. And all such nations operate under the physical protection of the legions, which are sworn to uphold the tenets of the Declaration.

'I should make one further point here, James. The Declaration is not universal; it does not claim that these principles should be applied across the globe. Indeed, it goes out of its way to refute any authority outside Europe – the future of Asia is an Asian concern, as Africa is an African one and so forth. The Declaration is a European document, aimed at Europeans for Europeans – nobody else.

'Unfortunately, a lot of our bureaucrats seem to me to be stuck in a time warp, still thinking like utopian members of the NWO plotting to bring the planet to heel for commercial exploitation. First and foremost, we are members of a nation; it constitutes our core group identity. That's why it is so important to safeguard and protect it, in the face of the NWO's attempts to blend humanity into a single soup for their own selfish interests. *Iuppiter immortalis,* James –this was the core issue that drove us to war in the first place.

'I'm a proud Frenchman: I love my people, my country, my history and my culture – but I'm fully aware of the attitude of some of those toffee-nosed elite up in Paris, who look down their beaks at small nations like Brittany, and the Basque country, as if they had no right to exist. They are the remnants of the old order, and the sooner they fade away the better. Look at the heritage of these smaller nations and what they represent to us Europeans. The Bretons, along with the Scots, Welsh and Irish, are the last of the Celtic peoples – one of the foundation peoples of our continent. Were you aware that the Welsh have the longest unbroken poetic tradition in Europe? Are they to be destroyed in order to keep some civil servant in London happy? Or to allow some multinational company to establish its factory there, so long as the wages remain low? Or what of the Basques? Theirs is the only surviving pre-Indo-European language still in existence; its importance is inestimable to Europe, but worthless to globalist corporations. Who's right? The Declaration says the nation is always paramount. Tell me, James, would you be prepared to fight, and if need be die, in order for some international corporation to make billions in profit? Would any sane individual? Yet democratic governments, stretching back centuries have sacrificed whole peoples, cultures and identities in the name of Mammon.

'I've fought and risked my life on many occasions, not for the NWO and its corporate tentacles, but the continuance of this continent and its unique peoples. This is my family's home, and the home of every one of us who is European.

'No, James, the Declaration treats all our nations as equals; every European nation has the right to a national life and national existence – bar nothing. I'm sorry if that makes your life harder, but if we are fighting for anything it's for the future of our peoples – all of them, from little Iceland and Estonia to the likes of mighty Germany and Italy.'

2.4 – Sentinel

It was nearly 22:30; Vasily drifted over towards Conrad Black and Tomasz Klukowski, who were dozing in a dark corner. He leant over and gently rocked them awake with his boot. As the pair got their kit together, Theo Dioletis came back from patrolling the warehouse perimeter and awoke Marco Bellini to start his vigil.

Alvero Vargas and Carlos Batista returned from duty, blowing out steaming clouds of warm breath in the chill air. Vasily enquired how things had gone; the pair answered that all was quiet – no sign of Jihadists. Within earshot a few of the men were still awake, either eating or quietly preparing kit.

Alvero and Carlos found a corner in one of the bays and started to make some food. Carlos decided to change the T-shirt he was wearing under his armour, after having been caught in a brief, icy shower during the watch. Across the way from the two Spaniards Theo Dioletis was chatting quietly about the prospects for tomorrow with Jan Eberhardt, while enjoying a smoke.

Suddenly Jan caught sight of Carlos changing his shirt and froze, giving Theo a nudge to look. Alvero caught their glances and smiled; he'd seen it all before. Carlos had a rather spectacular scar on his chest that never failed to excite comment among those who'd never seen it before. Alvero turned to Carlos and said in Spanish, 'You've got admirers again.' Carlos glanced over at Theo and Jan who looked away, embarrassed.

'When's the operation scheduled?' continued Alvero.

'Next month, in the legionary hospital in Vienna. I can't wait.' Although medically speaking Carlos' wound required no further operation it had been decided to clean up the scar with some plastic surgery.

The pair settled down as the vacuum-packed spicy sausage in rice with mixed vegetables slowly cooked on the portable burner. They were both dog-tired, but knew the morning would bring plenty to stir the blood and adrenaline levels. While Carlos busied himself looking for a dry T-shirt and some coffee from his pack, Alvero's mind returned to the deep scar on Carlos' chest and the circumstances that brought it about.

Two years earlier *Legio XXV Gediminas* had been one of four legions charged with guarding the Spanish coastline, from the Portuguese border in the West to the French border in the North. This vast area had been plagued by Jihadist raiders from North Africa, prompting a heavy response from the *Curia*. *Legio XXV Gediminas* had been given the task of defending the Andalucian coast. Although the real firepower was provided by helicopter gunships, supported by ground-attack aircraft, boots were also required on the ground. So it was that individual *centuriae* were given areas of responsibility, and in turn these areas were subdivided into sections small enough for individual *decuriae* to patrol. Pairs of *legionarii* would then be given sub-sections to sweep, with strict orders to call in support if contact was made.

However, Andalucía is a very large province with a very long coastline, and the men often found themselves having to improvise on the spot. Alvero's thoughts drifted back to the fateful day; it had been so hot …

Two figures moved slowly forward, cautiously navigating a course through the ruins of the hotel, their eyes searching for any sudden movement or telltale sign. The sun had already been up for a couple of hours, and was now streaming brightly through the building's skeleton. Heat shimmered off the bleached concrete, while a brisk, warm wind blew from the sea, catching pieces of nondescript cloth and plastic that billowed nosily, hooked by the spindly arms of rusting steel rods protruding from the jumble of broken concrete blocks littering the floor.

The pair had been threading their way through a labyrinth of deserted streets and abandoned buildings since dawn, tracking westwards along the endless shoreline. The contrast between the wreckage of an historic past, and the eternal beauty that is nature, was savage – even for those whose profession it was to enter such worlds. Standing on the seashore, facing the sea so that the tortured torso of the town no longer blighted the horizon, one could almost touch the old glory, sauntering the streets once again of this playground of summertime dreams and families slipping life's drudgery for a snatched week or two of escapism. Yet ultimately it wasn't the brochured fantasies that stirred the breast, but those intimate images of shared social existence in all their rich domestic humanity: mothers clucking over their brood, fathers fussing with gadgets, brothers teasing sisters and daughters taking their first lessons in the art of manipulation. Carlos had indulged in such daydreaming before, when sweeping through the smaller, more homely resorts down towards Motril; it was a dangerous habit.

Despite his training, and the unforgiving nature of his calling, he could no more stifle these urges than he could deny his identity. So it was that his thoughts began to wander yet again, if only momentarily, back to an age of innocence; for this place held happy childhood memories – indeed, this very hotel. As he blinked the sweat from his eyes, an image formed in his mind of Juanita leaping into the pool, giggling in her bright red swimming costume – followed by the pang of an even more poignant memory. There they were, he and she in their best clothes, dancing with their parents and the other guests in the cool evening concert to the familiar Castilian songs.

A flush of anger swept over him – all lost: and for what? He glanced down at the *Aquila Legionaria* embossed on his nano-tungsten breastplate, as a pang of an entirely darker nature gripped him. They pushed on dutifully into the core of the old wreck, Carlos peering out to his left towards the sea and the area where he remembered the pool having been. His gaze was met by a mound of rubble peppered with litter, framed in a deep azure sky populated by the occasional seagull, lazily drifting on the breeze. He could even see the tops of the beach palm trees, incongruously showing above the heaped debris.

His attention drifted towards Alvero, his partner, ten metres or so to his left. Heavily armed and clad entirely in grey, black and brown camouflaged armour, he cut an impressive figure – something that had never crossed Carlos's mind until this moment. It was not so much contempt that familiarity had bred as presumption. Both wore a carbon-steel battlefield *gladius* on their left hip, though its secondary duty as a symbolic image of *imperium* was lost on this deserted concrete wilderness. As experienced *evocati*, both also had another pristine, parade-ground *gladius*, safely tucked away back at base, in their polished *vaginae*, awaiting a more auspicious occasion. However, neither the battlefield nor parade-ground version were, nor had ever been, mere decoration.

A shadow blinked in the corner of Carlos' vision. His mind cleared instantaneously, leaving his left foot frozen in mid-stride as his eyes lasered into the skeleton's innards. They'd seen it all before, of course, dozens of times up and down the coast. There was no need for any orders. Without uttering a word Alvaro dropped behind a pile of broken bricks and concrete. Carlos silently took position under cover of a large concrete block immediately in front of him, bringing his GA-6 to the firing position – all the while scanning the derelict wasteland through the gun's sights. His well-drilled thumb expertly operated the computer-enhanced scope via the control pad just above the trigger. He zoomed in and out of suspicious shadows, flicking from infrared and back again according to the sun's brightness. All the while the GA-6's laser target finder, invisible to the naked eye but displayed as hairlines on the scope's internal HUD, followed Carlos's movements faultlessly. The seconds passed nervously....

Nothing.

The two remained motionless, the sweat from their bodies steaming up the inside of their *arma proeliaria*. It was heavy kit, covering most of the body – except for the face. Made of nanotech-derived tungsten with ceramic plate inserts, even the boots were of the same material, with inserts for the shin, ankle and base of the boot – in case one stepped on a mine. The only non-tungsten component was the composite steel helmet. Carlos could feel the heat escaping from the armour's vents at the back of his neck. He knew from long experience that by the time they got back to barracks the inside of the armour would stink – no matter what *Dietrich Munitionssysteme GmbH*'s blurb claimed; it would all need to be swabbed down and wiped with disinfectant before their next recce. In this heat it also chafed his crotch. To take his mind off the sudden urge to scratch himself, utterly impossible of course while incarcerated in armour, he glanced at the bottom left corner of the GA-6's HUD. It showed *automatice*. He moved his thumb onto the control pad and the HUD's display changed to *semi-automatice*, then *sole* and finally *tunde*. A slight humming noise came momentarily from the gun as its innards adjusted to the new setting. More seconds dragged by....

Nothing.

Carlos hated these games of cat and mouse. Why couldn't the bastards just stand their ground and fight – wasn't Allah supposed to be with them? Well, he couldn't wait much longer; a static target was a certain target. His right hand moved to the rim of his helmet where the controls for the COMS system were situated. He activated the communications hologram, which shimmered as a small rectangle just to his right at eye level. With the settings on *vicinia* he spoke softly into his helmet's built-in mic in Spanish: 'Alvero, keep alert; I'm going to circle around the back.' Alvero gave a thumbs up.

Carlos quickly readjusted the GA-6 to *semi-automatice* and slid out to his right, all the while keeping a low profile. He stepped from the shadow of the hotel's shell onto what had been the main entrance drive. He glanced up at the hotel's front – once so grand. Miraculously a few letters, 'SAB …', were still attached to the battered canopy, though Carlos had no need of clues to solve their puzzle, those familiar sentinels to a betrayed past. Anger was becoming a regular acquaintance, which in his business was a handicap.

There was no shade out here and the heat and brightness caused Carlos to pause as his eyes adjusted to the glare. He grunted a stifled *di immortales,* more in reaction to the sun's immense presence rather than a call to the Gods. He advanced again, rounding the side of the building moving towards the beachfront. Thirty metres in front of him was a jagged line of steel rods protruding from a gigantic slab of concrete that had once constituted the hotel's third-floor wall. Carlos scanned the area through the GA-6's scope – but the sun was so intense that even the technological wizardry of the *Klaus Zweig* optical scope, which sat atop the *Hirsch & Kalb GmbH* GA-6, struggled to cope.

He fingered the trigger nervously. He took another step forward, when suddenly a blur shot from the tangled mess of steel and concrete straight into the path of the blinding sun. In the bat of an eye Carlos had snapped the GA-6 into his shoulder and let loose a burst of *semi-automatice.* In the remainder of the three seconds the entire incident occupied he watched in shocked relief as the various dismembered parts of the cat descended to earth in a shower of fur.

He slumped down against an equally dismembered section of the hotel's third floor. He couldn't help himself, the release was immense; he began to laugh violently, venting his pent-up tension. Barely able to string a coherent sentence together, he half-blurted, 'Alvero!' into his helmet's mic, followed by a stumbling, chuckling, 'It was a fucking cat!'

But instead of Alvero's voice, Carlos's announcement was met by the distinctive crackle of a GA-6 firing on *automatice*, and the short boom of a grenade being discharged from its under-barrel launcher. Carlos grabbed his gun with his right hand, while smacking his left hand down hard on the floor as he levered himself powerfully to his feet. His backside had barely left the ground when a sledgehammer blow hit him square in the chest, knocking the wind out of his lungs and driving him sprawling backwards, beyond the remains of the third floor and onto the flat of his back. He lay there contemplating the sun, which filled his entire world, seemingly blazing directly into his eyes. Time oozed past viscously, taking on the consistency of treacle. He vaguely heard Alvero screaming at him in his earpiece, but as the passing of time ground to a snail's pace the sun's brightness dimmed, and the annoying crackling and banging drifted completely from his consciousness. His head seemed to sink slowly backwards, descending into the warm, silky embrace of the welcoming dark.

Alvero was hunkered down amongst the hotel ruins, his GA-6 on *automatice.* He had watched nervously as Carlos slipped out of the side of the building. It was hot and sweaty, and he was slowly being broiled in his own armour. He had no more love for this murderous version of hide-and-seek than Carlos; every nerve tingled, every muscle twitched – it was almost an exercise in masochism. It seemed like hours since Carlos had left, though Alvero was experienced enough to know that in reality it had been but a matter of minutes – time stretched like plasticine under the tension of imminent contact. The burst of gunfire sliced through everything, banishing all concerns in an instant. His mind clicked into battle mode while he scanned the rubble intently through the GA-6's scope. Various scenarios raced wildly through his head as he made a quick mental inventory of his weaponry: the GA-6 had the standard sixty rounds in the multi-mag, there were four more mags on his webbing plus twelve extra grenades for the under-barrel launcher – little wonder he was being broiled. 'Come on – where are you, Carlos?' The seconds piled up like Everest. He strained his ears for any clue as to what had happened, but except for the wind and the seagulls, all was silent. His hand started to move slowly towards his helmet's rim; he activated the COMS hologram. He was on the point of hailing his partner when through his swirling thoughts came the thick Cantabrian accent with which he was so familiar. 'Alvero! ... It was a fucking cat!'

The next few seconds blurred in front of his racing mind as the world exploded into a kaleidoscope of sound and noise. Alvero's mouth opened and

2.4 – SENTINEL

words formed in his mind, but even as the breath from his lungs passed over his larynx the words refused to emerge. They, and every other bodily function, froze as his brain struggled to respond to the images his optical nerves were frenetically relaying. Like some creature from a fog-bound swamp of horror fiction, there arose a figure of terror brandishing an Armalite AS-20 – not ten metres from Alvero's position. Behind the ominous silhouette a dozen other shapes could be made out, moving rapidly towards the beach. Gunfire broke out immediately.

Training has two levels. There's an initial mechanical level, the level where one is shown, childlike, how to perform a task, which one then imitates. The end result is an approximation of the original, perhaps carried out with determination, but inevitably bearing the mark of the apprentice.

However, there's another level of training, where seemingly simple tasks are repeated over and over again, under ever more difficult circumstances. This training goes on until the task can be carried out virtually subconsciously under almost any conditions. When one reaches this level of training other forces, beyond the mere mechanical, are engaged. The surface level of the mind is almost absent as the body responds to its now deeply ingrained programming – the hallmark of a master.

Were one to ask Alvero what exactly happened next, he could give a superficially coherent answer – but in reality his conscious mind had little to do with it. The GA-6 spat death on all sides, pumping grenade after grenade into the thicker groups of shadows. As he spun from one firing point to the next he barked savagely into his mic in Spanish, 'Carlos, speak to me; come in, Carlos.' There was no response.

Alvero was aware of bullets ricocheting around him, but nothing hit him directly. He swung from target to target, the scope's HUD ranging among the shadows, the crosshairs changing from green to red when on target, and then flashing red when locked – every time followed by the crack of the GA-6.

A flick of the thumb brought up the grenade ranger on the scope's HUD, displaying the target area as a white grid. Alvero zoomed in, hunting his elusive prey. The HUD turned red on hitting a potential target, and flashed when locked onto the target area. Three times Alvero sent out the electronic net to flash scarlet on some darkened jumble of concrete rubble. Three times the pulsating glow was followed by the thud of a grenade leaving the GA-6's under-barrel launcher. Three times the smoking launcher was answered with the crash of detonation, followed by the concussion blast racing over the shattered concrete at the speed of sound.

After what seemed an eternity the firing died away, as half a dozen shapes broke into the direct sunlight beyond the hotel, running down the beach.

Alvero dropped to his knee, lined up the nearest two on the GA-6's crosshairs and fired; both figures fell. The remaining four frantically heaved a concealed motorboat from its camouflage into the gentle Mediterranean breakers, the engine roaring even before the keel touched the water. Alvero flicked the scope's HUD to grenade launcher, only to be informed that the under-barrel launcher needed reloading. Swearing furiously, he fumbled to release three grenades from his webbing.

The spray from the outboard engine obscured the boat as the remaining insurgents headed back to Africa – they were out of range of the launcher by now, although Alvero continued to fire the GA-6 on *sole* until the multi-mag ran out of ammo. The boat had passed the furthest whitecap as he reloaded the GA-6 and scanned the boat again through the scope. In theory he could still hit them, but with the boat bouncing around at this distance it would be a waste of ammo; they were gone. He got to his feet and ran to the front of the hotel, fearing the worst. He found Carlos lying under blinding sunlight in a pool of scarlet. He fell to Carlos' side and ripped the med kit from his *arma proeliaria's* thigh compartment, while simultaneously knocking his helmet's COMS system from *vicinia* to *praetorium*. A voice confirmed connection. He immediately launched into a string of instructions snapped out in crisp Latin: 'Hispalis, come in: hello, Hispalis?'

'Hispalis here; report in, please.'

'Section R5 clearance team, man down, need immediate evac – direct hit on front plate. Pinpoint and confirm – over'

'Understood; location pinpointed, evac request acknowledged.'

Of course the helicopter would not be coming from Hispalis itself – Carlos would have been dead long before it arrived; no, this was obviously coming from the Almeria base.

'*Acceptum*, insertion cleared from Section R5; approx nine killed, four escaped by boat crossing the straits. Request hunt and destroy on remnants of insertion group.'

There was a short pause, then in impeccable Latin – though with a slight Dutch accent – the operator responded, 'Acknowledged; hunt-and-destroy mission requested on remnant of insertion group from Section R5 crossing the straits. Clean-up team for Section R5 has been ordered.'

Alvero unclipped the breast unit of Carlos' armour at the side and slowly opened it up, exposing the wound to his chest. The bullet had passed through the armour, but the ceramic plate had taken much of the sting out of its impact. Even so, Alvero reckoned he had no more than an hour maximum unless medical help arrived – it would be close. He did what he could with the basic equipment available, applying a battlefield dressing to the wound – a neat job if he said so himself.

There was little more he could do. He found a piece of old plastic sheeting – once such a common commodity in these parts – which he stretched over a crude timber frame to keep the worst of the sun off Carlos. It was an eerie experience: an entire town, an entire province, emptied of people and now inhabited by assorted feral cats and dogs along with an army of rats – of both varieties.

Once he was happy that Carlos was comfortable, or at least as comfortable as he was going to be under the circumstances, Alvero returned to the hotel. He clambered over a few large concrete blocks and came upon a body. It was lying face down. Alvero rolled it over with his boot, keeping the GA-6 trained on the carcass at all times – they had been known to take out *legionarii* with suicide bombs before now. If this cadaver so much as twitched it would get a fresh spraying from the GA-6.

The equipment was as expected: headscarf, armoured vest and dark combats – though the colour could vary. Next to the corpse he found the obligatory Armalite, highlighting the fact that virtually all the Eurab gear came from America. The Asians wouldn't supply them, but the Americans … that was a different story. All the weaponry and kit looked newish and in the pocket sewn into the armoured vest he discovered a satellite locator: another typical piece of kit found on insurgents. They were led to their targets by satellite – American satellites.

He went through the rest of the bodies, finding the same basic assortment of equipment as the first. Finally he came upon the corpse of the insurgent who had materialised so ominously at the very outset of the firefight. This one was somewhat different from the rest, sporting a holstered pistol in addition to the compulsory Armalite. He also had a non-standard hip pouch, in which Alvero found a map of the province. This was obviously the group's leader, though Alvero knew there would be no confirmation of this fact on the body – no insignia or written orders.

He wandered back to Carlos, his ear cocked for the sound of the expected helicopter, all the while studying the map. Unlike Carlos, Alvero had never been to these parts prior to the war, but even he felt the irony as he scanned the cartographical network of names and coloured lines. Here, under his nose, was the province as it had been: busy towns and villages, road and rail networks, with important cultural and historical sites marked by yellow symbols. He looked up from the map at the landscape before his eyes. In front of him was a roughly triangular-shaped facade, which had once housed comfortable apartments with shops and a restaurant on the ground floor. To his right, leading off into the distance, were streets of low, piled rubble, behind which stood tall, gaunt concrete figures – gaping holes for windows, burnt-out from within, their external surfaces a blotched patchwork of heat stains. Alvero looked down at the map again in an attempt to reconcile the paper image of ordered modernity with the timeless vision of Armageddon before his eyes. He felt like some Roman soldier of an earlier age, witnessing the destruction of Western civilisation by the barbarian hordes – only with one crucial difference.

Ancient Rome had lost her war; we were winning ours. Alvero smiled grimly and folded the map. Even so, Old Europa had not witnessed destruction on this scale in a hundred years; we had paid a heavy price for our arrogance and hubris. His eye caught a black speck in the bright sky, approaching from the east, and within a couple of minutes the sound of the 'copter could be heard clearly.

The helicopter landed on a piece of open ground just to the side of the hotel, guarded by the pockmarked shell of a giant fibreglass monkey – the sole survivor of what once had been a small amusement park. The medics ran from the Kamov Mi-97 towards Alvero, who was waving a ragged piece of plastic sheeting. He cried out in Latin to the medics, 'He's here,' trying unsuccessfully to raise his voice above the din of the Kamov. The paramedics got to work on Carlos immediately. Alvero looked on nervously as they carried him back to the 'copter and loaded his stretcher into a berth designed for the purpose. Alvero leapt aboard beside the medics. The roar from the Kamov's engines rose to a howl as it lifted off.

They headed back east along the coast. Once the 'copter levelled off, one of the medics turned to Alvero and, half-shouting in an effort to get his voice heard above the engines, said, 'Heard you've been busy,' in heavily accented Latin – Danish? Or Swedish perhaps? Alvero watched the second medic attach a plasma bottle to Carlos' arm. 'We're always busy,' he replied. 'They just keep coming; it's high time we took the fight to them, or we'll never see the back of these locusts.'

The medic smiled knowingly. 'Well, at least you took your fair share of them. I saw a lorry leaving base to pick up the remains of your handiwork as we lifted off.'

'What about him?' Alvero asked, nodding towards Carlos. 'He's taken a direct hit,' the medic replied, 'but I think we caught it in time, though we'll only know for certain once we get him back to base. If he does make it, I doubt you'll be seeing him back in your unit for a while.' Alvero nodded his thanks. They travelled the rest of the way in silence.

As the helicopter set down at Almeria, a crash crew ran forward and bundled Carlos into a waiting ambulance that whisked him to surgery in a babble of instructions, all in Latin, though the accents came from every corner of Europe.

2.5 – The Turning of the Tide

Alvero and Carlos, having finished their spicy sausage, settled down as best they could for some sleep; Vasily would soon be waking the whole *decuria* for the assault on Soviet City.

At 01:30 Conrad Black and Tomasz Klukowski returned from their watch, momentarily awaking some of the others as they bedded down. Sleepily, Alvero glanced over towards Conrad and Tomasz and gave the pair a wry grin before slipping back into deep sleep.

Tomasz wrapped a thermal blanket around himself as he tried to find a comfortable spot. However, Alvero's grin had jogged his memory and instead of falling asleep, he recalled various incidents from when he had first joined *Legio XXV Gediminas* some 18 months previously, during the legion's drive through southern France before passing into northern Italy.

Having already cleaned out the upper Rhône valley the legion headed south towards the viper's nest that was the Muslim Caliphate of Marseilles. Another five legions, *III Julian, XVI Dimitri, XVII Aetius, XXXII Béla* and *XXXV De Valette,* along with units from the reconstituted French army, advanced on the occupied city from different directions, sweeping the surrounding country clean of any remaining pockets of Eurab resistance.

Although Tomasz was fully aware of the enormity of the conflict being waged all around him – the greatest since the end of the Second European Civil War – it was the little things that stuck with him. His mind's eye conjured up a series of extraordinary, yet very personal, experiences: sharing a smoke with a wounded comrade under Eurabian fire in a Burgundian barn, or when the whole *decuria* spread out along the banks of a stream near Grenoble to soak their sore feet in the soothing cold water – much to the amusement of a group of passing schoolchildren. Then there was that mug of fresh coffee – the best he'd ever tasted – given gratefully by a relieved housewife standing outside her cottage after the liberation of the stunningly beautiful commune of Laffrey on an idyllic spring day. However, it was an incident of an altogether different hue that was seared deepest into Tomasz's memory – an event that encapsulated his belief that Europa had finally embarked on the path destined for her by the Gods.

Following some hard fighting around Lyon he'd been sitting with Alvero, atop a Finnish-built Sisu Mark III Mannerheim troop carrier, on a glorious summer's day, in a column half a mile long carrying 2nd and 6th *Cohortes* southwards. As the column pushed through a couple of villages north of Valence, some of the men set up a speaker system on their carrier and soon the epic tune *Promontory* began blasting out across the valley. The whole episode took on a surreal character – much like the *Ride of the Valkyries* scene in the film *Apocalypse Now*. All were affected; all felt the power of the music stirring their emotions, transforming them spiritually into woad-encrusted, torc-embellished Celtic warriors ready to pay, and to extract, the debt of blood owed for the *patria*. A couple of Irish lads – Breandan Ó Dubhthaigh and Lochlann Ó Nualláin from 9th *Decuria* (9-3-6, XXV) – got up on their carrier's turret and began dancing an informal jig in unison to the track's mesmerising pipes and drums, accompanied by the rhythmic clapping of their surrounding brothers-in-arms. A steel-tinged determination to reap a long-overdue retribution washed over the men, as the music filled them with a mounting sense of mission and purpose. They'd thrown off the alien shackles and at the eleventh hour had liberated Holy Europa from Hell's Spawn. Now they were closing in on Marseilles, every revolution of the Mannerheim's wheels bringing them closer to their goal, burning with resolve to complete the command of their resurrected Aryan Gods. It was one of those immortal moments indelibly imprinted on Tomasz's soul.

2.6 – Soviet City

At 05:00 Vasily woke Marco Bellini and told him to start waking the others. While Marco set about his task, Vasily raised 3rd *Centuria* on the COMS system and asked to speak with De Witt. The *centurio* was tied up finalising support details with 6th *Cohors*, so Vasily would have to be satisfied with Popovic, the *optio*. The pair rapidly went through the plans and Popovic confirmed the targets specified for 7th *Decuria*.

The men busied themselves preparing for the planned assault. Several had slipped around the back of the warehouse for calls of nature, while others packed away sleeping kit, checked their equipment or knocked up some rudimentary breakfast.

Vasily called all the men together and laid out a large map of the Soviet City complex on the floor. He showed their present location, and the route of their tab to the first target; other *decuriae* would be operating either side of them. They were scheduled to take out three warehouses themselves and to amalgamate with the rest of 3rd *Centuria* for the final assault on the huge building known as the Gulag, which in actuality was the main administrative block for Soviet City.

Three sappers from 1st *Centuria* had propitiously arrived in time to catch Vasily's briefing, carrying explosives and timing devises for blasting through the various warehouse walls.

2.6 – SOVIET CITY

That was the theory, according to De Witt's plan.

At exactly 06:00, 7th *Decuria* began their five-kilometre tab to Soviet City. It was still dark; the sun wouldn't rise for another 50 minutes at this time of the year. The air was sharp, their breath forming great clouds of steam as they pushed on in silence.

Thrace is a largely flat country with the odd ridge to break up the often-monotonous landscape. That morning the winds blew unhindered across the Thracian plains, bringing gusty showers that lashed the toiling *legionarii*. The sun began ponderously rising as the entire *centuria* reached a ragged ridge overlooking the main Soviet City complex. Through binoculars, or the sights on their GA-6s, the men scanned their target. The original, old-fashioned warehouses, made of dark-red brick, formed a massive monolithic block of structures around a kilometre to their front. In the muddy light of a raw October morning they were almost Victorian in their Satanic aura. Intelligence indicated that there were very few Jihadists in this original section of the site. According to De Witt's plan, 10th *Decuria* would enter the forbidding maze of buildings alone and sweep through its innards; little, if any, contact was anticipated.

Off to the left, perhaps two kilometres away, were the newer elements of Soviet City, namely grim, utilitarian warehouses even more vast than those in which the men had bivouacked overnight. Beyond these giants were a series of concrete-and-steel packing and shipping units. Once again these were very large structures, as long as the warehouses though not as high. It was in these buildings that the Jihadist forces were expected to be at their strongest. Far off, behind the buildings in the immediate foreground, could be seen the multi-storeyed Gulag, sitting within its walled compound.

Although the sun was slowly rising, the heavy cloud cover and wintry conditions meant visibility remained poor. The men advanced from one scrubby patch of stunted, overgrown bushes and long grass to the next; manoeuvring across rough, unmetalled, rock-strewn roads and around mounds of rubble and nondescript debris thoughtlessly left by Turkish workmen.

10th *Decuria* peeled off from the *centuria* and began working around the side of the old section of Soviet City. The other nine *decuriae* spread out and stealthily began their approach towards the newer units over the open, windswept terrain. De Witt activated his COMS system to check the support units. Both helicopters were within ten minutes' flying time, the 155 mm howitzers were ready, though far out of sight of any Jihadist. The two Wiesel III mobile mortar units and two BPM Kord heavy machine-gun carriers were much closer – so close in fact that De Witt ordered them to fall back lest they alert the Jihadists.

Everything appeared calm; Soviet City sat silent and desolate in the gloom of the overcast morning. The men trudged forward for another fifteen minutes, then across the COMS system came the news that 10th *Decuria* had entered the old complex. Everybody instinctively responded to the news by momentarily glancing at the warehouses to their right; the dark red of their brick walls offset by the blue plastic sheeting, used to cover their leaky roofs, boisterously billowing in the autumn wind whipping across the landscape.

De Witt advanced the remainder of the *centuria* for another five minutes, before bringing the men to a halt while he scanned the nearest half dozen buildings with his binoculars. He saw nothing. No guards, no sentries, no smoke or vehicles moving about: the whole place appeared deserted. None of this made sense; if anything it confirmed De Witt's suspicion that there were Jihadists here, who more than likely were fully aware of his whereabouts and had no doubt prepared a warm Jihadist welcome for them.

The men could sense the tension rising; they rechecked their weapons and positioning. Each *decuria* had a GPMG (general-purpose machine gun) firing 7.62 mm rounds, usually carried by a single man, though normally operated by a two-man crew. In 7th *Decuria's* case Jan Eberhardt had the GPMG, usually assisted by Theo Dioletis, whose job it was to lug around enough ammo to keep the gun firing for a reasonable length of time. Once contact was made, ammo had a habit of disappearing at a frightening rate.

De Witt ordered the three *decuriae* on the left of the *centuria's* line to peel off and seize the three nearest modern warehouses in a block of six, before pushing on to clear out the remaining three. In the meantime he would lead the other six *decuriae* into the gap between the new and the old warehouses, in preparation for the assault on the packing and shipping units.

Everybody waited in silence; nothing stirred as the three *decuriae* approached the first three modern warehouses, unmolested. De Witt's unease was rising by the minute; this was ludicrously easy – where were the Jihadists? He activated his COMS system and ordered the two reserve lorries of ammo provided by 1st *Centuria,* currently parked up five kilometres back near the battery of Caesar howitzers, to move forward under the protection of the two BPM Kord heavy machine-gun carriers.

While the three *decuriae* he'd already dispatched prepared to storm the first three warehouses, De Witt's attention switched to the six packaging units beyond the warehouses, where the Jihadists were thought to be concentrated. He grabbed his binoculars to scan the units before returning his attention to the sappers as they placed bar mines on the walls of the first three warehouses. Ready or not, he thought, things were about to get interesting.

A series of explosions boomed out across Soviet City, followed by the rush of *legionarii* through the blast holes made by the sappers. Immediately the sound of gunfire and grenade explosions could be heard. At virtually the same time the unexpected sound of machine-gun fire broke out from the old warehouses to the right and behind De Witt's position – what the hell was that?

In the twinkling of an eye Soviet City was transformed from a sleepy ghost town into an angry hornets' nest. From the nearest packaging unit heavy .50 calibre machine-gun fire opened up on the exposed *legionarii*, followed by the whoosh of half a dozen RPGs, causing all De Witt's men to dive for cover.

De Witt immediately ordered the two BPM machine-gun carriers to rush forward from guarding the ammo trucks and return fire on the packaging unit with their Kord heavy machine guns. Similarly the two Wiesel III mortar carriers were instructed to concentrate their fire on the same target. As the firefight developed along his front, De Witt became ever more concerned about the threat of Jihadists attacking from the rear. The mysterious fighting in the old warehouses seemed, if anything, to be intensifying. He activated his COMS system and managed to glean a few snatched pieces of information from Leon Mayer, *decanus* of 10th *Decuria,* who was embroiled in a fierce exchange of fire.

De Witt turned quickly to *Optio* Popovic, lying low behind a clump of bushes, and ordered him to send 7th *Decuria* into the old warehouses to support 10th *Decuria*. He then activated his COMS system and called in the Mil *Pilum* gunship to fire a PARS 4 air-to-surface missile into the Jihadists' positions. Popovic, crawled away from the bushes, and made his way on his belly towards Vasily with .50 calibre rounds flying close overhead. As he approached 7th *Decuria* he passed Dioletis and Eberhardt busy returning fire on their GPMG. The noise of battle was deafening. Popovic found Vasily sheltering behind a couple of old oil drums with the rest of 7th *Decuria;* he had to shout in order to be heard.

'10th *Decuria* have run into a spot of trouble in the old warehouses. It looks like there's a sizable Jihadist force in there; Meyer reckons around 70 to 80 fighters – they were undoubtedly meant as a little surprise for us. Take your men into the nearest warehouse, then work your way forward towards the firefight. Link up with Meyer and clear out the remainder of the block. Any questions?'

Vasily was about to ask about back-up when his eye caught a glint of light from a row of large storage and packing units beyond the immediate battle zone. Popovic had seen the glint too, and before Vasily could speak said, 'It's their reserve forces; they've been holding them back until their leaders could discern our disposition. By the looks of it they're ready to go; that's them now, loading up the pickups and open-top lorries. We'll be up to our armpits in Jihadists before long.'

Vasily looked aghast. 'What's De Witt going to do?'

Popovic smiled, and nodded sagely toward the far storage and shipping unit, where the Jihadists could just be made out as dark specks among numerous vehicles. Suddenly the whole rear end of the unit, including most of the Jihadists, erupted in a spectacular pyrotechnic display as six 155 mm high-explosive artillery rounds hit the building with impressive accuracy. Any remaining Jihadists were sent to *Jannah* by a direct hit from a PARS 4 air-to-surface missile fired from the Mil *Pilum* gunship called in by De Witt.

'That should keep them quiet for ten minutes, but they've not finished yet.' And to emphasise the point half a dozen columns of dust flew up with an ominous bang as the Jihadists starting lobbing 60 mm mortar rounds into the legionary position.

Popovic turned to Vasily with a steely look in his eyes, '*Decanus*, you're needed – go!'

Vasily hurriedly collected his men and headed for the old warehouses. As they cautiously approached the buildings the muffled sound of battle intensified; everyone was acutely aware that contact was imminent. They ignored the doors, which were assumed to be booby-trapped; instead the sappers placed bar mines on the warehouse's sidewall and blasted their way in. Tomasz and Axel were the first through, peeling off either side of the breach to assume covering firing positions. The rest followed smartly; Jan Eberhardt, with the GPMG, ran to the far wall with Theo Dioletis to establish a firing position in case of counterattack – but nothing happened. The warehouse was fairly large, though not on the same gigantic scale as the modern parts of Soviet City. Vasily ordered the men to secure the building and sent Rudi and Alvero to check the tightly packed neighbouring warehouses; the place was a real rabbit warren.

After around ten minutes Rudi and Alvero returned. 10th *Decuria* was holed up in the next warehouse but one. They had Jihadist-controlled warehouses on three sides, all of which were in contact. There had evidently been a number of attempts to storm 10th *Decuria*'s position, judging by the numerous corpses littering the ground, but to date the firepower of the *legionarii* had kept the Jihadists at bay. Vasily hailed Leon Mayer on his COMS system. There followed another snatched exchange under fire. The Jihadists, apparently unaware that 7th *Decuria* were already in the complex, had ignored the explosion caused by the sappers; after all, it could have been anything – mortar round, RPG, artillery shell or even an anti-tank missile. Leon was of the opinion that 7th *Decuria* could probably storm the Jihadist warehouses one by one from the rear; Vasily agreed. Leon would lay down as much fire as possible to cover each attack in turn. They synchronised watches; the first assault would commence in seven minutes. 7th *Decuria* found suitable cover, while the sappers slipped out to place bar mines on the external wall of the nearest Jihadist warehouse. With two minutes to go, Vasily warned Leon they were ready. 10th *Decuria* opened up with every gun and grenade launcher they had. The noise from the firefight among the close-packed buildings was thunderous; suddenly a shattering blast boomed out across the complex as the bar mine blew a large hole in the wall of the Jihadist warehouse. *Legionarii* leapt forward to pour through the breach, firing at everything and nothing – in this game you either fired first or were fired upon first; questions came later.

They found around a dozen Jihadists either dead or stunned in the debris from the blast; all were instantly dispatched. Two more Jihadists were scrambling unsteadily towards the adjacent Jihadist-controlled warehouse, but a short blast from Carlos' GA-6 brought them both down. There were numerous firing positions in the wall, through which one could see the warehouse occupied by 10th *Decuria;* Vasily hailed Leon on his COMS system to tell him that the first warehouse had been cleared.

The sappers exited the building to plant bar mines on the wall of the next Jihadist warehouse; the rest of the men duly took cover. The sound of battle continued to fill the air as 10th *Decuria* fired remorselessly at the two remaining Jihadist positions. Suddenly, across Vasily's COMS system one of the sappers called for help; they had come under small-arms fire. Vasily ran to the warehouse's main sliding doors, gingerly popped his head out and, following the noise of automatic fire, scanned left. He quickly caught sight of a handful of Jihadists, around 80 metres away, firing at the sappers with AK-47s. He called up Marco Bellini. 'Bellini, sort out those bastards before the whole operation goes tits-up.'

Without a word Marco slipped out of a side door and quickly found a firing position behind some packing cases. Two of the Jihadists returned fire with AK-47s; the third was busy loading an RPG. Axel, on hearing the exchange of fire, inched forward to catch a glimpse of what was happening. Before his eyes opened a spectacle that filled him with the deepest admiration and devotion for his fellow *legionarii.* Marco, steadfastly and with insane bravery, was calmly firing a constant stream of bullets at the enemy, while AK-47 rounds whistled and ricocheted all about him. Here, in the doorway of this grubby Turkish warehouse, Axel was witnessing a demonstration of the qualities that made European man the master of all he surveyed. Spellbound, he watched this embodiment of the selfless Aryan warrior, outnumbered but indomitable in defence of his land and people, trading blow for blow with the eternal enemy. At that moment the bond of brotherhood burnt fiercely in his veins as he realised just how important to him were his brothers-in-arms. These were men he valued as highly as any biological brother – men he was prepared to fight and die for, as Marco was doing now.

A colossal boom blasted through the air dragging Axel unceremoniously back to the here and now. He peered at the smoking, dust-filled hole newly opened in the next-door warehouse wall, but this time the Jihadists knew the *legionarii* were coming. Through the breach came a torrent of small-arms fire and even the crackle of a GPMG, making any attempt at storming the place a suicide mission. In a flash Vasily ordered smoke grenades to be thrown through the gap, mixed with the regulation high-explosive variety; there followed a series of bangs, with clouds of smoke billowing everywhere. The Jihadist fire intensified. Theo was only just pulled back in time by Conrad as an RPG flew through the breach, detonating on the next-door warehouse hardly twenty metres from where Marco was engaged in his deadly duel. Leon Meyer had been watching the stalled assault with mounting trepidation from his position in the warehouse occupied by 10th *Decuria*. He grasped Vasily's predicament immediately, quickly realising that if the logjam was to be cleared he would have to support 7th *Decuria*. He hurriedly gathered together six men from 10th *Decuria* and a couple of sappers, then surreptitiously sneaked around the side of the warehouse before crawling under the noses of the Eurabs in the third Jihadist warehouse, to approach the location of Vasily's thwarted attack but from the opposite direction. While 7th *Decuria* traded bullets and grenades with the Jihadist defenders, Leon ordered his sappers to place bar mines on the wall of the warehouse. The men of 10th *Decuria* dived for cover as another huge explosion rocked the complex. Leon then led the charge through the new breach, his men firing their GA-6s on *automatice.*

Although somewhat hampered by their own smoke grenades, Vasily simultaneously led 7th *Decuria* through the heavily disputed breach to catch the substantial Jihadist garrison in a murderous crossfire. Jan Eberhardt set up his GPMG among a jumble of rubble and started hammering the Jihadists hard; it was pure butchery, but before their extinction one lucky Jihadist burst found its target, Alvero fell wounded in his right shoulder and left leg – 'Man down,' screamed Carlos. A few more shots and the Jihadist force, perhaps thirty men in all, had been silenced.

Vasily ran over to Carlos, who had Alvero's head in his slap. Vasily activated his COMS system, switched to *praetorium* and called in a Kamov Mi-97 to evacuate Alvero. But the Kamov couldn't come – hadn't he noticed there was an aerial battle going on overhead?

Meyer was standing by Vasily's side, looking at Alvero bleeding profusely onto the warehouse floor. 'It's true – we've been watching the dogfights through the holes in the roof.'

Vasily glanced up; sure enough the roof was virtually open, the plastic sheeting having been blasted away during the fighting. Above his head Turkish F-22 Raptors were duelling with a legionary squadron of Sukhoi T-55 *Palashi*. Into this heady mix of aerial combat was added the occasional missile fired from mobile legionary Pantsir S-2E anti-aircraft units targeting isolated Turkish Raptors.

Carlos had already summoned a medic team from 1st *Centuria* who, aware of the moratorium on airlifts while the air battle raged, had called up a battlefield ambulance – not for the first time today. Leon tapped Vasily on the shoulder, 'We've got to push on – sorry, mate.'

'Yeah, of course,' said Vasily slowly.

'Batista, stay with him till the medics have loaded him, then rejoin the unit.'

Carlos nodded grimly, while the medics got to work. The shoulder didn't seem too bad, but the leg was haemorrhaging badly. They were soon slamming localised painkillers into his leg and shoulder; then, with a battlefield doctor online shimmering as a hologram giving live instructions, the senior field medic began to open Alvero's damaged leg.

In the other corner of the warehouse Leon quickly outlined a plan of attack for the final Jihadist warehouse, which Vasily immediately agreed to implement. 10th *Decuria* would blast a hole in the north wall, and simultaneously 7th *Decuria* another in the south. They synchronised watches – blasting in twelve minutes, which would give 10th *Decuria* enough time to get into position, 7th *Decuria* were already facing the enemy warehouse's southern wall.

As the sappers attached to 7th *Decuria* set out with another bar mine, Marco rejoined the unit; he looked fine, though there was a collection of grenade fragments embedded in his armour's left shoulder and upper arm. Conrad, who was closest to Marco, could see the jagged fragments clearly – some were still smoking. He needed no medic to tell him that Marco's shoulder and arm would have been shredded if he hadn't been wearing the full *arma proeliaria*.

10th *Decuria* had left their GPMG in its original position, with two men blasting away at the Jihadists in the third warehouse, while everybody else moved into position for the planned attack.

From opposite sides of the Jihadist warehouse Vasily and Leon glanced at their watches and counted down the seconds. Two blasts rocked the air simultaneously; anybody not under cover was knocked off his feet. Both *decuriae* hurled copious grenades into the warehouse to soften the position. Once again a whole series of blasts shook the building; then Leon, using the COMS system, snapped the order, *'Nunc!'* and both *decuriae* stormed the Jihadist positions. There was a short, sharp exchange of concentrated fire, then all went quiet; a jumble of Jihadist corpses and rubble littered the warehouse floor.

The men grabbed a quick breather as both *decuriae* assembled in the newly taken position; then Leon and Vasily dispersed the men to sweep every warehouse in the complex – but as they'd suspected, the place was now deserted. They pushed through to the far side of the block, emerging once again onto the windswept Thracian plain. Before them, perhaps two kilometres away, stood the steel-and-concrete Gulag, like some sentinel on its hill – albeit a smoking and very battered sentinel, as the 155 mm Caesars had obviously been pounding the place for some while. Off to their right the two BPM Kord heavy machine guns were firing on the compound wall surrounding the Gulag, while the bulk of the *centuria* appeared to be moving through the last group of packing and storage units before the Gulag, around a kilometre away to their left. Behind these forces stretched a scene from *Götterdämmerung*, with every warehouse and packing unit as far as the eye could see aflame; a huge, black pall drifted off towards Zorolus.

Leon and Vasily reported in to De Witt over the COMS system. They had cleared the old block of its surprisingly large Jihadist presence; what were their orders? De Witt instructed the pair to take their men over to the eastern side of the Gulag – to their right – while he would advance the main force from the west. As the two *decuriae* moved off to the east behind the BPM Kord units they came under small-arms fire, despite the frighteningly heavy counter-fire being laid down by the meaty Kords. Glancing towards the pockmarked and blasted Gulag compound wall, Vasily thanked the Gods the BPMs were on their side.

The two *decuriae* tracked around to the eastern side of the compound where they came across a semi-metalled road running past the Gulag and over the hill heading towards Constantinople. The two Wiesel III mortar carriers passed them and pulled up on a piece of open ground, preparing to add their fire to the pounding the Gulag was receiving. Suddenly a pickup full of armed Jihadists appeared on the brow of the hill, causing all the *legionarii* to fall automatically to one knee. Vasily realised immediately that the Jihadists had seen the Wiesels and were aiming to intercept them.

He watched the pickup come flying down the hill in a mixture of incredulity and awe – hadn't they seen the Kords? Apparently not. As the pickup got within a thousand metres of the Wiesels the nearest Kord turned deliberately from hammering the compound wall to fire at the pickup. It was carnage. The heavy Kord rounds literally blasted the Jihadists to pieces; in a shower of limbs and vehicle parts the pickup careered off the road, rolled over and smashed into a derelict tractor-trailer.

As cool as ice, the Kord simply turned back to the Gulag and resumed firing at the compound wall. Equally unperturbed, the Wiesels began lobbing mortar rounds into the compound. Vasily and Leon advanced their *decuriae* towards the pickup to clean up any unfinished business. There were human bits and spectacular splashes of scarlet littering the site – in particular a disembodied, bearded head staring up from beneath a tangled bush. A couple of shots rang out as the *legionarii* dispatched any survivors. Vasily glanced at the pickup itself. A huge, gaping rip in the bodywork had exposed the engine block, through which were two clean holes made by the Kord. '*Di immortales,*' he muttered.

De Witt began his approach from the west, while Leon and Vasily brought their smaller force around to the east. However, before any assault on the remnants of the Gulag could be made, a message broke over the COMS system for De Witt and the entire *centuria*: all the men were to take cover immediately. Everybody scrambled to find what cover they could – then they heard it. Out of the sky from the west a Sukhoi Su-39X was making its approach; slung beneath its belly was a large, long tube – a laser-guided 1,000 lb blockbuster. The Sukhoi roared overhead like some Angel of Death, while everyone held their breath. At first nothing happened; then suddenly the earth shook as a wall of noise engulfed the huddled men, who found the very air they breathed being sucked from their lungs. Anybody not under solid cover was blasted along the ground before the force of the explosion, rolling and flapping like pieces of demented tumbleweed. Slowly the real world re-established its hold on their frazzled senses and they felt confident enough to begin crawling from their hidey-holes.

To their utter amazement the Gulag's core concrete-and-steel structure still stood, though everything else – floors, walls and innards – was gone. The *legionarii* got to their feet and warily approached the blast site; here and there could be made out the outlines of where a wall or staircase might have been, but of the garrison there was nothing left.

It was over: Soviet City was theirs.

De Witt used the COMS system to thank all the men of 3rd *Centuria* for their professional action in clearing out this long-running sore in ExThrac's flank. He informed them that phase two of the operation could now begin: namely, a probing push around the Turkish southern flank by 2nd and 8th *Cohortes*. Soon there would be columns of Mannerheim troop carriers, Leopard 3B2 tanks, Caesar howitzers, BPM Kord carriers and all the rest of the supporting paraphernalia of war passing through the site; already the skies were becoming busy with aircraft and helicopters.

While 3rd *Centuria* was assembled in the vicinity of the Gulag, De Witt took the opportunity to give each individual *decanus* his instructions for securing the site personally. Vasily was instructed to position 7th *Decuria* on the brow of the hill by the road heading eastwards towards Constantinople. As De Witt turned his attention to organising the handover of Soviet City to 5th *Centuria*, scheduled for the following morning, he became aware that everybody was staring at something behind him. As if by magic, a young Muslim man had suddenly appeared fifty metres away, walking calmly towards the assembled *legionarii* with his hands held aloft in surrender.

Everybody automatically fell to one knee and took aim at the youth – but inexplicably, nobody fired. De Witt turned around slowly to face the youth, who had continued to approach despite the forest of GA-6s pointing at him. The sight that greeted the youth was a vision of the classic *centurio* and epitome of Aryanism – his eternal foe. De Witt was a big man; over six feet tall, he stood in full, if muddied and battle scarred, *arma proeliaria*. In his left hand he held that iconic symbol of *centurio* authority, his *vitis* – the olive-tree swagger stick presented to all new *centuriones* on passing out – which he tapped thoughtfully against his left leg. On his left hip hung a carbon-steel *gladius*, on his right a holstered Beretta M11 revolver. He moved his right hand to the holster, which he unbuttoned.

Still the youth advanced.

De Witt took a couple of steps towards the youth and pulled out his Beretta. The *decanus* of 1st *Decuria*, on his knee to one side of De Witt, barked savagely, '*Sta!*' – but the youth ignored the warning and continued to advance. De Witt could see clearly into the youth's eyes by now, and instantly knew; he instinctively levelled his Beretta while snapping out the command '*Accendite!*' But instead of witnessing a deadly volley the site was rocked by yet another detonation, as the youth disintegrated in an explosion of atomised body parts. De Witt took the brunt of the blast.

They found De Witt's left hand, still holding its *vitis*, 100 metres away. His *arma proeliaria* had kept most of his body intact, though he was dead before his corpse hit the ground. Five other *legionarii* were injured, one man losing an eye to a bone splinter.

Popovic immediately assumed command and began the business of clearing up and securing the site. As the shocked *decani* started dispersing, having received their new instructions, Leon turned to Vasily: 'These Muslims are insane fanatics; I just don't understand what makes the bastards tick.'

'Don't you? And you say they're the insane ones?'

'Of course: blowing themselves to pieces like that, they're completely unhinged, uncivilised animals.'

'I've seen this before in Chechnya, and I'm afraid I have to disagree with you.'

'What? You think this is normal behaviour?'

'I think you need a little lesson in reality. Everybody on the planet – except Western European man – recognises his fellow group members and strives to advance their lot. Muslims push Islam, Orientals strive for global commercial domination, Africans kill and drive out any alien who cannot defend himself. These feelings and actions are completely natural and normal in any healthy society; after all, it's this racial and cultural solidarity that allows society to function in the first place. Only in the West do people strive to push their own people down and to advance the lot of others, in the breathtakingly naive and arrogant belief that they can somehow rise above mere natural inclination; and in showing their supranatural abilities to embrace the "other" will become some sort of secular godhead for universal admiration and grateful thanks from the primitives they've brought into the light of modernity.'

'That's a bit harsh; we're just trying to be humane.'

'For the benefit of whom? You do it for yourselves and your inflated egos; you think you look all holier-than-thou because you help the weak and needy. The weak and needy don't give a fig for your feelings; they operate according to the iron laws of Mother Nature and once they are no longer weak and needy, they cut your throat, rape your women and steal your goods – for ultimately all mankind strives to advance its own kinship group. It's not the Muslims who are unhinged!

'We Russians have spent our entire history fending off Mongols and Turks; we need no lessons from stupid Westerners on how to protect our families, our peoples and our country. If we'd followed your lead we'd be extinct by now.

'That kid who blew himself to pieces understood the world far better than the vast bulk of Western Europeans. He knew that all of us are part of a unique ethnic group that defines our existence and identity – whether we like it or not. A Negro cannot stop being a Negro, even if he fancies becoming a Chinaman – Mother Nature has already decided otherwise. That bomber was standing in line, doing his bit for the greater whole, for his people, his culture and his identity. He wasn't a nutter; he was a realist. He didn't stick his head in the sand and start sprouting Marxist nonsense that we're all the same; he already knew otherwise. The Westerner is the true fool, putting his faith in fairy stories; then he compounds the idiocy by sacrificing his people, his country and the future of his children on the altar of Social Marxism – a creed, incidentally, not followed even by the ethnic parasites who devised it. You see, this ideological poison was only ever intended for one group – we Aryans – and we stupidly accepted the chalice and proceeded to drink deeply from its toxic contents.

'Yes, we're probably the most powerful people on Earth, but we are far from being all-knowing. There are many areas where simpler peoples can teach us basic home truths, especially about group loyalty and the reality of racial identity; as Ovid said, *fas est et ab hoste doceri*. Remember that kid and the sacrifice he was prepared to make for his people and culture; that's the eternal lesson of life which we must learn if we're to survive on this overcrowded and hostile planet.'

2.7 – End Game

Vasily finally got his promotion to *optio,* and soon afterwards starting preparing himself for the more exalted heights of *centurio* – the highest non-commissioned rank available. So it was that 18 months later he found himself once again in Nevers attending further lectures and reacquainting himself with the centre's staff, in particular Marcel Dubois. These were times of change, as the post-war world was being forged along lines very different from those pursued by the old NWO and their cronies.

As it happens, Marcel Dubois and Nevers were to play a small part in these paradigm-altering developments:

James Wilson slipped into the back of the auditorium with *Imperator* Thijs Visser; they had more or less agreed that Marcel was the man for the job, but wanted one more opportunity to hear him in action. They already knew the topic of today's lecture, so they settled down in anticipation of an insightful presentation.

Marcel was standing in front of the main auditorium in Nevers with around 150 *legionarii* in the audience; he was delivering this particular lecture for the third time that week:

'The whole concept of open-ended commercial ownership and control of a nation's media is nothing short of insanity – its repercussions truly frightening. These misgivings are particularly marked when contemplating the inability of a system as corrupt and morally weak as representative democracy to protect its population from exploitation. Under the de facto commercial dictatorship that money inevitably forges in these 'democracies', the media's function is not so much to serve the public, as to use them. The people become a resource, primarily commercial, but also political and even military – at the disposal of the controlling plutocratic elites. They are led, sheep-like, via a combination of television, films, newspapers and the radio to accept whatever standpoint, or dubious claim, best serves the elite's purpose. Such elites will always emerge to dominate systems as inherently ambiguous as representative democracy – for as we all know, nature abhors a vacuum. It was against these very corruptions – and their peddlers – that the Great Leader warned us all those years ago. The media becomes in effect a manipulation machine, whose controllers – not the politicians, and most certainly not the people – decide state policy via media-engineered social pressure.

'The existential threat is obvious. If, for example, Group A gains control of the media in Group B's territory, they could begin to influence, then steer, Group B's perceptions and thus opinions. The step from directing public perceptions to guiding state policy is relatively small, and easily achieved with a little largesse here, and favourable publicity there.

'We soon arrive at an Orwellian situation where the "truth" is bent to benefit third parties. Welcome to representative democracy. Who needs anything as crude as Communism, when both the media and the political elite are there to be bought?'

'Now, if Group A has a totally different ethnic or even racial composition to Group B – who are the natives of our imaginary country – any capture of Group B's indigenous media is potentially disastrous. Group A could then indoctrinate Group B, via its control of the media, to follow policies conducive to Group A's agenda. Not only would Group B find itself doing the bidding of Group A, but it would do so under the self-delusion that its actions were morally right, "democratically" endorsed and geopolitically necessary. This is exactly the situation that existed in Europe prior to the Eurabian War, and explains why your parents and grandparents were so powerless to resist.

'Needless to say, the Declaration of Rouen condemns unreservedly foreign ownership of national media outlets. No nation can conduct a healthy national life with its mass media in the hands of aliens. Let's be crystal clear: the media – in all its guises – must be controlled by natives; any government that either sits back, or worse still, condones foreign penetration of its national media lays itself open to a charge of *contra patriam*.'

Marcel went on to give various specific examples from before the Eurabian War, indicating how the media had constructed dialogues, then sold them to the public as moral and political imperatives. For all their evil intentions, one had to admire the art with which these operatives forged their fantasy worlds and sold them as reality – or at least as desired outcomes.

After the lecture James Wilson came down to the front of the auditorium to introduce his old friend to *Imperator* Visser. Marcel had seen the pair of them in the back and had been wondering what was afoot; he was about to find out. James and *Imperator* Visser were dutifully led down to the staff dining room for a coffee and biscuit, before being ushered into Marcel's private office.

Once everyone was ensconced comfortably, James took the opportunity to explain the position. 'Marcel, as you know, with the ending of the war a totally new global order is being established, based on regional blocks. It's early days yet, but that appears to be the wish of most nations, and is certainly the policy promoted by the *Curia*. Even as we speak, certain Far Eastern countries are putting out feelers keen to follow the example set by Europe; these are feelers we would like very much to nurture in any way we can – which brings me to our surprise visit today. You see, Marcel, we in Europe will soon be receiving a party of observers from some of these Far Eastern countries who wish to see for themselves the workings of the *Curia* and the *Legiones*. They have their own agenda, of course, but it's important that during this crucial visit we tell our own story succinctly, and make sure our guests understand our position and view of developments.'

Imperator Visser leant forward slightly to pick up on James' point.

'You see, *Legatus* Dubois, while we will be in a position to organise what our guests see physically, we will also need to present our case verbally concerning the post-bellum role of the *Legiones*.

'They are scheduled to receive several presentations covering these matters, one of which will hopefully be in your hands. We'd like you to give a presentation to our oriental guests on the Tigris Campaign and its aftermath. The lecture will be held here in Nevers, where our guests will stay for a night; all these arrangements have already been agreed upon. Would you be happy to deliver such a presentation?'

Marcel felt rather chuffed to have been approached by such a senior officer and asked to deliver what was self-evidently an important message in the *Curia's* push for global regionalisation.

'Of course, *Imperator*. I'd be honoured to play my small part in this great project. Could I just express my gratitude for the faith you've shown in my academic abilities?'

'If you wish to thank anybody, I'd suggest you thank Wilson here, as approaching you was his idea.'

'Well, thank you, James; that's a drink I owe you in the mess.'

Marcel was indeed honoured to have been asked to play a part in the reforging of the world's political structures. He, like the brass up in Bonn, supported the regionalisation project. However, Marcel was a strategic thinker, far more so than James, or any of the generals he'd come across. He, unlike them, saw some negative aspects to the proposed presentation to the Oriental visitors – but for now he'd keep his reservations to himself.

Nevers' Far Eastern visitors arrived bright-eyed and bushy-tailed on the appointed day, ready for Marcel's presentation, scheduled to start at 10:30 – the afternoon having been left free for informal discussions. At 10:29 Marcel ascended the stage and took up his position behind the lectern; having formally introduced himself as *Legatus* and senior lecturer at the Nevers centre, he launched into his presentation:

'I'd like to begin my analysis with some observations concerning our greatest asset: namely, the men of the *Legiones*. The success of the Thracian Campaign was built very much on the bravery and professionalism of these men, who bought us the time to strangle Turkey's supply lines and thus bring the campaign to a speedy conclusion.'

Marcel glanced up at the sea of oriental faces listening intently to his analysis. Is this wise, he conjectured? Will we not have to face the forces of the East one day? After all, they're the only ones capable of challenging Aryan dominance in global affairs. These thoughts had carried him off momentarily on a sea of speculation, when a sudden cough to his left broke the trance; he became immediately aware of the silence in the auditorium and the sea of eyes looking at him questioningly. He took a quick sip from the glass of water that sat on a shelf under the lectern's desktop, then proceeded. 'However, as you're no doubt aware, wars are ultimately won by the army with the greatest resources. Even if you have the best troops, as happened with the Confederates in the War for Southern Independence, or the Boers in the Anglo-Boer War, or the Germans in both the great European Civil Wars, you'll still be defeated if you cannot match your enemy's industrial output. Wars consume hardware at a staggering rate; that's why modern wars are often referred to as "industrial wars" – it boils down to a competition of factory against factory. Ideally, of course, one aims to have the best troops in conjunction with the strongest industrial base. Turkey's military output was very limited; the vast bulk of her supplies came from America, whose military output had remained formidable even if much of the rest of the economy had degenerated alarmingly.

2.7 – END GAME

'The problem for Turkey was the length of her supply chain, stretching halfway around the world; the legionary supply chain was much shorter. Nor was time on Turkey's side, for as the remaining pockets of Eurabian resistance were cleared, the entire continent – including Russia – could bend its surviving industrial capacity to supplying the legions. Bolstered by the ensuing upturn in European arms manufacture, the *Legiones* actively began to block the American airlift and naval conveys to Turkey. Tensions between the *Curia* and the US increased exponentially. The *Curia* massed its naval forces, *Classis XV Themistocles*, *Classis XVIII Codrington* and *Classis XLVI Exmouth* at Berehaven, in Ireland, to intercept US naval forces crossing the Atlantic. Another naval force, comprising *Classis XXIV Don John* and *Classis XXXIV Van Capellan,* was stationed in Naples to sweep the Mediterranean. A smaller force, *Classis XLV De Rigny,* operated in the Greek islands, having been given the task of sealing off the Turkish Mediterranean coast. There were fierce battles in the Atlantic as the US Navy tried to force entry into the Mediterranean. They managed to breach the Pillars of Hercules on several occasions, only to be met by our Naples force. In the air, large numbers of US military cargo planes were shot down during dogfights between US carrier-borne fighters and ground-based European interceptors – mostly over the Atlantic, but others as far east as Sicily and southern Italy. This was all a phoney war, of course: officially nothing happened – neither the *Curia* nor the US government acknowledged that a state of a conflict had ever existed.

'However, the gloves were about to come off.

'America decided to ramp up the ante by threatening direct military intervention in Europe, ostensibly to protect the oppressed Muslim population from the evil fascist forces, which the obviously xenophobic and militarist cabal in the *Curia* were nurturing. There was even a hint of a readiness to use the nuclear option if Europe refused to acknowledge the error of her ways.'

There was a slight pause as Marcel took another drink of mineral water, giving him an opportunity to scan the listening faces. James, representing the *Curia*, was sitting halfway up the auditorium, while behind him sat rows of senior students, such as officer candidates and those studying for *centurio* rank – amongst whom was a certain Vasily Nikonov. Marcel glanced quickly at his notes, then resumed the presentation. 'The *Curia* already had close links with Russia, which were about to get a lot closer. After a number of online discussions and flutter of flights between Bonn and Moscow, a retort to the American threat finally emerged from the Kremlin – to the effect that Russia fully supported Europe's efforts to regain control of her sovereign territory. Without being specific, Russia made it clear that her nuclear umbrella included all Europe, should the actions of any *ex-Europa* body pose a direct threat to the continent.

'As a result of this aggressive stance adopted by the US military, the administration in Washington found itself facing growing domestic discontent. All propaganda avenues were activated, mostly via corporatist-controlled news and press networks, in an effort to keep the American population on side. Initially, the bulk of the people tentatively swallowed the official line, though even then a large minority rejected it. There was already a substantial body of support for Europe's position, particularly among the Nativist White population. However, the threat of nuclear war with Russia proved a turning point for a critical mass of Americans; their support crumbled away, pitching the grand US project into very hot water.

'America reaped the whirlwind of this sterile diplomatic wrangling and military failure in the thwarting of her attempts to maintain supplies to Turkey. Without fresh munitions, the longer the fighting persisted, the weaker Turkish forces became. When Greek forces pointedly landed on the Asian bank of the Bosphorus, and pushed up to the banks of the Sangarius, the government in Ankara decided enough was enough. Already badly exposed by the American failure to maintain the arms flow, and acutely aware that any major landing of legionary forces on Turkey's Mediterranean coast would lead to internal collapse, they sued for terms. The *Curia's* demands were simple: Thrace to return to Greece, and a binding treaty to be signed by both parties recognising the new boundaries. The Marmara–Dardanelles were

2.7 – END GAME

mutually recognised as the natural border between Europe and Asia. Turkey was also obliged to vacate Cyprus – which finally achieved *enosis* – and return the two small islands of Imbros and Tenedos to Greece. With the new boundary having been recognised, the Turkish government formally renounced all claims to territories on the European side of the Marmara. Turkey, for her part, did not leave the negotiating table entirely empty-handed; the *Curia* recognised Turkey's right to her Asian territories renouncing any present or future claims to lands in Asia. Once these agreements had been ratified, the Greek forces on the Sangarius pulled back into Thrace.

'The *Curia's* recognition of Asiatic Turkey was important to Ankara, which faced two major internal problems. Firstly, Europe had taken the opportunity of the Greek penetration to dump around eight million people onto the far bank of the Sangarius in central Turkey, around half being Albanian and Bosnian Muslims, the rest mostly Gypsies and assorted non-Europeans. The native Turks had a modicum of sympathy for the Muslims, which in the case of the Albanians soon evaporated with exposure to their anti-social tendencies. Nobody, however, had much time for the Gypsies. All that can be said is that soon afterwards dark rumours of pogroms began circulating – the Turks had never been big on unrequited altruism. However, this was not the end of Turkey's problems; on her eastern and southern borders Kurdistan was expanding, reflecting the Peshmerga's successful efforts to exploit Turkey's military woes. Similarly, Armenia was striving to reoccupy her historic territories around Lake Van and Trebizond, having already overrun Nakhichevan. Crucially, Russia – a close ally of Armenia – was not bound by the *Curia's* recognition of Asiatic Turkey. Turkey might have lost her last toehold in Europe, and largest city to boot, but at least her western borders were now relatively safe – although of course, even as we speak the Turkish drama continues to unfold, as witnessed in the clashes with Kurdish forces reported from Edessa yesterday.

'With the Eurabian War slowly drawing to a conclusion, the *Curia* had to begin seriously considering Europe's long-term needs, in particular her supply of raw materials. It was decided to earmark three legions, *XXV Gediminas*, *XII Palaiologos* and *XXX Peiper*, for a new mobile task force of 15,000 men. The main concern was Iraq, where a recently agreed oil contract to supply Europe via a basket of named European oil companies was being threatened by the USA.'

Marcel paused momentarily to turn the page of his notes. However, he soon became conscious of the authoritarian visage of a certain gentleman in the front row – whom he subsequently discovered was the Korean ambassador – voicelessly chivvying him along.

He gave a short cough.

'America was by now in serious financial straits. The dollar's value had plummeted, and welfare programmes across the country were collapsing, releasing huge waves of social unrest and violence, particularly among the Black and Hispanic populations.

'Both the Washington elite and the cabal in New York clung on to the belief that a reinvigorated petrodollar would save the situation. However, Europe's recent deal with Iraq – priced in Europe's currency of account, the solidus used by the *Curia* for internal European inter-governmental business – undermined even that faint hope. The US responded by sending the XVIII Airborne Corps – which in theory could draw down up to 88,000 troops – to Iraq to block any further shipments of oil which were not priced and paid for in dollars.

'Delegates from every nation in Europe were called to an emergency session of the *Curia* in Bonn to agree a response; the rapid deployment force was thus mandated to protect Europe's sources of raw materials. This was the first time the *Legiones* had operated outside Europe. Yet another clash with the Americans seemed inevitable.

'The two forces landed in Iraq within 30 hours of each other. The Americans established themselves in Baghdad, sending a substantial force south to take control of the oilfields and shipping lanes using the Shatt al-Arab, while US naval forces converged on the Persian Gulf for the same purpose.

'Of course, all this alarmed Iran and her Russian and Chinese allies, both of whom sent their own warships to the Persian Gulf while offering Iran advanced weaponry.

'The Americans sent another force of around 40,000 north to seize the oilfields around Mosul, a dangerous manoeuvre, especially as the CIA was fully aware that the legionary task force had established a base around Mosul airport. Indeed, the Europeans had already begun probing southwards along the Tigris. The first clash between the two forces occurred near the industrial town of Baiji. At no time did the US or the *Curia,* or any individual European country, declare war or even acknowledge a state of conflict. Legally, the Tigris Campaign never occurred – just like the phantom naval and air clashes during the Thracian Campaign.

'From the very beginning the firepower available to the American forces was substantially superior to that available to our forces. The first day saw the legions pushed back around 50 kilometres to Ash Sharqat, having taken heavy casualties in the process. However, throughout the fighting fresh equipment was continually arriving from Mosul. The legionary HQ was defended by extensive SAM belts beefed up with a growing number of fighters and helicopter support units. Although publicly the XVIII Corps praised their men, highlighting the impressive advances made, behind closed doors the senior officers were not so sanguine. The casualties sustained by the Americans were almost as heavy as ours and, more worryingly, the legions had hurriedly deployed units of *Federschwert* that had begun to take a heavy toll of US helicopters and drones. US forces, used to operating under an umbrella of air superiority and on-call helicopter support, found their airborne umbrella thinning at an alarming rate. It soon became a case of "back to basics", gaining ground the old-fashioned way, inch by inch, corpse by corpse.

'The US commanders were also aware that the legionary units were battle-hardened, having seen plenty of action in the Eurabian War, and more recently against Turkey in Thrace – a fact whose repercussions were becoming self-evident on the field of battle.

'The second day superficially developed much as the first, with huge US pressure forcing the legionary units back another 30-odd kilometres as far as Rumanah; but behind the scenes American cohesion was beginning to break down. Equipment for the legions was still flowing in along with the first elements of five more legions sent to bolster the *Curia's* forces, namely the *IX Scipio, XVI Dimitri, XVII Aetius, XXXII Béla* and *XLIV Ingvar*. The Americans were being forced to battle for every yard, taking casualties the like of which had not been seen since the Second European Civil War. As the pressure mounted, so the composition of the two armies became ever more important. If political correctness was an absurdity in peacetime, on the field of battle it was a death sentence.

'The *legionarii* were – and remain – racially European to a man, fully aware of the cause for which they were fighting. The fear that gripped every *legionarius* was the nightmare of a return to mass immigration and corporate control of their countries. There was a widely held fear that should the NWO powers running the US administration defeat them, the evils which Europeans had spilled so much blood to expel would return anew. It was then, as the pressure reached unheard-of levels, that the ideology of the *Legiones* shone forth. All stood foursquare behind the doctrine of *Patria Europaea*; however fierce the fighting, however heavy the butcher's bill, no *legio* wished to be stained with the infamy of Paulus.

'In truth, as the military situation became ever tougher, so the *legionarii* bonded ever more tightly and fought ever harder. The US forces, in contrast, were an uneasy combination of mostly Hispanic soldiers, with a substantial Black minority and relatively small White component – although White European-Americans dominated the US officer corps. This was the much vaunted "strength through diversity" at work – but would it survive trial by combat?

'In practice, as the fighting escalated and the casualty list lengthened, the mistrust between the three racial groups intensified. Individuals began to turn on each other – especially between Hispanics and Blacks.

2.7 – END GAME

'By then the XVIII Corps had Mosul within striking distance; if they could push the legions out of the airport it would spell doom for the European forces, since no other viable supply route existed. The legions had been aware of the situation since the start of operations, putting some of their sharpest minds to work on the thorny problem of defending the airport.

'The third day saw further US advances, the outskirts of Mosul now clearly visible to those using binoculars. The fighting remained murderous. Time and again, legionary forces fighting from well-organised defensive positions took advantage of planned escape routes to secondary or even tertiary positions, all the while punishing the advancing Americans heavily. The SAM belts and Mosul-based Sukhoi T-55s kept the Raptors at bay, while the *Federschwert* batteries continued to reap their deadly toll of US helicopters and drones.

'However, despite the ferocity of the fighting the US forces pushed on, inching ever closer to their goal. By nightfall the battered legionary forces found themselves dug in around the perimeter of Mosul airport preparing a final stand. Things looked bleak; despite the mauling they'd given XVIII Corps, the unstoppable force had rolled on and looked set to deliver the *coup de grâce*.

'But it never happened.'

He glanced up again and straightened his back; the presentation was coming to its well-rehearsed climax.

'Puzzling dispatches had started to arrive from our forward positions: strange lights could be seen flashing behind the American lines, accompanied with the ominous sound of gunfire.

'More and more such messages poured into the legionary communications hub until suddenly at 03:00 a gigantic explosion thundered out from the American positions, causing the ground to tremble like in an earthquake. The blast was immediately followed by the eruption of a vast fireball so bright it could be seen fifty kilometres away. At first nobody understood these startling events, but subsequently we discovered that the forward ammunition dump of XVIII Corps had been ignited – but why?

'Within ten minutes of the explosion the first US troops reached our lines; all of whom immediately surrendered – and all of whom were White. Soon the staggering truth filtered back to legionary HQ. A childish spat in a forward canteen, between a Latino and a Black GI over a fried chicken leg, had spiralled out of control, resulting in the Black killing the Latino with a kitchen knife. The other Latinos, who had witnessed the fight, immediately attacked and killed the Black GI, decapitating the corpse and kicking the head about in a ghoulish game of football. Soon both sides were reaching for their guns and a full-blown shooting war broke out. Latinos and Blacks began killing each other on sight. Officers and NCOs trying to stop the fighting were simply gunned down. At one point a number of White soldiers tried to peaceably intervene, but they too were killed. The rest of the White Americans quickly realised it would be far safer to surrender to the legionary forces than wait to be butchered by their so-called "fellow Americans".

'Thus the US Army in Iraq disintegrated, signalling a crisis not only within US forces, but in America generally. The racial chickens were coming home to roost. Before long the *Curia* had thousands of White US prisoners on its hands, all of whom were anxious for their families and friends as the news from North America got progressively worse.

'On hearing the staggering reports from Iraq, Vernon Foreman of the Cemetery Ridge Foundation rushed to Bonn and pleaded to be heard by the full *Concilium Militare* – which request was granted after several backroom meetings had established clearly what Foreman intended to propose.

'The *Concilium Militare* consisted of seven senior generals, the chairman being Thijs Visser, who began proceedings as follows.'

Marcel lifted up his copy of Visser's words, taken verbatim from the official transcription:

2.7 – END GAME

"'Mr Foreman, we have convened this *Concilium* at your behest. It is important to note that this body is not usually at the beck and call of individuals, especially foreign individuals. However, after preliminary discussions it was felt that the ideas you have for our consideration are of such a magnitude that we would be failing in our duties were we to refuse this hearing. Mr Foreman, the floor is yours.'"

Marcel looked up once again to address his audience directly. 'Foreman got up and gave his famous speech, whose repercussions were to be so far-reaching. Here are his words:

"'Thank you *Imperator* Visser, and the rest of you eminent gentlemen. I should firstly like to express my heartfelt gratitude for granting me this hearing and the opportunity it represents for securing the future of our people. You may find my use of the expression 'our people' a bit odd – am I not an American, a foreigner – an enemy even? Well, politically yes: but if there has been one lesson to emerge clearly from the revolution that has reawakened Europe, it is that identity counts, and our primary identity – even superior to national identity – is to our blood and race. We are Europeans, all of us, be it here on the sacred soil of *Mater Europa*, or in North America, or Australia or South Africa, or wherever we Aryans have made a permanent home for ourselves. We are all Europeans, inhabiting a dangerous world where our people represent an ever-shrinking proportion of the global population, while the other races multiply at an insectile rate. This Malthusian tidal wave of alien humanity demands from us a hard-headed response. All these teeming races, numbered in the billions, seek – quite naturally – to benefit their own race and people. I put it to you, gentlemen: is it not right that we too stand together as Europeans – as Aryans – to hold our ground? Is this not the core message of the Declaration of Rouen, the founding document of this august body and beacon to us all?

"The bottom line for us as a race, gentlemen, is the core question of existence: namely, what will befall our people if we refuse to act? For I can absolutely assure you that our racial competitors will not waste a second's thought before trampling our bones into the dust of oblivion.

"However, I'm getting ahead of myself. Let me first congratulate you on the magnificent, inspirational rebirth of Europe, sweeping the continent clean of debris and re-establishing our people on their native soil. Your actions have been the most important achievement accomplished by European arms since the Siege of Vienna; you've saved the continent and the unique, superb peoples who inhabit its pleasant lands and cities. I salute this glorious achievement and thank the immortal Gods for our deliverance.

"However, as I've already touched upon, the remit of European man does not end at the Urals, or on the coast of Ireland. Our lands stretch from North America to the Argentinian pampas, from the Australian bush to New Zealand's snow-capped Southern Alps and South Africa's high veld – where our Afrikaner kin cling on tenaciously in the face of orchestrated genocide.

"The USA and Canada are collapsing fast; racial war rages across the continent, Whites flee to ethnic enclaves guarded by ad hoc militia, while the evil and corrupt central governments sink ever deeper into impotence and torpor. Let your revolution be exported, gentlemen; take the legions to all our lands and free your Aryan brothers from the threat of extinction everywhere. I'm not asking you to shed more European blood; we Americans - and Canadians - can fight our own battles. All I ask is a helping hand with equipment, training and transportation. Allow me to organise these American prisoners from Iraq and form new American legions, which in due course will make a second landing on Plymouth Rock and retake those lands snatched from us by a pernicious and poisonous ethnic plutocracy. Allow us Americans to sweep our lands clean of the human debris that now engulfs it – as you have done here – and once again establish a European homeland on American soil.

"If you grant me this request, I feel I must warn you that I have no intention of re-establishing the USA as it once was – a vast, bloated monster, too big to be aware of the parasites eating away its guts, yet big enough to bully the world into following insane policies dictated by the greed of Mammon. I intend to establish at least two nations on the former US lands, if not three. I certainly intend re-establishing both the Confederacy and the Union; no doubt other subdivisions will appear in due course.

"So there you have it, gentlemen; with your permission I intend to take these fine American soldiers and form Eagle Legions, to forge a new Union, and Cotton Legions to resurrect dear, sweet Dixie."'

Marcel, who had watched the video of Foreman's short speech dozens of times, remembered clearly the slight pause in his delivery at this point as he cast a glance at his wife Maybellene, sitting in the viewing gallery.

"'As many of you gentlemen are aware, Dixie is the second greatest love of my life – as no doubt your native lands are to each and every one of you. Come, gentlemen; let us agree and resolve here, today, to re-establish European man and European civilisation on North American soil. Then it's on to Australia, New Zealand, South Africa and all our blighted lands crying out for succour. What say you, gentlemen?'"

ACT THREE:
PHOENIX

3.1 – Rebirth

The European Space Station *Mercurius* was connected to Earth via a space elevator anchored in the Sierra Nevada mountain range. The anchor point, situated between La Veleta and Mulhacén peaks, lay some 3400 metres above sea level, every extra metre of altitude decreasing the strength of the Earth's gravity. Over the past decade the nearby ski resort village of Pradollano had virtually doubled in size, owing to the increased traffic generated by the space station, which was scheduled to grow even further with the burgeoning European space programme. The anchor point itself was reached via an underground maglev track, cut through sheer rock to Veleta Base, the engineering and dispatch centre, which controlled and maintained the space elevators operating over their 36,000 kilometre-long ribbon of carbon nanotube. Owing to the harsh weather conditions at this altitude the actual base was situated below ground level. The carriages, that traversed the elevator were fairly substantial affairs, with sleeping quarters, toilet facilities, kitchens, etc., all of which were needed owing to the vastness of operating in space – for although the carriage travelled at speeds averaging 350 kph, it still took around four days to reach *Mercurius*.

The carriages might have been slow compared with a rocket, but they were also far cheaper, far safer, had virtually no payload restrictions and could be turned around on arrival at their destination. They operated as a train service, using a fraction of the fuel rockets gulped down, while suffering none of their re-entry problems.

There were similar such elevators in Russia, China, Japan and North America with rumours of an Indian entry in the offing, though to date nothing had emerged from the subcontinent.

The maglev train to Veleta Base ran from the Space Station's operational control centre some 30 kilometres away, just outside Granada – with one additional stop at Pradollano. Travelling on its magnetic cushion the maglev train could rapidly reach speeds of 250 kph even on a comparatively short hop, like that between Granada and Veleta – though it tended to slow considerably in the steeper mountain sections. The journey typically took sixteen minutes, including the stop at Pradollano.

That morning, around the large conference table in the Granada centre's main conference room, there sat the strategic steering group responsible for co-ordinating Europe and Russia's space programmes. On one side sat three representatives of the European Cosmological Programme (ECP); next to them were two high-ranking officers of the *Legiones*; and finally three further delegates from the *Curia*. Facing them was the usual invited Russian delegation, mirroring the Europeans with a senior scientific representative, a three-star general and member of the Russian cabinet, all of whom were accompanied by a posse of high-ranking members of the Russian government.

Discussions were held in Latin, a language everyone present spoke fluently. The main topic under consideration was the delay in the *Argo* project, the deep-space manned expedition to the planets Saturn and Jupiter and their moons, planned as a follow-up to the earlier successful unmanned probes conducted by both the ECP and Russian Space Agency. The *Argo* itself was being assembled in the main dock on *Mercurius,* but the time taken to transfer material from Veleta to *Mercurius* had become a major issue, with research teams from both the ECP and Russia working on various schemes to improve the elevator's performance.

The Russians had been looking at methods of boosting the power available to the carriage and its climbing mechanism, with energy being transferred via laser beam. The early trials had been positive and the ECP's representatives were keen to help in every way possible. With greater energy the apparatus could be beefed up considerably, attaining far higher speeds; the only concern was the extra pressure this would put on the carbon nanotube. The material's strength was legendary, and all calculations indicated that increasing velocities by up to 300 per cent would still fall comfortably within the nanotube's theoretical tolerance.

The Japanese had been running an alternative system using two carbon nanotubes – one for the carriage and the other for power. The *Curia* had looked closely at the Japanese design, but to date had favoured the Russian solution as being more effective and easier to control and maintain.

The space race was real enough and Europe, via the *Curia*, had decided to commit fully; though expensive, it focused ambition, hugely boosted scientific and engineering progress while culturally it complemented Europe's Faustian spirit of exploration and adventure.

The meeting moved on to discuss the construction of a solar power station. Plans were already well developed for a space-based solar-power array, using a specially engineered variant of the carbon nanotube to transfer solar energy directly to Earth without the problems and dangers inherent in trying to transfer energy via wave technology. The initial plans had been to establish an experimental station somewhere in Scandinavia – northern Norway or the Kola Peninsula being the favoured locations.

The discussions proved fruitful, with both sides agreeing on the need to push forward with both projects. The considerable catalogue of potential future projects, such as the manned long-range space vessel, and the deep-space probes to the nearest twenty systems, were all given a provisional green light. Both the European and Russian scientific teams had agreed to closer co-ordination, which it was hoped would see projects completed quicker and at reduced cost. Everything was progressing well, giving rise to considerable confidence within both teams for the future of joint ventures.

All those present were aware of the momentous developments in Asia that would inevitably impact on their work and future plans. The collapse of North Korea and the long-awaited reunification of the peninsula had opened the door for the formation of a new grouping under the terms of the Shanghai Protocol. This agreement, originally signed by China, Korea, Hong Kong and Japan, had since expanded to include Taiwan, reluctantly awarded observer status under the pseudonym 'Taipei', followed by Vietnam, which became an associate member.

The creation of the Shanghai Protocol, mirroring Europe's formation of the *Curia*, was widely seen by most observers as the birth of modern global regionalism – the hoped-for antidote to the madness of the NWO project.

Another region beginning to re-establish itself was North America. The North American Congress had recently been formed in Albany by the six countries that emerged following the Wars of Secession and the War of Reconquest: they were the USA, the CSA, the Republic of Columbia, Canada, Québec and the Atlantic Provinces.

The old USA had been all but destroyed during the Wars of Secession, which saw the country ruthlessly carved up into autonomous racial blocs. The death of the money economy following the Global Meltdown heralded the disintegration of the entire state apparatus maintained by government expenditure – including both the police and the armed forces. In the social and racial chaos that ensued, all the South West fell to Latino irregulars – spearheaded in urban areas by armed Latino gangs. This rapidly expanding zone of Latino control, coalesced politically into the People's Republic of Aztlan, whose independence had been dramatically declared live on Mexican television. Tellingly, the declaration occurred in El Centro's Council Chamber, in what had once been southern California. The new republic of Aztlan was totally controlled by *La Rasa,* with barely concealed backing from the Mexican government. A select core of front organisations soon came to dominate the administration, the foremost of which was the Sons of Quetzalcoatl, commonly believed to be a front for CISEN (Mexican Secret

Service). Areas that fell to Aztlan forces were systematically cleared of Whites, and in urban areas of Blacks, whom the Latinos were particularly keen to expunge. Most Whites on the West Coast fled north to the relative safety of the North West Republic, an Aryan ethno-state unilaterally declared by White nationalists, who were busy consolidating their grip on an expanding area of Washington State and Oregon.

Outside the Deep South, the Negro population had concentrated in urban areas. As a result, numerous Black-majority cities, from Detroit, Baltimore and Jackson to Birmingham, Memphis and Miami, had degenerated into third-world hellholes. The remnant White populations in these blighted wastelands were either butchered, or fled into one of the independent and well-armed White communities that were springing up all over the country. Once the process had begun, it rapidly snowballed into a universal phenomenon, the whole country – indeed, the whole continent – dividing itself along racial lines. Huge numbers were left either dead or homeless in its wake. Atrocities were commonplace.

The collapse of the dollar meant the collapse of the social-support network financed by the state. The cutting of this financial life-support system hit urban areas hard, especially the disorganised Black communities. These people could no longer be fed, causing vast waves of mostly Negro marauders to leave their urban neighbourhoods to fan out into the surrounding countryside to forage for food – and loot. However, with few exceptions outside the South West, such agricultural districts were protected by White paramilitaries, heavily reinforced by ex-police and armed forces personnel. The resultant clashes were savage in their finality; however, 95 per cent of these actions saw the better-organised and better-trained White forces scattering the marauders, who were then hunted down and dispatched. Starvation soon gripped the rump urban Negro population, which started dying off in droves; those that survived, instead of co-operating for mutual self-preservation, turned on each other, squabbling over meagre resources, which merely led to further rounds of internecine mass slaughter.

This liquid political situation only began to stabilise with the landing of the two forces of American Legions, signalling the beginning of the War of Reconquest. Strictly speaking there were actually two separate wars, and they only affected the formation of the USA and the CSA, since the Republic of Columbia established itself independently of legionary assistance. Similarly, in the ex-territories of Canada, the initial break-up of the old state and subsequent ethnic clearance of non-Europeans was all accomplished by local forces.

The South won the race to officially reconstitute itself as a political entity. When the two Cotton Legions waded ashore in the Charleston sunshine of June, 2788 AUC, the entire Southern White population erupted in ecstatic celebrations; the Confederate legionaries were greeted like conquering heroes – Robert E. Lee himself wouldn't have received a warmer welcome. The Confederacy was formerly reconstituted ten days later by declaration at Columbia, South Carolina – the name heading the list of the declaration's signatories being that of one Vernon Foreman, honorary commanding officer of the Cotton Legions.

Two years later Vernon Foreman gave a famous interview to the *Richmond Enquirer*, in which he described his feelings as he signed the declaration of independence in the state dining room of the Governor's Mansion at Arsenal Hill, Columbia:

'I can't begin to describe the emotions that were coursing through me that day; even now my legs go weak just thinking about it. The honour and gravity of the occasion were truly overwhelming. I remember clearly that my vision was blurred and my hand shook as I approached the table to sign the declaration. I know this sounds melodramatic, but I could feel the presence of Jeff Davies in the room, looking on benignly as we breathed life back into the Confederacy.

'With impeccable timing the band on the Mansion House lawn struck up *Bonnie Blue Flag* the moment I put pen to paper. On the completion of our task all the signatories filed out to greet the people who spontaneously broke into a thunderous rendition of *Dixie*.

'Let us not beat around the bush here: this was one of the great turning points in the history of our people – a second revolution, a second bite at the cherry of independence, the implications of which, both for the South and for me personally, were epoch-making.

'I think I can say without fear of contradiction that no man on this planet, no matter what he achieves, or what success he enjoys, can ever surpass the distinction that fell to me that day in the realisation of Confederate independence. How many men can boast they've fulfilled the pinnacle of their life's ambition – and in such a glorious manner?'

The Federal Legions, operating in the North, were aware that the South had gone, but where exactly the Union's borders would rest was still unclear. A number of states had split loyalties, like Missouri, Kentucky and Maryland, whose final destination had yet to be decided. In the West, a furious row broke out between those who wished to remain in the Union and those who wished to follow Dixie and declare independence. It fell to the Rocky Mountain States to bring the arguments to a conclusion, when they cast their weight behind independence. The Republic of Columbia came into existence as a consequence of the decisions made during the Great Western Congress, held over four days in Eugene, Oregon. Controversially, San Francisco was designated capital of the new republic – much to the chagrin of many Rocky Mountain delegates who had favoured Denver. The irony of the situation lay in the fact that, at the time, San Francisco was occupied and formed part of the People's Republic of Aztlan.

From its inception the Republic of Columbia (RoC) had envisioned itself as an Aryan homeland, in which only individuals of European extraction could become citizens; miscegenation was illegal, as it became once again across the continent. Having been formally established, the RoC turned its attention to the militarily powerful North West Republic. A series of frank negotiations were held in Portland that resulted in the North West Republic agreeing to join Columbia, thus making its heavily armed and highly motivated militias available for deployment. The first act of foreign policy enacted by the RoC was to declare war on the People's Republic of Aztlan. Immediately on declaring war, the RoC's new president – Norton Harper of Utah – made a nationwide broadcast in which he committed Columbia's forces to retaking all the territory lost to the Aztlan offensive since the collapse of the old USA. Within two days of Harper's announcement, the People's Republic of Aztlan signed a treaty of friendship and cooperation with Mexico, a package that included the training and arming of Aztlan forces by the Mexican Army. Thus began the Aztlan–Columbian War.

Canada also succumbed to powerful centrifugal forces, with Québec finally declaring independence, an act that virtually obliged the remaining four English-speaking eastern provinces of Newfoundland, Nova Scotia, New Brunswick and Prince Edward Island to form the smallest of the North American states – Atlantic Provinces.

Having decided it was time to forge a new future, representatives of the six North American capitals – Washington, Richmond, San Francisco, Ottawa, Québec City and Halifax – came together at Albany in upstate New York, where the North American Congress (NAC) sat for seven weeks thrashing out the details of the agreement. Both the Declaration of Rouen and the Shanghai Protocol were at hand to be used as models, or points of reference, though ultimately the Treaty of Albany which formalised the North American Congress was a unique document tailored specifically to the new reality facing the six nations of North America.

The revolutionary atmosphere many observers felt in Albany during those seven weeks was heightened by the uncertainty surrounding the future of the six political entities. At the time of the Congress, the RoC was locked in a deadly war with Aztlan, its designated capital San Francisco still in Latino hands. For the duration of the negotiations the government of the RoC was located in Eugene. The USA had problems of its own, with the fate of Maryland hanging in the balance owing to the strong support for the

Confederacy in the state. The loss of Maryland would have made Washington untenable as a capital for the US.

Further north, the final fate of Alaska had yet to be decided. Although the population tended to support remaining part of the USA, the geographical barriers made such an option a virtual non-starter – something even the US acknowledged. The same was true of Hawaii. After the formation of the NAC both Canada and the RoC made tentative approaches to Alaska, with neutral commentators voicing the obvious conclusion that union with Canada would be the most practical solution. However, after toying with the idea of independence, Alaska decided to join the RoC, mainly for historical reasons. Hawaii plumped for a semi-independent existence, becoming a protectorate of the RoC. Fiscally, however, it adopted the Columbian dollar as its legal tender.

The NAC acted as guarantor of the independence of its six member states, each of which was legally recognised as a constituent part of the Congress and its framework. Much like the Declaration of Rouen, all member states declared themselves ethnic states, whose citizenship was confined to people of European Caucasian blood; the Treaty of Albany specifically condemned civic nationalism as a recipe for instability and ultimately genocide. The remnants of the non-European populations – mostly indigenous Indians, and a rump Negro population in Dixie - were given their own territories, outside which they had only limited rights.

The Congress voted to keep a minimal bilingual secretariat in Albany, where in theory the NAC sat in permanent session. All six governments maintained an ambassador in Albany to oversee NAC business. The importance of the NAC organisation and secretariat would only increase with time, as the new reality of global regional blocs emerged from the carnage left behind by the failed NWO project.

3.2 – Castel di Guido

Oriana slid into the back of the modern, glass-and-stainless-steel university auditorium in time to catch the second half of Anton Dubov's lecture on Marxism and globalisation within the larger NWO project; this took her back a few years. Dubov was world-famous, of course, the leading theoretical architect and high priest of the emerging global network of regional blocs. His native Russia was looked upon by some as a bloc in its own right, though the links between Mother Russia and the *Curia* grew by the day, with most assuming that sometime in the future a more formal relationship between the two would be penned. This was the first time Oriana had seen the great man in the flesh; he struck an imposing figure, with his left hand gripping the lectern while he gesticulated authoritatively to the assembled audience with his right, speaking in heavily accented Latin. He was a large man in his late fifties, with rather untidy hair and a full beard, his once black locks having turned grey as they thinned. He explained, with surgical precision, how the descent into the Eurabian War was an inevitable consequence of the megalomaniacal policies pursued by the ethnic financiers and social engineers behind the NWO disaster. The blind conformity of European society to what was self-evidently a campaign of genocide had to be considered one of the greatest civic failures in all European history. This sobering observation prompted him to look skywards for inspiration as he exclaimed, 'By Perun! For the sake of our children's future, let's hope and pray that the lesson has been learned.'

He finished off with a selection of comments by leading post-war figures concerning the depravity and evilness of the NWO concept – all of which he dismissed by saying, 'Wisdom after the event is merely stating the obvious – a trick any dog can learn. Those who deserve our fuller admiration are the ones who predicted this disaster before it occurred. You've all got a sheet of quotes on your seats, take a look at item "C" – isn't that a fascinating insight? Particularly when one considers its age and provenance; allow me the indulgence of reading these portentous words:

'*Thus it* – meaning Marxism, of course – *denies the individual worth of the human personality, impugns the teaching that nationhood and race have a primary significance, and by doing this it takes away the very foundations of human existence and human civilisation.*

'We've come full circle, have we not? It's been a bloody and painful journey to confirm something already known and understood by our forebears. Okay, I hope you've enjoyed today's lecture and have come to appreciate the enormity and scope of the NWO project – easily the most evil and pernicious development ever witnessed in the course of human history.'

Oriana, like everybody else in Europe, had seen plenty of Dubov over the years, his vision of a global network of regional cultural and racial blocs having caught the world's imagination. He appeared frequently on television, and was consistently being written about in newspapers and magazines as some sort of geopolitical messiah. He'd written numerous books, which had been translated into dozens of languages; indeed, she had copies of several of them in Italian.

Her visit to the auditorium had been a trifle fortuitous as originally she had a blank diary, condemned to kick her heels around town for a few hours, while her scientist boyfriend Pascal tried to finish a research paper he'd been writing. They were scheduled to catch the 6:00 pm maglev from Paris to Rome, and as she had a huge weekend planned, missing the train was simply not an option.

However, that morning when she woke up in Pascal's flat and turned on the radio to listen to *Radiophonia Latina,* she was greeted by the unexpected news that the famous Russian political scientist, Anton Dubov, was to give an impromptu lecture at the Sorbonne that afternoon. She checked the time of the lecture – it was just possible if she hurried. She would miss the beginning, but could catch the second half – it would be worth it. She managed to sneak in on her press card; the security was fairly lax, more concerned with student hotheads than some Italian journalist. The question-and-answer session at the end of the lecture had been especially helpful in getting a feel for the scope of Dubov's influential ideas. She had become engrossed in the discussions as Dubov fielded questions from the inquisitive students making the most of their opportunity to quiz the great man, forgetting she was on a tight schedule herself. She casually checked her watch – damn! – the maglev would not wait: she had to fly. Time was now against her; she hurried out of the university to collect Pascal then sprint for the train.

She found him in the college staff canteen, deep in conversation with a gaggle of fellow scientists; she slid in beside her boyfriend and kissed him lightly on the cheek. It was a slightly unusual situation for Oriana as all the scientists were French, and so spoke in French. Most of her time professionally was spent covering *Curia* affairs, which were held in Latin. Unfortunately, her French wasn't the best, making it difficult for her to follow the scientists' conversation – she spoke Latin to Pascal. He glanced at her and smiled. Across the table, between mouthfuls of pasta, a middle-aged man was expounding on the current state of CCS technology. CCS – Carbon Capture and Storage – was one of the energy options being pursued in Europe and already several major experimental projects were under way in Germany, Holland and Italy. More and more data and experience were being collected and a working CCS plant was in the offing – indeed, a site near Toulouse had already been earmarked, a step that excited all those around the table. Any potential reduction in Europe's consumption of oil would be a godsend for the continent's long-term economic future, while decreasing exposure to the continuing geopolitical tension that surrounded this troublesome resource.

Oriana leant forward and whispered, 'It's time, darling; the maglev leaves in half an hour. Are you ready?' Pascal nodded and duly made his apologies, before grabbing his coat and bags as the pair departed the institute.

The journey to Rome would take just over five and a half hours, enough time for Oriana to make last-minute arrangements for the weekend over the phone, while Pascal could finish his paper.

The development, and rapid expansion, of the maglev network had revolutionised transport across the Eurasian landmass. At a fraction of the cost aircraft charged, one could cover substantial distances at very high speed – perhaps not enough to beat the plane, but close enough to tip the balance towards using the maglev. The greatest impact had been felt in the transportation of goods. Russia had become a huge commercial hub, with goods from Europe and Asia using the intercontinental maglev network as their primary mode of transportation. In just under 24 hours, vast, ten-mile-long maglev cargo trains could deliver goods from the Beijing Intercontinental Terminal into Moscow, and vice versa.

There were plans afoot to expand maglev into India, and even under the Bering Strait to Alaska, and the entire North American market. While most praised the maglev revolution, it had not been a universally positive experience – in particular, for those involved in merchant shipping, whose Euro-Asian traffic had evaporated as a direct result of maglev expansion.

The maglev pulled into Roma Termini on time; the pair collected their luggage and quickly headed for the main entrance to find a taxi to take them to Castel di Guido, just outside the city.

Oriana's family had an impressive villa in Castel di Guido, with spacious grounds and landscaped gardens. Recently she had begun researching a new book concerning the collapse of the NWO project in Europe, with particular reference to the demise of the centralist EU dictatorship and the attempted White genocide through mass alien immigration. It had been over ten years since the destruction of the one, and expulsion of the other, allowing Europe to readjust to a new and infinitely superior reality. She had invited a group of selected people for a long weekend at her villa in order to discuss the aftermath of the war, and Europe's evolving future, which she hoped would produce plenty of material for her upcoming book.

She had bracketed the guests into two groups: three she considered her main contributors, owing to their position, knowledge, age and authority, while the other three could bring important inputs in other key areas and add a little balance to the party. That was the theory. It would all begin tomorrow – Friday morning.

The first to arrive with the lark was Jörg Zander, a leading financial correspondence with the *Völkischer Beobachter,* who had extensive knowledge of currency matters, economic policy and the long-term economic patterns developing within the *Curia* nations. In his late forties, Zander was a big man with long, swept-back blond hair and a well-trimmed beard, which was beginning to grey. He was dressed in a smart dark-blue suit with a provocative red silk tie. He had something of the pirate about him, thought Oriana, as he exited the taxi, smiling to her over his shoulder and puffing nonchalantly on a large, expensive Cuban cigar.

Oriana gesticulated to Pascal, who in response hurried down to the taxi by the villa's front gates to help carry Jörg's stylish leather travelling cases. Jörg gave Pascal a nod of thanks before turning to Oriana with a broad grin and theatrical spreading of his arms as he strode towards his host. He proceeded to sweep Oriana up in an ostentatious bear-hug, leaving Pascal to follow in his wake, lugging Jörg's two main cases plus a travel holdall slung over his shoulder.

'Oriana, darling, what a fantastic place you've got here; thank you so very much for the invitation to visit such a beautiful spot,' announced Jörg in his accented Latin.

Oriana smiled back. 'Oh come on, Jörg; I'm sure you've been to plenty of places far more impressive than my modest little abode.'

Jörg glanced up at the eight-bedroomed villa, then at the three acres of well-groomed grounds along with the pool and tennis court – 'modest little abode' was not quite the description that sprang to mind. 'It's magnificent: a real Roman villa – I'd bet Caesar himself would feel at home in such a splendid place,' he said; then, waving his hand towards the rolling Roman hills, continued, 'And all set in this iconic countryside – it's simply stunning.'

'You're far too kind,' said Oriana, threading her right arm through Jörg's left and leading him up to the front door of the villa, where the maid was waiting to show him to his room. Jörg was glad to get inside the air-conditioned villa, as the Roman sun was already beginning to hammer down, even this early in the morning. Pascal arrived, hot and sweaty, with Jörg's fancy travelling bags just as Rosa, the maid, opened the door to Jörg's suite. Jörg, catching sight of Pascal, suddenly remembered his luggage. 'Thank you; I'm sorry, I should have helped – were they heavy? I forgot where I was.' Absent-mindedly he came within an ace of putting his hand in his pocket to tip Pascal. Luckily, he pulled back from making what would have been a blistering faux pas.

'It's okay. They weren't that heavy,' lied Pascal unconvincingly, before dumping Jörg's bags unceremoniously on the bed and turning on his heels. Playing lackey to rich Germans was definitely not part of his job description. He found Oriana on the veranda, looking down the long, sweeping drive to the electronic gates – the same drive along which Pascal had just toted Jörg's expensive baggage.

The next three guests all arrived at the same time, having travelled from Roma Termini in the same taxi – a rather smart Mercedes people carrier with leather upholstery. Although they had journeyed on different trains, all three had fortuitously arrived within 20 minutes of each other.

Initially, none had been aware of the identity of the others, which led to a rather comic situation as they all tried to hire taxis to the same destination simultaneously. Once the penny dropped, they quickly decided to share a taxi. On arrival, instead of dumping his fares at the gate, the taxi driver sensibly waited for the electric main gates to open, then drove up to the villa's front door. The three guests disembarked and carried their own bags into the villa's spacious reception area, where Oriana and Pascal greeted each in turn. First through the doors was the English lawyer Hannah York, who specialised in the legal repercussions of the Declaration of Rouen on national legislation. Youngish, at around thirty, she had shoulder-length brown hair and a broad face, set off by large, round, hazel eyes. Dressed formally in a smart, dark business suit with black patent shoes, Hannah made a beeline for Oriana who greeted her with a smile, asking in Latin how the journey from London had gone.

As Oriana and Hannah started swapping niceties, the second guest slipped unobtrusively through the front doors. A tall, powerful man in his late twenties, the new guest strode into the reception area carrying a huge, blue holdall as if it were a ragdoll, with the words 'Alabama State' emblazoned on its side. Pascal recognised him immediately from the description Oriana had given on the maglev. 'You must be Robert Foreman,' he enquired in Latin, and in less-than-perfect Latin with a broad Dixie accent the young man replied, 'That's correct, sir; nice to be here in Italy. I've been looking forward to this weekend ever since I received the kind invitation from Miss Perotti.'

Oriana broke off from her chat with Hannah to extend her hand to the young man. 'Robert, so nice to meet you at last; thank you for coming over. You can drop the "Miss Perotti" – just call me Oriana. It's quite an honour to have a representative of such a distinguished family with us. I'm sure you'll enjoy the weekend and find the experience beneficial.'

The third, and final, guest from the people carrier sidled in behind the bulk of the young son of Dixie – exposing the silhouette of the taxi driver hovering impatiently by the door. 'Pascal!' hissed Oriana. Pascal, becoming inured to his role as porter and general dogsbody, glanced resignedly at the front door before squeezing past the third guest – with profuse apologies in French – on his way to pay the waspish taxi driver.

On his return he found Oriana shaking hands with the third guest, a man of medium height, well built, in his early fifties with receding hair that gave him a prominent forehead and slightly protruding lips. He obviously knew Oriana well; the two of them gossiping away in Latin oblivious to those around them. Again, from the description given him, Pascal deduced this was José.

Rosa was standing at the edge of the party, waiting to show the guests their rooms. Oriana, catching Rosa's eye, abruptly brought her chat with José to an end and stepped back to face her guests. 'We're nearly all here now; Rosa will show you to your rooms. Please feel free to explore the villa and grounds; lunch will be served at around two o'clock on the veranda' – which she indicated by pointing past Rosa to the long veranda running down one side of the villa, giving a stunning view of the well-groomed grounds and pool.

Rosa took Hannah off to her room, while Oriana helped José to his suite and Pascal led Robert to his rooms at the rear of the villa, overlooking the plush tennis courts and rolling Roman hills.

The various guests disappeared into their rooms to unpack and freshen up in preparation for the long weekend. Soon individuals re-emerged, all having changed into more comfortable attire, to form little groups that began exploring the villa and venturing out into the warm sun to admire the grounds. Oriana and Pascal did their best to answer questions about the villa's history. Oriana's grandfather had bought the original parcel of agricultural land on the edge of the village of Castel di Guido fifty years ago. Her father had subsequently built a modest little villa on the land as a weekend retreat. Later, having acquired the funds and the ego, he decided to bulldoze the old building and raise the current opulent spread – all paid for by the profits from his plastic-moulding business up in Turin.

The final guest had yet to arrive, but just before 2:00, as if by telepathy, a sleek, bright red Alfa Romeo coupé pulled up by the front gate. A short conversation ensued over the gate intercom system, the ornate gates swung open and the Alfa drove in, pulling over into the secluded parking bays tastefully screened off by a row of cypress trees.

So it was that at 2:00 on a balmy Friday afternoon on the outskirts of Rome, all Oriana's guests were present and correct as they sat down around a long table shielded from the sun by a huge, flamboyantly swish canopy that ran the whole length of the veranda. Oriana sat at the head of the table as the host, with Pascal to her right. While the guests made themselves comfy, Oriana took the opportunity to introduce everybody and explain the purpose of the weekend.

She rose to her feet and in the distinctive Latin spoken by all Italians, began to address the group. 'One way or another, you are all known to me. Some of you are long-standing friends and acquaintances; for the others, while acknowledging this may be our first meeting, you have all been recommended to me by colleagues who hold your work and opinions in high esteem. As most of you know, I'm both a freelance journalist and author, and it is in my capacity as an author that I've invited you all to this, my family's villa at Castel di Guido.

'I'm intending to write a book concerning the fall of the NWO project, the aftermath of the Eurabian War in Europe and its epoch-changing impact on the rest of the world. You've been chosen because each brings unique knowledge of specific sectors of European life – which will become clear as you're introduced. We're about to eat, so there's no need to give your life histories: just introduce yourselves and state your specialist field.' She turned to Pascal, nodded, then sat down.

Pascal remained seated while introducing himself. 'I'm Pascal Faurot; as most of you know, I'm also Oriana's partner. I'm a scientist, currently working in the École Normale Supérieure in Paris. I shall be speaking about the current state of scientific research and development in Europe, but perhaps more importantly, I'll be giving some insight into the long-term goals of Europe's scientific programme.'

'Thank you, Pascal – short and sweet, as requested.' Oriana smiled, then nodded to Hannah, sitting next to Pascal.

Hannah, taking her cue from Pascal, also remained seated. 'Hello everybody: I'm Hannah York, an English lawyer currently working in Cambridge and London. My field of specialisation is the Declaration of Rouen. Its clout is huge, stretching even into areas where formally it has no legal power. Generally speaking, the considerable impact of the Declaration on English Law is replicated in the legislation of most European countries, despite their different legal structures and modes of operation – as I hope to demonstrate during my presentation.'

'Thank you, Hannah. Jörg, do you mind?'

'No, of course not, Oriana. I'm Jörg Zander, a business and financial correspondent with the *Völkischer Beobachter*. I've been invited to Oriana's lovely villa to discuss the state of European business and the substantial financial developments which have transformed banking practice across Europe – which will probably overlap with certain aspects of Hannah's expertise, since the driving force behind these changes also comes from the Declaration of Rouen.'

'Thank you, Jörg. We now turn to my left; José, I believe you're next.'

Before the new speaker could introduce himself, Rosa appeared by the sliding doors with two serving girls to start laying out the food. It was to be an informal buffet affair – though the food laid out so attractively on fine ceramic platters looked anything but informal. All the weekend's food would be prepared by Salvatore, a local chef who specialised in function catering. Having carefully placed their platters within easy reach of the guests, Rosa and the serving girls returned to the kitchen for the remainder of the buffet. While the ladies were away José took the opportunity to make his brief introduction.

'Hello, everybody: I'm José Pinho. Before discussing my field of interest I'd just like to thank Oriana for the kind invitation to attend this important event. I've known Oriana for some years, having crossed her path during various religious conferences up and down Europe, which she covered for the Italian press. I'm an academic from the Universidade Catolica Portuguesa based in Oporto, specialising in Theology. Although the university is Catholic and much of my work is grounded in the concept of Christian revelation, the Pagan revolution has not passed us by completely unnoticed. There has been a great deal of time and effort invested in trying to understand the shifting religious sands in Europe; indeed, I've written several academic papers on different aspects of contemporary Paganism.'

Just as José was about to expound further the ladies reappeared from the kitchen with more goodies for the table. Oriana glanced at the hungry faces salivating at the feast laid before them and decided to finish the introductions. 'Thank you, José, but before we start our lunch I think it only fair to allow our last two guests to say a few words – Robert?'

The young man smiled broadly at Oriana, then launched into his introduction. 'My name is Robert Foreman, son of Vernon Foreman, whom I suspect you've all heard of. Dad was the driving force behind sending European-trained and armed American legionaries into North America – which in effect saved the continent for White Americans. By now, of course, there are six nations in North America. I'm a proud citizen of the Confederacy, but I have a good knowledge of all the North American states, even Québec. As Oriana has explained, I'm here to talk on behalf of North America and our new future within the North American Congress.'

Oriana thanked Robert then quickly turned to the final guest. 'I know you want to start eating, but let Marcello speak for a minute; he's our last guest – Marcello?'

'Thank you, Oriana, and hello everyone, I'm, Marcello Salerno, member of the Italian cabinet – we advise President Bellucci on various policy positions and legislative decisions. I've been invited to explain the political system in Italy, which is similar to the systems used in many European countries – though not all. There is overlap, once again, with Hannah since the

Declaration throws such a long shadow over everything. It can't be ignored, because it's held almost as holy writ among the general public, who see it as their ultimate protection from corrupt politicians and administrators. Believe me, as a politician myself, I'm under no illusions as to our reputation.'

'Thank you, Marcello, and all the rest of you. I have one more piece of information. We will be joined tonight by Concetta Leoni, a journalist like myself who wishes to do a piece on this meeting and its importance, as Europe faces the challenge of the post-NWO world. Okay, that's enough talking for now; Salvatore's gone to great lengths to prepare this spread, so please – enjoy: *buon appetito.*'

They settled down to a relaxed lunch, washed down with plenty of red wine. The afternoon drifted on lazily as everything slowed down under the accumulated effect of the warm, early-afternoon sun, full bellies and a generous intake of alcohol. Oriana cast an impish eye over her content guests and decided it was time to poke a stick into the hornets' nest. She knew José worked for a Catholic institution but had, at the very least, sympathies towards the growing Pagan movement. She also knew he had attended a few Pagan ceremonies following the Roman tradition – all in the name of academic research, of course. At one time José had confided to Oriana that he had a marked affinity with Mercury, and at times could almost feel his presence.

Robert, the young Confederate, came from a strictly Christian background, Southern Baptist, though how much was belief and how much culture, Oriana couldn't tell. A bit of fishing was called for.

She placed a couple of olives in her mouth and chewed over the problem, 'Robert, tell me,' she began, 'as a good Christian what's your take on all these European Pagans?' She kept an eye on José as she asked the question – he in turn focused on Robert for some insight into an outsider's view of native Aryan religious practices.

'To be honest, I'm not entirely sure what's going on. There are Pagans in America, especially in the more northerly territories – Odinists and the like. In Dixie it's mainly Christian: the Baptists are very strong – you could say it's almost our national religion. Having said that, I understand why there was a backlash against Christianity in Europe. It lost its relevance; it spoke for everybody and therefore for nobody – as Frederick the Great famously observed – owing to its universalist credo, which in turn led to it welcoming immigrants into Europe. To be honest, although the Baptists preach the same Christian universalist ethos in Dixie, when it comes to practical matters you find some of the most ardent Baptists are utterly opposed to all forms of universalism, including immigration. Of course, there is no immigration into any of the nations of the NAC; the laws throughout North America have been tightened considerably. I'd say we're more or less back where we were before Kennedy and LBJ threw open the gates. Perhaps somebody could give me a clearer picture of Paganism in Europe?'

Oriana turned her head. 'José?'

Everybody's attention was now on José. He took a mouthful of red wine, then began: 'There's been a simmering anti-Christian undercurrent in Europe for centuries, mainly animated by the authoritarian tendencies inherent within Christianity's orthodox Nicene credo. However, it was the use of Christian teachings on equality to give a veneer of moral authority to mass third-world immigration that really stoked the popular backlash.

'I suspect it was the general rejection of universality as a concept by Europeans, following their nightmare experiences under the NWO project and the horrors of the Eurabian War, that led many to search for a more pertinent spirituality – a more European spirituality.

'They also rejected the rudderless concept of atheism – though of course there are still plenty of individual atheists around today. However, most have grasped the moral dangers inherent in a society bereft of a higher social code. Rampant hedonism might be fine and dandy while you're young and single, out for a good time, but where does it leave the more mature individual who wishes to raise a family? As we all realise by now, hedonism and the social cancers that follow in its wake all fitted nicely into the NWO's plans for mankind's ultimate destiny as mindless units of consumption. Let's be clear about this: you either accept that humans are entities with their own agendas and dreams, which inevitably encompasses their friends and kin – a construct commonly referred to as "society" – or conversely, we're just a haphazard collection of undifferentiated automatons, easily sated with glitzy showbiz trinkets, casual sex, copious booze and drugs, all tied up with an utter lack of responsibility.

'Therefore, I'd argue that spirituality cannot die, for we will always need a higher spiritual authority; indeed, I'd say that a meaningful society is impossible without the anchor of a spiritual dimension. The vast majority of Europeans have come to the same conclusion, thus explaining the rapid growth in the movements advocating a return to our indigenous Pagan roots.

'No doubt you're aware of the *Liber Iuliani* – the Book of Julian – referred to erroneously by Christians as the Pagan Bible. This book was completed fairly recently in accordance with the wishes of the Roman emperor Julian the Philosopher, who back in the fourth century AD defined the philosophical corpus fit for a pagan priest. True, there was a slight delay of some 1600 years between Julian first expressing his opinions and our modern response in collating these works into a single volume. However, the work has now been completed and named in honour of the man who inspired its compilation – thus the Book of Julian.

'The book in its basic form is primarily a collection of Greek and Latin philosophy. However, in full editions there are also copies of the epic poetry of Homer, Hesiod and Virgil, given as classic exemplars of the Gods at work. Homer has two pieces in the collection, the *Iliad* and *Odyssey*, as does Hesiod with his *Theogony* and *Works and Days,* while Virgil has to be content with one, namely his mighty *Aeneid*.

'The composition of the Book of Julian naturally echoes the emperor's instructions, containing philosophical collections by Pythagoreans, Platonists, Neo-Platonists, Stoics and the works of Aristotle. The Book also contains the critical works of Plotinus, Porphyry and the Neo-Platonist Sallustius, plus the relevant works of Julian himself. Incidentally, Julian's not the only emperor whose work appears in the book; the Stoic writings of Marcus Aurelius are also present. Julian was very specific in rejecting Epicurean philosophy and the works of Pyrrho, a wish that has been honoured. Overall the book presents a powerful collection of works that delve deeply into the nature of man and divinity.

'Although by today there are numerous schools of Paganism in Europe: Germanic, Slavonic, Roman – or 'Imperial' – Greek, Celtic, Baltic, Hungarian and Finnic, they all make use of the Book of Julian as a philosophic and intellectual reference point.'

The young Southerner suddenly interrupted: 'But don't they also use their own sacred texts, like the *Edda,* or the Ulster Cycle among the Irish Celts?'

'That's an interesting point. The mythological tales are far more complex than the basic stories in their raw form might suggest. Sallustius mentioned mythology in his treatise, *On the Gods and the Universe*; he recognised how the simple rustic would grasp the myth merely at its face value, whereas the learned man would see deeper into the underlying message – which was the real point of the myth in the first place. Many myths can be understood on multiple layers. However, your basic point is right, Robert; these texts are very important to modern Pagans, though there is a problem of Christian corruption due to the late date of their being committed to vellum – in most cases this occurred under Christian cultural hegemony.

'There are many today who have grasped the multi-layered nature of mythology, recognising they're not mere fictional fairy stories, but allegorical windows into the minds of the Gods and are to be treated as such; that certainly appears to be the attitude of Spiritual Norse Pagans, among others.

There's a deep tendency among those raised in the world of monotheistic divinity to automatically belittle other belief systems – without even coming to some understanding of such beliefs.

'Interestingly, I characterise Julian himself as one who sought the Old Gods while still entwined in the mindset of monotheistic Christianity; he was raised a Christian and turned to the Old Gods for spiritual succour. He's a fascinating man, very intelligent, as his writings clearly demonstrate; one wonders what might have been if he'd lived longer – he was killed early in his reign, fighting the Persians. His promise of a restored Paganism must rank as one of the greatest "what ifs?" in European history.

'However, to get back to your original point, these stories, myths, are not theological in the sense we in Europe have come to understand the term under the influence of Semitic belief systems like Christianity and Judaism. For those seeking a deeper understanding of the nature of the Gods, I would suggest taking a spiritual journey under the tutelage of a Pagan shaman; it's a journey well worth the effort.'

Oriana, rather surprised, interjected, 'José?'

'So I've heard, shall we say?' Oriana was not convinced, but left it for another day.

José continued, 'Of course, as many Christian apologists continually remind us, the absurdities of Pagan mythology are put to shame by the obvious truth as revealed in the Bible. You know what I'm talking about: things like Jonah living inside a whale, or the Israelites bringing down the walls of Jericho with trumpet blasts, or Yahweh turning Lot into a pillar of salt and so forth. I'll skip over Sodom and Gomorrah, talking bushes or walking on water, feeding 5000 with a couple of fish, curing blindness and coming back from the dead. For some reason these examples of Jewish mythology are held to be true by many in your country, while dismissing our native mythology as nonsense – though of course we Europeans have always recognised our mythology as mythology, unlike our Semitic friends who continue to argue for the veracity of their myths.

'This sounds awfully anti-Christian, which was not my intent, though I have to admit a recent paper of mine was savaged by a certain French bishop, which does tend to colour one's view. Ultimately, whatever the truth of the material in the Bible, one cannot ignore the vast contribution Christianity has made to the formation of European identity. Many have been critical of this legacy, blaming Christianity for everything from the fall of the Roman Empire and the grim religious purges of the Middle Ages to the disastrous French Revolution and all the subsequent horrors that owed their existence to the demons released in that insanity. Once again, whether all these ills can be laid exclusively at the door of Christianity is at best moot; however, one can say that blindly attacking the Church only hurts Europe, since the legacy of these events is indelibly stamped on us all. My personal opinion is that we should recognise the contribution of Christianity, for better or for worse, and move on. If the Church really is the way – as it claims – then in time it will re-establish its authority naturally. If, as some argue, the Church only acquired its dominant position through state sponsorship, then one suspects Paganism will reap the new dawn. Time will tell, one way or another.'

Oriana had been listening carefully to José's words and finally asked a few questions of her own – questions which had been in the back of her mind since her childhood days at Sunday school. 'José, is there one god or many? And has God, or the Gods, always existed? Is the universe the work of the divine or the result of the laws of physics?'

José guffawed loudly, 'Do you always ask such simple questions?' With some effort he managed to regain his composure; then, looking intently at Oriana, began his response.

'Your question is very much in the Judaic tradition of the one almighty godhead – though of course, you do realise that Yahweh himself actually admits the existence of other gods in the Old Testament? Reread the story of the Tower of Babel carefully; you'll be surprised. All religions have a creation myth – no, that's not true – the vast majority of religions have creation myths, but I would argue the place of these myths within the religion tells you more about how these religions view themselves in relation to man. Paganism has a number of such myths; certainly the Germanic and Greek traditions have quite famous myths on the creation of the world.

'However, are these creation myths genuinely cosmic in their reach and importance, or merely stopgaps to get back to the core of the religion – namely, the relationship between man and the gods? You could take a step further and ask, do these religions accept a state before man, where their god or gods existed in a universe without man? Genesis appears to suggest that everything was created for man; therefore has Yahweh any purpose or function without man? Would an uncontrolled nuclear war that killed all mankind also kill Yahweh?

'Pagan Gods are often attacked for being too human – fighting, loving, scheming and so forth. Although, as I've already mentioned, these are mythological tales, they do appear to lead one in a far more human direction than is the case with the Semitic godhead. The Pagan Gods are portrayed very much as human gods, tied to humans. How is this? I would posit that it grew out of Paganism's linking of the manifestations of the Gods with Nature and her various aspects. Having said that, Paganism still holds the Gods to be as otherworldly as the monotheists' God; after all, they're described as being eternal, unbegotten, incorporeal, et cetera. Yet for all this, Pagans still look to Nature almost as a bridge between them and the eternal power that is the God or Gods. Monotheism has no such bridge, no link between our world and that of God – he's a very alien entity, don't you think? That's why there's such an emphasis on faith, blind or otherwise, and obedience to the Church's teachings. Both of these aspects of monotheism are generally absent from Paganism.

'You asked about the creation of the universe. The Semites would claim their god Yahweh, or Jehovah or Allah, created everything. To me, this position of itself begs a question or two. If you accept that the universe came into existence around 14 billion years ago, and we – that is *homo sapiens sapiens* – have been around for at most 200,000 years and perhaps only as little as 100,000 years, what has Yahweh been doing during the intervening 13 billion, 900 million, 800,000 years? Incidentally, as for us higher, Aryan humans, who constitute the most recent evolutionary development from the primitive earlier versions that still inhabit substantial parts of the planet, it appears we emerged as recently as 30–40,000 years ago, according to some scientists.

'The classic Greek Pagan creation myth gives a far more subtle account than the crude Semitic model found in the Bible. It has insightful depth, with various Gods looking after different aspects of creation: those who made the world, those who animate it, those who harmonise it and finally those who maintain it. These are the Gods of the world, but there's another class – the Hypercosmic Gods, who create such things as essence, thought and the soul. Of course, I'm being ludicrously simplistic here, but you grasp the level of complexity involved in certain Pagan creationist mythologies.'

Oriana switched off the little solid-state recorder she would be carrying around all weekend. That was a good start, she mused, but there's more to come from both José and Robert – early days yet. As the afternoon drew on, some guests retired to their bedrooms for a *siesta,* while others wandered back to the gardens, where Hannah, Pascal and Robert were sitting under the shade of a cypress tree. Hannah and Robert had been chatting in English, but once Pascal arrived they switched to Latin. Oriana watched the three from under the awning shading the veranda at the side of the villa. Hannah was the youngest woman present, and although in Oriana's opinion her attire was less than chic – all Italians consider anybody from north of the Alps to be a philistine when it comes to dress sense – this minor fault didn't seem to have diminished either Pascal's or Robert's ardour for her company.

Oriana took a closer look at Hannah; she was a fresh-faced creature who appeared to be enjoying the men's attention. Oriana took one more glance at the group then decided it was time for her to join her enamoured boyfriend.

She walked slowly towards the group, with Pascal very much on her mind. Oriana had recently turned 34, one more heavy milestone that merely underlined the fact that her biological clock was steadily ticking away precious time. If she wanted a family, she'd have to act soon. Pascal, her current lover, was actually two years her junior. She was acutely aware that this painful dilemma was all her own doing. She'd spurned previous opportunities to start a family, in particular the long-term relationship she'd had with Massimo Gargini, son of the owner of a Pescara haulage company used by her father's business in Turin. That excruciating break-up had occurred following an ultimatum from Massimo, desperate to start a family. She refused, of course; she always refused.

If she was at last going to bite the bullet, this little weekend gathering, and any ensuing book, could well be her swansong, as a baby would change everything and make her current hectic lifestyle impossible to maintain. She had much to chew over. She sat down quietly close to Pascal, who was discussing computer systems, mainly with Robert – though Hannah listened carefully, this not being one of her areas of expertise.

'The *Curia* is actively widening its policy of self-sufficiency, which has dominated military procurement since the formation of the *legiones,* to include strategically important sectors such as computer hardware and software.

'The big project currently being pursued is the creation of an operating system that can be used throughout Europe and be as user-friendly as the current commercial packages from the RoC. Rather than reinventing the wheel, the project leaders made it clear from day one that the new operating system would be a Linux-based program, but cleaned up and simplified for Joe Public, who's no computer buff, nor has much interest in becoming one.

'Once it's ready, and the word is it'll be out later this year, the new system – called *Euclid* – will be free to download, certainly in Europe. It'll come with its own packages, such as an office suite, that are normally expensive bolt-ons for the commercial systems.'

'That'll hit the likes of Microsoft and Apple hard,' voiced Robert.

'I think that was part of the idea, Microsoft had a horrendous record, like most of corporate America, in supporting and promoting the entire NWO poison. Turning our back – as a continent – on such corporate monsters was always going to be part of the *Curia's* ethos.'

'That's right,' interrupted Hannah. 'The Declaration of Rouen states openly that Europe should strive to maintain a domestic commercial base in every field of business and innovation, otherwise the continent will fall prey to third-party manipulation – which is basically what you've just been saying regarding Microsoft.'

'Do you think *Euclid* will be available in the Confederacy?' queried Robert.

'I doubt very much if distribution beyond Europe's borders has been a priority for the *Curia*. However, as there will have to be an English-language version I'd say not only the Confederacy, but the Aussies and the other English-speaking countries should be able to get hold of a copy easily enough – though the spelling will be in British English, rather than the American variety.'

The group slowly broke up; some drifted back to their rooms, others found new conversations to join. Oriana took Pascal's arm and led him off to a secluded corner of the grounds, where they could relax together in private under the shade of a fine stone pine. There was no rush as the long, hot afternoon meandered on; the evening meal, far, far away, would not be sighted until 9:00 pm, when the sun had gone down and the welcome evening had brought some relieving freshness to the stifling Roman climate.

The early birds started drifting into the dining room next to the veranda at around 8:00 – just in time to see the late arrival of Oriana's extra guest. Concetta Leoni was an Italian journalist who'd heard of Oriana's fascinating project through her connections in the Italian press. She had contacted Oriana asking if she could attend the weekend, with a view to writing an article on the New Europe based on her observations. Oriana, judging that such an article might well prove beneficial to her new book's sales, agreed to the request.

Concetta was a striking woman in her mid-forties. She had dark blond hair, a round, lived-in face with big dark eyes and strong features. One wouldn't have called her beautiful, but she had that look of worldly experience that so many men found alluring. Even the two small moles on her face, one above her lip, the other on her chin, played their part, enhancing her air of raw, natural womanhood – no plastic-and-paint Barbie doll: she was the real deal. As everybody started to drift slowly towards the veranda, where Rosa was setting out the places for the evening meal, it was noticeable how Concetta never lacked for male company.

The evening meal finally began, accompanied by even more wine as the guests settled down for a very long and leisurely Roman banquet that would undoubtedly stretch into the wee hours. One aspect of the meal novel to the non-Italians was the bowl of pears that always appeared at the end of the meal as a finisher. Some, like Marcello, automatically took hold of a small knife to skin the pear before eating – a practice soon followed by Robert and Hannah. Others just ate the pear like an apple, skin and all.

Oriana, as usual, was steering events and decided that Pascal could use this Friday evening to expound on the state of science in *post-bellum* Europe. She made sure her recorder was on, as did Concetta: then invited Pascal to say a bit about his area of expertise.

'Since the end of the War and the emergence of the global regional blocs – in particular the Shanghai Protocol grouping – it has become imperative that Europe not only keeps abreast of current technological development, but instigates new areas of research.

'As Europeans we need to grasp the fact that the *Curia* looks upon competition from the Shanghai Protocol nations – and indeed the NAC – as healthy and beneficial to Europe's scientific progress. Without competition we stagnate, and once-energetic institutions become moribund, content to harp on about past glories; this is not our way, and the *Curia* is determined it will not be Europe's fate. I strongly suspect that these three entities, Europe – including Russia – North America and the Orient, will ultimately fight out their great scientific duel in space. It's a vast canvas, on which none will want for a challenge. I'm not talking about war here; the coming of global regionalism has guaranteed peace to a far greater degree than the unnatural, engineered dictatorship of the NWO's uniform homogeneity could ever have aspired to achieve. The nuclear arsenals held by the three major regional blocs would turn any all-out war into a declaration of mutual suicide.

'This is not to say there won't be unofficial conventional clashes from time to time, like those between the *Curia* and the old USA in the Atlantic and later on the Tigris. These, of course, were "Ghost Wars" – wars that didn't occur officially, even though men fought and died in them.

'Outside the three main blocs the other areas of the globe are, for all practical purposes, of no consequence; they are not in a position to compete now, and frankly there is no obvious or likely path for them to reach a position where they could join the great game at any foreseeable time in the future – biology seems to have passed them by. Any serious struggle for future supremacy – in whatever field – will be between Aryans and Orientals.

'As you're all aware, the ECP and Russia already have an ambitious space programme in operation, a programme which will undoubtedly grow and expand with time. This may be an expensive pastime, but treading water is simply not an option – unless you can guarantee that the NAC and Shanghai Protocol countries will do the same. If we, as a people, as a race, want a future, we need to compete.

'In other areas Europe is repositioning itself to be a major player in all sectors of scientific and technical advancement. I was talking to Hannah and Robert after lunch about Europe's significant entry into the computer software market. However, what I did not mention was the parallel development in hardware design and manufacture. These are areas traditionally dominated by North American and Oriental concerns, but in both areas Europe has accepted the challenge and responded with far-reaching programmes of research and manufacture.'

Concetta decided it was time to make her presence known with a question. 'Tell me, Pascal: what's your understanding of the position with genetically modified crops – an area dominated by the Americans?'

'The question of agricultural commercialisation was touched upon in the Declaration of Rouen, I believe.' He glanced towards Hannah, who nodded in confirmation.

'There are various problems with genetically modified crops, principal of which is the ownership and production of individual foodstuffs. These doctored crops – or their seeds, to be specific – have been copyrighted. Therefore the corporations that own the rights to these seeds also own the market in the resultant foodstuffs. Do I need to state the obvious? After water, food is the most basic requirement of human existence – yet we're happily allowing whole varieties of foodstuffs to become the private property of commercial concerns. If the Declaration of Rouen considered the private ownership of utilities to be unacceptable, how much stronger do you imagine is its position in opposition to the effective private ownership of any given variety of food? It's immoral, and highly dangerous, to put such power into the hands of a small clique of men for their own financial gratification. Indeed, I'd go so far as to say that the commercial manipulation of genetically modified foodstuffs constitutes the greatest condemnation of the NWO project it's imaginable to make.

'The selling and distribution of genetically modified foodstuffs has been banned throughout the *Curia,* while domestic research in crop production has been designated a continent-wide concern. By today agricultural research programmes are in operation right across Europe; even the smaller nations are investing in their long-term agricultural development. The whole question of global corporations, and their homogenising tendencies, will no doubt be covered by Jörg in greater depth later on.'

Oriana had a question for her partner. 'What's happening in Europe to safeguard energy sources, and what is the future of energy for us in Europe?'

'The acquisition and safeguarding of strategic *ex-Europa* resources, meaning raw materials, is the concern of the *Curia*. Indeed, as I think you all know, the non-war in Iraq between the *Legiones* and the old USA was fought over oil. This situation continues today, Africa being an interesting case in point. Africa is a continent of vast wealth in terms of natural resources, and historically was a part of the world where European influence used to reign supreme. By today it is the Shanghai Protocol countries that rule the roost – China, in particular, has her claws deep into Africa. We are beginning to slowly reassert ourselves, especially in the south of the continent, where the new *Suid Afrika* was established with *Curia* support. I believe Marcello will discuss this further on Sunday.

'To a degree, the growing ties between the *Curia* and Russia have changed the game for us; Europe now resources a large proportion of its basic needs in raw materials from Russia.

'However, there are a number of promising projects currently under way that potentially could transform the way we generate and use energy. Obvious examples of this include advanced battery technology for the rapid charging and storing of electricity; the ongoing advanced research into nuclear fusion, a development which would revolutionise energy production; and CCS – Carbon Capture and Storage – another area whose potential is enormous.

'I could go on for hours, since somewhere or other in Europe there's an institute engaged in scientific research touching every conceivable field – from the war on cancer and the enticing promise of genetics, to deep-space exploration, robotics and the whole complex field of AI.'

3.3 – Saturday

The following morning, after a pleasant breakfast on the veranda, Robert Foreman gave an account of the situation in North America. He had prepared a presentation that would cover the functioning of the NAC, the War of Reconquest and the RoC's successful prosecution of the Aztlan–Columbian war – in which the CSA fought as an ally of the RoC in order to retake Texas – plus a general round-up of the reclaiming of North America by Aryan forces.

Robert made himself comfortable, then began his narrative. 'I'll start over on the West Coast, where two new states, the Republic of Columbia and the People's Republic of Aztlan, were at war with each other for domination of the old state of California. This had been a tough war for both parties, but the RoC slowly gained the upper hand. It's perhaps misleading to label this as a purely RoC war, since the Confederacy also fought against Aztlan, to retake Texas, most of which had fallen to Aztlan-controlled militias. As the RoC army pushed ever southward, the vast Latino population of immigrants retreated with the defeated Aztlan forces, petrified of the bloodthirsty reputation the hard-core North Westerners had for dealing with Hispanics. With both the RoC and the Confederacy in the ascendancy, the Aztlan project faced total annihilation. It was during this time that talks began in the NAC to solve the bigger problem of Latino penetration across the continent. The RoC and CSA were not the only member states to have significant Latino populations; if the NAC countries wanted to stay true to their founding principles as Aryan homelands, all the Latinos would have to go.

'Once the last of the Aztlan forces had retreated across the Mexican border, both the RoC and Dixie decided to round up the remnants of their Latino population for deportation. The military brass of the RoC and Dixie met at Fort Hood and came up with a plan to create a territorial bubble inside Mexico into which these remnants could be repatriated. And this is exactly what happened. It was nothing huge: just a hop over the border to Ciudad Juarez, which under the old corrupt USA regime had been a "bi-national metropolitan area" with El Paso – can you believe it? Legalised treachery! A government sharing its own national territory with a foreign, and if I may say, alien nation. Needless to say, under the Confederacy absurdities like "bi-national metropolitan areas" were swiftly disbanded.

'Both the Confederacy and Columbia sent troops to occupy Ciudad Juarez, which was deserted as most of the locals had fled on the approach of our forces. We threw up a defensive perimeter around the city, and told the NAC we'd hold our position for seven days. If any other member state wished to expel its Latino population, it had this brief window in which to ship them back over the border. The US still had a fairly substantial population, even after the heavy losses the Latinos incurred during the barbaric urban wars against the Blacks, and their eventual crushing by the Eagle Legions, supported by Union militias.

'Soon sealed and heavily guarded trains – along with convoys of buses – were running down to El Paso from the US and Canada in relays, full of Latinos for deportation. This human cargo was disgorged into holding zones outside El Paso, then systematically moved into designated areas of Ciudad Juarez. You should be familiar with these tactics; we got the idea from the *Legiones'* dumping of Albanian Muslims and Gypsies over the Sangarius into central Turkey.

'However, the situation in Ciudad Juarez started to deteriorate badly. The Mexican military were pressing hard from the outside, while the seething millions now filling every nook and cranny of Ciudad Juarez were becoming highly aggressive towards their jailors. There were some pretty nasty incidents, I can tell you, resulting in a large number of fatalities, most of whom unfortunately were civilians.

'In the end it was decided we couldn't hold the city for seven days. It wasn't so much the Mexican Army we couldn't contain, as the heaving sea of urban Latino dregs in Ciudad Juarez. We came to an agreement with the Columbian government and withdrew all our men after five and a half days – and that's when the really interesting stuff began to happen.'

'Which was what?' interjected Marcello.

'The attitude of the Mexican Army; they had absolutely no time for the rabble they found dumped in the city. After a brief tour, the commanding general – Jorge Obregon – ordered the dispersal of the population across the country. However, the angry mob refused to move from the Confederate border. Obregon, incensed at being thwarted and having little patience with what he considered to be worthless Chicanos, gave the order for his troops to clean out the human dross. They slaughtered on a Biblical scale; to them these people were the absolute bottom of the barrel, and frankly were no loss to Mexico.

'Contrary to what might have been expected, the hard-line attitude towards the border and population movements, adopted by both Richmond and San Francisco, were understood and applauded by Mexico. Clarity of purpose is always appreciated by those trying to operate human social systems.

'The joint RoC/CSA border with Mexico was designated a military zone and very heavily fortified – again, something you're familiar with in Europe, having experienced the Berlin Wall. A triple fence was erected along the entire length of the border: a twelve-foot, electrified razor-wire fence in the front, then a solid concrete wall with live machine-gun towers every 1,000 metres in the middle, and finally an alarmed barbed-wire rear fence. Attack dogs are free to wander on either side of the concrete wall. In front of the razor-wire fence, a half-mile deep minefield was laid. In the case of the Confederacy this minefield lies along the Confederate bank of the Rio Grande. For the Columbians – who have no natural geographic marker – the minefield is just a clearly designated, fenced-off area in front of the razor wire fence.

'There are now only three official crossing points between North America and Mexico – all heavily policed and tightly controlled. Anybody trying to cross the border anywhere else is likely to get themselves shot and killed.

'In both the RoC and the Confederacy, local volunteer militias back up the official border forces, patrolling behind the triple fence in case anybody gets through, which does happen occasionally – mainly through tunnelling. Everybody caught, without exception, is deported and given a life ban from whichever country expelled them.

'The Negro population is another long-standing problem that has bedevilled North America, ever since these people were first brought over from Africa. In truth, the importing of Negroes into the Americas – for whatever reason – has been an unmitigated disaster. With the exception of physical labour, they have consistently shown themselves incapable of functioning constructively within advanced societies as found in Aryan North America.

'Blacks fared particularly badly during the Wars of Secession. There had never been much love lost between Blacks and Latinos, who used the war as a smokescreen to hunt down and exterminate urban Blacks by the million. It also needs acknowledging that during the campaigns conducted during the War of Reconquest, numerous Aryan militias criss-crossed the continent cleaning out any remaining population concentrations of Negroes and Latinos. There were many local battles during these campaigns, but the better-organised and better-trained Aryan forces almost always defeated the disorganised and unprepared Third Worlders. I'm not claiming it was pretty, or particularly noble, but county by county, state by state, the Negro population was expunged.

Hannah interjected: 'But I've seen Negroes in North America, when I attended a conference on, "Membership of Regional Blocs".'

'Really: where was that?'

'Raleigh, North Carolina.'

'Yeah, that makes sense. The urban Negro population has gone; I'd say 95 per cent were either killed or died from starvation and the rest fled. In the rural areas, mostly in Dixie, they managed to survive a little better – perhaps as many as 25 per cent came through the war. Those that survived have a status similar to the Native Indians. At the end of the war the remnant Negro population was given the option of returning home to Africa, after the NAC had bought, and taken control of substantial portions of Grand Kru and Sinoe counties in Liberia. All who went got a generous financial package and practical help in building a home. The Liberian government also got a bonus for every Negro from North America who settled there. Alternatively, they could move onto reservations for Negroes, where they had to remain unless issued a pass by the local authorities. Around 80 per cent opted for the reservations.

'This situation remains unsatisfactory to many in the Confederacy, where the bulk of these reservations are situated. Most suspect that in the future, perhaps by the time our grandchildren or great-grandchildren are adults, some soft-headed liberal will restart the campaigns for "equality", with all the lessons from the Wars of Secession and War of Reconquest having been conveniently forgotten. There's currently a lot of speculation concerning proposals to move the rump of the Confederacy's Negro population to the Caribbean Islands; we'll see, but that appears to be the direction of current thinking on the subject.

'The other major non-European population was the Asians – Chinese, Japanese, Koreans and Vietnamese. Quite simply, they were told to leave within a given number of days, which varied according to the circumstances of the individual. This all sounds rather draconian, but they were given plenty of warning – typically six months – in which to sort out things like property, business arrangements, travel plans and so forth. The Asian population was heaviest in Columbia and Canada, though most of the repatriation arrangements were organised through the NAC, which explains the uniformity of policy across the continent. Those who refused to move had their property confiscated and were simply deported. Those that ran were given over to bounty hunters; this happened everywhere within the NAC – even in the Atlantic Provinces.

'The same sort of thing happened with the other non-European population groups – Muslims, Turks, Indians, whatever – they all went the same way as the Asians. Of course, there was one other long-standing problematic group, but I'll leave them to Hannah, as we used the same technique as the *Curia* to deal with that particular clique.'

Concetta took the opportunity to jump in with another question. 'So are we to believe that the "Great American Melting Pot" has stopped blending?'

'Very good question; yes, you are – though I'd take issue with your opening premise, which in my opinion is completely false. The whole idea that America was ever a melting pot is farcical. Until LBJ's lunacy in dismantling the old USA's border controls, the only people coming into America were Europeans. Now, Europeans may have different ethnicities, but we're all the same race – European Caucasian. And before the late nineteenth century, the categories of Europeans that were allowed into the country were even narrower.

'Take a look at the brave men who fought and died in the War for Southern Independence; look at their names and ethnic backgrounds – for most of them it could have been the English Civil war for all their ethnic diversity. This "Melting Pot" label is complete hogwash, dreamt up by one particular ethnic tribe who have their own nasty little axe to grind.

'As for the countries of North America today, I'd say we're very close to the position we were in at the turn of the twentieth century. It's not as good as our position in 1850, but it sure beats the horrors that existed prior to the Global Meltdown.

'There's one last thing I'd like to say before break-time. The whole atmosphere in North America has changed fundamentally since the wars of Secession and the War of Reconquest. The old monolithic USA has gone; the new North America of the six nations has emerged, and I'd say for the better. We now enjoy co-operation and genuine discussions, since no single entity can now dominate proceedings. The new USA is still the largest nation in North America in terms of population and wealth, but its lead over the other countries is marginal. As the NAC calls on all members to defend the integrity of each other's territory, the USA couldn't retake its old southern and western states even it wanted to – it's simply not strong enough to take on the CSA, Columbia, Canada, Québec and the Atlantic Provinces simultaneously.'

Taking advantage of a pause in proceedings, Oriana announced a short break for refreshments and the chance to stretch stiff legs before the next presentation – which would be Jörg's.

Everybody took the opportunity to grab a cool drink and find a bit of shade from the oppressive summer heat. Concetta, in a primrose dress of light, summery cotton with buttons down the front, circled around the guests making a mental note of groupings and seating arrangements – keeping a particular eye on Jörg. Once she had established he was sitting alone, under some olive trees not far from the tennis court – apparently making a few notes before speaking – she disappeared to powder her nose.

When she reappeared, freshened up and invigorated, both Oriana and Hannah spotted that the top and bottom buttons on her dress were undone. She headed towards the tennis courts, where she 'bumped into' Jörg. The pair soon fell deep into conversation, with much flicking of eyelashes and crossing of legs from Ms Leoni.

After twenty minutes or so, Oriana drifted over to the tennis courts to ask Jörg if he was ready. In the strong sunlight Oriana noticed how Concetta's dress became almost translucent with the sun behind it – which by coincidence happened to be the case – and the conspicuously empty chair to Jörg's right, sitting forlornly under the shade of a Mediterranean oak. Jörg nodded his consent, and Oriana turned to make her way back to the villa. She hadn't taken half a dozen steps before glancing around to check whether Jörg was following or not. Concetta had stood up as Jörg got to his feet, the sun catching her primrose dress fully from behind – it was quite a revelation, as Oriana had to admit. What effect it had on Jörg she could but guess.

For Jörg's talk the group had retreated to the air-conditioned comfort of the Green Lounge, which overlooked the swimming pool, the whole vista set off by rolling green hills basking under the hot Roman sun. As the guests settled down on the stylish fabric easy chairs, Jörg got his things together, and Oriana noted that Concetta's buttons were all now firmly done up.

Oriana turned on her recorder – as did Concetta. Jörg took a swig from his tumbler of orange juice, then began:

'I'm going to discuss some of the developments which have transformed the monetary and commercial situation in Europe beyond all recognition from that which existed prior to the Global Meltdown. As I mentioned yesterday, many of these developments are the direct result of the philosophy, if you will, delineated in the Declaration of Rouen. I hope, therefore, that my little presentation doesn't undermine anything Hannah had planned for us this afternoon.

'Let us begin with banking and the knotty question of what role money should play in our societies. Since the Middle Ages usury, which is the practice of lending money for profit, or "interest" as it's coyly termed, has been practised throughout most of Europe. The justification for this charging of interest is said to lie in the fact that the lender has taken a risk in loaning money to a given individual or concern, and therefore is entitled to claim some recompense for exposing his finances to possible default, or even loss. Now, although on the face of it such an arrangement seems equitable, within such a concept lurk many long-term dangers. The function of money slowly changes, from being a convenient means of allowing the free exchange of goods and services, which obviously benefits society as a whole, to becoming a commodity in its own right.

'Commodities are owned and controlled by individuals, or interested parties; they do not, as a rule, belong to society generally. If an individual, or cabal of individuals or concerns, control a commodity, they control the market for that commodity – something touched upon earlier in the discussion on genetically modified foodstuffs.

'With the advent of powerful central banks – largely the construct of one family in particular – came the era of commodity control over the issuing of currency. The outcome was utterly predictable, as a certain member of this family once quipped, "Permit me to issue and control the money of a nation, and I care not who makes its laws."

'And he wasn't joking.

'The ethnic dynasties that dominated the global central banking system at the time of the Meltdown were easily the most powerful financiers that have ever existed in human history. Their actions eventually led to the Eurabian War here, the Wars of Secession and Reconquest in North America, and a death toll numbered in the tens of millions.

'One can gauge the power exerted by these clans in the events behind the collapse of the Gold Standard under President Nixon. The public has this naïve vision of the US sitting on a mountain of gold stored at the famous Fort Knox. This gold had been accumulated to support the dollar, the two being mutually-exchangeable in theory. However, Nixon was obliged to abandon the Gold Standard for the most basic of reasons, namely that Fort Knox was empty. Where had all the gold gone? Nobody knew, officially, though the betting was that most of it ended up in Fed vaults – the Fed, of course, being an entirely private concern established and owned by a cabal of the usual suspects.

'The central banks subsequently began issuing *fiat* money, which they conjured from pixie dust and moonbeams. Now, I'm not saying that the issuing of *fiat* money per se is a bad thing. Whenever governments have adopted this system in the name of the state the results have been spectacularly good. However, the return of money creation to the state was the last thing the bankster clans wanted to see, as it constituted the basis of their astounding wealth and power. Unsurprisingly, they opted for defending their control of the global money supply with every weapon at their disposal, heedless of any moral implications. It should come as little surprise, therefore, to learn that they have reputedly been responsible for the assassination of three US presidents – and the failed attempt on a fourth – one British prime minister plus numerous Russian tsars.

'Any major national central bank that succeeded in breaking free from their clutches was forced back into line with extreme violence. Alliances of slave nations still shackled to usury were engineered by the puppet masters, all marching in tandem under the flag of 'freedom' – meaning the freedom of ethnic central bankers to bleed their prey dry. In order to sell their version of reality to the public, a compliant and controlled media was required – which money duly provided. Thus it was that black became white, up became down: the whole world turned topsy-turvy, and the banksters got their wars of acquisition.

'The nineteenth-century campaign to reassert ethnic control over the Banque de France, and the twentieth-century campaigns to do the same with the State Bank of the Russian Empire and the Reichsbank, cost us millions of Aryan lives. Of course, the true victors in all these wars didn't do anything as menial as fighting and dying themselves; that was a job for the *goyim*.

'I've already given you one quote from the foremost family among these predators; here's another by the mother of the original brood: 'If my sons did not want war, there would have been none.' You have to give it to these people – you can't fault their *chutzpah*.

'While *fiat* money works well for states, it is a lethal weapon of social deconstruction in the hands of interest-charging private bankers. Under a system of private, *ex nihilo* money generation debt is built-in; the very act of creating currency also created debt as the central banks charged governments interest on the tender they issued – the more they issued, the more they profited. The end result of this lunacy was an ever-expanding mountain of debt; it was debt on an intergalactic scale, which ultimately led to the Global Meltdown.

'The Declaration of Rouen rejected all of this. It rejected the concept of money as a commodity, it rejected money creation by private concerns, and it rejected usury. One needs to grasp the fact that all the pre-war central banking institutes, like the Fed in America or the European Central Bank in Frankfurt, were either owned or controlled – directly or indirectly – by private concerns, something not widely understood at the time.

'By today, as most of you are aware, all the nations of Europe run a system of national banks that are wholly owned and controlled by national governments. These high-street institutions issue loans free of interest – though most charge a nominal administrative fee. Currency is also issued directly by national treasuries; within the *Curia* private central banks are illegal. Indeed, any member state reverting to the old private banking system would be expelled, since its actions would be deemed *contra patriam*.

'Within the *Curia*, a mechanism for conducting interest-free currency exchange had to be implemented, since all members paid towards the upkeep of the *Legiones* in their own national currencies. The *Curia* established its own unit of exchange, the solidus, based on a weighted basket of the member states' currencies, against which other European currencies were – and are – exchanged free of charge.

'Business practice has also changed hugely since the Meltdown. The NWO was very much about the commercialisation and acquisition of every asset on the planet. Trojan Horse organisations like the EU were used to destroy national entities, allowing unrestricted commercial exploitation of territories and their peoples in the name of free enterprise and choice. The high-water mark of this process was the infamous US–EU TTIP trade agreement, which allowed corporations to sue national governments if the state's actions to protect the domestic economy, or workforce, impinged on the corporation's "right" to turn a profit. Needless to say, the level of corruption and bribery involved in forging this agreement was staggering.

'The Declaration recognises the responsibility of national governments to operate for the benefit of their people – indeed, it's more than a responsibility: it's a duty. Take, for example, state expenditure policy. Under the old EU dictatorship, commercial considerations held absolute precedence. If your police force needed new motorcycles, the EU would force you to buy the "best" deal from whatever source. This was heralded as a great boon to the long-suffering taxpayer, who got the best goods at the best price – right?

'Not quite. What would have happened if the Republic of Lilliput had tried to buy its motorcycles from the local Lilliputian Motorcycle Co.? The EU would say, "Look, the bikes from the neighbouring state of Brobdingnag are cheaper, and therefore constitute a better deal for the hard-pressed taxpayers of Lilliput." Superficially that's true; in the context of the immediate transaction Lilliput gets a better deal. However, in the context of the overall economic health of the state, Lilliput gets a lousy deal. The workers at the Lilliputian Motorcycle Co. don't get the order, don't get paid and the money that would have ended up in the pockets of Lilliputian workers, to be spent in Lilliputian shops and businesses, thus boosting the Lilliputian economy, is redirected towards boosting the Brobdingnag economy and motorcycle industry.

'You might argue, well if the Brobdingnag motorcycle industry can produce superior goods for a cheaper price, why should the Lilliputian government spend money on overpriced, inferior goods? There is some substance in this argument, particularly if the goods being produced in Lilliput are substantially inferior to other similar goods on the market. However, a government is not a private individual; a government's duty is to the people of the nation and to enact polices, and direct expenditure, in a fashion that most benefits the nation as a whole. Even a basic cost-benefit analysis of the two buying options available to the Lilliputian government would show how superior economically was the option of retaining the funds within Lilliput's own economy.

'To be frank, unless there is a major disconnect in quality or price, one would always expect a government to direct taxpayers' money towards the domestic economy, where it would do the most good.

'Needless to say, such a common-sense and realistic position was completely at odds with the ethos of the EU tyranny, whose goals were directed towards the interests of a global financial plutocracy. There was nothing new in any of this; every major geopolitical and economic upheaval to have rocked Europe since the French Revolution has had the advancement of international finance at its core.

'Now, I've been rambling on for a while. Are there any questions before we head into the second half of this presentation?'

Pascal perked up. 'Jörg, I've heard things like this before, but I've never been able to get my head around what those pieces of paper in our wallets represent. What exactly is money?'

'They are, Pascal, exactly what they seem to be – pretty pieces of paper that claim to have some nominal monetary value; of themselves they are worthless. Back in the time of the emperor Augustus, coins were issued in silver and gold; that money was genuinely valuable, as a currency and as a real metallic commodity. Those bits of colourful paper in your wallet can be viewed as IOUs, issued by governments; your task, I would advise, is to judge whether or not our governments are trustworthy. Can they come good on their IOUs, and with what? Before the Meltdown, all the circulating currencies were *fiat* money – their true worth as great as the pixie dust that created them. By today, all of Europe's central banks operate on a revised version of the Chicago Plan, where the state is the sole issuer of currency. The scope for traditional commercial banking has narrowed very significantly with the effective outlawing of usury. Most countries have a system of either state or joint state and selective commercial high-street banks dealing with the public. The only charge these institutes can levy – as I've already indicted – is a nominal service fee. In the majority of countries the banking role is now entirely in the hands of the state – albeit via a separate agency from the actual government.'

There followed a short break. Rosa brought through a large pot of coffee and some light snacks, which were most welcome. Jörg stretched and went over to the window to take a more considered look at the beautiful Italian countryside; he loved this country. One of his great joys was driving down from Munich in his BMW, and crossing the Alps into the eternal glory of this ancient land. As he gazed at a tractor chugging away in some distant field, Concetta sidled up to him, pretending to admire the agricultural earthiness of his tractor. She was a fascinating woman, admitted Jörg to himself, and despite his better judgement he couldn't help but feel flattered by her poorly concealed interest. He glanced down at her. The open button at the top of her dress allowed a clear view of the silver amulet nestling snugly in her ample cleavage.

This was only a short break as the schedule was tight. Before Jörg and Concetta could pick up on their previous tête-à-tête, they were called back to the villa. As Concetta crossed the room to her seat, fumbling with her top button, she became aware that Marcello, sitting by a coffee table with Robert, Hannah and Pascal, was watching her carefully. She sat down, pointedly ignoring his glance and took out her notebook and recorder.

'We're going to finish this stint with a short review of current commercial and technological developments in Europe,' announced Jörg.

3.3 – SATURDAY

'As I mentioned, the Declaration of Rouen places a burden on European governments to develop their nations to the best of their ability; this includes such factors as industrial evolution and building a broad-based economy. There's one country in particular where these tenets have had a significant impact – England. England was perhaps the classic example, in a European context, of a nation giving itself, body and soul, to the diktat of international financial orthodoxy under the old *fiat* regimes – a country that in recent history had a significant manufacturing base, producing cars, lorries, aircraft, ships and railway engines: indeed, you name it, they did it. All of that was lost, most of it sold off to competitors. These evil and self-defeating developments, were not unique to England – or Britain generally – but more than in any other European country the dismantling of a functional economy in the name of financial expediency went the furthest, due entirely to the pernicious influence of the financiers in the City of London over the country's deeply corrupt political elite and policy makers.

'If pre-war Britain fell the furthest, post-war England has been in the forefront of showing the way out of the abyss left by the NWO.

'One of the iconic stories from England revolves around the rebirth of its automotive industry. Rebuilding whole sectors of an economy is an expensive business, requiring much thought. The English decided they needed a serious engine manufacturer, to make every sort of engine for every sorts of vehicle; they did not want a plethora of different companies, just one specialist manufacturer. The government decided to buy the rights to an old diesel company called Gardiner. This name and brand – so famous by today – became England's universal engine manufacturer, sucking in engineering specialist from across the country – even from neighbouring countries, like Scotland, Ireland and Wales. Then they decided to buy the rights to several historic car brands – Austin, Napier and Jensen – and set about re-establishing them in different sectors of the car market, using the new generation of Gardiner engines.

'Since then England has resurrected other companies in other automotive sectors, such as the lorry company Scammell, and the agricultural equipment manufacturer David Brown, to name but the most famous. It's the scale of the reindustrialisation in England that's made it an example worth noting, though by now we see similar restructuring programmes in many European countries.

'I've almost finished, but there is one final point worth mentioning – again trespassing on Hannah's territory. The fundamental nature of capitalism has been questioned by the Declaration – albeit indirectly. While acknowledging that capitalism in its basic form is both natural and healthy, in its later, mature forms, capitalism turns cancerous. Almost without exception, this turning point occurs when the original founder and family members have either died or been removed. The resultant body is a Frankenstein – a legal personality with no human dimension. The only loyalty such a body possesses is to its own survival through profitability. Nothing, and I mean *nothing*, is allowed to stand in the way of this blind pursuit. The antihuman nature of globalist corporatism has long found a working partner in that other source of societal decay: Cultural Marxism. Together these powerful bacilli laboured tirelessly to break down Aryan social structures, as was graphically witnessed prior to the War. Our people, shorn of the bonds provided by a healthy, organic society began to degenerate into a debased, rootless rabble at the mercy of corporatist predators and cultural Marxist commissars.

'Contrary to their claims, large international corporations are not powerhouses of progress and development; they're typically fat and bloated, using their vast financial assets to buy up genuinely innovative smaller concerns.

'Since corporations pose an existential threat to the societies in which they operate, the *Curia*, taking its lead from the Declaration, has a triple-layered attitude towards capitalist concerns. Domestic businesses operating solely within their own home nation are largely left to their own devices, with as little unsolicited state interference as possible. Companies that operate within a single global region, in our case Europe, are kept under tighter scrutiny – often paying higher levels of tax. It depends upon the business, but the bigger they get the more dangerous they become, requiring ever-tighter scrutiny.

'The final category is for the truly global corporations – which are trusted least of all. Such bodies are kept under very close observation and regulation. When they step out of line, any infraction is automatically pursued to the full extent of the law. Among the membership of the *Curia* the imprisonment of corrupt and criminal executives is considered a necessary deterrent, which should always be followed through to its final judicial conclusion. Other sanctions available include the break-up of the guilty corporation, or even its nationalisation. Remember, impersonal, vastly powerful corporate bodies are inherently hostile to any act in defence of human social identity.

'As I mentioned earlier, under the aegis of the Declaration it's assumed that a government's preference in purchasing goods and services will always follow a pattern of turning to local companies first, then regional businesses, and finally global corporations as a last resort. For an advanced region like Europe, were it to be discovered that certain products or services were unavailable anywhere on the continent, somebody in the *Curia* would start asking some pertinent questions. Much the same process occurs among the Shanghai Protocol countries. You'd only expect basic technological or commercial shortages to occur in the less developed regions of the world.'

Lunch was approaching and most headed for their rooms for half an hour or so. Oriana and Pascal lingered in the Green Lounge for a while, talking privately, while Concetta, who had no room to go to, wandered out to the Mediterranean oak to find a bit of shade from the afternoon heat.

She sat talking to her office in Rome on an expensive mobile, mulling over the best way to present the weekend meeting and its importance to her potential readers. Her involved discussion meant that the figure moving behind her, around the back of the stately Mediterranean oak, went unnoticed. Concetta, half-listening to her sub-editor's suggestions, was suddenly taken aback by a man's voice, speaking in Italian. 'Hello, Concetta; you're a hard one to track down on your own.'

She pointedly broke into her sub-editor's verbal flow. 'Sorry, Tommaso, I've got to go – something unexpected has cropped up.'

Without turning to face the interloper she responded dryly, 'Hello, Marcello: I didn't think you wanted to speak to me.'

'And why would you think that?'

'As I recall, you made it fairly clear that you didn't want to see me again.'

'That's hardly fair, Concetta; I said I wasn't prepared to carry on as we were, with you working full-time and gallivanting all over Italy – all over Europe, in fact.'

'So now you're dictating how I should spend my time and what work I ought to do?'

'It was you who said you wanted something permanent, something settled in your life; it was you who bemoaned the shallowness of those hectic relationships you flitted between. I know, from my own failed marriage to Ariana, that the two simply don't mix.'

'What doesn't mix?'

'The bright lights and stable relationships.'

Concetta was about to respond when Pascal came out from the veranda to announce that lunch was served.

Still far from happy with Marcello, Concetta made sure she was sitting next to Jörg for lunch, the two soon slipping back into their previous cosy conversation. Marcello, not quite so comfortable, spent lunchtime in the company of Oriana and Pascal.

'How do you think the weekend's going? Are you getting enough material for your book?'

'Oh, I think it's going well – isn't it interesting how people feel so strongly about certain aspects of the *post-bellum* world? I was taken aback by the depth

3.3 – SATURDAY

of José's interest in the Pagan movement; then from the tone of Jörg's voice it was obvious that he strongly supported the economic changes since the Global Meltdown. What about you – what's taken your interest?'

'Well, I hadn't fully grasped the extent of the changes in North America; Robert's account of the various wars was a bit of an eye-opener for me – especially the racial situation. How about you?' he asked, turning to Pascal.

'I've been struck by all the presentations; it's given me a far wider insight into our present situation than I had previously – though I must admit I'm looking forward to hearing from Hannah later today.'

Marcello nodded in agreement. 'Yes, her presentation should touch all the other topics we've discussed so far, as essentially the Declaration of Rouen was the driving force behind all of them.' He glanced over his shoulder; Concetta was showing off her silver amulet again. Oriana followed his gaze and sighed inwardly – what complex webs we weave.

After lunch it was far too hot and oppressive for presentations. Some returned to their pleasantly cooled rooms, Pascal and Robert went swimming, while José discovered the villa's library, tucked away in the back of the complex. Delighted to discover a rich collection of the classics, he was soon engrossed in a copy of Lucan's *De Bello Civile*.

Once again Concetta was at a loose end; Hannah wouldn't be speaking until 6:00, and the evening meal would not begin before 9:00. She decided to seek out Oriana for an interview, which lasted around half an hour. She went through the expected questions: why had Oriana organised the weekend, what had she learnt, did she feel it been a success and when would her book see the light of day? Concetta thanked Oriana for the interview, then headed out for the Mediterranean oak and a cigarette. She was an occasional smoker, usually when under pressure; a packet of twenty would normally last a good week. She leaned back on her chair, pulling heavily on a *Diana,* blowing out smoke rings, a trick she'd mastered while still at school. This time she saw him coming.

'Would you like some company?'

'Suit yourself.'

Marcello sat in the shade, seeking a little solace from the stifling air. He picked up the conversation from where they'd left off.

'Why won't you consider my offer? It was given in good faith and I think it would work. It would certainly be better than anything either of us has at present.'

'So say you. But I'm not your little *Hausfrau* – I'm a serious journalist who has been on the shortlist for journalist of the year. I have a career to think about.'

'Yes, I know,' voiced Marcello cautiously – her nomination had been seven years ago – 'but is that what you really still want? What's your schedule for this week? Bellucci's giving an important policy speech in Milan on Tuesday, so what does that mean? A maglev up north, two nights in a hotel, a quick report for the paper – then what? Off to Bonn for the annual *Legiones* report due next week, then up to Hamburg for the tests on the new carriages for the *Mercurius?*

'You've been on the same merry-go-round for what, twenty-five years? Twenty-six? No husband, no children – haven't you had enough? That's the impression you gave me.'

'How dare you!' Concetta stood up immediately. 'You have no idea how I feel or what my ambitions are.'

'Then tell me,'

She threw down her cigarette butt and started for the villa.

3.3 – SATURDAY

'Where are you going?'

'There's somebody I need to see.'

Marcello grabbed her by the arm. 'Don't be so stupid. What will that achieve? Even if he takes you up on your offer you'll only feel cheap afterwards, like some call girl – Concetta, get a grip!'

With tears beginning to well up, she pulled her arm free from his grasp, turned on her heels and headed out to a clump of cypress trees on the edge of the cultivated part of the grounds. She slumped down, her back resting against a trunk, and took out another cigarette. Marcello looked on sadly from afar, before returning to the villa for a sorely needed shot of Famous Grouse.

The hot afternoon dragged on. Concetta finally retreated from the sun, seeking the air-conditioned relief of the villa. She entered through the veranda; there was nobody about, other than Rosa sorting out the cutlery and crockery in the dining-room cabinet. Concetta walked slowly to the bar in the Green Lounge and made herself a tall glass of lemonade with ice and lime – and a large splash of vodka.

It had gone four; Hannah would begin her piece within two hours. Jörg's room was just down the corridor, overlooking a beautifully ornate garden leading to a colonnaded marble temple. She threw back the vodka and lemon, then began the process of self-justification. She reasoned it was merely a matter of professional thoroughness that she – an investigative journalist – should fully evaluate and explore the attitude of the financially most important member of the weekend party. For Jörg was only a part-time journalist on the *Völkischer Beobachter*; the rest of the time he sat on the boards of at least three major German manufacturing concerns. It was his knowledge of advanced battery technology that really interested Concetta – she was sure there was a story to be had if only she played her cards right. It was time. She sauntered down the corridor and gently knocked on the door. The door opened.

'I was expecting you earlier,' he said.

She entered and caught sight of the beautiful gardens and temple, 'I was tied up with something. Well, we have a bit of time now.' She sat down on the edge of Jörg's bed, her hand slipping surreptitiously into her handbag to activate a hidden, solid-state recorder. Jörg had a jug of cooled orange and bottle of champagne in the fridge under the dressing table. He prepared a glass of cold Buck's Fizz for the pair of them; more of Concetta's buttons opened – it was a hot afternoon.

The two toasted each other with a pregnant 'chin-chin', before Jörg set himself down beside his enticing guest on the edge of the bed. How many times had she been in this position before? But how else does one get scoops to become Journalist of the Year? Sacrifices need to be made and she'd decided she needed to know about those batteries. Smiling, with both top buttons now fully open, she turned to Jörg and, slightly dropping her posture to make the most of her cleavage, wrapped her finger around his ear and whispered in Latin, 'Come, Jörg – let's get to know each other a little better …'

Jörg had seen it all before, of course; being a man of both knowledge and power he was constantly being targeted by agents of either the media or commercial competitors. Concetta was merely a far more experienced and alluring prospect than most of the clueless young things sent his way. In truth, he was a married man with three healthy kids, so his days of ploughing through the proffered females flung in his direction had all but come to an end in recent years; it was far too dangerous for his reputation and the stability of his marriage. Concetta was something of an exception because of who and what she was, but even as Jörg enjoyed the silky pleasures she had to offer, he speculated this could well be his last bite of the forbidden fruit – in which case, he might as well make the most of it.

He duly gave up a few secrets concerning the batteries, as Concetta had given up something far more personal. Although Jörg didn't say anything, he was acutely aware that the information Concetta had worked so earnestly to acquire had a very short shelf life. Next month's *Elektrotechnik* journal would be publishing an article covering all the details he'd just given up. Ultimately, of course, this was Concetta's problem; as an experienced journalist she understood the game better than most.

She slunk out of Jörg's room just in time, Hannah's presentation was almost upon them, but her comings and goings did not go entirely unnoticed – Robert, hurrying back from the swimming pool, almost collided with her outside Jörg's door.

As usual at such times she was torn with mixed emotions. She had her all-important scoop, but even without Jörg warning her, she knew it wouldn't remain a scoop for long. However, for the here and now, at this magical moment, she held a scoop – a fact that filled her with professional pride and a sense of achievement. Yet simultaneously she also felt the degradation of her calling, undermining her sense of self-worth. Marcello had been right; she did feel like a call girl.

Ten minutes later all were back in the Green Lounge, as the temperature began slowly to fall to more pleasant levels. In the background Rosa and the other maids could be heard busying themselves in the kitchen under Salvatore's instructions, and setting out the veranda for the evening meal.

Hannah thanked everybody for their company and explained that the Declaration of Rouen constituted a huge field in its own right. Therefore, she would only be touching on certain aspects of its influence during her talk.

'I'd like to start my exploration of the Declaration of Rouen with the question of language. I've chosen to begin with language, as I've recently delivered a short paper on the topic to senior government advisors in London – indeed, I was talking about this very point with the education minister, Walter Elliot, as we crossed Powell Green on our way to the House only last Thursday.

'So, here we all are in Rome, hailing from various far-flung corners of Europe – and indeed beyond, with Robert here. Yet we communicate easily enough through Latin, which has become a widely understood tongue throughout

Europe – and that begs certain questions. I'm sure this situation may seem superficially similar to that faced by the settlers in North America, with its history of blending Europeans from many nations to create a new entity that bonded strongest around language. This new-found unity was sealed linguistically in the English language. Much the same occurred in South America with Spanish and Portuguese, and to a lesser degree with French in Québec. This linguistic uniformity was supposed to have forged a sense of commonality among the population; of course it failed, but we'll discuss that in a minute.

'From the standpoint of an American, therefore, it would make perfect sense for the whole of Europe to adopt Latin as its official language. The advantages are manifest, are they not? And it would be far simpler than our current Tower of Babel. What is it, 37, 38 languages used officially within Europe? Surely a single tongue would solve so many problems?

'Well – yes and no. The adoption of Latin has allowed the formation and functioning of the *Legiones*. It is also the only official language in the *Curia*, thus presenting all members with a level playing field; they've all got to learn and use Latin.

'However, all this superficial practicality misses the point. The Eurabian War, and the crafting of the Declaration of Rouen by a group of mostly French visionaries, all occurred for the same reason – to save Europe. Europe is not merely a geographical region; it's a culture and a racial identity – including its indigenous languages, histories and religions. We did not fight the suffocating rigidity of Islam, and the genocidal programme of population replacement, merely in order to supplant Europe's indigenous ethnic histories and identities with a reconstructed Roman Empire spouting Latin.

'This reality is recognised in the Declaration. To become a member of the *Curia* you need to be "self-constituted". What does, "self-constituted" mean in the context of the Declaration? Well, it means that the nation must be operating as a mature unit, using its mother tongue as its main language, teaching its own history – in short, being a healthy, fully fledged national entity. I'll give an example.

'When the *Curia* was first constituted, most of the political states of the time tried to join, but several were surprised and shocked to find their membership rejected. The Irish Republic was one. Back then the Irish Republic operated almost exclusively through the English language; this, as I've just explained, is not an example of a "self-constituted" nation. They were told to go away and return once they'd normalised the situation with their national tongue – which, of course, they've since done.

'Ireland wasn't the only nation rejected; so were Britain, Spain and France. You must understand, the *Curia* is largely blind as regards political states: it operates as a collection of national entities. The German people, the Danish people, the Polish people sit in the *Curia* – not the German state or Danish state, et cetera. Now, for many the two are synonymous, but in states like Spain and France that is not the case. In Spain, for example, the Basques and Catalans have limited self-rule, but as I've explained, it is the nation that counts to the *Curia*, not the state. If a nation's not "self-constituted" it can't join – and this cuts both ways. The Castilians – the Spanish, if you will – couldn't get membership either, as oppressors of other European nations, namely Catalonia and the Basque Country. The *Curia* will not grant membership to a European nation that suppresses another European nation. And how could we? Political expediency simply doesn't cut it when men from the oppressor nation and the oppressed nation are supposed to fight side by side in the *Legiones*.

The *Curia* tries not to interfere in the internal affairs of states, but for a unit like Catalonia to attain "self-constituted" status while remaining an integral part of the Spanish-speaking Castilian state would be very difficult. To give you some idea how difficult this can be, let's consider the Jutland Peninsula in Denmark. For a very long time prior to the War, the Danes had complained that Germans had been buying up large chunks of Jutland as holiday homes and changing the composition of the population – this problem, incidentally, was very widespread across the whole continent. At the time the Danes had no redress; they simply had to accept their own demise on their own native soil due to the diktat of the NWO's local enforcers – namely the EU. Situations like this the Declaration condemns unequivocally; governments are to do everything in their power to protect their native people and the territorial integrity of the nation.

'If an imaginary situation had arisen whereby Denmark suddenly became politically part of Germany – as Catalonia is politically part of Spain – any action to defend Danish Jutland against German land buyers would in effect become a case of one group of German citizens taking action against another group. Such a situation highlights clearly the absurdity of civic nationalism and the ideology of making a political structure – the state – the centre of loyalty. In Spain, Basques and Catalans were supposed to be loyal to a Castilian state, just as Celtic Scots and Welsh were supposed to give loyalty to an English state in the old Great Britain. States are political and legal constructs; they only deserve our loyalty when they correspond to our national aspirations as a unique collection of people inhabiting a specific geographic location. States that fail to meet these basic requirements are merely paper constructs; and speaking personally, I wouldn't be prepared to give either my life or the lives of my family members for a legal construct backed by a parcel of windbags.

'Hopefully, the reasons why the *Curia* operates in nations rather than the muddy legal waters which are states is a little clearer.

'The post-war Danish actions to curtail and reverse German settlement in Jutland are not anti-German, so much as pro-Danish. The Danish government is merely fulfilling its duties under the Declaration of Rouen to safeguard its population and territorial integrity from third parties.'

As Hannah took a sip of water, Oriana raised a probing question. 'How far do you take this national idea? There are some European linguistic groups that are tiny, or geographically scattered. What does the *Curia* say to groups like the Vlachs, Sorbs or Manx?'

'In theory the *Curia* supports all European ethnic groups; however, as far as membership is concerned, we have to have a viable population on a recognised territory. You might ask, "What's a 'viable population'?" A good, though technically difficult, question to answer. However, even among the present membership of the *Curia* there are some quite small population groups: Estonia has one and a half million people, Malta under half a million and Luxembourg some six hundred thousand. Generally speaking each case is judged on its own merits.

'I'd like to speak next about citizenship and its consequences for the states within the *Curia*. Before beginning, I think it needs making clear that the *Curia* has no power over member states; each state must act as it sees fit for the benefit of its own people – in fact that's an obligation laid down in the Declaration. Having said that, the Declaration's tenets have become so deeply ingrained in the European psyche that most governments act in accordance with them as a matter of course.

'Citizenship within Europe is, by today, universally ethnic in character – civic nationalism as a concept is stone dead. To be a citizen in any European state you need to be connected by blood to its people – things like immigration, asylum seeking, economic migration and all the other scams pulled off before the War are gone. Indeed, governments do not have the right to open borders or accept non-nationals without the consent of the population by referendum.

'Even if by some miracle this could be accomplished – and no national population has ever voted in this fashion – the change in the composition of the nation's population would endanger its membership of the *Curia*. The *Curia* is at heart an assembly of European nations, a nation being a unique collection of people defined both racially – by DNA if need be – and culturally. The influx of non-Europeans would turn a nation – defined by blood – into a state, defined as a random collection of individuals connected by bits of paper issued by a state bureaucracy. Pure states cannot be members of the *Curia*.

'Learning from the disasters inflicted on Europe during the NWO years, all European nations have very strict laws concerning the ownership and control of the media and core elements of the economy. I think I'm right when I say that utilities are held in state hands, by law, in every nation in Europe.

'The key to understanding the Declaration of Rouen, and indeed the actions and attitude of the *Curia* in general, is to grasp its basic priorities. As with the Great Leader, the Declaration and the *Curia* hold the people to be their highest concern. When I say "the people", I don't mean any people: I mean the people who belong to a country. For example, the most important element in Germany is the German people. And when I say "the German people", I don't mean people living in Germany; before the War half the people living in Germany were Turks. These Turks were not, and never could be, members of the German nation; they were holders of state-issued citizenship papers. They were political creatures, whose rights to occupy another's lands rested entirely on a corrupt state. When that state failed, so too did any excuse for these aliens to remain in Germany.

'The real German people – the German nation – are the northern, Indo-European, European Caucasian peoples speaking a West Germanic dialect, known as High German, who have lived on the lands known and recognised as "Germany" since before the Roman Empire. Germany is their land – nobody else's. The Declaration will always work to protect Europe's native peoples, and expects the government of Germany, and every other European government, to operate for the benefit of their respective peoples.

'While talking about the make-up of populations, it's interesting to note how the Great Leader always considered the small farmer to be the backbone of the nation. It's a feeling reciprocated in the Declaration – not in its original form, but the amendments made during the post-War conference held in Bonn, which established most of our current inter-governmental working practices. In amended Footnote One, you'll find a call to all European governments to succour and defend small farmers – not merely for their agricultural output, but their healthy attitude towards tradition, culture and the nation.

'Population size is one obvious area where the interests of commerce and biology collide. One can see it now, as the continent gets closer to full employment: the old calls to allow immigration are heard once again in commercial quarters – but nowadays they must be careful. Such calls could be construed as incitement to genocide.'

Hannah's mind drifted back to an event that occurred three months earlier. Sir John Bagnall, chairman of the EBF – English Business Forum – had approached Paul Fisher, member of the National Chairman's cabinet with responsibility for business and commerce, with a complaint from his members. Their order books were full, but finding enough staff to meet their needs was proving ever more difficult.

'Well, invest in further automation; upgrade your facilities,' suggested Fisher.

'Do you know how expensive that would be? A minor easing in the draconian immigration laws would allow us to bring in willing workers from abroad.'

'From where? Poland? Bulgaria? Albania? Their economies are growing too, you know.'

'No, not Europe. I was thinking of Bangladesh and Bolivia. One of our senior members has offices in various third-world countries and could easily acquire workers, who would work for half the wages our indigenous workforce demands.'

'You're asking me to suggest in Cabinet that we open the door to immigrants from Bolivia and Bangladesh?'

'Not immigrants: guest workers, who we can get rid of once the current staffing problems have passed.'

'Like the Turkish "guest workers" in Germany, who almost overran the entire country during the War – that sort of guest worker, you mean?'

'No, no, you're getting all excited over nothing – just a few workers, not an invasion force. Listen, Paul, I think you need to get closer to English business in order to understand our position. Is that not a reasonable suggestion, especially as you hold responsibility for our well-being in the Cabinet? There's a vacancy currently available on the board of Royal Deeside Chemicals (RDC); it would only be a couple of meetings a month and would allow you to see into the workings of a major industrial concern and grasp the day-to-day problems we encounter at the coalface. It's also quite lucrative, if you follow my drift – and one door tends to lead to another. Just think about it, that's all; it's just an innocent suggestion.'

Fisher eventually managed to fob off Sir John Bagnall and his demands for a relaxation in immigration controls. However, shocked by the cavalier attitude displayed by Sir John, he decided to contact Martin Tyndall, the National Chairman, to seek advice.

After listening to Fisher's report, Tyndall made a crucial decision. As he reasoned later on, the old Britain had a horrendous record for financial manipulation and monetary shenanigans – the City of London having been one of the NWO's main nodal points. All this had to stop, and more importantly the mental attitude behind it had to be challenged and struck down. Tyndall would not allow the re-emergence of the sanctimonious posturing, so typical of the plutocratic democracies, used to justify naked commercial exploitation of the nation on the spurious basis that whatever benefited the "right people" also benefited the nation. Tyndall ordered Fisher to refer Sir John Bagnall to the Nürnberg Commission.

The news that the chairman of England's leading business forum had been referred to the Nürnberg Commission left the EBF stunned. Martin Tyndall went on television to explain publicly that the EBF had approached the government, with an eye to reopening the borders in order to import cheap labour from Bangladesh and Bolivia. The EBF replied via the press, stating that their position had been grossly distorted and they had merely wished to bring in a handful of temporary guest workers – but nobody believed them.

Hannah, whose legal studies specialised in the workings of the Declaration, had gone out to Nuremberg to listen to Sir John's case, and see how the Commission would deal with the EBF's actions.

She remembered entering the impressive chamber; three high-backed leather chairs sitting behind a high, inlaid oaken bench. The presiding judge was Heinrich von der Reingruben of Germany, assisted by the Scottish judge, Flòraidh Moireach and the Latvian, Gundars Usins. The whole case subsequently became famous in England as an exemplar of "the old versus the new". Sir John and the EBF represented the attitudes of commercial dominance that existed prior to the Eurabian War, while the Commission represented the new Europe of the peoples, embodied in the Declaration of Rouen.

She recalled the worried expression on Sir John's face as the case began. 'Do you consider it acceptable to import workers for your factories from third-world countries, like Bolivia and Bangladesh?' opened von der Reingruben.

'Yes, as long as the numbers aren't excessive, and they don't impact unduly on the local native population. They'd only be temporary – guest workers – who'd be obliged to leave once their contract expired.'

'Tell me, Sir John: what brought you to the conclusion that it was necessary to import these third-world workers in the first place?'

'There are two main reasons. Firstly, with the country moving towards full employment, it's getting very hard to find suitable labour.'

'And secondly?'

'Native labour is very expensive. These hard-working Bangladeshis and Bolivians would work for half the English wages – an important cost consideration in a competitive marketplace.'

'I see, and how do you intend to guarantee that these aliens won't have a negative impact on the local population and culture?'

'By keeping their numbers low.'

'If the numbers are that low, what was the point of importing them in the first place? If they're so few, you could have offered a bit more to native workers and met your labour shortfalls without resorting to immigrants.'

'But as I've explained, that would cost a lot of money – native Englishmen expect a certain minimal wage.'

'Tell me, Sir John – who's going to pay for these Bolivians and Bangladeshis to come to England?'

'They'd pay for themselves.'

'How could they afford it?'

'That's a good point; we would like to see some government assistance with migrant transportation costs. However, barring such help, an advance on their wages could be arranged. We've discussed this option during policy meetings of the EBF.'

'You would advance their wages?'

'Well, yes: how else could they get to England?'

'And where would they live?'

'Rented accommodation; then hopefully council property, once they'd settled.'

'You would expect local councils to extend public housing to aliens?'

'Once they're working in the country they're part of the workforce, aren't they? I don't want to be accused of teaching my grandmother to suck eggs, but does not the Declaration of Rouen say it's the duty of every national government to support the economic development of the country?'

'Yes.'

'Well, can't you see, that's exactly what we're trying to do? We're creating competitive businesses whose success will ultimately benefit the whole country.'

'Thank you for the insight, Sir John. Might I ask, where exactly is the factory or business that requires these migrants?'

'They're everywhere. The labour shortage is getting very serious across the whole country, though I admit my own business could do with some extra labour in our fabrication plant in Nuneaton.'

'And where do you live?'

'Claverdon.'

'Would your Bangladeshis and Bolivians be based in Claverdon too?'

'Good God … I mean – no; unfortunately it's too far from Nuneaton, and in any case no suitable accommodation exists for them in Claverdon.'

'But you live there?'

'Yes, but I suspect they would find the price of property a little expensive in Claverdon. It takes me almost three-quarters of an hour to drive to Nuneaton of a morning – it's highly unlikely they could afford cars.'

Judge Moireach now picked up the questioning.

'Sir John, you said earlier that these would be temporary workers, and you claimed they would return home at the end of their contract. I have two questions for you. Firstly, what happens if they do not go home at the end of their contract? And secondly, who pays for their return ticket? After all, you've already admitted they would be living in cheap, rented accommodation, and would not be able to afford cars – so how could they afford to save for an air ticket?'

'I said they should only be allowed to enter the country as temporary guest workers – for a fixed period. Once that period's up, unless they left they would become illegal immigrants.'

'Meaning what, exactly?'

'That the police and border agencies would deal with them.'

'The government would sort out the mess?'

'Yes.'

'And what of my second question: what happens if they haven't, or can't acquire, plane tickets?'

'Well, it's basically the same position. They would become illegal aliens, who'd have to be rounded up and deported by the authorities.'

'Does that mean the authorities would also have to pay for their air tickets?'

'If that was the only way to remove them from the country, yes.'

'Thank you, Sir John.'

Judge Usins finished off the Commission's interrogation.

'Sir John Bagnall, you mentioned earlier that only a small number of "guest workers" would be required.'

'Yes, just a few to tide us over until the labour market settles down.'

'Yet, Sir John, you also said there was a widespread demand for this labour from many of your members in the EBF – is that correct?'

'Well, yes, but these migrants would be dispersed across the country; they'd only exist in small groups, as and where our members' businesses required them.'

3.3 – SATURDAY

'Would there be restrictions on their movements?'

'Perhaps, I hadn't thought about it.'

'And who would enforce that?

'Well, the police, I suppose.'

'Would these restrictions hold even in areas of high commercial activity?'

'I'm not sure what you mean; could you explain, please?'

'The English West Midlands is a manufacturing hub, is it not?'

'It is.'

'So if, as you claim, there is a widespread call for these migrants from among your membership, would that not result in a concentration of these migrants in locations like the West Midlands?'

'It might, yes.'

'Would that not lead to the almost inevitable creation of migrant communities in the poorest districts of the West Midlands, which, as you've already explained, is their most likely destination? Indeed, Sir John, it could be no other way, since one of the main reasons for the EBF's request to import this human material into England is to keep wages low – did you not say that?'

'Yes. Though I don't see any problem; these people would be confined to certain areas where the authorities could keep a close eye on them.'

'So once again, you're placing the control of migrants, who you and your members wish to import, in the hands of the authorities?'

'Well, isn't that their job?'

'Thank you, Sir John.'

Judge von der Reingruben brought the session to a close with lunch approaching.

'Sir John Bagnall, we will deliberate the case and deliver our verdict later today. If for any reason we fail to come to a decision today, you will be given a new date to appear before this Commission sometime in the near future. Commission adjourned.'

After lunch Sir John found himself back in the chamber looking at the stern faces of Judges von der Reingruben, Moireach and Usins – they'd come to a decision. After briefly checking with his colleagues, Judge Heinrich von der Reingruben began his delivery of their unanimous judgment:

'I'm glad that so many representatives of the press from England and the neighbouring Celtic countries are present to record this verdict. Hopefully the message from this chamber will spread far and wide, so that similar cases will not have to be heard by the Commission in the future.

'Sir John Bagnall, you stand today before this Commission, as chairman of the EBF, charged with deliberately inciting actions likely to bring about the physical destruction or atrophy of a native European ethnic group on their historic territory. I hope you realise the gravity of the charge, Sir John: a charge made even more serious by the fact that these actions were undertaken at the behest of an organised group – the EBF.

'You've outlined the position held by your members, which in strictly commercial terms makes much superficial sense. You want cheap labour, which you claim will lead to higher profits and therefore greater commercial success for your members – which you also claim will ultimately benefit the English people. You have pointed out that the Declaration of Rouen charges European governments to nurture and develop their national economies – which is quite correct. You have then taken these two points and linked them by claiming that the importation of cheap labour will indeed benefit English commerce, which was a desire of the Declaration; therefore these proposed actions must be good and equitable, since a successful business sector makes for a prosperous nation.

'Unfortunately, Sir John, both you and the organisation you represent have misunderstood the *raison d'être* for the Declaration of Rouen at its most basic level. The Declaration is fundamentally about people. It is their interests and well-being that come above everything else; for you see, Sir John, the people *are* the nation.

'You say the Declaration holds governments responsible for economically developing their countries – it does. But you seem to have lost sight of the "why" somewhere along the line. So why does the Declaration place this burden on governments? In order for the people to prosper and live decent lives; businesses and commercial concerns are merely a means to an end, not an end in themselves – and that is where you err most seriously.

'You almost take the position that your business, and the rest of the businesses within the EBF, operate in a social vacuum. You should be free to do whatever you consider beneficial for your businesses; the impact of such actions is apparently not your concern or responsibility. That's the job of the government – to clean up any mess you create. Now, this is an illogical standpoint to adopt since its inevitable consequences run counter to your stated reasons for supporting immigration in the first place.

'You claim these migrants will be cheap because they're willing to work for low wages, yet once their contract is finished it appears the government foots any subsequent bill. The government appears also to be responsible for policing these migrants, and even hunting them down once their contracts have expired – all of which will require heavier taxes, paid by the entire nation so that you can exploit cheap labour.

'In practice you're asking the entire English nation to subsidise your company for the benefit of you and your migrant workers. Why should England do this? Where's the benefit?

'The people are not here to serve you; in a very fundamental sense you are there to serve them. Your factory in Nuneaton makes metal kegs and casks for the brewing industry, I believe. You might not like the idea, but were your factory to disappear tomorrow another business would arise – in a very short time, I suspect – to take the place of your concern. While for you personally this scenario might be disastrous, in reality the fate of individual businesses is not intrinsic to the well-being and continuance of England.

'However, the continuance of the English people is the only way in which England, as a nation, can survive and thrive. With no English people, the term "England" becomes merely a geographical expression – a position we came perilously close to realising prior to the Eurabian War.

'The profits or otherwise of your business cannot, and never will, override the needs of the national group. Can I just reiterate once more? – England is the homeland and property of the English people. If your business is struggling, that's your problem, not that of the English people. If you are incapable of solving your problems without damaging the nation, leave the market for somebody who is capable of operating successfully under prevailing social and economic circumstances – that's real competition.

'The sanctions open to this Commission are severe; your actions can indeed be construed as genocidal – population displacement is genocide. Sir John, we find you guilty as charged.'

Sir John turned pale and felt his knees begin to shake.

'We feel that a clear message needs to go out from this chamber that corporate felony will not be excused in the name of financial gain. We have decided, therefore, to sentence you to five years in the European Penitentiary in The Hague. Hopefully this sentence will act as a deterrent, and the business sector in England and across the British Isles generally will learn from this experience. Your native peoples come first; profit from business is a by-product of efficiency and serving the people well.

'As this sentence constitutes an official warning to the British Isles from the Nürnberg Commission, individuals and corporate bodies must guard against committing similar infractions in the future. Any repeat offence will be interpreted by the Commission as a disregarding of this warning – which would be construed as contempt of court. Those deemed responsible for pursuing commercial gain to the detriment of the native population will be dealt with severely.'

The memory of that day remained sharp in Hannah's mind. She refocused on the group and with a smile said, 'Right, I've been warbling on for a bit, and I think Rosa is almost ready for us.' She glanced enquiringly over at Oriana.

'We've got ten minutes yet – have you anything else you'd like to mention?'

'Many things spring to mind, but for now I'll confine my comments to the thorny question of dual nationality. Dual nationality concerns all those with a theoretical right to take up residence in another country; even if the option's not taken up, its mere existence still has consequences.

'There are European nations with particular overseas connections, like the various British nations with Australia and New Zealand, or Italy and Spain with Argentina, or France with Québec. These relationships can normally be handled fairly easily, especially when we're talking about those of the same blood.

'Then there are simple cases of mixed marriages – meaning between two Europeans from different countries. Miscegenation is of course illegal throughout Europe; such marriages are neither permitted nor legally recognised.

'With ordinary mixed marriages there is no legal power obliging governments to accept citizens from other states, just because they've married to a native. States can, and frequently do, block partners from bringing in foreign spouses. Governments will always act to safeguard the bloodline of their own populations; therefore those contemplating marrying somebody from another country should spend some time quizzing the relevant officials as to their chances of gaining entry for their partner.

'Needless to say, any European marrying or cohabitating with a non-European will not receive entry permission for his or her partner into any European nation.

'Now we come to a certain problematic ethnic group mentioned by Robert this morning. He very kindly left it to me to explain how they were handled, due to the NAC having wisely decided to follow the *Curia's* lead. All members of this group held the right to claim citizenship of a particular foreign, non-European country. True, many in this community never took up the offer; however, the existence of this political umbilical cord, and the group's attitude towards the foreign state, meant their loyalty was always in question. Indeed, leading members of the group routinely made it clear that their ultimate identity, and therefore allegiance, lay with the aforementioned foreign state. This attitude, in conjunction with the fact that these people constituted the most powerful, subversive and dangerous alien bloc within Aryan society, resulted in the decision by the *Curia* and NAC to repatriate these people to their spiritual homeland. The procedure adopted for this task echoed that used with the Orientals and Muslims in America. However, owing to the vast economic and financial power exercised by this group, their assets had to be seized in order to maintain economic stability; as most of you are aware, these assets were subsequently nationalised. Right across the *Curia* and the NAC there exist today very stringent regulations concerning the ownership and control of financial and commercial enterprises; these far-reaching measures were enacted largely in response to the activities of this group.

'Finally, we have those who are exceptions to all these rules – namely, the ex-*legionarii*. Members of the *Legiones* have free movement throughout the *Curia*, and owing to the plurality of nationalities in their ranks often have non-native spouses. They have the right, earned through serving in the *Legiones*, to settle anywhere they wish within Europe on the completion of their tour of duty. As you all know, there are "Latin Quarters" in all the major cities of Europe, where Latin-speaking populations live and work. They're never short of work, as the call for their linguistic skills is considerable. They're an interesting phenomenon, viewed with mixed feelings by many.'

Pascal butted in here. 'We have a large Latin Quarter in Paris – besides the historic area of the same name. You're right about people's mixed attitudes, but I'm not aware of any animosity towards them; if anything they're more pitied as outsiders, not being true *Parisiens*. Yet at the same time they're also admired, since most have fought for us in the *Legiones*. Then there's something a little deeper. They're revered as the true representatives of pan-Europeanism, speaking Latin on a daily basis and all that; they're the heartbeat of the new Europe – it's all rather schizophrenic, I'm afraid.'

'No, don't apologise; we see the same range of responses everywhere.'

Rosa appeared by the door. 'Food's ready,' she announced in Italian; everybody understood.

Concetta watched the guests file through to the veranda, giving both Jörg and Marcello the merest nod, before catching Oriana's arm.

'I've got to go, I'm afraid, and I was so looking forward to enjoying Salvatore's gastronomic excellence – it's a delicious-looking spread. Please forgive me; I'll see you tomorrow after breakfast.'

'Of course, Concetta; nothing untoward's happened, has it?'

'No, no, just something that's unexpectedly arisen at the office; I'll have to sort it out, otherwise there'll be trouble tomorrow.' A taxi was already waiting for her by the front gates. She headed back to her flat in the knowledge that she needed to write her article on the new battery technology quickly before it went stale. She strongly suspected her window of opportunity would be brief – it promised to be a long night.

3.4 – Dies Apollinis

The following morning Pascal, Oriana and Marcello were up with the lark, sipping coffee and eating breakfast by 7:00, with Robert and José joining the rest by ten past. Most were heading for the local temple of Apollo, situated down in the village by the Via Aurelia. Marcello, however, would be heading in the opposite direction to the Corpus Domini Catholic Church, a journey of around ten minutes in his Alfa. The church was a simple, modern building that he'd visited before, tucked away among the houses – he rather liked its relaxed atmosphere. Robert had a longer journey to the English Baptist Church in Rome itself, located on the Piazza San Lorenzo in Lucina.

Hannah had half promised to accompany Robert, but she'd drunk a bit too much the night before.

José mused on the Christians among the group who were about to leave for church. They accepted unthinkingly that Sunday was their holy day, but of course it wasn't. He knew this was actually *Dies Solis* – Day of the Sun – the holy day of Apollo. If this was indeed a holy day, it was a Pagan holy day. Jesus, being a good Jew, had kept the Sabbath on Saturday, like all Jews, and of course so had the early church of Paul.

José's Christianity had worn very thin over the years. His official status as a Christian scholar had become ever harder to maintain with each new encounter with the Roman Gods. Today he would be frequenting a Roman

Pagan invocation of Jupiter. He had been looking forward to this event all weekend, for the celebration was to be held in the iconic Temple of Antonius and Faustina in the Forum. This magnificent temple had already seen considerable restoration work since the Catholic Church relinquished its grip on what was one of the best-preserved temples in the Eternal City. The restoration of ancient religious monuments had become a very hot potato in recent years, as more and more Pagan groups wished to restore and reuse pre-existing sites. The authorities were not sure how to proceed, but some temples were being renovated, under strict supervision from archaeologists to make sure the restoration was in line with the temples' original appearance. It made the work extremely expensive, though the results had been visually impressive.

By midday everybody had returned from their various spiritual encounters – along with Concetta, who was eager to see what the final day would bring. Smart as always, she wore a simple, if exquisitely cut, white blouse, and a summery, patterned blue skirt. Still tired from the long shift she'd put in knocking out her scoop, she drank a couple of glasses of fresh orange juice, chased by a large black coffee in an attempt to generate some energy.

The group gradually congregated on the veranda awaiting Oriana, who finally emerged with Pascal to welcome everybody to the last day of the weekend. She hoped they'd had an enjoyable and informative time at her little chalet, and were ready for two more presentations: one from José and one from Marcello. Since there was a distinctly religious air to the day following the morning's visits to temples and churches, Oriana had decided to start with José's second stint.

José found a nice spot, sat down with an iced fruit juice and began:

'This shouldn't be as long as my previous talk, but since then several of you have come to me with further questions which need addressing. First of all, I'm sure you're asking yourselves, why has Oriana asked me to speak again – has she some sort of religious fetish?

'No, I don't think so; it's more a case that she, like me, understands the role and importance of religion in human societies. Some atheists think their position of disbelief in the divine only arose following the scientific revolution, which apparently from the age of Kepler and Newton onwards has seen the pursuit of scientific knowledge steadily displace the primitive need for the supernatural.

'That's all nonsense, of course. There have been many historic periods when man has either embraced something not far short of disinterested agnosticism, or gone the whole hog in rejecting the supernatural in all its forms. Examples of such attitudes can be found in the ancient world, both from Greece and Rome, while widespread religious disinterest reared its head on numerous occasions during the Middle Ages.

'In reality, atheism is neither a child of the scientific revolution, nor is it new. Once one grasps these facts a far bigger question rears its head: why has atheism always faded away, always failed to become the norm? Even in the period prior to the Eurabian War, when religious affinity among Europeans was at a historic low, the people were not so much affirming their new-found atheism as showing a chronic lack of spiritual interest in anything being offered. The consequences of this spiritual disengagement soon impacted on society, which drifted like a rudderless ship on stormy seas. The inevitable shipwreck duly occurred and Aryan society went into freefall. Families ruptured – if they existed at all – while the young and the old were left to fend for themselves. The entire edifice toppled into a hideous dog-eat-dog nightmare of unrestrained hedonism. It was nothing less than the engineered atomisation of European society.

'However, as the Americans say, "what goes around comes around". In reaction to this disintegration of Europe's societal framework a spiritual backlash occurred, mostly harvested by a reborn and reinvigorated Aryan Paganism, though Christianity has also experienced some stabilisation of its perilous position.

'All of you, even those who now follow Pagan paths or hail from atheist homes, were originally raised culturally as Christians. Since the basic shape and functioning of Christianity is already ingrained in you, I will restrict my comments to the position of Paganism, as it's often misunderstood. It also appears to be gaining the ascendancy in Europe.

'I spoke before about some of the problems modern Pagans face with the corruption of their core historic texts due to the influence of Christianity. I think I mentioned the *Edda,* which concerns the various strains of Norse and Germanic Paganism, though it's equally true of other schools of Paganism. For example, last summer I visited the Welsh Druidic centre at Cae Braint on Anglesey, and spoke with one of the leading Druidic leaders there, Huw ap Nisien. He showed me the main text they use, the *Mabinogi,* but mentioned that it too had been corrupted, in much the same way, and for the same reason, as was the *Edda.*

'So, the question becomes, "Is reading books like the *Edda* or the *Mabinogi* a waste of time for German and Celtic Pagans?" No, it isn't. Do you remember how Sallustius described the Gods? They're "eternal and incorporeal" – and there's the problem. Humans have severe difficulties with incorporeal divinities – even our all-embracing, universalist monotheistic varieties. None of the monotheistic brands describe their God; indeed, all hold that he's unknowable and beyond mere human form. Yet look at any pictorial depiction or film portraying their "God" and you'll find an image that looks uncannily like Zeus.

'Huw ap Nisien spoke to me about the hurdles facing those who seek to know the Gods. He didn't deny that the Gods are incorporeal, but this is of little help to us mortals – we need a hook on which to hang our beliefs, otherwise they fall to the ground and are lost. The *Mabinogi* and *Edda* may have flaws, but the core of what they have to say rings true, as does their portrayal of the Gods, in both form and character.

'Those seeking a relationship with the immortals find it much easier to deal with an entity they can envisage, rather than having to grapple with Sallustius' ghostly, incorporeal beings. As Huw commented, "It's much more likely to happen if you can imagine it," and a human form – as portrayed in the *Edda* or *Mabinogi* – makes imagining far easier for the average seeker of the Gods.

'This question of imagery brings me onto another point: something mentioned to me in passing by Robert, who's noticed all the striking painted churches here about. In point of fact, these striking buildings are all ex-churches, which have been converted into Pagan temples. All across Europe, as Christianity has retreated Paganism has expanded to fill the void. In consequence, Pagans have bought substantial numbers of old churches and chapels to turn into temples. What's fascinating with these reborn Pagan temples is the way the various branches of Paganism have chosen to decorate them. Almost all have adopted a policy of external plastering and painting, using the building itself as a backdrop for their mural work. Once plastered and given a base colour – normally white – they set about decorating the temple with illustrations from their mythological texts, usually in a highly stylised fashion related to their particular tradition. For example, Pagans here in Italy – like those back in Portugal – follow the Roman tradition. What's striking about these temples is their colour. Most are painted ochre, then painted with scenes from Roman mythology in white and black. The Celtic temples I saw in Wales were superficially similar to the far more common Germanic examples I'm sure you've all seen. However, the style and motifs of the external illustrations were markedly different, using intricate Celtic-knot designs as borders for illustrations depicting scenes from the *Mabinogi* – again, all accomplished in a very striking Celtic style. You'll find similar buildings and designs in the other Celtic lands – Ireland, Scotland, Brittany and so forth.

'I hope, Rob, that helps explain the colourful buildings you've noticed on your travels.'

'Yeah – thanks, José. So if I travel to other parts of Europe – say Poland, Greece or Ireland – I'd see different-coloured temples with depictions of the local Pagan beliefs painted on the walls?'

'Yes, and I would particularly advise you to go to Poland, or any of the Slavonic countries, to see their unique paintings and designs. They're very distinctive, especially if you've only seen Germanic versions, or the typical Roman variants you get around here. You must also visit Lithuania and Latvia, historically the last strongholds of European Paganism, and arguably still the beating heart of the continent's reengagement with the Old Gods.

'Now, I wish to say a quick word regarding kin and family – a central theme in all forms of Paganism. In a general sense, Pagans view us as standing in the chain of life, which extends beyond birth and death. This is not just mere religious dogma; it's biologically true. Our being stretches back through our forebears, and forward through our unborn offspring – who will carry our DNA. For Pagans, therefore, we are not just self-contained units; we are the product of generations of our forebears – as indeed will be our future generations. In line with these beliefs, Pagans take lineage very seriously. All branches of Paganism honour their bloodlines and celebrate their forebears, dressing their graves at Hallowe'en, or Samhain as the Irish call it. Huw told me the Welsh call it Calan Gaeaf. It's important that the Celtic branches of Paganism are mentioned here, as it has been their influence that has seen these practices expand into other European Pagan traditions.

'Paganism, therefore, conceives us as the sum of all who have gone before – which brings me back to an important battle ranging in certain sections of Germanic Paganism.

'This battle revolves around the nature of Paganism. Is it a folk religion, which the widespread veneration of ancestors would indicate, or is it merely a polytheistic version of the existing universalist, monotheistic cults? Odinists are firmly in the folkish camp, while the universalist position is held by a number of followers of Ásatrú – which explains why so much bad blood is directed in their direction. To many – the majority in fact – the stance taken by some within Ásatrú seems to belittle our ancestors. In adopting universalism Ásatrú ignores the folk by accepting all sorts – not merely the non-Germanic, but even the non-European – as members of their version of "Germanic" Paganism, which frankly I find ludicrous.

'By and large, all the various branches of Paganism followed in Europe today accept the folk nature of their belief system; it's a case of blood, soil and the Gods. Universalism has had its day in Europe; nobody wants to revisit the horrors of the Eurabian War – and nobody is in favour of throwing open Europe's front door to any vagrant who happens to be passing, in the name of universalist pipe-dreams. It seems to me that Ásatrú's attempt to be a polytheistic version of monotheism is doomed to failure – if you want universalism, join one of the monotheistic cults.

'Other issues confronting Paganism are similar to those faced by all belief systems. The most fundamental divide lies between the seeker and the follower. Some wish to get out into the woods and mountains – or wherever they feel closest to the Gods – to encounter the Divine personally. From this group emerge Paganism's leaders, shamans and priests. In contrast, the followers – who in a mature religion constitute the majority – may like the idea of communing with the Gods, but haven't the drive or commitment to make it happen. Their requirements are different; they need sheepherding through ceremonies that allow them to feel part of a greater whole. It's ironic, but the stage-managed ceremonies enacted by Ásatrú priests, so fiercely criticised by Theodish groups for their superficiality and lack of true spirituality, are exactly what passive followers need. The same split can be seen in Christianity.'

José turned to Marcello and gave a nod; Marcello took up the narrative with a few words concerning the political consequences of Paganism's growth:

'Since the end of the War, with the rapid growth of Paganism, there have been several significant international political developments. The most notable example of these changes has been India's growing friendship with Europe – all of which stems from the religious developments José has been expounding upon. Hinduism views Paganism as a sister belief system – indeed, the closest religious relative Hinduism has on the planet.

'Of course, these developments cut both ways; staunchly Catholic South America views the growth of European Paganism very darkly. I'm not entirely sure how the North Americans view things – Robert, do you have any observations on this point?'

'Well, many leaders among the non-Conformists, like the Baptists, and the likes of the Mormons and Jehovah's Witnesses, condemn Paganism as Satanism; therefore openly hostile views towards Paganism do exist fairly widely. I myself have heard people back home in Dixie refer to Europeans as heathens – used in its derogatory sense, not shorthand for Germanic Paganism. However, in truth, many of the schools of Paganism José's been discussing are thriving in America, especially further north in the US, Canada and the Atlantic Provinces. Odinism is getting pretty big, and a lot of the Irish – believe it or not – are turning to the Irish and Gaelic branch of Druidism up around Boston.'

The discussions came to an end and everybody settled down to a late lunch, enjoying the pleasant weather, which was noticeably cooler than Saturday. Lunch was provided buffet-fashion, with individuals filling their plates then dispersing around the grounds to enjoy each other's company and Salvatore's excellent food, all packaged in a truly beautiful setting.

Marcello had been one of the last to load his plate, having been busy discussing political developments in Italy with Oriana. Over in the shade under the Mediterranean oak, Concetta was sitting with her legs crossed, eating lunch and sipping from a glass of white wine.

Jörg was nearby, viewing Concetta's legs with interest. She had kept herself in fine fettle, he mused, and these particular assets extended all the way to the promised land, as he recalled fondly. He had half an idea that as this was probably his last opportunity for high jinks, he'd like to stop over for the night in Rome. He could book a nice hotel – something decent, like the Boscolo Exedra or Splendide Royal, where Concetta could enjoy the opulent luxuries such establishments could provide – while he would get another chance to appreciate her finer points.

He sauntered over to Concetta, his mind full of various erotic scenarios located in plush hotel bedrooms. He placed a hand deliberately on the nearest of her shapely crossed legs, then very slowly began to inch his way up her thigh. Concetta went rigid, her eyes wide-open in blind panic – what did he think he was doing? Jörg leaned forward and said softly, 'How does a night at the Boscolo Exedra sound, or somewhere else if you prefer? I've heard the food's stunning there.'

Concetta recoiled internally, her mind racing wildly, seeking an exit strategy. Who does he think he's dealing with? He'll be putting me on speed-dial next. She put on a false smile, and gently removed his hand from her upper leg. 'That sounds wonderful, Jörg; the Boscolo Exedra is a lovely hotel and normally I'd love a night there.'

'So you'll come?'

'It would be divine, but unfortunately I need to get back to the office straight after finishing here – there's lots to do and deadlines to meet. I'm sorry, Jörg, but thank you for your generous offer. Perhaps the next time you're in Rome we could meet somewhere nice.'

Marcello, slowly moving towards the Mediterranean oak, had witnessed from afar Concetta's lifting of Jörg's hand from her thigh. Having been rebuffed, Jörg moved away, catching sight of Marcello as he turned for the villa. He was disappointed that his erotic fantasy had burst, but ultimately that's all it ever had been – a throwaway gesture. Even as he crossed the lawn Concetta had already faded from his immediate thoughts, sliding into his catalogue of subjects for idle sexual daydreams that he accessed whenever he felt a little frustrated. Much to his relief and quiet satisfaction, his family began to fill his mind. Perhaps it was all for the best: it would have been a wasted night in Rome with a one-night stand, when he could have headed home to his loving wife and three kids.

Marcello and Jörg passed each other unacknowledged on the lawn, Jörg heading back for more food, Marcello heading for the clearly angry Concetta. He slid silently into the chair by her side.

'Did you see that? That man tried pushing his hand up my skirt like some sleazy bar tart – what exactly does he think I am?'

'I would have thought that was fairly obvious.'

Concetta tuned sharply and glared threateningly at Marcello.

'And what would that be?' she said softly, in a tone of steel.

'What do you expect? You can't act like that and walk away unscathed.'

'Sorry – what are you referring to?'

'Robert saw you leaving his room yesterday.'

Her face was suddenly a picture of horror; unbelievably, she blushed scarlet – something Marcello had never seen before.

'Does everybody know?' Her voice quivered in suppressed shame.

'Nobody knows, except me – and Jörg, of course.'

'You said Robert saw me.'

'He did, but he doesn't understand. He just thinks you were lost – looking for a drink or the powder room.'

Relief washed over her; she'd escaped again. 'Oh Marcello, what have I done? How many times have I found myself asking this selfsame question? I'm not sure how much longer I can carry on like this.'

'Then don't, Concetta. My offer is genuine; come back with me and become mistress of Villa Ombrosa – please. The good people of Volterra won't know what's hit them. You'd make me a very proud and happy man, and the old place needs a mistress. You could redecorate and modernise to your heart's content.'

'I'm a city girl; living out with the cows and farmers isn't my scene.'

'Now that's not true, is it? Remember that week we spent up in the hills above Saccaggio? You were feeding chickens, herding sheep and haggling in the market like a local, all your city frills and make-up abandoned. I've never seen you so happy; you loved every second of it.'

An unintentional grin broke across her face as she leaned on Marcello's arm and hugged him. They sat like that for five minutes listening to the crickets in the long grass, before Oriana called everybody back to the villa.

Somewhat differently from Friday and Saturday there would be a session in the afternoon, because people needed to get away before evening. As they crossed the lawn towards the villa, Marcello told Concetta it was his turn to speak. She pulled on his arm again, and kissed him affectionately on the cheek. 'Good luck!'

Oriana introduced Marcello, who began his talk on the political situation in Europe following the Eurabian War.

'This topic can be approached on two levels: the domestic and the international – I'll start with the international. Incidentally, when I say "international" I'm referring to *ex-Europa* territories; internal European developments are regional affairs.

'The birth of the *Curia*, as a voluntary confederation of self-governing nations, changed the way the world saw itself and thus its proposed future trajectory. Prior to the War, the NWO was pushing for global bodies, giving them free rein to implement their poisonous corruptions worldwide. Interestingly, once the idea of regionalism had been planted, other regions saw its advantages and wanted to followed suit. The Orient came first, forming a well-defined regional group under the auspices of the Shanghai

Protocol. Since then, North America has also joined the movement under the banner of the NAC, and other parts of the world have also organised their own regional groups – though to be frank, other than as sources of raw materials none of these second-string groupings is a major player.

'These observations may appear harsh to those of a sensitive disposition, but they conform to reality. It's people who forge nations and advance themselves to the best of their abilities. The Great Leader understood this, noting how some societies research nuclear fusion and build spacecraft, while others are content to squat in mud huts counting their goats. Our position among the planet's leading peoples is a direct result of our qualities as Aryans; as the Great Leader noted, "Economics play only a second or third role, while the main part is played by political, moral and racial factors."

'The wider cause of Aryan welfare beyond Europe was first brought to the *Curia's* attention by Robert's father, Vernon Foreman. This led to the formation and deployment of the famous legions that retook North America. However, the Aryan cause stretches beyond America to include our southern hemisphere homelands. It was natural, therefore, that the *Curia* agreed to send four legions to South Africa, to save our people and bring the long-running genocide there to an end. These forces successfully cleared the Bantus from South African territory, driving their remnants north – from whence they'd first invaded the south. The *Tuisland Oorlog* – as the Afrikaners called the war – entailed fighting across a mixture of terrains, ranging from grim urban battles to fierce bush campaigns, where legionary forces were, crucially, backed up by powerful Afrikaner Kommando units. The Bushmen and Cape Coloureds were allowed to remain, neither group having much time for the Bantus.

'Australia and New Zealand proved much easier to deal with. The ruling plutocratic elite, in the last outpost of the NWO project on Aryan soil, held on to power in both countries by a media-induced thread. The news that the *legionarii* had landed in Western Australia caused the whole edifice in Australia to collapse without so much as a shot being fired – I'm sure you all remember the news clips showing the rats scuttling out of Canberra in their government limousines. Much the same occurred in New Zealand when we landed on the Northland Peninsula.

'Australia and New Zealand have since held Commissions, much like the Nürnberg Commission here in Europe, incarcerating their NWO plutocrats in the Tasman Penitentiary located on Norfolk Island.

'Coming back to European soil, one of the great lessons learnt from the excesses of the NWO project, and its inevitable descent into the Eurabian War, was the failure of democracy as a functioning political philosophy. The bulk of the population is not interested in larger issues of policy and is easily herded with a mixture of government bribes, via the welfare state and behavioural conditioning delivered by a controlled and ideologically charged media – which since the end of the Second European Civil War had been in the hands of the enemy.

'In most European states today – with a couple of exceptions – single-party rule exists. Nobody is claiming that this arrangement is perfect; such things as perfect political systems only exist in the realms of myth and fairy tales. All these single-party entitles are nationalist in sentiment, the strength of this sentiment varying with the nation. They are also all parties of mass membership, meaning anybody can apply to join and take part in the party-political process. They all operate along broadly democratic lines internally. For example, in Italy I was elected as representative for the region of Tuscany by local party members, and subsequently voted onto the National Steering Committee before being offered a position on the National Cabinet.

'Naturally, those not interested in politics don't join, but since there are no open elections with different parties promising all sorts of expensive goodies from the public purse – another example of democratic corruption – more serious concerns tend to get a better hearing. Single-party rule allows long-term planning, while remaining fairly flexible in reflecting public concerns, as ordinary members tend to elect regional representatives who most closely reflect their views.

'Owing to the internal nature of a single party's functioning, it's far more difficult for external and alien bodies to exert influence on the national government's policies. This political stabilisation, in conjunction with the financial stabilisation that's occurred with the adoption of the Chicago Plan across Europe – as Jörg described yesterday – has led to levels of social stability and contentment not seen since before the First European Civil War.

'Owing to its inherent weakness, and ease of corruption, I would suggest that open-ended democracy is a dead letter for the foreseeable future. It's instructive – if not entirely surprising – to note that current levels of public satisfaction with their governments are the highest ever recorded, and are substantially in advance of any figures ever returned under democracy.

'The system I've described, which operates here in Italy, is pretty common everywhere. All branches of the party send delegates to the National Congress, where the National Chairman is elected along with the membership of the National Steering Committee (NSC) – around two hundred members. Incidentally, the members of NSC become paid, full-time politicians. From this group the National Chairman chooses his Cabinet, which ultimately is responsible for running the country.

'Nicolo Bellucci is our current National Chairman, and I have the honour of being a member of his Cabinet.

'A quick word regarding membership of the party. Anybody can apply; however, they'll need the support of three existing members to make an application. They will then be on probation for a year. During this time the new recruits will be assessed and given training – normally via weekend courses – on the ethos of the party, everything being solidly grounded in the Declaration of Rouen.

'There is much more to the running of the state than I've touched upon here, but you get the general idea. There has been a lot of criticism of this system for not being "democratic" – meaning not allowing other parties to exist. This is true, but in practice, when canvassing the population at large, democracy is not the topic that excites them most. Our system, like every other that exists today, or frankly has ever existed, is dependent on being accepted by the population if it's to govern. The great danger to us, and all systems of governance, is corruption. With corruption comes loss of public support – a state of affairs that had reached epidemic proportions in Europe prior to the Eurabian War. Corruption, left unchecked, will eventually lead to the collapse of the state, which explains why so much time and effort are invested – both domestically, through the Italian prosecution service, and regionally by the investigative officers of the Nürnberg Commission – to combat its influence. Now, let's not be naïve here: where you have power and wealth you have corruption – it's a bit like rats. You can keep them under control, but you're never going to eradicate them. It's a never-ending battle, and those caught with their hands in the till are severely punished – quite rightly so, in my opinion.

'I know Oriana wishes to finish off before we all leave, but there is one last aspect of our experiences during and after the Eurabian War that needs mentioning. Around seven months ago I was lucky enough to be invited to a weekend seminar at the *Legiones'* teaching centre at Nevers in France. The seminar's title was, "Aryan and Semite – The Eternal Struggle". I must admit, before the seminar I'd never grasped the overarching struggles behind the façade of our individual national view of history. Yes, there is such a thing as French history, or Danish history, or Czech history – but behind it all lies a far grander narrative. I'm not sure if the American, James Henry Breasted, was the first to broach the age-old struggle between Aryan and Semite, but certainly his ideas dominated the seminar in Nevers.

'In prehistoric times our ancestors, the Indo-Europeans, lived on the northern grasslands which today lie mainly in the Ukraine. To the south, on the Arabian grasslands, lived the Semites. Over the ages these two groups gradually expanded and occupied the lands surrounding them, leading eventually to the Aryan flow from the north coming into contact with the Semite flow from the south, along a line roughly delineated by the

Mediterranean and the Fertile Crescent. This meeting of Aryan and Semite was to herald the beginning of a struggle that continues to this day. In the early rounds the Semites were in the ascendancy; on the Eastern Front the Semitic Assyrians and Babylonians ruled mighty empires, while on the Western Front the Phoenicians expanded throughout the Mediterranean as far as Spain.

'However, the Aryans were not content to merely sit on their hands. In India our peoples burst through from the north to conquer the Dravidian sub-continent and found a whole new Hindu civilisation. The Aryan Persians arose to eclipse the earlier Semite empires, while with the birth of ancient Greece, European man at last entered the lists. With the rise of Rome and defeat of Carthage the western Semites were crushed – but not destroyed. For a long time the Roman Empire faced the Persian Empire: the ancient world's two superpowers. Both these mighty peoples were Aryan – though the earlier Semitic empires had left a cultural imprint on the Persians.

'It is in the context of our ongoing war with the Semites that one has to view the decision by Constantine to adopt Christianity as a strategic mistake. It's both ironic, and tragic, that this non-conformist Jewish denomination came to be adopted by the greatest Aryan empire ever to have existed.

'As a result, 1500 years later, we find so much of Europe's history and culture intertwined with this alien Semitic religion that it's almost impossible to untangle them. Incidentally, for those wondering, I go to church because my parents went to church, as did their parents and so forth back through history. Ancestors of mine are recorded as members of the church of San Francesco in San Gemini in the mid-fifteenth century – that's a lot of history, and a powerful family connection to the church as an institution.

'We almost wriggled out of Christianity's grasp when Julian became emperor; the last Pagan to don the purple. If Julian had managed to keep himself alive long enough to have seen through his far-reaching Pagan renaissance, we might have avoided the interminable cultural and religious wrangling endemic to a monotheistic sect like Christianity – and Judaism would not have enjoyed easy entry into European culture via the Bible.

'The weapon of religion has proven very effective for the Semites. First the Roman Empire fell to Christianity; then all of Europe. This murderous policy was effected through the persecution and physical destruction of indigenous Aryan religious practices. Our tragedy lay in the fact that these infamous deeds were enacted by Aryans against Aryans, in the name of an alien Semitic religion.

'But of course, soon the Semitic religious onslaught mutated and gave birth to yet another branch – Islam, which in turn conquered the other great Aryan empire, Persia.

'Under the banner of their newest religious incarnation, the Arabic Semites launched a huge offensive on Aryan homelands to the north. The Greeks lost all their Asian provinces, France hung on grimly, while Spain and southern Italy faced centuries of perpetual fighting to regain their territories.

'This great war continues still, though by today the struggle is waged primarily through cultural and social channels. The Semites attack via a combination of faith, the media, social engineering, population displacement through mass alien immigration, political gerrymandering and international finance. Our weakness is our ignorance and lack of understanding – we don't recognise the beast even as it stares back at us from our TV screens, our pulpits, our classrooms and lecture halls.

'Hopefully this explains why I support the new Pagan dawn breaking over Europe while still cherishing my historic and cultural roots, which paradoxically I manage through attending church. Nobody ever accused us Aryans of being a simple people.

'Let us be clear: everything we associate with the poison of the NWO and the resulting Eurabian War was merely the latest twist in our struggle with the Semites. They will come again; the struggle is never-ending and we are locked together for eternity as foes. The greatest mistake we, or future generations, could make would be to refuse to recognise the truth of our predicament.'

3.5 – Aryan Dawn

Oriana got up to thank everybody for their time and input over the weekend; she reckoned she had enough material for ten books. Before the taxi came to take her guests to the maglev she had time to summarise some of the main points covered since Friday.

'Much of what I intend to say you've obviously already heard; these words therefore, are merely a means of emphasising the more important aspects of the weekend's various presentations.

'Firstly, I'd like to highlight the concept of competition. This priceless commodity is key to our future in that it obliges us to match, or even surpass, our rivals. Without this competition we would stagnate. The West stagnated almost to death prior to the War. We'd become so cocky that we imagined we could serenely carry on as before, even as we committed racial suicide, glibly believing there would be no repercussions to our actions. There are always repercussions. You notice the Shanghai Protocol countries never had any truck with the NWO death cult.

'We face competition on two levels. There is the straight challenge issued to us both scientifically and culturally by our closest rivals in the Shanghai Protocol bloc and the NAC. Then there is the more insidious, and I'd say more dangerous, menace posed by the various branches of the age-old Semitic threat.

'It's becoming ever clearer that our ultimate field of competition will be space. This vast project will focus attention and set goals the like of which we can only dream, but it is a canvas worthy of man's abilities and thirst for knowledge. Once again, it will undoubtedly be a competition dominated by the Big Three, though it's not inconceivable that other players could make an appearance, perhaps India, or the southern territories of the Aryan peoples working in conjunction – who knows?'

She glanced over towards Pascal. 'Already two unannounced competitions exist between these three blocs, primary of which is to be first to get a probe to the Alpha Centauri system – the closest to us at around 4.4 light-years. The second competition – and most ambitious – is to find and then send a probe to the nearest planet capable of supporting life. I'm right, am I not?' She glanced again at Pascal, who confirmed that both contests already existed, even if neither had as yet been officially made public – though their existence had been the subject of general European media speculation for months now.

Oriana checked a few notes before continuing. 'Another element that has emerged from the War, and was of course central to the Great Leader's philosophy, is the recognition that not only does race exist as part of the human condition, but that more than any other aspect of our make-up, it defines our identity. Race overrides everything in the end; we are what we are. Our race – the Aryans – has a magnificent record; with the possible exception of the Oriental peoples, no other human grouping has come remotely close to matching our achievements. This is a fact we can be proud of. I'm not saying we should go around sticking our superiority into the faces of everybody else – but, in my opinion, we Aryans are simply the most accomplished group of humans that has ever existed. However, I'm not predicting this will always be the case. The Oriental peoples are keen to take our crown, and are currently making great strides in realising their ambition; remember they've fought no Eurabian War, or had half their urban infrastructure flattened.

'There are obvious dangers in competition, especially competition against worthy opponents in which victory is not assured. The Oriental countries may ultimately triumph and gain technological superiority over us in Europe

– or indeed our cousins in North America might reassert their twentieth-century superiority. I personally don't think that will be the case, as in my opinion a properly harnessed European population can achieve anything, but time will ultimately produce a victor – if such a thing is possible when contemplating an infinite entity like space.

'There exist other dangers of a different nature, touched on by Marcello – namely, corruption and loss of focus. We live in a post-war society, yet already easier-going social attitudes are afoot, as is always the case following war. This of itself poses another challenge: that of finding a task big enough to focus society generally. As I've already mentioned, I feel space exploration is a prospect, and cultural canvas, with sufficient kudos to fill this void.

'War is not an option for competition – not among the three major regional groupings. We ourselves, along with the Oriental powers and those in North America, are all far too powerful militarily to engage in warfare. Since we all have major nuclear arsenals, any contemplated declaration of war would be tantamount to a suicide note. However, this merely places more emphasis on space as the focus for the future – for without a worthwhile focus, bored fingers and minds drift, and soon cynical hubris and corruption take hold; it's a societal cancer against which we all need to remain eternally alert.

'The Eurabian War acted as a wake-up call to all Aryans, both here in Europe and across the globe. It taught us unequivocally that the attitudes and actions of our forefathers, who built the great empires of Britain, France, Portugal, Holland, Spain, et cetera, were correct in their treatment of local non-European natives. They tended not to mix with them, and the natives for their part, both understood and condoned this state of affairs that respected the core distinctions Nature had bestowed upon us as separate groups.

'I intend finishing off now. Religion has played a large part in this weekend's proceedings. Religion is a foundational element in any society; societies without religion crumble and die, normally falling to other societies that do have religion. Marcello spoke about the penetration of Aryan societies by

Semitic religion, in particular of Rome by Christianity, and Persia by Islam. It is in the light of this greater Aryan vs Semite clash that I welcome the rebirth of Paganism in Europe. A Europe enslaved to Semitic mythology will never function to its full potential, as witnessed in the collapse of the advanced Greco-Romano civilization, built on Aryan Paganism, into the primitive Christian Middle Ages. One could argue quite convincingly that Christianity cost Europe the best part of a thousand years in retarded progress.'

Oriana lifted up her glass of orange juice and toasted her guests; it had been a marvellous weekend full of insight and surprise. The taxi for the maglev arrived; she and Pascal stood by the double front door saying goodbye to each guest personally. One by one, Hannah, José, Robert and Jörg filed out to the de luxe Mercedes people carrier, heading for Roma Termini and a maglev home. Robert would be staying in Paris for a few days before catching a flight from Charles de Gaulle to Braxton Bragg International, North Carolina.

As the Mercedes departed, Marcello walked over to Oriana and Pascal to bid *adieu*. Concetta stood by his side, looking very content and a touch sheepish. After mutual hugs and kisses the pair headed for Marcello's red Alfa and a new chapter in both their lives – a successful weekend indeed, thought Oriana.

After Marcello and Concetta had gone, Oriana and Pascal hurried to get ready themselves; the evening maglev for Paris departed at 6:30 and neither had finished packing.

As it turned out, they found themselves outside Roma Termini with plenty of time to spare. Pascal disappeared into the main booking hall to check times and any delays. While he was gone Oriana waited under the large statue of the Great Leader by the station's main entrance – there were similar such statues all over Europe. She had much on her mind; she'd already decided to broach the idea of marriage and starting a family with Pascal, confident that she had a pretty good idea of his likely reaction. The approach of motherhood filled her with cautionary apprehension and a deep sense of natural fulfilment – Concetta wasn't the only one facing a new chapter in her life. She glanced up at the fatherly warmth of the Great Leader's face, then read the words embossed on the statue's plinth:

The most precious possession you have in the world is your own people. And for this people, and for the sake of this people, we will struggle and fight, and never slacken, never tire, never lose courage, and never lose faith.

GLOSSARY

Adhan
    Call to worship for Muslims, normally made from a minaret

Aper (pl. *Apri*)
    = Boar – see: *centurio*

Aquila Aureua
    = The Golden Eagle – in-house magazine of the *Legiones*

Aquila Legionaria
    = Legionary Eagle. The spread-winged legionary eagle is the symbol of the *Legiones* and can be seen on most items of legionary equipment

Arma Proeliaria
    = Battle Armour. Full legionary battle armour made of nano-tungsten with ceramic inserts – see: *Dietrich Munitionssysteme GmbH*

Armanx
    Anglo-Italian company making communications equipment for the *Legiones* – see: COMS

ARC
    = Anti-Racist Coalition

Ásatrú

> Branch of Germanic Paganism, strictly speaking worshipping the Æsir (senior Gods), based on the mythology delineated in the *Edda*. High Council is located in Iceland. Like all branches of European Paganism, intellectual and philosophic teachings are based on the *Liber Iuliani* (q.v.)

AUC

> = *Ab Urbe Condita* – since the establishment of the City (Rome). To get AUC date, add 753 to A.D. date, e.g. A.D. 1945 + 753 = 2698 AUC

Automatice

> = Automatic (fire) – see: GA-6

Blót

> Communal offering to the Gods as practised by various Germanic Pagan groups, such as Odinists and Ásatrú – see: Ásatrú and Spiritual Norse Paganism

Bollingen & Sartori

> Swiss defence-systems company supplying the *Legiones* with low-altitude defence systems – see: *Federschwert*

Boubou

> Grandiose West African garb of plush, flowing robes

Burqua

> Full Muslim garb worn by Muslim women, covering them from head to toe with no part of the body visible

Centuria (pl. *Centuriae*)

> A hundred legionaries, commanded by a *centurio*

Centurio (pl. *Centuriones*)

> = Centurion. Senior NCO in charge of 100 men, denoted by *aper* motif on arm

Chicago Plan
>A plan first aired by University of Chicago economists in 1933 which proposed the elimination of fractional reserve banking for 100% reserve banking issued entirely by the state, which would be the sole source of currency. Under the plan fluctuations in the market decrease substantially, inflation largely disappears, there's a huge reduction in all forms of debt and bank runs are eradicated. The plan's efficacy was confirmed in a detailed 2012 study by Benes and Kumhof

Cohors (pl. *Cohortes*)
>= Cohort. A grouping of five *centuriae*, giving a nominal strength of 500 men. There are ten cohorts in a *Legio*

COMS
>Battlefield communications systems. The legionary system was developed by CMCS (Cambridge Military Communication System) based in England – see: Armanx, *vicinia* and *praetorium*

Concilium Militare
>= Military Council. The military decision-making body attached to the *Curia* (q.v.)

Contact
>Military term for engaging the enemy

Contra Patriam
>= Against the fatherland. A legal term emanating from the Declaration of Rouen to describe actions contrary to the well-being of Europe's indigenous peoples. Such accusations would typically be referred to the standing Nürnberg Commission – see: Declaration of Rouen and Nürnberg Commission

Copiae Legionariae Europaeae
>The legionary forces formed to protect Europe, usually referred to simply as the *Legiones* or *Curia,* after the controlling body. First constituted in

Bonn, the *Legiones* accept recruits from all nations that are members of the *Curia* and Russia. The *Legiones* do not accept men from outside Europe or non-Aryans – see: Declaration of Rouen and *Curia*

Cui Bono?
To whose benefit?

Curia
Literally = Senate House. Name of the confederacy of European nations, based in Bonn. The *Curia* operates within guidelines set out in the Declaration of Rouen. The *Curia* was originally established as a successor to the P-EC (Pan-European Conference), the initial body formed in response to the cross-border Jihadist campaigns waged during the Eurabian War. The *Curia* is responsible for controlling and directing the *Legiones* and operating the solidus, an internal unit of account formed from a basket of *Curia* currencies against which all member states can exchange their currencies free of charge. The *Curia* is not a parliament: indeed, non-independent entities cannot be admitted to the *Curia*, whose membership is based on the nation, not the state – see: Eurabian War

Dashiki
Colourful West African loose-fitting garb worn by men over top half of body

Declaration of Rouen
Pivotal document written in Rouen in France by a group of nationalistic academics, which defined European identity and the concept of fatherland – *patria*. The Declaration became the foundation document of the *Curia* and the Nürnberg Commission – see: *Curia* and Nürnberg Commission

Decanus (pl. *Decani*)
Junior NCO rank in charge of 10 *legionarii* = a *decuria*

Decuria (pl. *Decuriae*)
: Unit of 10 *legionarii* – smallest unit in a *legio*

Di Immortales!
: Immortal Gods!

Dietrich Munitionssysteme GmbH
: German manufacturer of the *arma proeliaria* (full battle armour) – see: *arma proeliaria*

ECP
: = European Cosmological Programme

Eurab
: Muslim living in Europe

Eurabian War
: War fought between Europeans and Muslim, Negro and other racial colonists that erupted following the Meltdown – see: Global Meltdown

Evocatus (pl. *Evocati*)
: Senior *legionarius* – denoted by single *gladius* motif

F-22 Raptor
: Main US fighter plane

Federschwert
: = Longsword. Bollingen & Sartori's low-altitude defence system used by the *Legiones*; especially effective against helicopters and drones – see: Bollingen & Sartori

Fiat
: Third-person singular, subjective present tense of the verb 'to be' in Latin – basic meaning: 'let it be'. In financial circles it describes the way money is created by central banks – out of thin air: 'let it be'

Flobert
> Small-arms manufacturer based in Wallonia

Freya
> Germanic Pagan Goddess of such elements as love, fertility, magic, war and death. A member of the Vanir group of Gods

GA-6
> Standard legionary rifle, with four settings for fire control: *automatice, semi-automatice, sole* and *tunde*. Gun manufactured by *Hirsch & Kalb GmbH* with advanced scope and control system designed and manufactured by *Klaus Zweig* – see: *automatice, semi-automatice, sole, tunde, Hirsch & Kalb* and *Klaus Zweig*

Gladius (pl. *Gladii*)
> = Short Roman sword – modern military model made with carbon-steel blade and polypropylene grip, guard and pommel

Global Meltdown
> The global economic crash that occurred when the US dollar imploded owing to excessive debt fuelled by *fiat* money creation. With the end of social payments, immigrant populations across Europe revolted, sparking the Eurabian War – see: Eurabian War

GSS
> = Global Social Strategies

Hijab
> Veil or scarf worn over head of Muslim women

Hirsch & Kalb GmbH
> German arms manufacturer and supplier of the GA-6, standard weapon of the *Legiones* – see: *Legiones*, GA-6 and *Klaus Zweig*

HUD
> = Heads-Up Display

Hummer HX
> Military version of Hummer off-road vehicle – American manufacture

Imperator
> = General. Commander of units greater than a single *legio*

Imperium
> = Empire. In general sense used to describe a nation's natural independent evolution: its unique path as defined primarily by the genius of its people and their culture

Iuppiter immortalis!
> = Immortal Jupiter!

Janbiya Knife
> Curved Arabian dagger

Kamov Mi-97
> General-purpose helicopter used by the *Legiones,* Russian manufacture

Klaus Zweig
> German manufacturer of optical equipment used by the *Legiones* – in particular the advanced scope on the GA-6 with HUD technology and automatic targeting – see: *Hirsch & Kalb* and GA-6

Legatus
> Senior officer, normally commanding a *Legio* (q.v.)

Legio (pl. *Legiones*)
> = Legion. Comprising 5,000 men subdivided into cohorts of 500 and *centuriae* of 100 men – see: *centuria, centurio* and cohort

Legionarius (pl. *Legionarii*)
> = Legionary

Legiones
> = Legions. Plural of *Legio,* but also used in a more general sense to mean legionary forces; shorthand for the 'army'

Leopard 3B2
> Main battle tank of the *Legiones* – German manufacture

Liber Iuliani
> = The Book of Julian. Named after the last great Roman Pagan emperor, Julian the Philosopher, who stipulated the appropriate body of philosophic works suitable for a Pagan priest. The book primarily comprises a collection of Greco-Roman philosophical texts. This hefty tome opens with the seminal works of three great poets – Homer, Hesiod and Virgil – before laying out the teachings of each of the philosophical schools: the pre-Socratic philosophers, Socrates, School of Plato, the Peripatetics, the Neo-Platonists and the Stoics, finishing with the works of Julian himself. The *Liber Iuliani* is used by all Pagan traditions as their philosophical base, with the added bonus of forming a bridge between the traditions. The book has been translated into all the European languages, while a 'full' *Liber Iuliani* refers to a copy written in the original Greek and Latin

M5-106 Obama
> US main battle tank named after the watershed president

Maglev
> = Magnetic Levitation. A form of transport where the carriage travels on a magnetic cushion above the ground – free from ground friction, maglev trains can achieve very high speeds

Meltdown
> See: Global Meltdown

Mil *Pilum*
> Attack helicopter used by the *Legiones,* Russian manufacture, built by the Kamov Company – see: Kamov Mi-97

Multi-mag
> Standard magazine for GA-6, holding 60 rounds – see: GA-6

Mjölnir
> Thor's hammer and symbol of Germanic Paganism – see: Ásatrú and Spiritual Norse Paganism

MSM
> = Main-Stream Media

Niqab
> Veil worn by Muslim women to cover the face

NPG
> = National Provisional Government – name of successor government in Germany, responsible for initially approaching Russia to intervene in Eurabian War – see: Eurabian War

Nürnberg Commission
> Standing tribunal (sometimes referred to as Nuremberg II) where corrupt democratic leaders and allied business and financial figures are tried for the attempted genocide of the European peoples and various other acts of treason against the nations and peoples they theoretically served. Death sentences given to worst cases, others incarcerated in the *Curia's* penitentiary located in The Hague – see: Declaration of Rouen

NVD
> = Night Vision Device – various electronic enhancements that allow night vision through binoculars and other sighting equipment

NWO
> = New World Order – grand scheme for universal global control of business, finance and politics closely linked to the state enforcement of Marxist social models. Chief backer of scheme was the old US plutocratic elite, though project largely conceived and controlled by same ethnic group that controlled global central banking – see: Nürnberg Commission

Optio (pl. *Optiones*)
> Next rank up from *decanus*, denoted by triple *gladius* motif worn on arm. *Optiones* typically found as second-in-command to a *centurio*

Pakul
> Pork-pie-shaped woollen cap worn by Afghan men

Pan-European Conference
> Forerunner of the *Curia,* responsible for all the early key decisions, like the use of Latin, military buying policy and the adoption of the Declaration of Rouen as the continent's guiding ideology – see: *Curia* and Declaration of Rouen

Pantsir S-2E
> Russian-built mobile anti-aircraft system used by the *Legiones*

Patria Europaea
> = European Fatherland. Concept derived from Declaration of Rouen: namely, that Europe is the home of European man and should be defended and made safe for the continuance of the European peoples – see: Declaration of Rouen

Pillars of Hercules
> = Straits of Gibraltar

Porcus (pl. *Porci*)
> = Pig. Legionary nickname for centurion – see: *aper* and *centurio*

Potomac System
> Low-altitude defence system used against helicopters and drones built by VAC, American corporation – see: VAC

Praetorium
> = Headquarters. Setting on legionary COMS equipment for contacting base – see: Armanx, COMS and *vicinia*

Robespierre's Orphans
> A term used to denote those who betray their own patrimony, heritage, culture and people

RoC
> = Republic of Columbia

RPG
> = Rocket-Propelled Grenade

Semi-automatice
> = Semi-automatic – see: GA-6

Shalwar Kameez
> Two-piece garb consisting of long shirt worn outside pyjama-style trousers – common throughout southern Asia

Sole
> = Single (shot) – see: GA-6

SPG
> = Swedish Provisional Government, successor state to failed democratic order in Sweden

Spiritual Norse Paganism

    Spiritual Germanic Paganism built around the individual's personal relationship with a God or Gods – sometimes referred to as Theodism

Stain of Paulus

    Reference to the infamous general. The Stain of Paulus is a fear that grips every legion and explains the tremendous tenacity of legionary forces when in action – none wish to fail, or bring shame onto their ranks through surrender

Successor Governments

    Name for the national governments that arose across Europe in response to the collapse of the corrupt, plutocratic democracies following the outbreak of the Eurabian War. Although each nation has its own variant, most are single-party constructs with a president or chairman chosen by a council. Council members are typically elected by party members from each region of the country. Mass membership of the national party is strongly encouraged. All of Europe's successor governments base their policies and national constitutions on the Declaration of Rouen and send representatives to the *Curia* – see: *Curia* and Declaration of Rouen

Sukhoi T-55 *Palash*

    Russian-built combat aircraft, main fighter used by the *Legiones*

Tab

    A long military march carrying kit, normally done at speed within a set time period

Telnyashka

    Iconic striped Russian military vest/T-shirt, with different-coloured stripes denoting different branches of the military: Black = Marines, Dark Blue = Navy, Light Blue = Paratroopers, Light Green = Border guards, Maroon = Internal Troops

Tunde
> = Thump. The GA-6 has an auxiliary percussion cap magazine that feeds into the firing chamber when the gun's set to *tunde*. The extra percussion drives each round at maximum velocity and impact, but the gun can only fire singularly on *tunde,* and only as fast as the gun's mechanism can feed, then eject, the extra percussion caps – see: GA-6

VAC
> = Vannevar Aerospace Corp. – American aerospace corporation specialising in defence systems – see: *Potomac* System

Vicinia
> = Local. Setting on legionary COMS system for communicating with fellow *legionarii* in the immediate vicinity – see: Armanx, COMS and *Praetorium*

Vagina (pl. *Vaginae*)
> = Sword sheath

Vitis (pl. *Vites*)
> = Vine shaft. Swagger stick issued to every *centurio* on passing out. These iconic sticks are the hallmark of a *centurio* and badge of his authority. The *legiones* have contracts with a number of small growers in Spain, Italy and Greece, to supply suitable *vites* – see: *centurio*

Nomina Legionum

I	Augustus	Roman
II	Caesar	Roman
III	Julian	Roman
IV	Roland	French
V	Sobieski	Polish
VI	Ferdinand	Spanish
VII	Isabella	Spanish
VIII	Degrelle	Belgian
IX	Scipio	Roman
X	Leonidas	Greek
XI	Alexander	Greek
XII	Palaiologos	Greek
XIII	Godfrey	French
XIV	Lazar	Serbian
XV	Themistocles (Classis)	Greek
XVI	Dimitri	Russian
XVII	Aetius	Roman
XVIII	Codrington (Classis)	English

XIX	Kléber	French
XX	Sarmiento	Spanish
XXI	Miltiades	Greek
XXII	Zrinski	Croatian
XXIII	Vlad	Romanian
XXIV	Don John (Classis)	Austrian
XXV	Gediminas	Lithuanian
XXVI	Tancred	French
XXVII	Hardrada	Norwegian
XXVIII	Charles Martel	French
XXIX	Gurko	Russian
XXX	Peiper	German
XXXI	Roger Bosso	French
XXXII	Béla	Hungarian
XXXIII	Dimitriev	Bulgarian
XXXIV	Van Capellan (Classis)	Dutch
XXXV	De Valette	French
XXXVI	d'Aubusson	French
XXXVII	Trajan	Roman
XXXVIII	Minotto	Italian
XXXIX	Giustiniani	Italian
XL	Chard	English
XLI	Xenophon	Greek
XLII	Silva	Roman
XLIII	Törni	Finnish
XLIV	Ingvar	Swedish
XLV	De Rigny (Classis)	French
XLVI	Exmouth (Classis)	English

XLVII	Fenet	French
XLVIII	Wrangel	Russian
XLIX	De Flor	Italian
L	Titus	Roman
LI	Agrippa	Roman
LII	Hypatia	Greek
LIII	Raud	Norwegian
LIV	Daithi	Irish
LV	Vata	Hungarian
LVI	Skorzeny	Austrian
LVII	Ivan	Russian

Classis = Fleet

Nationalities listed on the right refer to individual after whom the legion is named – not its make-up. Legionaries are drawn indiscriminately to individual legions from every country in the *Curia* plus Russia.

Basic Legionary Organisation:

Unit — Commander & Motif

Decuria (10 men) — Decanus (twin gladius)

Centuria (100 men) — Centurio (single aper)

Cohors (500 men) — Tribunus (single wreath)

Legio (5000 men) — Legatus (triple wreath)

Intermediate Ranks

Evocatus (single gladius)

Optio (triple gladius)

Primus pilus (twin aper)

Tribunus militum (twin wreath)

Printed in Poland
by Amazon Fulfillment
Poland Sp. z o.o., Wrocław